THE INVASION OF SAND

A Selection of Further Titles by Bel Mooney

THE INVASION OF SAND

Bel Mooney

This first world edition published in Great Britain 2005 by
SEVERN HOUSE PUBLISHERS LTD of
9–15 High Street, Sutton, Surrey SM1 1DF.
This first world edition published in the USA 2006 by
SEVERN HOUSE PUBLISHERS INC of
595 Madison Avenue, New York, N.Y. 10022.

British Library Cataloguing in Publication Data

Mooney, Bel, 1946-
    The invasion of sand
    1.   Single women - Australia - Fiction
    2.   Landladies - Australia - Fiction
    3.   Australia - Social conditions - Fiction
    I.   Title
    823.9'14 [F]

    ISBN-10 : 0-7278-6318-5   (cased)
               0-7278-9157-X   (paper)

Typeset by Palimpsest Book Production Ltd.,
Polmont, Stirlingshire, Scotland.
Printed and bound in Great Britain by
MPG Books Ltd., Bodmin, Cornwall.

3 1984 00238 7544

For

Eva Learner

No pilgrims leave, no holy-days are kept
for those who die of landscape. Who can find,
even, the camp-sites where the saints last slept?
Out there their place is, where the charts are gapped,
. unreachable, unmapped, and mainly in the mind.
Randolph Stow

aircraft recognition charts pinned to my bedroom wall
the smell of paint on toy soldiers
doing paintings of Spitfires and Hurricanes,
Lancasters and Halifaxes
always with a Heinkel or a Messerchmitt plunging helplessly
into the sea in the background
pink light in the sky from Liverpool burning fifty miles away
the thunder of daylight flying fortresses high overhead
Adrian Henri

He who loses his dreaming is lost.
Aboriginal saying,
(quoted by Cynthia Nolan in 'Outback')

One

Bernie Molloy thought that if she had been seeking God at the bottom of a can of beer, it would be an excuse for still working in this place. Maybe once she'd believed the old man in the sky might hang out in the most unlikely places, to surprise the unwary. Imagined him loving the lost ones, the drifters, the bruised. But not any more. *Godforsaken* was the word that fitted.

Now she saw her whole life in terms of mirage. You walk out into the shimmering heat and see the water in the distance, getting closer as you stumble forward. But as your tongue slips out to moisten parched lips, it's gone. Left there alone, staring at the sand all around, you hear a voice cry. 'I didn't think my life would be like this.' Nothing to be done, Bernie thought, as she reached behind for a glass, and poured the chaser.

As usual the grimy bar was packed.

'Blue can – wait – make that two. You gonna let me in tonight, Bernie?'

'In your dreams, mate.'

A voice murmured, 'Best lookin' woman in the territory.' Wanting her to hear.

Bernie smiled the usual smile, accustomed to compliments and abuse in equal measure. She knew her job was to slam the booze down on the bar and keep quiet, nothing else to do, night after night, all of them like this one, with the yells coming from the screen in the corner, and the faces leering at her.

Bernie contemplated the faces of her customers, which bared broken yellow teeth. Sweaty hats were pushed right back, singlets streaked with red dirt above tight shorts, shiny at the crotch. They weren't regulars, the men she was serving now. They'd picked up her name only to feel they belonged. From a road gang, she guessed: the hard, ugly ones who live only to slurp up their graft in strange bars. You couldn't guess their

1

age, because the sun had dried them up, dirt caking every pore, transforming skin into soil, so that men became one with the earth. No choice. Sometimes she thought that was why you couldn't hate them, despite their ugliness.

No longer believing in divine intervention, Bernie was still surprised by the kindness that lurked within herself. But there was never any time for it, not here. The noise was deafening. Somebody said something she missed.

'Tell you what, mate, you'd come out with a few fingers missin'.'

'You reckon?'

'Yeah. Whose shout is it?'

'Yours, Skinno, you tight bastard.'

'Same again, Bernie, and I'll shout you one yourself if you'll step out the back.'

'Second thoughts, don't even bother to dream,' she said.

Frank Massey loomed over, a fresh scar pink on his cheek. The bouncer fingered it tenderly. 'Somebody giving you trouble, Bernie?' he asked, the East London accent giving edge to his menace. The strangers looked wary.

'Nothing I can't handle, Frank,' she said.

'Feel free to handle me, anytime!' squealed the man they called Skinno, nearly shaking himself off the stool, as his two friends slapped his back.

The bouncer hesitated. But when Bernie shook her head, he shrugged and stalked across the bar. It could have ended then. But the devil got into Bernie some nights, despite herself. Breaking her own rule, she leaned forward and whispered, 'So you want some handling, do you . . .? What's your name? Skinno?'

'You on?'

The lolling dog's breath of him, corroded by beer and nicotine, caught in her nostrils. Not dropping her gaze, Bernie reached beneath the bar and located the rubber gloves kept for cleaning up. Pulling them on with elaborate stagecraft, she peered over towards his shorts, then narrowed her eyes and shook her head.

'OK, so I got the protection – but how am I going to find it without a magnifying glass?'

The hackneyed jibe worked. The man's two friends turned their mirth against him, and a third poked his head over and jeered, 'Tell you what, mate, no wonder she can't see it – you've worn it away with all the bashin' you give it.'

'Always pulling it cos he never gets lucky to push it,' Bernie chimed, and the laughter increased.

Hatred flashes across the eyes as fast as a switchblade. 'You frigid bitch!' the man Skinno spat, moving as if to strike. But Bernie didn't flinch and her gaze was steady. She knew dogs will always drop their eyes and slink off. She'd seen it all before.

The place was known as the 'Zoo', although somebody nostalgic for the old country had called it the 'London Tavern', and had even had a traditional pub sign painted, which survived bombardment by beer cans and blistering sun. Nobody knew when it became the worst bar in town, the one where the hardest people – roadworkers, crims, drunks, losers, psycho nutcases, drifters from the stations – liked to drink, knowing it could only add to their reputation. From time to time complaints were made, and the police shook their heads to say we warned you. There was the time the young tourist in search of real life had been frogmarched to the riverbed and subjected to a 'train', but nobody could prove anything, and in any case, she was asking for trouble, they said, being so stupid as to go to a place like the Zoo in the first place.

That was long before Bernie Molloy drifted back into town, running, as so many did, from the accusations of her dreams. At the age of eighteen, just after the St Patrick's Ball, she had left wanting – no, *needing* – the city, starting the long dirty journey from the bungalow her mother kept so clean, and messing up badly along the way. She couldn't go home after that: it was too far, too expensive, and the reproaches were terrible. But when they died at last, Ma and Da, so suddenly – with Patrick and Siobhan in England, and baby Lou in California, all doing well for themselves and hardly ever writing – Bernie, as the eldest, got the house in Dean Street and went back for good.

By that time she had given up pretending she was in control. Knowing there was no longer anywhere to hide in the city, she packed two nylon holdalls, to journey for what seemed like an eternity of days and nights and face up to her guilt. Her mouth grew dry. Her nails flaked. She stared out of the window for hours and hours, recognizing the arid vacancy of sand which stretched for thousands of miles and whispered that it *knew* her, and would never let her go.

How could she have known that all the time her tiny

3

nightmare sprinted beside the tracks, or fluttered above the moving train under the Southern Cross – making its own little pilgrimage into the vast emptiness, where the light glittered and the earth was as scarlet as sin?

There was to be no escape.

Then it was the double funeral: black hole in red sand, and the snuffling all around not hers. Sometimes Bernie wondered if she would ever cry again. For a while she shared the bungalow with Suzanne Angelini, who moved up because she'd done something she shouldn't and somebody was on her tail. The two of them went way back, hanging out with the bikies in Bondi, and Suze knew all her secrets then. They had fun, sure enough. The old home didn't know what had hit it. There were men and parties, booze and dope. The hangovers grew so big it took a whole lot more medicine to drive them away. But now Bernie lived alone and mocked her own residual dream that somebody might walk into the bar and offer her a cure.

The Zoo roared about her. Men, and one or two women, clustered beneath the large screen in the corner. The mud wrestlers jumped into the ring, and the match began, ooze slurping over flesh as they pulled hair, slapped, locked arms, tumbled and heaved, on and on, to grunts and yells and screams, until finally they tore off each others' bikinis and the bout was over, the filthy naked women leaving the ring empty for the next two. Then 'Hurricane Helen' and 'Annie the Animal' were slithering over each other like brown snakes in a hole.

'Slags,' said Frank, pausing by the bar and glancing up.

'How d'you know?' Bernie asked, slamming the cooler door.

'Stands to reason, innit?' he shrugged.

'What would you know about reason, then, Frank?'

'What?'

'Forget it.'

It would not be wise to irritate the bouncer, since he stood so often between her and drinkers maddened by the ice behind her eyes. Frank Massey was quiet about his background, yet once boasted that people back home wanted him dead, and Bernie suspected he had married his blowsy Australian girl for escape as much as love. She no longer believed that people did things for love, since there was no justification for it in the world she'd come to inhabit, and too much in the one she left behind.

4

Bernie watched Skinno. His mates had moved away, and he sat there, glowering at his can and occasionally looking up to give her such looks of loathing she'd have been alarmed, if there was room in her heart for such weakness. Instead, in a flash of light, she suddenly saw the whippet-skinny road-worker as pathetic. Without his friends and his foul words, he was nothing – a crude and ugly atom who'd probably – no, certainly – never been loved.

But then, she reminded herself, why would you . . .?

And the light faded.

At that moment a huge man lurched through the door, clothes caked in conte red, brown skin warmed by the all-pervasive dust. His broad flat face and scarification gave his origins away. Behind him stumbled an aboriginal woman, probably in her forties, although the ravaged face and stooped shoulders bore the weight of centuries of misery. One skinny hand was held out in front of her, whether in pleading or defence it was impossible to say. Her palm was like an old rose.

'Kiwi . . . wait . . . Hey, Kiwi!' she called, swaying as she stood. '*Kiiiiwiii!*'

The man glanced over his shoulder and laughed – the sound taken up by the group he joined, and ricocheting about the yellow ceiling. Winking, he cupped his genitals through his jeans, as if restoring them to their proper place, then ostentatiously wiped his hand on his rear. The mirth redoubled.

'Hey, Kiwi, hey big guy, you promised you'd shout me. You said so, you bastard . . . Mister Kiwi . . .!'

Nobody took any notice. The woman's hands were by her side now, plucking at the grubby flowered cotton of her dress. Her eyes rolled round the room as if they had long forgotten their aim, and in any case, the man had gone, disappeared amongst the other bodies, his debt unpaid.

'Shhh . . . shomebody buy me a drink,' the woman mumbled, raising a hand to her wild hair.

'OK, Lizzy, that's enough for one night,' said Frank.

'Let me stay, and I'll . . . Let me stay, big guy, and I can show somebody . . . somebody'll shout me . . .'

Then she noticed Skinno, crouched morosely on his stool. The place next to him was empty, so she tottered across, barely able to climb up because of the spindly shortness of her legs, clutching the bar to prevent herself from falling. Frank stared at her for a moment, then heard yells outside and moved to the door, leaving Lizzy free to pursue her quarry.

'You, mate, you want – be my friend?' she slurred, a hand on Skinno's shoulder.

Bernie waited, but the man said nothing. Tense, she leaned forward. 'Listen, love, I shouldn't bother. Why don't you get yourself home, now?'

Lizzy jerked her head up and bared her teeth. 'You tryin' to take my man off me? You jealous of me, white girl? This is my man, here, an' I love him. I love him good. What you called, sexy man? You better'n any fat Kiwi . . . Wha' you called, lover? Tell Lizzy . . .'

Skinno swigged hard from his can. The woman was leaning heavily on him now, trying to twine both hands round his neck, the tip of her tongue tracing the shape of her lips in a mime of seduction.

'You want to fuck me? I fuck you so good – better'n fat Kiwi. You shout me a beer an' Lizzy'ull fuck you so good, you keep standin' an hour . . . Come on, just one beer . . .'

He hardly bothered to turn his head, but the movement which hit her hands away was sharp as a snake's bite. She swayed perilously, then caught the edge of the bar again. His voice was venomous. 'Get off of me – I wouldn't touch you, right? Go and fuck yourself, you dirty old gin. You makes me sick.'

Skinno's friends were back now, reunited in laughter. The woman's gaze travelled from one to the other, her eyes glazed, and puzzled.

'So you want to take us all on?' said one of Skinno's cronies, flicking her flattened breast with his thumb and forefinger, so that the woman drew back with a slight moan, shaking her head from side to side.

'Stinks somethin' rotten,' sneered Skinno.

'Give it a wash then,' said the other, reaching for the can on the bar, and beginning the action of upending its dregs in her lap.

Bernie's hand got there first, closing over his wrist with a grip so hard he looked up in surprise. Taking advantage, she wrenched the can away and threw it behind her. 'OK now, that's enough of all this crap,' she said firmly. 'I want you lot out of here right now – you hear me, *now* – or else I'm going to get friend Frank to help you on your way. And if I tell him

I'm mad, he'll get mad too, and you wouldn't like that, eh?'

'There's three of us . . .' muttered Skinno.

'Listen, mate, I wouldn't even think about it,' said Bernie, performing a laugh. 'If you'd been in this place before, you'd know that Frank breaks wrists for a hobby. And I've been known to do the same myself – ask anyone. Now leave this *lady* alone, and get the hell out of here.'

Lizzy slumped forward, her face in a puddle of beer, and began to cry. Tenderly Bernie wiped the bar around her head.

'Dirty bitch,' said Skinno's friend.

Bernie folded her arms and balanced her weight on the balls of her feet, staring him down. 'You talking to me, or to her?'

'Some bloke needs to teach you a lesson, you dry snatch.'

'Listen, mate, where I come from women like me spit out losers like you before breakfast.'

Controlling her trembling, she watched them slink away towards the door, then stand in a huddle. Then drinkers made their demands, and she did not notice the men leave.

Bernie Molloy, christened Bernadette thirty-nine years ago, had given up believing that the universe would repay sweet-ness in kind. Ma and Da knocked the first glimmering of the gospel out of her when they took the cheap fare and landed them all here, not Pommies but 'Irish bastards', trying to make it in the building trade in this godforsaken place and succeeding beyond their dreams. But only after a while. For years they were poorer than in Skibbereen, and Bernie still cringed at the memory of the other kids laughing at the clothes her mother (God rest her penny-pinching soul) ran up from remnants, telling her pride was a sin.

'Jaysus, Colleen, the girl never stops whining so.'

'They call it whinging here, Sean, and God knows ye're right.'

'Jaysus, Colleen, it's hot so.'

Well, it would be hot, wouldn't it, if you'd travelled across the world to a dried-up hole of a place like this? Nobody could understand why she hated it so much. This is the lucky country, they said, God's own, where your men eat steak every day, while your women lie on the beach and burn themselves to beauty. And lamb chops for breakfast, while nobody ever thought of serving a beer that wasn't steaming with the cold.

Oh, it was beautiful all right. Yet she hated it. You think they speak your language, but they don't, really.

She never belonged then, or later, even before she started running. Bernie was always homesick, but sometimes she thought it was for a place she'd never known. She would look in the mirror, widen her grey eyes, stroke the cheekbones Zippo used to say made her look like one of those Greek sheilas, sculpted in marble – and wonder what tribe she belonged to.

At last, the long, identical hours finished, Bernie cleaned the bar, swept her share of the mountain of cans into black sacks, lit a cigarette and went outside. Distant violence rumbled in the night. A flash on the horizon. Shouts fading as Frank shoved the last ones out, she crossed to the old white Holden, desperate for a shower to wash herself clean of the smell of beer, smoke and people. Gaunt figures slipped into the darkness like ghosts, walking towards the riverbed. But Bernie did not look behind her, not ever.

She revved and pulled away, picking up speed along the main street. Treeless car park, bitumen lots, K-Mart, rows of shops with plate-glass fronts, selling tourist tat – the frontier town had been transformed since the Molloys arrived in 1955, sharing a wood and iron hut with the O'Donnells for a few dollars a week, and clearing the bush land as best they could, the kids using sticks for tools, to make a small space for potatoes. The development had already begun then, although Sean Molloy and Pat O'Donnell found it hard to break in at first; the groups were too tight, and anyway, you couldn't get hold of building materials even if you had the money for the sites.

The next year Virginia McKenna came to the town for the premiere of *A Town Like Alice*, and Bernie went to the Phoenix with the other kids to rubberneck at this mad, beautiful woman in a strapless evening gown on a freezing July night. But she was a star, and she had come to the Never-Never and the town would be famous – everybody said. So, as more and more bush land was cleared, the sand retreated, and the hotchpotch of buildings grew. The town rejoiced in its library and civic pool, but the dead were still carried to the cemetery in the back of a battered Ute.

Bernie turned into Dean Street, slowing down because of the neighbours. They'd complained about her and Suze so many times, but Suze had been in Sydney for well over a year

now, while Bernie had reached her thirty-ninth birthday realizing that she didn't want to be wild any more. She lived alone
in the the old, dusty bungalow with the wide verandah, not
minding its ghosts too much, except sometimes at night.
Slowing almost to walking pace, Bernie glanced around,
allowing the peace of home to slide towards her, and smelling
blossom she still could not name on the night air.

Suddenly a pickup roared away from the end of the street,
disappearing in a cloud of dust. She thought she recognized
it as belonging to one of the bar regulars, but wasn't sure.
Another car, a battered dark-blue Honda, was parked just past
the entrance of her house, barely visible beneath the sweep
of branches. Bernie felt the hairs on the back of her neck stir.

She pulled into the short drive, jumping down with her fists
balled, and holding the bunch of keys in one so that metal
poked out between each knuckle. Insects scraped at the walls
of the night, but apart from that familiar sound there was
nothing. Still she stood in the darkness and listened, feeling
the universe fold round her briefly, as if in protection.

After a pause, Bernie returned her keys to their proper func-
tion and let herself in, closing the door quietly behind her. She
paused in the long hall, without switching on the lights. Then
she tensed again, flaring her nostrils. There was a faint smell
of sweat, and something else she could not identify. As if through
her whole body, not just her ears, she caught a small sound,
somewhere outside, through the back maybe, in the garden –
a cough or a sigh, or even a dry laugh, hidden in the trees.

Bernie would not let herself be afraid. She walked forward,
her rubber soles making no sound on the lino. The hall led
straight across the square bungalow, bisecting it neatly to lead
through the back into the overgrown garden. Reaching the
glass door, she paused to peer through, then unbolted it, stepping out into the darkness, where the crow with a damaged
wing scratched in his cage.

He cawed demands, making her jump.

A dog barked in the distance. The sky was heavy with stars,
and the thick air seemed stale, even at this time of night, with
the perfume of too many overblown flowers. Bernie felt isolation fall around her shoulders. There was nobody she could call.

But maybe now, lurking in the dusty undergrowth, in the
wilderness of shrubs and untamed grass that was her garden,

9

there was somebody who did know where to find her. And perhaps that was all right. No worries. You would stride forward to meet your death, saying, *G'day, I always knew you'd come along, you old bastard! What took you so long?*

'Ah, who gives a fuck?' she asked the garden, but there was no reply.

A car door slammed. Bernie jerked her eyes wide, ran back to the back door, and along the hall. The Honda was turning the corner as she reached the gate. Her call died behind her teeth. The echoes receded, dust settled in silence, and the night poured back, leaving her panting with disappointment.

She went into the kitchen and poured a glass of white, grimacing at the near-squalor of the room. Ma had always kept it so clean; she would breathe on a surface and rub it with her sleeve, giving a little sigh of martyred satisfaction. Bernie grew to hate phrases like 'wearing my fingers to the bone', and years later, dizzy with independence, it pleased her to let the dirt ball up in corners and the dishes pile in the sink – just to assert her distance from all she had left behind.

'Tomorrow,' thought Bernie, drawing a heart in the dust on the window sill, then obliterating it with a bad-tempered swipe. 'I'll clean up tomorrow.' Always the fresh starts lined up in front of her, like drinks on a bar.

She downed the wine, sighed, and crossed the hall to her bedroom, desperate to strip off and shower. In the doorway she stopped. The sense of something wrong blasted from the darkened room like a force field, to hold her there. And then it hit her full on – the unmistakable human smell, strong now, and disgusting. Trembling, sweat running down her sides, she slammed on the light and saw the window half open.

Her gaze travelled across to the mirror of Ma's veneered dressing table.

The message was scrawled with her own pink lipstick. Above the debris of tissues, creams and a full ashtray, large misshapen letters spelled out: FUCK YOU.

A nerve started to twitch in her right eye, splintering the room for a second, before she saw the large human turd placed with precision right in the centre of her pillow.

Two

A cross town, in the same heavy darkness, a man lay in his bed, and cried. Struggling to stifle his sobs made him sweat the more in the room's dense heat. His pyjamas were thick cotton. He wore them because *she* had bought them, and packed them in his case when he left. Too hot. Yet how could his grandmother have known what it would be like here? You can't imagine it, when you're at home.

He curled like a foetus and crammed a fist into his mouth. Where would he go now? Another landlady had snapped she needed the room 'for a rellie', and John Roper didn't know what he'd done wrong. She was just like the rest of them, she wouldn't give a chap a fair crack of the whip, she was prejudiced.

The woman asked too many questions anyway. Where he'd come from, how long he'd be staying . . . and now she was telling him he couldn't lock his door in the daytime, because she needed to clean. Poking around his things, moving his letters . . . like all of them, blowsy and red-faced, with that nasal whine, and the conviction that she was better than him. She looked like the sun had dried her up from the inside. She even pretended not to understand him half the time, just like so many of them, and although she never said 'Pommy bastard' to his face, he knew she thought it. He knew.

At last he slept, and woke with his eyes crusted, a terrible tiredness weighing every limb. He showered in her bleak little bathroom, then crept downstairs, although the temptation to stomp was strong, to wake her early. He would find somewhere else to live, somewhere better. It had been like that for the last year. Leaving. Moving on. Hoping the homesickness would run out of him with the sweat, as well as the tears. John thought how lucky it was Nan believed he was doing well, and getting a raise each time, instead of taking all this

11

cheek from the bloody locals. For those few minutes he wrote, he could believe all the good-news stories himself.

The drive to the airport took about twenty-five minutes in the clapped-out old Moke he could barely afford. The morning light was soft and blue; the air cool before the hairdryer-blast of the day; the streets empty. This was when he felt most nearly himself, with nobody to ask questions, or tease, or laugh, and the prospect of time in the air making him happy. Waiting for the point when the drumming faded and he hung there, in perfect silence, above the earth. That was the moment he had always dreamed of, and the first time it had happened he'd drawn in his breath so sharply it made him cough, and his instructor asked, 'You crook, mate?'

When he arrived at work he nodded at the others. He never bothered to chat, for there was nothing to say. Steve Brass asked coolly, 'Getting the hours in now, mate?' He nodded, signed the papers, and turned on his heel. He knew he wasn't popular, and didn't understand why. He wanted somebody else to intervene and explain that shyness turns your tongue into a stone blocking the cave of your mouth. But they all found it easy to chat and be mates. It wasn't fair.

The Cessna 210 was a thing of beauty – poised by the hangar, nose slightly in the air, as if in contempt for the two men in overalls loading the sacks. A small functional plane, like a car really, with little style, and yet he loved it. He almost trembled when he thought of easing himself into the cockpit; never changing that fantasy of years ago – when the bicycle was not a bicycle, but a spitfire barrel-rolling across the sky.

'I'm running late,' he said.

His voice was curt, and the world shifted briefly into black and white as, without noticing the gesture, he smoothed his moustache. Glen Miller was the style, and he was proud of it. Nan said a moustache made a man debonair, like Clark Gable and all the other stars she loved. John dropped his hand to fiddle with the one of the epaulettes of the white shirt they supplied (with navy slacks) as company policy. He took a deep pride in what he considered his uniform. If she could see him, Nan would be proud.

The two other employees of Abbott-Air exchanged glances, raised their eyes to heaven, and grinned. One of them raised his hand to twirl an imaginary moustache, and the other clicked his heels together with Nazi precision. But John Roper noticed nothing, which peeved them. The last bag went in with a particularly eloquent thud, and a small cloud of dust rose in the pearly air.

The airport workers stood back as the engine roared, and watched in silence as John Roper taxied away, a map of the red centre on his knee. Then they turned back to the long low white building, exchanging looks full of contempt.

'What would it cost him to say "See you later"?'

'That Pom wouldn't give the time of day to his own cock before his morning piss.'

Back in the office they stopped to have a yarn with Steve, who shared their views. Nobody at Abbott-Air liked the Englishman. He'd arrived from Wyndham as good as demanding a job, and as bad luck would have it, one of the guys on the mail run had shot through with his neighbour's wife, leaving no address, needless to say. So there was a vacancy, and at the time – with old man Abbott ill, and his son and heir expected from overseas – there seemed no reason not to give it to Roper. But there was something uptight about the man that got up everybody's nose. He strutted, he fiddled with the moustache that aped some RAF bugger from a dozen war films, and he didn't even talk like a proper Pommy. It didn't take long for word to reach even the canteen staff that Roper was a bit of a pain. When he talked at all it was to hint of great ambitions, so the name 'Roper-the-Hoper' stuck, the mocking emphasis heavy on the last word, as if they knew.

Far above, he climbed up and up into the bowl of the morning, to meet the sun. The buildings of the tiny airport dwindled to 00-gauge toys, and even its office 'tower' (a recent addition of which Abbott-Air Pty was inordinately proud) was reduced to a flash of plate glass. He glanced down and smiled briefly. The drumming of the engine filled the cockpit and soothed him to a sort of peace.

Shadows of mulga stippled the plain below, black dots on reds and ochres. Gullies filled with scrub resembled the tracks of a huge animal, slithering across the landscape. John looked down on ridges of land that settled into their patterns like the folds on the neck of an old man ruined by years of hard living. Yet after six weeks of doing the run, between charter ferrying, he noticed little about the land beneath, beyond what he needed for the routes between stations. He observed only that the plane's tiny, cruciform shadow was the only thing moving in this vast emptiness, crawling across the cinnabar plains and reminding him that he was there, and would always be there, free between heaven and earth . . .

And the shadow *was* him too. The little boy in grey short pants, stretching out his arms and roaring, round and round, then up and down the street, until Billy from next door shot him down – *Duh-duh-duh-duh-duh-duh . . . Crash!* Rolling over and over in the gutter, until Nan came to the door and shouted down the street, 'You – our Johnny! You get in here now!' Then he would be brushed down and swiped at with the dishcloth, as she moaned under her breath, 'Look at the state of these clothes, just look . . .' And she wouldn't let him out for a while, not if he was going to get his clothes dirty.

She said dirt was a sin, and he wondered where it came from – her obsession with scouring and polishing, until the floor and all the surfaces in that tiny house were so clean you could eat off them, which did not prevent her from starting over again, day after day.

'Nan, tell me about me mam and dad,' he said.

'Look at the state of the place!' she moaned, eyes swivelling around the room.

'Tell me, Nan!'

A little shadow, wings outstretched, travelling across the land, with nothing and no one to threaten it. Not up here. He and the Cessna were one.

It leapt now, whacked by thermal currents, and John let out a yelp of delight, feeling the air catch them both again, playing games, throwing the plane and him up and down, careening across the sky . . .

His joy filled the cockpit. Then it was as if the universe itself held them suspended, as if by wires, dead still above the arid red heart of the continent.

Three

A week later, Bernie slept late in the stifling bedroom which still smelt of disinfectant. It hadn't been so clean since the day her parents died. Out in the back garden the damaged crow began to caw loudly in his cage, wanting his ration of raw kangaroo. The harsh demands penetrated the layers of her consciousness, making her turn and pull a pillow over her head.

After being sick then running down the road in impotent rage, as if the perpetrators were likely still to be hanging around waiting for her, she'd burnt the defiled pillow in the garden. Then, smelling of sweat, wood smoke and burnt feathers, she had half-drowned herself in a shower and scrubbed at her skin so hard it hurt for days. She double-locked front and back and closed every window tight. During that long night, Bernie cursed the mixture of laziness and poverty which had prevented her organizing the air-conditioning most people now expected in a decent home.

The crow shrieked when the telephone rang. She jumped naked out of bed, and ran into the hall.

'Yeah, what?' she snapped.

There was a silence. Bernie slammed the phone down with a curse. All week she had been expecting this. Her enquiries at the bar had not increased her quota of friends. Skinno and his mates had not been seen again. But somebody local had led them to where she lived, and Bernie wanted to know who. There would be a score to settle; she passed many hours of frantic boredom – as she dispensed cans in the hubbub and sharpened her wits on the dross – pleasantly fantasizing about how. Sometimes her own aggressiveness shocked her a little, as if, within her tough exterior (she had no illusions about that) lurked a real monster – a genuine grade-A freak – only kept in check by the height and hardness of the walls.

15

Ah, but no – that wasn't who she glimpsed sidelong in the mirror on her wardrobe. There she saw a gentle, pretty child, opening her grey eyes wider and wider to look into the future – little Bernadette, saying her prayers each night, knowing nothing at all.

Bernie was pulling a singlet over her head when the phone rang again. She picked it up and waited. After a couple of seconds, a tentative voice repeated her number. She exhaled with relief.

'Sure . . . hey, er . . . you ringing about the . . .?'

'In the paper?' he said, as if this were a mystery that had to be solved.

'That's *right*. You interested? There's two rooms in fact, but one's better, so since you're the first, well, you can come and see. See what you think. The rent and everything, I put that in, didn't I? We'll just have to talk about the kitchen and stuff like that. Some kind of working arrangement . . . er . . . agreement, you know?'

She heard herself babbling foolishly into the silence. That's the trouble with living alone, she thought, you lose the habit of speech. She waited, but the man said nothing. Unreal quietness fell from the receiver in her hand . . .

'Well, d'you want to come and see the place or not?' she barked.

'Yes.' He sounded hesitant.

'Listen, mate, if you got some problem . . .?'

There was a click, and the line whirred.

The old fridge shivered and groaned as Bernie pulled it open and wrinkled her nose against the stink of the crow's food in its plastic box. She plucked out a couple of gobbets, and opened the back door. Eucalypts shaded the garden but already the sun was reaching towards its punishing height.

The sound of the bird was ugly: a harsh sawing *kraaa–ak,* devoid of recognition, let alone affection. It spoke only of the primitive grasping need for sustenance which is, Bernie knew, at the heart of all things. Two months ago she'd found it walking to and fro, trailing the wing, and wondered whether to put it out of its misery. But she remembered an old cage her brother once kept a couple of pigeons in, and dragged it from under the verandah. Now they tolerated each other, though the savage peck which took the first dark gobbet from her fingers also nipped her skin. As if excited by the unexpected treat of inflicting pain, the creature hopped frantically

16

from side to side on his perch, the broken wing giving him an ugly, lopsided hunch.

'G'day, Crow,' she said.

The bird cocked its head on one side and looked at her. The eye was glassy and cold, and looked past her into its memories of flight.

'Careful now, you vile old bastard,' she grinned, holding out the second chunk of meat. The heavy grey beak made its hammer blow; she saw the naked pink of the maw and the throat bulge grossly as the meat went down whole.

'You're my mate, Crow,' she whispered. 'Just you and me against the world, hey?'

It glared at her with a discordant, '*Kaaa kaaa–ak.*'

Then the telephone shrilled once more and Bernie turned back to the house, hoping this caller might be serious. But taking lodgers? She had serious doubts about the wisdom of this plan.

It had been Suzanne's idea.She responded in amused outrage to the phone call (a rare occurrence now, though there was no reproach) which had woken her on what Bernie called The Night of the Long Turd, and suggested that Bernie let the two spare rooms. 'You might as well have somebody there with you,' Suze said. 'That way, apart from the rents – which you could use, OK? – you'll have people around when you aren't there. It'll put the pigs off – in case they get off on crapping in your bedroom.'

'But turning into a *landlady*! Makes me sound real old,' Bernie said slowly.

'No, babe, just wise,' came her old friend's reply, distant down the line.

She made an effort to make her voice sound welcoming as she picked up the phone again.

'I'm sorry . . .' said the same light voice.

'You the guy rang about fifteen minutes ago?' she asked.

'Yes, I . . .'

Again, silence lapped against her ear, making her nervous. This voice was so quiet, as if, like her, it had forgotten how to speak. She could form no picture of its owner; only wonder that such shyness could survive in a town like this.

'Why'd you hang up?'

'Ran out of change.'

'You want to see this room, or not?' asked Bernie.

'Today?'

'No worries! Come by in about thirty minutes? Hang on – no, an hour? Tell you what, come at twelve for a beer – OK? I'm Bernie Molloy and it's 65 Dean Street – top end of town . . .'

She put the phone down and realized that she had not asked – nor had he volunteered – his name.

Carrying a bucket of water and a mop, Bernie contemplated her task. The truth was, she no longer went into the two rooms they'd all shared, she and Patrick in bunks in the larger one, and Siobhan and baby Lou in the other, on the little iron cots. She remembered Ma and Da waltzing down the hall with the triumph of this move: their own house, the step up from yearning at last, the proof that they were as good as 'them'. They'd made it in the lucky country.

When Bernie thought of her childhood she wondered when loss first sticks its claw into life, hooking you, so you're never the same again. And was there a point at which you could stop it? Long before she came face to face with death it was there, pricking her like conscience. From the other side of the world she heard Father Mullen:

'Listen to me, children, and imagine the hottest fire you've ever known. Well, believe me, that is as nothing compared with the fires of hell. The fires of hell are a million times hotter than your fires at home, and if you sin and fail to repent, you will be in there forever, burning in the fires of hell. Forever.

'And what is forever? What does it mean? Think of a beach, the biggest beach in the world. You go there and you pick up one grain of sand and you take it away. You go back a year later, and you take another grain of sand, and the next year and the next. How long before you have removed all that sand from that beach. How long, Bernadette Molloy?'

'A million years, Father.'

'No, a billion years, Bernadette. A billion years to remove the sand, and a billion years to burn in the fires of hell. That is forever, children.'

Patrick was happy to get out of all that. At fourteen he thought himself a man and wanted nothing more than to be a builder like Da, besides which, he had read enough Western comics to like the idea of a frontier town, even if it was in the wrong continent. Bernie's protests drew clucks from her mother, as if she was trying to deny the whole family a better

18

life. Colleen Molloy snuffled as Bernie yelled it wasn't fair to be transported (she'd read about the convicts) across the world where you ate your Christmas chicken and gravy in the sun, and the bugs were so big you were afraid to put your foot out of bed in the night . . .

And anyway, what sort of a God invented the *kangaroo*, so? She'd never fit in, she cried.

That's where it started. The ache of homesickness so strong that even the memory of Father Mullen's bulging eyes looking into your soul at the sin he knew was there – even that was better than eking an existence in the land of fire and sand that seemed the nearest thing to hell this side of the grave.

She finished cleaning, threw open the window, made up the bed with old purple sheets, and finally surveyed the room. It would do. She was curious about the person who was due to arrive, and the novelty of becoming a landlady. The rents might pay for a trip to Sydney . . . or perhaps she'd give up the bar – and not a moment too soon. Eight months off her fortieth birthday, Bernie Molloy brooded on time. She stared at herself in the mirror, and pinched the skin on her arm, noticing how it no longer sprang back to smoothness.

Noon came and went. Bernie wandered restlessly, giving in at 12.30 to crack a beer. She'd been sure the phone would ring all morning, promising company as well as rent. Why the silence? Must be a lot of vacant rooms in the town right now. She gave in to the cigarette too, despite her vow to cut down. Still, this was the first since the breakfast one, and she knew the first couple of draws would make her shiver, like vodka straight from the icebox, hitting the gut.

Twelve forty. *Bloody hell.*

She was staring the crow out when she heard a rattle from the front door. 'Didn't the fool see the bell?' she said aloud to the bird, flicking at the chicken wire so it was deluded into thinking food was imminent, and jumped from side to side on the perch.

'Poor grounded crow!' she said softly, and turned towards the house.

The young man who stood in the porch was tall and lean, with slim brown legs poking from faded cut-offs, and a beige singlet that revealed wiry arms. Somehow his clothes, skin and hair all shared the same tones, like the beaches she remembered from her childhood, when wind and rain whipped the sand into corrugations of ochre and brown which dried greyish-yellow in the sunlight. His hair stood up in little accidental corkscrews, and the eyes that stared at her from beneath thick straight eyebrows were as pale, soft and distant as the winter sky in Cork. A small gold hoop glinted in one ear.

She tried to guess his age. Twenty? No – from the lines at the corners of his mouth, he might have been approaching thirty. His face was bony and intelligent, but wary.

'G'day, uh . . . My name's Eddy?' he said, as if unsure.

'The room?'

He nodded, and waited.

She said nothing. Nor did she move.

They looked at each other. Bernie found herself glancing down at his feet, dusty in old red thongs, noticing how long and thin they were, to bear that gangling height. She took in the loose upward swing of his wrists – which seemed to replace speech, as if by this sudden half-gesture of resignation he might be understood. Disconcerted by his steady gaze she glanced beyond him to the ancient pushbike leaning against her fence. No car. She wondered if he could possibly afford the rent.

'Eddy Carpenter,' he said at last, as if he had just discovered the fact.

'Bernie Molloy,' she replied. 'Come in before you take root.'

He passed. To her slight surprise there was not the stale, unwashed smell she half expected, just the faintest suggestion of grass, leaves and soil.

'Which way?'

'Turn left – that's the room. I mean, one of the two – the biggest one, I told you . . . Then I'll show you the rest of the place.'

They stood side by side, looking at the purple and black paintwork, the poster of Hendrix, the ramshackle assortment of furniture. Bernie was assuming it must seem the height of luxury to this man, when he gave that non-committal shrug again, and murmured, 'I might have to move things out.'

'I know it's not . . .' she began. Then irritation snapped in. 'Why?'

'I just like space.'

'Don't we all?'

'You got the whole house?'

20

'Yeah – my parents' place. Then they died.'

'Ah,' he said, as if he knew.

She turned and he followed her from the bedroom, his feet making little slapping noises. Knowing it was absurd, even crazy, to let a total stranger into her house, Bernie still walked in front of him to the kitchen. He might have a record for all she knew, or be an axe murderer.

In the kitchen she turned. 'This is weird, isn't it?'

As if he had been reading her mind, he said quietly, 'I'm OK.' Then he smiled for the first time, and that sudden curve of his wide lips made her turn her face away, dazzled by sudden beauty. Such sweetness was out of place in her grubby house.

Bernie showed him pans and cupboards and said there would be a shelf free in the fridge, but that he should not cook his meals when she was in the kitchen, and must be careful because the washing machine was temperamental on account of its age. He followed it all gravely, making no response to the sentences which tumbled with increasing rapidity from her mouth. 'And there's a TV in the lounge room,' she went on. 'I suppose we share that. Tell you the truth, I've never done this before and . . . Oh hell, we'll just have to see how it works out . . . Beer?'

He shook his head.

'OK – well, do you want the room? You saw what I'm asking?'

He nodded.

'Does that mean you took the rent in, or that you want it?'

'Both,' he said.

'Not much of a one for talking, are you?'

He shook his head, and then smiled again. Full lips curved upwards wryly over slightly uneven teeth, transforming his face, making it more vulnerable. Still he said nothing.

Bernie grinned back. 'Yeah – well, I suppose most of us spend our lives going on about sweet FA. I know I do.'

'Why?' he asked.

Surprised by the challenge, she shrugged. 'I dunno – I suppose it's like . . . your words are bricks, you know? Pile enough of them up all round you, and nobody can get in.'

There was a short silence.

'Can I see the garden?' he asked abruptly.

Bernie flinched. She had just let something slip about herself which should have been followed up. But he'd ignored it. And with that realization she was overwhelmed by loneliness – like she stood on a strip of land, and had just noticed the crack beginning to open in the narrow spur behind.

Without another word she led him outside. He stood still, looking at the luxuriant growth. Bernie knew the place was neglected, like the house, and saw it clearly through the eyes of this stranger – weed-choked and dusty, paths fissured by growth.

'I could . . .' he began, then waved a hand around – reminding her of the ungainly but endearing movements of a marionette. 'It needs . . .'

'Feel free,' she said shortly.

Then he moved across to where the crow sat regarding them balefully from his wire-fronted home. As Eddy approached, he scuttled sideways, trailing the wing, and let out a hostile *'Ka–arak'*. The young man bent his head to the cage to murmur something, then glanced back at her with a shadow of a frown.

'Why d'you keep him?'

'I found him one day, just walking around out here. Don't know what got his wing. But he was only young and . . . I thought of wringing his neck but . . .'

'Too soft?'

'No,' she snapped. 'I just reckoned it'd be cool to see if I could tame him. I mean, why not?'

'Can't tame wild things,' he said, matter-of-factly.

'He's an old bastard but I've got used to the sound of him.'

Eddy Carpenter grunted, and she felt judged.

'How'd you earn your keep, anyway?' she asked.

'Odd jobs when I can. Here and there. Shelves and things. Only been in town a few weeks – and I got work labouring at the golf club they're making – you know? Soil's coming next week – from the north.'

She laughed. The idea of the golf club amused her, as the town's most incongruous nod in the direction of Old Country pretension. Still, anyone who could look at the area of dry scrub and visualize it green deserved a medal.

She grinned. 'If you don't shoot through, you can do what you like with the garden. Me – I can't be bothered.'

He nodded gravely.

As she showed him the bathroom, the full implication of Suze's plan made her cringe. This boy might well be in the shower when she wanted to be. It used to be bad enough when some guy stayed the night; always she wanted them gone when the act was done, even before the sweat had dried. But politeness meant you let them stay, and offered breakfast, and pretended that it had all meant something, when in reality there was nothing left to say or do. Conversation – she once said to a particularly keen man called Pete who came to work for the new tourist office – is an overrated activity. Certainly this Eddy would agree with that.

She looked at her plain bathroom and frowned. 'Haven't had anyone living here for a while. I s'pose I'll get used to it.'

'Have to get used to things,' he said.

The telephone disturbed their awkwardness. Relieved, Bernie ran to pick it up. 'Good afternoon – is that the person with a room to let?' The accent was English.

'Yeah, it's still going.'

She wondered why she didn't lie. Two of them! It was a ridiculous plan, and she felt angry with herself for being panicked by a turd – she, Bernie, the rough and tough, who needed nobody and was afraid of nothing. But since that night her real fears had been laid bare, here inside her parents' house. The violation from the outside only served to remind her of the private horror that lay within. Two strangers could surely do little to allay it, but at least there was a chance.

As she gave directions to the man who said his name was John, Eddy Carpenter was backing away towards the door, telling her he'd go and collect his stuff.

Four

Later Bernie would remember that she had quite fancied the other bloke at first. He stood on the step and tried to smile, but she saw the shyness that stiffened his limbs. Not much taller than she, he was broad-chested, even chunky. She liked that in a man.

John Roper had a square, ruddy face, given height by hair brushed neatly back in the style of Humphrey Bogart – or somebody. A pilot, she thought, he looks like a pilot! The epaulettes and short white sleeves gave it away, and the unnatural crease of his synthetic navy trousers. In this heat? She didn't like the moustache, though. Zippo had a cool Zapata back then; this guy had an apology for facial hair. He was younger than Bernie, but then (she thought with a pang) most people seemed that way these days, and it would get worse. Not as young as Eddy Carpenter though, and so maybe more likely to become a mate, if this crazy house-sharing worked . . .

The thing that bothered her, put her off, was the fact that John Roper was standing on her step, holding a large fibre suitcase, with the air of an expected visitor, sure of his welcome.

She looked down pointedly.

'You've come to check out the room, not move in, mate!'

Unfazed, he held her stare, and she was momentarily disconcerted by the darkness of his eyes. He said, 'There's been a problem, you see. I had to leave my other place.'

'Didn't pay the rent, then?'

She folded her arms. The man was unmistakably English – with speckled forearms, that unhealthy burnt-meat quality to the skin, and a look in the eyes of panic at distances too great to comprehend.

'I paid my rent,' he answered shortly, 'but the landlady wanted the room for a cousin who'd moved to town.'

'Oh.'

'There was nowhere to leave this. If you don't want . . .'

His voice tailed off, making Bernie feel guilty. She stepped back, allowing him to pass, drifting a too-sweet aftershave in his wake.

'John Roper,' he said, with a slight bow of the head, like someone in an old film.

'The name's Bernie Molloy.' The hand she took was surprisingly limp. 'Put the case in the hall. Then it's ready for a quick getaway if things don't work out!'

Anxiety flashed across his face.

'What might not?'

'No worries,' said Bernie, with a wave of her hand. 'Come in and check it out. Not that there's much to look at.'

The man walked into what had been Patrick's old room,

24

and stared at the ceiling. A large crack reached from west to east, like the horizon. Bernie saw his eyes follow it, to and fro. Then, without dropping his gaze or examining the furniture, he nodded. 'It's fine,' he shrugged.

In an indifferent staccato she told him the house rules she'd just devised. He nodded with an enthusiasm that did not match her tone, and smiled for the first time. She saw his relief; he had nowhere to go. The smile revealed good teeth, and she realized he definitely had a look of Bogart.

Yes, she thought, not bad.

Then – no you don't, my girl; the last thing you need is to be rolling in the cot with the lodger. It would be a good yarn for Suze, mind . . .

For about the sixth time that day, it occurred to Bernie Molloy that she might be going crazy. From tonight onwards she'd be sharing her precious space with two complete strangers. Oh Jesus.

'Listen, uh, John . . . it's a fortnight's notice – OK? I mean, if it doesn't work out, you can find somewhere else in a fortnight?'

'I'll bring the case in,' he replied.

She spread her arms wide, palms upwards, and grinned, despite herself. 'Might as well – since you brought it along. By the way – what do you do?'

'I work for Abbott-Air. On the mail run.'

'I thought you looked like a pilot! It's that shirt . . . My dad knew old man Abbott years back. It's a good place, yeah?'

He stroked his moustache, and slightly raised one shoulder. 'It does for now. But I'm not sure I'll stay. Maybe the company's too small. I've got ambitions . . .' His voice chimed assertively.

She cut him off.

'Good on you. At least I won't be worrying about the rent then!'

He said he would fetch his case, but paused, as if abstracted. 'Something wrong?' asked Bernie. The bloke was standing looking at her as if he wanted her for breakfast, and she didn't like that. Amused, she reckoned she'd have to lock her bedroom door at night.

'If you don't mind me saying, you remind me of a film star,' he said, shyly. 'Rita Hayworth. She had hair like yours, and she—'

'I don't go in for old films,' said Bernie.

'I'm sorry.'

'You were going to get that case?'

Fascinated despite herself, Bernie lounged in the doorway as he heaved the dented suitcase into the small room.

'What you got in there – rocks?'

'Books – and stuff. Makes it heavy.'

'*Books?*'

'Books about flying, and the war.'

She gazed at him with curiosity. 'You're really into all that stuff then?'

'It's what I wanted to do since I was little.'

The case was in the middle of the floor. He unclicked the rusting metal catches and flung back the lid. Inside, everything was packed, Bernie noticed, as if by an elderly lady. He looked up from the neatly folded clothes, met her inquisitive stare, then swung the lid down again.

'My father was a pilot,' he said shortly, and waited.

'Well, I'll leave you to get on with it then,' she said, taking the hint.

She'd reached the hall when he appeared behind her at the threshold of his room and rattled the handle with its old-fashioned latch lock. 'Is there a key?' he asked.

'Somewhere – yeah. There's a whole pile of them in a jar in the cupboard under the sink. Nobody's used them for years. Why'd you want to lock up?'

'I just . . . When you've moved around you like your privacy.'

'Nobody here'll poke about among your stuff, mate,' she retorted.

Face shuttered, he insisted. 'That's as may be, but still . . .'

Bernie strode into the kitchen, and knelt down by the sink, throwing open the doors with a crash. Silverfish scurried into crevices; somewhere in the murk at the back she heard the dry scrabbling of cockroach legs. A drum of scouring powder parted company from its rusted base and scattered congealed lumps among the dessicated corpses of spiders and flies. The rusting can rolling on its side evoked the countless morning hangovers of her past. A festering rash of dampness bubbled and flaked on the back wall, filling the small space with the stink of neglect. Gloomily Bernie picked up the single rubber glove that lay beneath the U-bend and it stretched itself into perished yellow Emmenthal in her hand.

26

Suzanne used to call the gloves her 'rubbers', and laugh. It would never have occurred to Ma to protect her rough red hands. Bernie imagined her mother kneeling there on the floor, just as she was now, rump poking out, big red arms going like the clappers as she scrubbed. A smell of vim and bleach always, and even the bottom of the washing-up bowl scoured to white. Poor Ma.

What an apology you are, Bernie Molloy, said the voice inside her, as if it were Ma's voice – soft and sweet with that rain-washed sound of home. But reproaching, as always.

'We always did the best for ye, Bernadette.'

'Will ye try to settle down so?'

'Will ye not be coming home?'

'Your Da and me, we'd feel the better for seeing ye at Christmas.'

And you're lying in some guy's bed, not remembering his name from the night before, with the stale, damp smell of him on your body and the hangover rising in your throat, thinking about your mother's hands, wrinkled from the washing water, laying out your clean knickers each morning. Little piles of clothes, folded, on the chairs in our room. And the shuffle of her old slippers down the hall at night, checking everything was all right.

The large jam jar was right at the back, still there after all this time, rattling with keys that unlocked doors nobody cared about any more. Bernie pulled it out, walked through to John Roper, and smacked it down in front of him.

'OK, mate, be my guest. Lock yourself up if you like,' she said.

Five

There was no sign of Eddy Carpenter the rest of that day. Hearing John Roper moving about in his room behind the closed door, Bernie took three more phone calls, and regretfully told the callers the rooms had gone. Two of them were women. She realized she had gone about it the wrong way, but it was too late now. She cursed herself for being so dumb as to give the room to the first guy without taking a dollar as deposit or getting an address. It was as if he was already merging into the dust of the road outside her house.

But if he didn't come to claim his room, she'd be left alone in the house with the English pilot with the war books, the moustache and the locked door – and Bernie wasn't sure she could handle that. Unless he turned out to be the love of her life, or at least a goer in the cot. There you go again, she thought. You always dream the man who met you before you were born would walk into the Zoo and know immediately you were made for him. It wouldn't matter about the dead-end job, or the clothes you wore, it wouldn't matter what you said or what you smelt of, because you'd both know. Then the music would swell and not a dry eye in the house.

'Pile a crap!' Bernie jeered at her own reflection.

Then she piled up her hair on top of her head, appraising this way and that. At least there was some consolation in knowing that the outside of you was still beautiful. But for how long? Only months before I'm forty, she thought grimly, and then it's the long slow slide towards the black hole.

No sound came from John Roper's room when she passed. She wondered if he would feed himself, and if so, with what? But for a hunk of cheese and a solitary tomato, and the festering kangaroo meat for Crow, her fridge was empty. She imagined him poking around in her kitchen, judging her.

She rapped on his door.

'Come in.'

'Thought you'd have locked it,' she said dryly.

'I didn't mean to cause offence.'

John Roper was lying bare-chested on the narrow bed, arms folded behind his head, legs stretched out and crossed. He was wearing khaki shorts like her own . . . Bernie averted her eyes from his solidity, because she liked that kind of build, and didn't want to. But his body was grub-white; the sun that reddened his face, neck and forearms had never been allowed to touch the skin beneath the pilot's shirt.

'Don't mind me, mate, I'm not used to having people around. You lock yourself away, and be my guest!'

'My last landlady . . . she was nosy. You know.'

'Not me,' Bernie said, resisting the impulse to stare around

28

at the plain little room, and see what he had done with it. But what could you do? It was like a cell; a room you might die in, realizing that it was all you deserved.

'You don't have to stand at the door,' he said, swinging around so he sat on the dge of the bed, looking up at her. She folded her arms, and planted her feet apart.

'Settled in then?'

'It doesn't take long.'

'Best to travel light. Where's home?'

He hesitated, then shrugged as if it did not matter.

'Sound like a Liverpudlian to me,' she said, surprised.

He looked down briefly, shaking his head. Then looked up again, focussing on a point just over her shoulder.

'Well I am, really, in a manner of speaking,' he said. 'But that was a long time ago.'

She noticed his accent change a fraction, straight-jacketing itself into tight vowels as it had done before. Who's he trying to kid, she thought, what's he got to hide?

There was an odd pause, then he added, 'I left, you know.'

'That's what you have to do,' she said dryly, 'unless you want to stay tied to your ma's apron strings.'

'My mother's dead.'

'Oh Sorry, mate. So's mine.'

'And my father.'

'Me too.'

He looked at her eagerly. Bernie guessed what was required.

'It happens,' she added.

'An accident . . .'

'Yes – it was. How did you know?'

'No, I meant *my* father,' he said.

Years of experience taught Bernie that few strangers want to hear your own tale, true or false. They scatter their lives before you like seeds.

John Roper rose abruptly, heading for the shelf that ran along the wall behind the door. About twelve books were lined up. She glimpsed a title: *The Spitfire in World War Two*. Then he was holding something out towards her. Light glinted on glass. 'This is him,' he said.

She took the small photograph in its scratched wooden frame, and examined it carefully. It was black and white, faded to a near-sepia tone, and creased as if once thrust carelessly into a wallet, so that no amount of smoothing could erase the cracking across one corner. Bernie squinted at the poorly focussed image. Cap at a jaunty angle, a pilot was grinning at the camera, mouth just about defined by a moustache, cigarette hanging from one corner.The features were indistinct. Behind him was a grey unidentifiable mass of a plane.

'That's a Fortress,' John Roper said. 'A B17.'

'What?'

'The plane behind him. It's a Fortress – good plane. The Americans flew them, and they helped us win the war, no doubt of that!'

Bernie peered at the image, wondering how anybody could identify the aircraft, since it was barely visible. Just a shadow, like the indistinct contours of the young man's face.

'This is your father? So he was an American?'

'Yup.'

Bernie heard the accent switch again, one jaunty syllable transporting Hollywood to her house, and pitied him for reasons she did not understand.

She handed back the fuzzy image in its battered frame, and watched him stand it tenderly on the shelf. There were two other framed pictures too, and she waited for him to show her.

John spoke as if to himself. 'Rotten luck, that was. He shoots down God knows how many enemy aircraft, ditches in the drink himself, up next day, at 'em again – and then he goes and buys it on a peacetime run because his 'chute got tangled. Pretty bad show.'

Bernie Molloy wasn't used to feeling out of her depth. Each night in the Zoo she handled the nutters and the drunks and the straightforwardly nasty ones who should have been put down at birth, and knew it was her role in life to cope. Yet this stocky Englishman, talking in his different accents as if the pale heart of him had no knowledge of itself and so roamed the byways of the universe looking for a voice – this stranger was now in her house and therefore a part of her life. The customary wisecracks died on her lips.

'My parents were killed in a car crash,' she told him.

'Bad luck,' he replied absently.

'I was away.'

'But *I* wasn't born,' he said, with the faintest air of triumph, as if nothing could cap that for tragedy.

'Who's this?' she asked, picking up one of the other photographs, the nearest. It was a round-faced woman with grey hair, wearing what looked like a hand-knitted cardigan. Something about that anxious expression, the attempt at a smile, reminded her of somebody else.

'Oh, that's my nan. She brought me up.'

'What's her name?'

'Lily. Lily Roper.'

Bernie handed it to him. 'Looks like my ma, mate! Hey – maybe we'll have a barbie tomorrow. Make you welcome – if this other guy turns up . . .' She hesitated, then grinned broadly. 'Jeez, I don't know how this'll work out. Never saw myself as anybody's landlady!'

He flushed. 'Well, to be perfectly frank, you're not much like any landlady I ever met.'

The room felt smaller and hotter than ever. Sweat gleamed on his pale chest.

Better be careful, girl, better get out of here, she told herself, and turned away with a careless, 'Catch you later,' feeling his eyes burn her back.

The Zoo was owned by Dick Springville, known in his youth as Springing Dick, because of his hyperactivity in bed. They said there wasn't a woman in the Territory he hadn't lusted after, and it was only geography got in the way. Those closest to him were privileged to examine the pits in his buttocks, where the irate husband of one woman peppered him with shot as he escaped through the window, leaving his pants behind. Dick was over sixty now, tough and strung out as a piece of old wire on a fence. His cropped hair was steel-grey. Pale mean eyes looked at you without blinking, but would sometimes close in a threatening wink if the talk got dirty enough or the woman was good-looking. He was short, skinny and almost bow-legged, and his right arm bore a tattoo of a skull with hoop earrings and a rose in its teeth, and the caption, 'She Ansered Back.' Few people he met had the intelligence to notice, or else the courage to point out, the mistake.

Nobody else could have run the Zoo and gone through three wives at the same time, treating women and customers alike with contempt or expansiveness, depending on his mood. Even the bouncer kept on the right side of Springville, because the darkest stories said that those who'd walked the other side long ago didn't come back, but in those days and these parts nobody knew or cared. A long scar up his left arm, and a set of white weals across his right knuckles were the nearest, he said, to anyone ever beating him in a knife fight. Springing Dick was respected.

But Bernie had a handle on her boss. It had been part of her privilege as the wanderer come home, to meet people who were always around when she was young, and see them for the first time. She remembered Dick Springville and his reputation, and the fact that Ma and Da dismissed him and his type as the worst aspect of the town, to be avoided by anybody 'daycent'. After the funeral, when she decided to stay, Bernie knew she was no longer decent and nothing mattered any more. So she sought him out to ask for a job.

He'd touched the small butterfly tattoo on the front of one of her shoulders with his nicotine-stained forefinger. 'Don't take much of a bloke's weight to crush one of them little things now, does it?' he said.

Holding his stare, she replied, 'Not usually, Dick, but this one's a steel butterfly.'

'Got tickets on yourself, eh?'

'Too right!'

'Goodonya!'

Later, knowing she was watching, Springville tightened his fist round the beer-hand of the troublesome ringer who'd tried to chat her up, so that the man paled beneath his tan as the can collapsed, squashing his hand in its tin folds.

Dick cleared the bar more quickly than usual that night, manhandling the last couple of drinkers out with powerful shoves and kicks – 'Go on, you bastards . . .' – before turning to face her with a grin. 'How'd you fancy a shot of something decent, Bern? You wouldn't let a feller drink alone?'

She'd shrugged. 'I'm on for anything, Dick.'

'Goodonya!'

He came through the bar, carrying two squat glasses and a bottle of Bells and sat next to her. Pouring himself a generous slug, he pushed the bottle over, as if to serve her would be an intolerable exhibition of gentility. She seized it, and sloshed in twice as much as he'd poured for himself – without removing her eyes from his.

'Goodonya!' said Springing Dick again, showing his yellow teeth.

'So – can you take me on, Dick?'

He raised his eyebrows in reply. There was an awkward pause. Bernie slugged whisky like medicine. Then, as if dredging from somewhere deep within himself a remembrance of social nicety, a sense of form, Dick Springville arranged his face into lugubriousness and said, 'I was sorry to hear about your ma and pa, Bernie.'

She shook her head and said shortly, 'That's why I got to find a job.'

'Come back to stay now, have you?'

'Reckon there's nothing to keep me in the city.'

'What you been doing?' he asked.

'A bit of everything. Worked in some tough places too, Dick, so this'd give me no problems.'

He nodded, staring at her. 'Ever get married?'

She shook her head vigorously, eyes fixed on the golden liquid in her glass, knocking some more back quickly as if the sound of her own swallowing and the fiery hit of it would stop the noise in her head.

'No way.'

'All the women round your age I've known, they start wantin' blokes and babies like blokes want Fosters and fucks. Get the old ring on the finger, you know what I mean?'

He did not see her hand shaking as she fumbled for a cigarette from her open pack, and bent to light it, so that the curls fell over her face. Somewhere in her mind the keening started up again, high and desperate.

Bernie picked up her glass and held it high. 'Cheers mate!' she shouted, and he clinked his noisily against hers. 'Here's to a good working relationship, eh?'

'I'll drink to that, love. And I'll drink you up too, if you give me half a chance.'

She looked down at the gnarled hand on her knee, then tipped back her head to empty her glass in four or five long swallows that set her head on fire. The shelves behind the bar, stacked with bottles, glasses and cans, were all circling her now, like a gang of predators waiting for the kill. She leaned back slightly, forgetting she was on a stool, and nearly lost her balance. Dick Springville's hand gripped both her arms tightly and held her fast.

33

He spoke urgently. 'Come upstairs with me, Bernie. What you say? Come upstairs and cop a bloke a favour. Know what I mean? Get acquainted, eh? You're a big girl now, Bernie – know the score . . .'

The whole place was bucking and swooping. She let herself be led to the door at the side of the bar and up the narrow stairs to the room Dick kept for when he was too drunk to drive home. He lived in a bungalow on the outskirts of town but four nights out of seven slept up here, in a chaos of old soft-porn magazines, boxes of booze, overflowing ashtrays and the rank smell of unwashed sheets on the small double bed shoved up in the corner.

Dick Springville crushed his face into hers as if his next meal was somewhere halfway down her throat, grinding his teeth and tongue and tearing at her zip at the same time.

'Half a mo . . .' she said, pulling free, and slipping out of the dress to save him the bother. She wore no bra, and after grabbing her breasts with scratchy hands, he pushed her back on the bed. She lay, eyes closed, listening to the sound of his clothes dropping to the floor.

Bernie tried to shut off as he worked away giving small moans close to pain. Every so often she absentmindedly made an answering noise, the smallest display of panting, to give him encouragement. She'd learnt that was required.

She thought about Zippo, her Bondi bikie, the man she loved way back when she was twenty. They'd lie on the beach beside his Triumph and there wasn't enough of him, or her, or the universe, for the wholeness of it, the happiness. In the hot, fat night, with sweat and slick and surf crashing in as the sky exploded with dope and sex and stars, he gave her something more brilliant than she'd dreamed of back home, haunted by the sound of Ma's Singer. That was when she met Suzanne, and the days and nights merged into one long party, as the Stones snarled in the background and Janis sang 'Freedom's just another name for nothing left to lose'. Me and my Zippo – lighting up my gut every night. That was real loving, and she knew it at first sight. Oh God, and we'd lie in each other's arms, sharing a joint, and talking about the kids we'd have one day, because he thought family was cool, and loving was cool, and none of it should stop, even when you got old. And the weeks drifted into months – until the Bonneville spilled him over the highway and she watched him hang on for two days until finally his light went out, and she knew she had to find her way in the dark.

Dick was on top of her now, fumbling away with his hand between her legs. 'Oh fuckin' Jesus,' he muttered.

She heard the catch in his throat. Astonishment sobered her. 'All right, Dick – happens to the best of you,' she said.

Springing Dick's spring is sprung, she thought, wondering how many years he had been failing to get it up, and avoiding women in case his secret was out. No wonder the guy was desperate. He was like a primitive tribe that suddenly saw its gods crumble, leaving an empty universe in their place.

'Reckon we better let sleeping dicks lie, eh dog?' The words were out when she heard herself, and the laughter began to bubble.

But his mouth moved, painfully shaping the one word, 'Sh–orry'.

'No worries, mate.'

Still he covered his eyes. 'Never used to happen,' he muttered, and she saw a trace of moisture on one cheek beneath his hand. 'Too much booze.'

'C'mon, Dick, you weren't that pissed tonight,' she said quietly. 'Maybe you've got to face the fact that you're not as young as you was, and settle down with some nice cosy lady who'll cook you meals. You don't want to be trying to get in the pants of every chick twenty years younger who walks into your pub. Do you? That's no way for a man to live. That's no way for a man to be happy. You don't want to be livin' like *this*, mate.'

With moist eyes he followed the wave of her hand, taking in the dingy room and coming to rest on the old calendar that hung from a nail on the wall opposite. The naked blonde was kneeling with splayed legs. 'I mean, looking up at that'd give any bloke the droop. Imagine finding that pair of nutcrackers in your bed, Dick! Bloody terrifying, I call it!'

She giggled, and after a few seconds he joined in. Their laughter softened the empty squalor of place and time, smoothing the cracks. As if at an unspoken signal, they both eased themselves up, and turned away to dress. Then they were sitting side by side on the creaky bed, smoking cigarettes.

'I won't—' Bernie began.

At exactly that same moment he whispered, 'Keep it to yerself like a good sheila, eh?'

'I got nothing against you, Dick,' she said.

'Goodonya,' he said sadly. 'Start work Monday?'

She did. He was impressed by the way she drew a schooner, two smooth movements making the perfect head. She could change a keg good as any man, and attracted business too, since one man in two thought himself in with a chance with 'Springing Dick's new stunner'.

And just four weeks later the town buzzed with the news that Dick was trying to pass himself off as Richard Springville, and had asked Joanie McPherson to marry him. Joanie was a plump, fifty-five-year-old widow who kept a rooming house, and had been after him for years. The new Mrs Springville cooked for him, and cleaned him up, and Dick never stayed upstairs at the Zoo any nights now. He filled out, lost that edgy look and people said he had never appeared so damn pleased with himself, even when he was up every skirt in the town.

Dick greeted her now, as she swung into the Zoo. 'You late, Bern – got yourself a man to keep you busy at last?'

'No such luck, Dick, they all heard I was coming and left town.'

'Take a real man to tame you, Bernie Molloy.'

'Yeah, and the only one left in this dump is the one I'm talking to, and he's spoken for! Wouldn't want to get the wrong side of Joanie!' she grinned.

He chuckled. 'Goodonya!'

She told Dick about her lodgers, explaining, 'Need a bit extra, you know?'

'You asking me fer a rise, Bern?'

'Wasn't what I was saying, Dick.'

'Maybe one of em 'ull make an honest woman of you at last.'

Bernie looked at him through narrowed eyes, in mock aggression, and stuck fists in her hips. 'Listen, Dick, one more crack like that . . . If you think I'm that desperate I'm going to jump into bed with a Pommy pilot who looks like he's been too long in the sun already, or this kid who didn't even come back, then you'd better sack me as a sad bitch bad fer business!'

Dick looked her up and down, slung an arm around her shoulder, and winked at Frank, who was preparing for the evening by cracking his knuckles with intense concentration.

'Looking at you, Bernie, I'd say you're bloody brilliant for business!'

When he moved away, the smile died on Bernie's mouth. She sat down near the door, lit a cigarette and watched the wraiths of smoke, like the joss sticks she sometimes burned, filling her room with incense smells far sweeter than Father Mullen's. The thin cloud dispersed into the sunlight slanting in from the high window above her head. Was that what happened when you died, she wondered – your self and soul dispersing like sand blowing across the desert? Ma and Da were lying in the same grave not far away, dust to dust, but what about the rest of them? You couldn't believe it, no matter how much you wanted to. Ha! Imagine Ma meeting Zippo . . .

She had screamed at the nurse to leave her alone with him.

She had shouted to the priest to get out.

Sometimes at night, haunted by the intolerable sounds – crying, Ma's soft shuffling slippers, then the crying again – she would wonder how the universe could contain all the millions and billions and trillions of dead souls accumulated since the beginning of time, with that vast teeming space always being topped up, each day, each hour, each minute, with more. How could you find the ones you knew, among so many? Was it lonely there? And if you were little, how would you find your way? Who would find you, to look after you there?

A vibration sang deep within her throat, like a tremor that shifts the glasses and pictures in a room, making people glance at each other nervously, not knowing if the avalanche will sweep them all away, or the earth turn itself inside out to welcome the new dead.

Ohhhhhh. Bury it. Bury it.

Bernie gripped the cigarette between her teeth and shut her eyes tightly, blotting out the bar and the curling smoke. She wanted it to stop. She wanted to return to the blank stillness she had worked so hard to achieve. Hands balled, hard nails digging into her palms, she rocked forward and back, like someone with a bad stomach cramp, until – by sheer will – she managed to stop her own sound. Then she slumped back again exhausted, and opened her swimming eyes to see ash spread across her thighs.

'You all right?' Dick asked.

'Fine.'

Dick unlocked the door, and the first regulars walked in, crying out for recognition in the shape of the usual tinny in its holder. Bernie heaved herself up and went to her place behind the bar, as ready as the punters for another night in the Zoo.

A couple of hours later, hot and busy, she became aware of somebody watching from the end of the bar. At first she ignored the pull of the eyes because it didn't do to show you noticed. Then at last she looked up. For a few seconds Bernie could not identify the oddly familiar figure. She took in somebody tall and tan, before nodding in sudden recognition. Eddy Carpenter hovered as if he did not know what to do, bobbing behind the heavy drunks like a moth.

'Hey – you didn't show!' she accused.

'There were things . . .'

'Might have phoned, mate!'

He gave that odd little shrug. 'Lost your number.'

'Serve you right if I'd given the room away already.'

A small smile lifted the corners of his mouth, as he shook his head as if to say he knew she would not have let him down.

'How did you know I worked here?'

'Maybe you said.'

'I didn't.'

He looked embarrassed. 'No? Er . . . well, I saw you in here once. The day I hit town.'

'You were never in here!' she accused.

'Just that once. And I remembered . . . on your doorstep, I remembered. You. Here.'

Hands flat on the bar, he set his mouth in a narrow line, like a man who has decided to reveal no more. She saw the red dirt in his fingernails, and splashes of orange, white and black paint on his bony fingers. Suddenly she felt amused by the snub nose, the curly light-brown hair that had not seen a comb for years, the broad lips that could not help but curve in a smile to match her own. How could you not like him, she thought? And he's . . . the strange word 'beautiful' flashed unbidden across her brain.

'OK,' she said.

'OK.'

'You want a drink?'

38

He shook his head. 'No – nothing. I'll come tomorrow then? Bring my stuff?'

He was already turning away when she nodded assent. She called, 'Not too early!' but he showed no sign of having heard.

Eddy Carpenter turned away and drifted out through the crowd, which seemed to part before him, as if instinctively daunted by his stillness. He was not one of them, and she liked him for that. Bernie lit a cigarette and noticed the grace of her new lodger's movement, hips, spine and shoulders as flexible as a young eucalypt.

Six

Lily Roper wakes at five, and as usual her first thought is of John, wondering what he is doing. But this morning the ache knocks her back on her pillow, making her catch her breath. Light from the street lamp outside slashes through the gap in the thin curtains.

Lily arches her back, squeezes her eyes tightly shut, and pants, counting each shallow inward rush of breath.

. . . twenty . . . twenty-one . . . twenty-two . . . twenty-three . . . twen— Ahhhh, it'll be all right, John, in a minute . . . you'll see.

It's passing, as always. Sweat chills on her forehead. She sighs and settles back into the pillows. Hilda Rawlins, three doors down, keeps nagging her to go to the doctor's, but Lily doesn't believe in them. You have a bath, put your best underwear on, then wait for three-quarters of an hour only to be in and out of there in five minutes flat, with another bit of paper in your hand for the tablets.

She hears the milkman's glassy clanking in the street below. When John was little and couldn't sleep, they'd be sitting in his room having a cup of tea, nice and sweet to calm him, and the milk float would go by, and John would say, 'Nan? What do you get if you cross a cow with a boat?'

'I don't know, love,' she'd smile. 'What do you get?'

'A milk float!' he'd yell, and she'd laugh, each time.

'Listen, Nan, there's this man sitting next to this pilot, and he points out the window and says, "Look at them people down there, they look like ants!" And the pilot says, "They *are* ants. I haven't taken off yet!"'

She reaches for her glasses and his last letter, fumbling to unfold the thin blue aerogram. Maybe he's writing so big this time because he doesn't have much to say, and doesn't want too much space on the blue.

She reads:

Dear Nan,

I hope you are keeping well. I'm not so bad, though the heat is getting bad again, and gives me a headache. I can't say I like the idea of another Xmas in the sun, but it can't be helped. Funny to think of you all complaining becos of the rain!!!

I'm just about to move so will write with a new address when I know it. The rent sounds OK – but soon I'll get the rise and won't have to worry.

I'm keeping well in general and hope you are too. Please, Nan, don't send me anything for Christmas, because what with the move I don't need anything – but you can look out for the postman!

That's all for now, from your affectionate grandson,

John

Lily smiles as she folds the letter, opens the drawer, and puts it back on the pile. Then, very slowly, she heaves herself up, and sits on the side of the bed to catch her breath. Look at the weight on me, she thinks. No wonder me heart's playing up. John used to call me Nellie the Elephant when he was feeling cheeky.

He always found it hard to sleep. There were shadows beneath his eyes during the day, and he yawned in class. She'd be fast asleep and hear him yell, 'Naaaaaann!' Another bad dream. His nerves were bad. So she'd bring him the tea, and one of his comics, but he always wanted her to stay and talk.

It takes her twenty minutes to dress, the cold seizing her

up now, so it's almost impossible to bend. The one good thing about the pain is – it makes you burn inside. That's what she told Hilda, who put on that face of hers again – long as a wet weekend. Lily can read it easily. It says – *Poor old thing, shouldn't be living there alone, and that grandson of hers just buggered off because all he could think about was learning to fly. What do ordinary folk like us want with them fancy ideas?*

She's heard them talking about him. Things like he used to put that funny accent on, because Scouse wasn't good enough for him, was it? And the endless flying talk. He never meant any harm, all that saying 'Wilco' and 'Over and out', was what he'd learned from the comics.

Later, all that funny stuff he'd come out with, it was just him pretending – trying to get over his disappointment at getting nowhere. Such a shame. All those nights in the Air Training Corps, and him so smart in the uniform, even though the other children laughed at him, right in his face. But the nobs turned him down in the end and he stayed in his bed for a week, he did. Who'd have thought you'd need exams to fly a plane!

He never took to shop work. Then he read about what it's like over there, wide open with chances for lads like him. Out there they think of flying like we think of jumping on the 81. So we looked into the whole business and found he could get help in getting out there. Assisted passage, they call it. Oh he saved and saved . . .

He said, 'Nan,' he said, 'you have to have ambition and I know I was meant to be a pilot, like me Dad.'

That's what he said.

Poor John.

John Roper's grandmother opens the door of his bedroom, setting her teeth against the damp air that swirls out to meet her, and stands there for a few moments watching the little Spitfire twirling on its thread in the middle of the room.

Seven

With a cry she jerked awake, and stared across the room. The long mirror on the wardrobe door reflected nothing but blankness. Bernie squirmed down and groaned aloud. Pandemonium of birds in the garden, punctuated by unmelodious cawks. It was too early to be hooked by the grief which pulled her up from the dark depths to the unwelcome light on the surface.

Bury it, bury it, bury it . . .

She went back to sleep at last, despite the nightmare. Later, she heard the doorbell – a short burst only, as if the person on the doorstep was unsure.

'Shit!' she mumbled, fumbling on the night table for her watch. It wasn't there. She reached to the floor, picked it up in a handful of dust and fluff, and cursed more loudly.

'It's . . . too . . . bloody . . . early,' she protested.

The doorbell sounded again, more loudly this time.

Bernie was starting to heave herself out of bed, when footsteps passed her bedroom door. She froze for a moment in shock, then remembered the presence of John Roper in her house. Another stranger. What had she done to her freedom? It would be better to sell the place and move to Sydney than share this space with two . . . what? Two drifters, was the phrase that flitted across her mind, although she knew she too was a drifter. At least they'd all have something in common, if she let them stay long enough to find out.

She heard the voices clearly. John Roper asked Eddy what he wanted and Eddy explained he had come about the room.

'Afraid it's gone, old chap,' said Roper.

'But I thought . . .'

'Bad luck.'

Bernie burst out of her bedroom, tying the belt of her kimono. 'If you don't mind, I'll answer my own door,' she snapped, barely able to look at the man in the checked cotton dressing gown who stood squarely as if he owned the place.

'Sorry, I thought you were asleep,' John said, standing back to let her pass.

'I *was*,' she replied, transferring her hatred to the apparition on the doorstep.

Eddy Carpenter wore a yellow sweatshirt too thick for the morning's warmth, and loose denims hung precariously off his narrow hips. A bedroll was strapped on his small rucksack, and on one shoulder he carried a long tubular bag of coarsely woven red cotton.

'I said not to be early!' she snapped irritably.

He flinched, and glanced down at a non-existent watch on his wrist, then looked up again, more worried than ever. Satisfied, she turned on the other man.

'Why are you telling him the room's gone? He's the bloke I bloody well let it to!'

'I didn't know . . .'

'For someone who doesn't know things, you act pretty cocky to me!'

Bernie saw something approaching panic in John Roper's eyes. He shuffled his feet while Eddy Carpenter stood still.

Twenty minutes later they were sitting on the back verandah, around a shaky wooden table, watching the crow hop to and fro. Craving a cigarette, Bernie poured tea. The two men waited for her to start the conversation – which (she thought glancing from one to the other) was as demanding a task as kicking the drunks out of the Zoo on a Saturday night. Eddy Carpenter wore silence like a mask, but John Roper was at the blocks, just waiting for the signal to release his nervy litany.

'You two are going to have to get to know each other,' she said at last. 'We could play it like one of those alcoholics' meetings – which in my case ain't far from the truth!'

John laughed, too loudly. Eddy stared at her as if she had said something deeply puzzling to him, and faintly disturbing. He turned towards the crow.

'You fed him?' he asked quietly.

'Won't do the old bugger any harm to wait.'

He stared at the bird in silence for a few seconds. Then he turned to her, his pale eyes opaque, and just raised his eyebrows. Bernie felt judged and did not like it.

43

'Bad enough for him to be in there. With that wing.'

Before she could protest, he stood up and disappeared into the house. She heard the fridge door open, and shut, and felt unsettled by the impudence of the stranger, who reappeared quickly with a sliver of black meat between finger and thumb. She and Roper watched as he leaned against the cage, making soft clucking noises deep in his throat, and the bird shuffled on its perch to take the meat from his fingers. '*Kar-ark.*'

'Sure,' whispered Eddy, 'Kuk-kuk-kuk-kuk.'

As Bernie watched, he thrust his finger into the dull beak of the grasping injured creature and allowed it to nibble – but gently, as she had never seen it behave.

'Just as well he likes you,' she said sarcastically. 'Take your finger off otherwise.'

'Oh, they *know*,' he said.

'We used to have a budgie when I was little,' said John, 'and my grandmother tried to teach it to talk. She spent half the day by that cage saying, "Joey, Joey," but it never spoke. Then one day it got out, and the window was open, and that was that.'

'Good on it,' said Eddy, folding himself back into the rickety chair.

Bernie glared at him. 'No harm in keeping things,' she said shortly.

'Depends who's doing the keeping and why,' said Eddy.

'*Kaa-ark,*' said the crow, cocking his head towards them so the sharp, malevolent eye looked straight at Bernie, carrying ancient curses.

She reached for her pack, shook out a cigarette, and took a long time lighting it, while she surveyed her lodgers under the shadow of her hair. They were a weird pair, she thought – the red-faced Pom with his stiff mannerisms, and the golden Aussie with his sinewy limbs and silent insolence. For that was what it was, she thought – to go and get the crow's meat like that. Who did he think he was? She blew smoke into the air across the table, challenging them not to like it.

Half-heartedly she waved the pack around, to be rewarded by two headshakes. 'That's good!' she laughed harshly. 'One person smoking in the place makes it stink enough.'

Bernie imagined days like this – meals, bumping into them outside the bathroom, someone else's programme on the TV – and felt dispirited. But she wouldn't show it. She turned to

44

John Roper with a try at enthusiasm. 'OK, so back to the beginning. Why don't you tell us how a Pom comes to be flying planes around this godforsaken country?'

'Wilco! But I warn you – it's a long story,' said Roper, lifting a shoulder as he swivelled towards her, as if to ward off a blow.

'No worries. We got time,' said Eddy Carpenter.

'I always wanted to be a pilot – since I first remember,' John said, cradling the mug of tea and staring down at the strong liquid. 'Nan says it must be because of my father. She brought me up, it was just the two of us all the time, and at first she tried to put me off. He was American, a pilot – she says he was a bit of a hero. Flew B17s, you know them? They called it the Fortress, big plane, had this plexiglass nose where the navigator and bombardier would sit – must have been really cramped, stuff sliding all over the place. Cold too. But my dad, he was the pilot, sitting up there with the co-pilot, and I bet he hardly ever let him take over! I bet they showed Jerry what's what!'

His face shone. He was leaning forward now, mug put down, right hand reaching as if for a joystick. There was a long pause.

'About your dad . . .?' Eddy prompted.

'Stationed in Suffolk. The Mighty Eighth. That's where he met my mother. It was the usual story. Pretty waitress, handsome flier – you know. But this was right at the end of the war, and he stayed on for a while – some of them did, had to wind things up . . . Nan says it was a real romance, like in a film. But she thought nothing would come of it. Johnny – they called me after him – went back to Minnesota, but kept on writing. Nan says he looked like a film star – and my mother too, somebody called Veronica Lake? She couldn't believe it, Nan says, because those chaps . . . well, you know know what they were like. But Johnny wasn't. He wanted to marry my mother . . . and . . . he came back to see her . . . and . . .' He looked down.

'What?' asked Bernie softly.

His mouth stiffened. 'She got pregnant, but Nan didn't worry, because he'd gone back to get things ready, y'know, for the wedding. But – this was the rotten luck. He'd flown the Fortresses in all those missions and then what happens? He's flying peacetime at home, has to bale out, but the chute gets tangled . . . and . . . that's it.'

Eddy leaned forward intently. 'God, mate, that's bad. So what then?'

45

John shook his head. Looking miserable, yet strangely pleased, he seemed to shake the question off with a twitch of his shoulder. 'Nan's always kept pretty mum. Understand why. But to cut a long story short, my mother had me, but went into that depression – what's it called . . .?'

'Postnatal,' said Bernie, swallowing hard.

'That's it. She was only twenty and I wasn't two months, and she just walks out the house one day, and doesn't come back. She was on tablets, Nan says – didn't know what she was doing – went and jumped off a railway bridge, and that was that. '47, this was.'

'Mother of God, the poor girl,' Bernie sighed.

'What was her name?' asked Eddy.

'Lily – same as my Nan. *She* never got over it – well, you wouldn't, would you? She left Suffolk because she wanted to forget it all, and for some reason we ended up in Liverpool. She said she wanted a new start, so . . .'

His voice tailed off. He spread his hands out, then let them drop on his knees, as if it were too much effort to keep them in the air any longer.

'And so . . . you wanted to be a pilot like him?' Bernie prompted.

He nodded, mouth set in a thin line, then rose abruptly as if standing to attention. 'I'll get the photos,' he barked, and disappeared inside. Oh God, thought Bernie, can I face this? She glanced across at Eddy, but he was still staring intently down at his clasped hands, head on one side. Insects buzzed. The crow scratched at its perch.

John Roper came back and pushed the small framed picture at her, forgetting she had already seen it in his room. Politely she studied it, then handed it silently to Eddy, who cradled it in cupped hands.

'And *this*,' said John Roper in the voice of someone who expects a response, 'is my mother.'

This photograph was slightly larger, in a metal frame. Bernie contemplated an image almost as misty as the one of the pilot. The young woman was smiling, her eyes narrowed against bright sunlight. She was posing by what looked like a front door, one hand up on the frame, the other on the hip thrust out beneath the flowered dress with puffed sleeves. She wore laced platform shoes, and her long dark hair was dressed in a roll around her head, like a halo.

'She looks pretty,' said Bernie.

John nodded and offered the snapshot to Eddy, who held the images side by side – the flier and his girl, one in each hand, making of them a diptych before which he bowed his head. He sighed.

What do you say? Bernie thought. She wanted to cry.

At last Eddy placed the frames on the table in front of their owner, so that the debonair pilot and pretty girl stood peering from their grey mists, across time, towards their son, John Roper, who was gazing back at them with an expression neither Bernie nor Eddy could read.

'Good to have the pictures,' Eddy said tightly. 'Good to have something left.'

'Well, I reckon we all need a beer after that,' said Bernie, rising awkwardly to her feet. As she passed behind John's chair, she laid a hand on his shoulder and murmured, 'OK, mate.'

When she had disappeared inside the house, John Roper leaned forward. 'Don't you think she's a bit – well – gorgeous?' he whispered.

The sudden change made Eddy gape. 'Can't say I noticed,' he said.

'My last landlady looked like a rat!'

'Oh.'

'Where did you live before here?

'All over the place – travelling around, until I came to town a month ago. Somebody I met on the road gave me a floor.'

'Got a job?'

'Yeah – at what's going to be the golf course.'

'Doing what?'

'Labouring. They've just got all this soil from the north, mountains of it. Good stuff, too. There's no soil round here – not proper earth, only sand.' John Roper looked blank. Eddy forced himself to continue, 'Once the soil's laid we'll sow the grass seed. Has to be a special strain, because the water round here – way down – is salty.'

'Ah.'

John Roper tilted his chair back and gazed upwards, his attention wandering out and beyond the verandah, up to the sky, far above a man who raked soil.

Eddy grinned and leaned forward, hands dangling between his splayed knees. He watched the ants' frantic activity around his thongs, noticing the patterns of their dance, and saw how the wood was rotting and splintering all around them. Once the house had been painted dark green; now the paint hung in greyish curls, and the wood beneath was bleached and grainy. The builder in him assessed all that needed to be done.

Eddy saw, but could not know the full extent. Within that wood, and the ruined paint, and the very dirt beneath the rotting floor he sat on, were recorded, as if on tape, all the complaints of Colleen Molloy, visiting the house every couple of days, to see how the building was progressing; weeping and shouting when Sean made excuses; setting her moaning brood to pick up bits of rubbish that blew into the site; and laughing, after nearly a year of waiting, with the excitement of removal into her own house at last. Mrs Molloy's hopes were painted on the walls of that building and her tears washed through the pipework – when none of her children remained, and the bad daughter Bernie refused even to write from the city, where she was up to Lord knows what sort of sinful things. Colleen Molloy's prayers still whispered in the shadows, and hung in curls of paint.

Bernie came back with a small tin tray, on which she had placed three cans and a bowl of crisps.

'It's quiet out here,' she said.

Both men looked up. John Roper rose politely to take the tray. Eddy immediately returned his gaze to the ants, and said quietly, 'There's plenty of time.'

'Not when you're coming up forty – like yours truly.'

'Well, I hope you won't mind me saying, but you don't look anything like that,' said John Roper with open admiration. 'More like thirty, I'd say!'

'For *that* you can live here as long as you like!'

After a short pause, during which they each made much of tipping cans and crunching crisps, she asked if they were hungry. At the same time, helplessness settled on her; as she realized this was a new life and she had no idea how to live it.

John Roper looked at his watch. 'Well, I will be when it gets to dinner time,' he said gravely, looking disgruntled – as if his feelings and appetite mattered.

'We can go out and buy something,' said Eddy. 'Take your car.'

'Oh God, it's too hot. We'll have to work out this meal thing,' she said, looking bothered.

They both nodded.

'What about weekends?' Eddy asked.

She frowned. 'Depends on my shifts . . . but seems stupid for us all to be cooking meals at the same time and eating separate. So . . .'

'We could have a rota,' said John. 'Take it in turns . . .'

'Can you cook?' she asked.

'No – Nan did all the cooking.

'I can cook,' Eddy said. 'I'll make something.'

'Like spaghetti an' a tin of tomatoes?' she said, relieved. 'I never been much of a housewife. Living with Ma you got homemaking stuffed down your throat 'til you wanted to be sick!'

Eddy glanced up. Spider webs were grey with dust under the sagging verandah roof. Bernie followed his gaze.

'Bit of a dump.'

'Just needs a coat of paint, a bit of maintenance. Wouldn't take long.'

'Trying to offer in exchange for rent?'

Eddy bridled. 'I'll pay your rent,' he said quietly, 'and do odd jobs for you for nothing. Houses need a bit of care. Like people.'

Ashamed, she ducked her head for a cigarette. Her hand trembled as she lit it, and she sucked in smoke as a starving person gobbles food. But when she threw back her head to send a cloud up to the webs, the laugh was harsh. 'Oh, pull your head in, Eddy! Do all the odd jobs you want, if you feel like it! But who's going to pay for the paint – Father Christmas? Me, I'd rather sit on my bum and work my way through a cask.'

Eddy shrugged and rose. He stood for a second looking down at them both, then turned to walk into the house without another word. Through the back door screen he heard her clearly. 'Bit of a drongo, eh? Oh well – I always could pick 'em.'

John Roper laughed.

Eight

When John Roper arrived for work on Monday morning he had a new boss. But here they did not play such roles overtly; the philosophy of 'mateship' made that unacceptable. Democracy in the lucky country had to be seen in action: they clapped you on the shoulder, called you 'mate' and then gave orders.

John Roper was afraid.

He was summoned to Greg Abbott's new office at the top of Abbott-Air's new low-rise office tower, in one corner of the airport above the hangars. The young man sitting at the desk was his age, John reckoned. But the only son of the legendary old man 'Ace' Abbott, pioneer of flight in the outback, entrepreneur and founder of Abbott-Air Pty, was fitted by birth and training to instruct. As a result he rarely raised his voice, or caused offence to the most prickly of employees.

After listening downstairs patiently while his wife gave birth to four daughters at home, old man Abbott had at last been rewarded, thirty-four years ago, with the birth of the son who would take over the family business. The celebrations went on for days. People used to say the old man shouted the whole town.

When he was four Greg sat on his father's knee in a Cessna, put his chubby fingers over Ace's brown hands and felt, through his father's body and his own, that sweet pull against gravity. By the time he was ten he knew all the controls as well as he knew his multiplication tables, and when his school friends were coveting motorbikes and cars, Greg was flying with a finesse that reminded everybody of old man Abbott himself. It isn't just a question of getting the machine in the air and bringing it down safely, Ace used to say, it's a matter of *feeling* the air, and knowing how to control it, to ride it – like a horse.

Ace Abbott's pride in his boy was as legendary as his prowess. Greg would have the best of everything, but an education too; science at university, then a further degree in business studies, a postgraduate diploma in management, a few months, public-relations experience . . . He would go overseas too, groomed to expand Abbott-Air Pty even beyond his father's dreams. Now he was back for good, summoned after his father's illness, to gain experience of each department, so that at last Ace could fully retire knowing his life's work would be continued.

'G'day!' said Greg Abbott, indicating the chair in front of his desk. He leaned back, arms folded behind his head, and grinned at John Roper, who sat on the edge of the chair and studied the veneer of the desk.

Stories about the heir apparent had filled his ears. Now, opposite him, sat the perfect specimen of Australian manhood, and the resentment which framed that phrase in his mind could only make John Roper hunch his shoulders and avoid the open, friendly gaze. How could he match it? He had no idea what to say, what might be expected of him. Shyness ossified his tongue.

It was not just women who thought Greg Abbott perfect, although his height and build, fair hair, tanned skin and blue eyes had caused enough girls and women in cities around the world to succumb. The man had a grace which turned even his reluctant leave-takings into promises, while giving other men the reassurance that it was possible to be rich, good-looking and successful without sacrificing one iota of mateship.

'Greg 'ud shout any bloke a drink anytime,' was the kind of thing John had heard. He failed to understand the symbolic importance of the phrase, and wondered what the fuss was about – because somebody like *him* would always buy his round too, if only they would let him.

'How's it going, John?' Greg asked.

'Very well, thanks.'

'No, I mean, you haven't been here long, so how are you finding us?'

'Yes . . . very well.'

Greg leaned forward, and explained that he wanted to try to get to know a little bit about all his father's employees. He opened the file on the desk in front of him, and John Roper saw his own letters, three of them, asking for a job.

'Got to hand it to you, mate, you didn't give up, did you? But there's not much here to go on – you're a bit of a dark

51

horse, eh? So just fill me in a bit, will you? How come a Pom's working for us in what's really – y'know, no offence – a junior bloke's job?'

John Roper stiffened. The man at the desk was only his age yet he was in charge, so patronage came easy. Pretending to be friendly, he mocked – and used the term of abuse John Roper hated most, the one he heard in the echoes of his footfalls. *Pommy bastard.* They didn't like him, and this man must have picked it up already. Golden boy, in his beige shirt and shorts, he knew he could glitter at the Pom and put him in his place . . .

'I'm happy to get the hours in,' John mumbled, 'then . . .'

'That what brought you out here?'

'Since I was a boy . . . I wanted to be a pilot, but at home . . . costs too much and they seem to think you need a pile of exams.'

Greg Abbott nodded sympathetically. 'Must be – the place is so small you need a physics degree to calculate your landings!' he joked. 'One mistake and you're off the other end and into the drink!'

John Roper knew for a fact that the perfect specimen of Australian manhood happened to have a physics degree himself. So he heard only mockery in the pleasantry and sat unsmiling.

'It says here you worked on the trams in Melbourne,' Greg prompted, glancing down at the folder. 'How long was that?'

'I was saving up for Cessnock,' said John shortly. 'Took a long time – more than a year. I did some taxi driving too. Nights.'

'Yeah . . . that's what it says here. But you enrolled in the end, then had to drop out for a while. Was that money worries, mate?'

John nodded. 'Affirmative.'

'But in the end you got the flying trophy in your class – pretty good going, mate! My dad always says that if a bloke's determined, he'll make it.'

'You have to decide what you want.'

'And with you it was flying all the way, hey?'

'A chap has to live up to his father,' John said.

Greg Abbott looked up sharply, his smile widening. 'Was your old man a flier like mine? Strewth, they put you through it, the old bastards, don't they?'

'My father was killed in 1946,' said John shortly. 'In Minnesota.'

Greg's smile faded. He grimaced and spread out both hands in a gesture of surrender. 'Put my foot in it, didn't I? Sorry mate. Bad luck too. I dunno, a bloke doesn't know what to say . . .'

'Best to say nothing.'

'They told me you were a nutter when it came to flying, and now I can see . . .'

'*Who* said that?'

'Oh, the blokes talk. All they mean is, you're obsessed. No offence.'

When John Roper made no reply, Greg Abbott frowned and went on, 'But while we're on the subject, I wasn't going to raise it this time, but there were a couple of complaints after that charter you did two weeks ago? So watch your speeds and keep it smooth, eh? And listen – if you're asked into one of the stations for a cuppa, keep it short, OK? Out there in the bush they don't go too much on all that RAF stuff . . .'

'What stuff?' mumbled John, his face reddening in blotches.

'Ah, mate, the talk, you know? Listen – your old man, was he in the RAF?'

John shook his head. The corners of his mouth twisted into the faintest semblance of a smile. 'No – he was American. Based in the UK, in Suffolk, where all the bases were. He flew hundreds of missions over Germany – daylight bombing. Nearly bought it God knows how many times.'

Greg Abbott raised his eyebrows and whistled. 'I read about all that . . . and hey, those guys were brave as hell. But I thought the record was something like twenty-four missions? Then they went home?'

John Roper shook his head, too vehemently. Greg stared at him, opened his mouth to speak, then closed it again. He recalled the irony of the nickname, 'Roper-the-Hoper', and immediately understood it. Ruddy, with slicked-back hair and pencil moustache, the man looked out of time. Greg Abbott didn't get it.

'OK, maybe one day we'll have a drink and a yarn and you can tell me more. But just for now, I'm curious to know why you left the Mount Isa charter job. What happened?'

Twisting in his chair so that his right shoulder pointed at Greg, John now directed his words at a spot somewhere by the picture window which showed the vista of runways, with the ring of mountains beyond, and a new Beechcraft Baron taxiing for take-off.

'Nothing happened. I just got tired of it and left, that's all. Thought there'd be more opportunities here, that's all.'

There was a moment's silence. Then, as if somebody slipped a new mask over John Roper's head, he seemed to recollect who was sitting behind the desk, and why. Still looking past Greg, he went on, 'But anyway, your father's famous, isn't he? Everybody wants to work for him! I thought it would be better to work for a company like *this*, started by someone like *him*, even if it meant working up from the bottom. I mean, just to say you're with Abbott-Air . . . I thought that would be a pretty good show.'

Greg Abbott thought the man's attempt to please worse than his hostility. It made his neck itch, although he could not understand why. For the first time since returning, he found himself nonplussed by one of the employees he had set himself the task of welding into the happy family which made his father wax sentimental, especially after his third shot.

They're right – this guy is just a bit weird, he thought.

He sprang to his feet, thrusting out a hand to grasp John Roper's unexpectedly limp paw. 'OK, mate – that'll do for now. Good to meet you! Catch up with you later, OK?' He paused, looked at his watch, and forced a grin. 'They'll be wanting that mail!'

Roper stood. 'Over and out,' he said, with an attempt at a grin.

Watched by Greg Abbott, he turned and walked into the tiny outer office where Hazel Cartwright sat at her desk, typing with four fingers, the tip of her tongue protruding between white teeth. The pink nails moved slowly; she was aware of the halting sound and wished it could be faster. Seeing the pilot emerge, she was glad to stop and reach for the envelope on her desk.

'John – could you take this down to dispatch for me? Save me a job?'

'Wilco,' he said, not slackening his pace as he seized the package from her outstretched hand.

Hazel glanced up to see her boss leaning on the door frame, hands in the pockets of his perfectly pressed beige shorts. His ribbed knee socks were white. She averted her gaze from the golden mist of hair on well-shaped knees and thighs. At eighteen, Hazel knew men in their thirties were far too old for her, but nothing could stop a girl admiring Greg Abbott. As her friend Leanne, the siren of bookings, said – even your old gran wouldn't be a real sheila if some little bit of her didn't fancy Ace Abbott's son.

'So – what do you think, Hazel?' Greg was asking.

'W–what about?' she stammered, growing pink.

'The Pom. What'd you make of him?'

She looked at the door that led to the stairs. They could still hear the echo of Roper's descending footsteps – tramp, tramp, tramp, down to the ground. As Hazel pondered her response, the outside door squeaked open, then shut. A squawking blur of rose and grey passed the window on the landing, then the galah wheeled off to join the rest of the flock.

Greg observed the painstaking process of her thought. She could easily have replied with a fast judgment, a cliché, but the girl was actually bothering to consider the Englishman. Her earnestness impressed him, like the simple skirts and blouses that refused to entice, and the open, un-made-up face speckled with a veil of freckles which only added to her prettiness.

'I feel a bit sorry for him,' Hazel said at last.

'Why?'

'I don't know . . . The others, they all laugh at him? They call him Roper-the-Hoper – have you heard that, Greg?'

He nodded again and waited. She grew pinker under his gaze, not quite sure what else was required of her, but aware she did not want to fail. Taking a breath, she continued, 'He's the sort of bloke who . . . well, he's shy but he tries hard, and somehow he gets it all wrong. He doesn't know how to . . . be . . . Does that make any sense?'

'It makes sense, Hazel. I heard this from other people.'

'So that's why I feel sorry for him.'

'You don't think he's just a pain in the neck?'

'No, not really. It's like he came here to find some kind of dream, and every day he wonders why it hasn't made him happy. If he could only be like everybody else – relax a bit – he might be all right. Get a girl – you know? But you never know what he's thinking. He always stares past you. The blokes downstairs say he looks like he's not quite the full two bob.'

'That'd be right,' said Greg Abbott, his mind already wandering.

'What I don't understand is why he comes out with all those funny things. What was it he said just now? "*Wilco*" . . . what's that mean?'

'It means – Will carry out. I'll do it. It's flying slang – how they talked in the RAF in the war.'

He met her eyes – clouded with concern for John Roper, and wanting to understand him with all the earnest curiosity of her eighteen years. Greg could visualize her putting her dolls to bed and treating their headaches and coughs, dressed as a little nurse with dark pigtails hanging over the cot. Witnessing her questing pity for an oddball Pommy pilot, he felt a sudden surge of tenderness for this kid, chock-full of kindness, of innocent questions, whose life must surely turn out as good as she deserved.

'But he wasn't *in* the war,' she whispered.

Nine

Hilda keeps telling me I need the home help, well, I'll be in my box before I let some stranger into my house. You can't trust people nowadays; it's not like it was. Why would I want some woman poking her nose in my things, pretending to be cleaning? If our John got to hear I had to get some help in, he'd be home like a flash – I told Hilda that. And what did she say? 'Good thing too.' It was under her breath but I heard it clear as day: 'Good thing too.'

'What was that?' I says, looking at her straight.

She looks back at me, in the eye (I'll give her that), and says she didn't think our John ought to be out there having a good time and leaving me here on my own.

'You need looking after, Lily Roper!' she says.

I know she means well, and she's the only one of the old lot left in the street, so we can't fall out. I told her we have to let the young ones fly, not keep them ringed and cooped up like pigeons.

'That may well be true, Lil,' she said, 'but – I have to speak as I find. You spoilt that boy rotten, and how does he pay his nan back? By buggering off to Australia to play bloody Biggles – pardon my French.'

I just walked away at that, came straight home. It'll be all right tomorrow. We'll bump into each other in the green-grocer's and it'll be as if nothing was said.

They used to say I put our John on a pedestal. I taught him to talk nice and dress nice, and they don't like that. That's why he stood out. When he was fourteen and got the bus to Allerton for the training, they'd hang round the bus stop and shout things at him. Poor lad – there was me saying how smart he looked in his uniform, and them calling him for everything . . .

I liked that nice air-force grey, not too much blue in it, and when he got the little silver star to wear on his tunic, he was that proud. That made him a senior cadet, he said. He was made up, he was. Yes . . . clever, our John. Knew all his planes, how to read maps, the lot.

All he'd be doing of a Saturday was fiddling around with his kits, so the place smelt of paint and that terrible glue, and if you didn't open the window you'd go dizzy sometimes, what with the coal fire too. He'd crouch over the table for hours, with all the bits of plastic spread out, some of them so little you'd wonder what they were for, and then he'd make a Spitfire or a Camel or whatever they were called, and paint it in the camouflage colours, and I told him – they were little works of art, they were. We had them all over the house once . . . but the dust on them . . .!

Always planes, planes, planes.

And whose fault was that, Lily?

Ah . . . Where's his postcard? Look at that colour! You'd never imagine soil that red . . . Mind you, he doesn't like the heat at all. He says it fries your brains, and that's why they're all so mad out there.

The new place he's living in sounds nice, and he'll write to me properly with all the news when he gets back from the expe-dition. I forgot to tell Hilda that. He must be doing well for himself if his boss is trusting him on a real flying expedition in the desert, to look for gold. Prospecting, he called it. He told me before he went out, that they find gold out there, like in the Westerns . . . Jewels too. Gold and jewels all over the desert.

John Roper glanced at the map on his knee, then down to where the row of humpies shone dully in the sunlight. As he circled lower, dark stick-like figures emerged, and began to walk across the scrub to where the rough landing strip made a scar on the earth's face. Children scampered, surrounded by leaping dogs, all like ants. The sun in his face made him squint as he turned, and his eyes watered behind cheap sunglasses that did nothing to keep out the rays.

Lower and lower, with a throbbing intensity of heat and noise, until at last the wheels crunched to the ground, and he bumped along the runway, his bones juddering. A bad landing. He thought of Greg Abbott and sweat poured down his face.

The Cessna jolted to a halt beside the fuel can, which the station owner had added legs to and a horned bull's head made from scrap iron. Its eyes were like targets; daubed letters spelling out *Brookfield Station* wobbled in white paint across its side. In the sudden silence after the engine, John contemplated the name. It conjured up a vision of English landscape, a brook gurgling over stones, and a field green and moist, starred with daisies and dandelions, beneath the purple haze of mountains he remembered from that one cadets' summer camp in Wales. He would never be so happy again. To get away from the lads in their street, and spend a whole week talking about planes with people who understood . . . And the sound of the helicopters whirring overhead and all of them looking up, as if they had seen God.

John Roper stared at the cow. Its target eyes goggled back at him, making a farce of memory. *Brookfield* mocked too, here in the Never-Never Land of arid wilderness, where the aboriginal children and their parents circled his plane, caked in flies and red sand, while their mangy dogs yelped and snarled at the metal thing that had dropped from the sky.

There was no air, even when he undid his belt and reached back to push the windows. He wondered if Greg Abbott would look so cool and crisp in his beige if he was out here doing the lowly mail run that was a junior bloke's job.

'G'day!' called a woman's voice.

Evie Brookfield was like no farmer's wife he had ever imagined. She was tall with golden skin and long blonde hair in a single fat plait. She always wore khaki or denim shorts with a white Aertex or a pale blue singlet – and the hairs on her arm were the colour of the sun. John tried not to look at her athletic brown legs. Beneath her faded Akubra, the wife of Dave Brookfield was the female equivalent of Greg Abbott, but John Roper did not resent perfection in the woman. It was the stuff of any man's fantasies. The only thing that bothered him was that it was wasted on the cattle-owning Australian who, on the one time they met, treated him with silent contempt, turning away to talk business with a black stockman as soon as John had introduced himself.

He clambered down and stretched his arms. 'Good to be on terra firma,' he said.

Evie Brookfield giggled.

'And how are you today?' John said politely over his shoulder, as he reached in the back for the bag. By now the straightening of his syllables into what at home they would have called 'posh' was second nature. Nan would have been proud of him.

'I love it! That Pommy accent is just unbelievable. Yeah, I'm doing just fine. You got much for us this time?'

'Quite a lot. Shall I carry it to the house for you?'

He pulled out the bag, and held it out, pleased it was indeed bulky. But Evie shook her head. 'No worries, I'm a big girl! I can manage. Here . . .'

'But you've got the baby to carry too . . .'

The aboriginal women and their children stood looking at them, one or two talking and laughing amongst themselves. They made John uneasy, although these were not like the ones you saw in the town, staggering about, or lying comatose on the pavement. In their lively eyes he saw curiosity and amusement. One of the women held out her hands to Evie without speaking, and took the child, straddling him on her own hip with a smile.

'See? No worries,' Mrs Brookfield said.

Her teeth flashed; she held out her hand for the bag. John hesitated. The prospect of a brief respite in the air-conditioned cool of the bungalow was more enticing as it receded.

'Do you think . . .?' he began.

'Don't be embarrassed, mate – you want to use the facilities?'

The Brookfields' bungalow was an oasis. Screams came from the two older children, splashing in the raised 'pool' like a gigantic vat, which stood to one side of the house. The verandah that surrounded the whole building was equipped with fold-out screens which would divide it off into rooms, so the family could choose to sleep outside. The rooms inside were cool and dark, all opening off a central living area furnished with big sofas and colonial cane chairs, and dominated by an enormous television set. It was the most luxurious home John Roper had ever visited. Last time, when Evie invited him in for a cup of tea, it reduced him to gawping, wistful silence.

She left him in a side corridor with a cheerful, 'Last door on the right – OK.'

One wall of the lavatory formed a huge pinboard, on which Evie pinned scores of family snaps. He saw a younger Evie and Dave riding a tandem, Evie with the first baby, Evie on horseback, the family in a studio shot, coiffed and all wearing white, Evie in a bikini, holding the last baby. And so on. John bent to examine the last picture carefully, admiring her breasts, the undulations of stomach and thighs, her legs . . . Slowly he reached out his index finger to touch the image, convulsed with envy for the naked child she held against her skin. He turned to splash cold water on his face, and peered at his own reflection in the mirror. It looked back at him, hot and blotchy.

At last he emerged, and stood in the darkness of the hall. He could hear a radio playing, and followed the sound of Simon and Garfunkel into the kitchen.

'*And here's to you, Mrs Robinson . . .*' Evie Brookfield was singing, swaying in front of the plump toddler in the high-chair as she dangled a biscuit before his outstretched hand. She was oblivious to the man who stood in the doorway and stared at the easy rhythm of her body. Seconds passed. The baby reached up and gurgled.

John coughed. She turned.

'OK?'

He nodded, desperately searching for what to say next. In the silence, the Simon and Garfunkel selection continued with 'Bridge over Troubled Water'.

'I like this one,' he said.

There was no alteration to her catch-all smile but she reached to turn down the volume, so that the song whispered tinnily. He waited for her to suggest a cup of tea, but no offer came, not like last time, and he wondered why. He moved from one foot to the other, and wiped his forehead, even though the room was cool.

'You want a cold drink?'

'Oh . . . that's kind of you. Yes please.'

Without being asked, he pulled out a kitchen chair and sat

near to the child, who stared at him impassively. Awkwardly he waggled his fingers by the tray of the highchair, but the little boy flinched, and his face creased. Silently John Roper begged him not to cry, and watched Evie's buttocks as she stood with her back to him, pouring iced water into a glass.

'There you go,' she said, plonking it down on the table. After a few seconds' thought, she sat down too, and he relaxed. This is what he craved. She had to talk to him now.

'So – how's it going then?'

'You mean the job? It's reasonably suitable. For a while.'

'Got your sights on better things, eh?'

'Affirmative,' he nodded, and she suppressed a grin.

'So what's the plan, then? You going to take over from Greg?'

'You know him?'

'Doesn't everybody? My Dave was at boarding school with him, though Greg's a couple of years younger, of course. Good bloke – the best.'

'I'd hardly be able to take over from him, since his father owns the business,' said John stiffly.

Evie's laughter tinkled around him. 'Go on, mate! I know that! I was only teasing you – you know?'

His face changed then, as if he had remembered something, and he settled back in his chair, looking straight past her as if in a sudden trance. 'Last year I met a man in Adelaide who was going to start a flying school. Had the finance in place and everything. He was very impressed by me, even if I say it myself. Did I tell you that, apart from the year prize at Cessnock, I went on to get a grade A instructor's certificate, you know, and with special commendation?'

He sounded like a speak-your-weight machine, but Evie Brookfield nodded encouragingly and said, 'Not bad, eh?'

'So anyway, he told me that if I came out here and built my hours up, I could go back down pretty soon and manage the whole school for him. He said he needs someone like me, with management skills. Anyway, I heard from him the other day. I'll be going back quite soon, and then . . .'

'The sky's the limit?' she said, smiling at her own joke.

He frowned. 'You could put it that way,' he said coolly, hunching his shoulders. 'What I do expect is to have several instructors under me. There comes a time in a man's life when he doesn't want to take orders from anybody.'

'Ri–ight,' she said, drawing out the one syllable into two, and looking thoughtful.

'And what time's that?' said a voice behind him.

Dave Brookfield stood in the doorway. He was a man who made Greg Abbott look almost small. John could smell his sweat, and the aroma of dust and animals that hung about him. On his last visit he had heard from the proud wife that Dave was a famously tough outback farmer who had once survived being gored by a wild bull, even walking into the house holding his own fist to the hole in his side to staunch the blood.

'Get me a glass of water, love?' he called to his wife, who leapt up to obey. 'So, mate – give us a tip – *when's* the time a bloke ought to stop taking orders?'

'Oh, when you get into your thirties, I suppose,' he answered.

'No kidding? Funny thing is, I got stockmen of forty and fifty who know everything there is to know about the animals, they can smell water ten foot down, track a goanna twenty miles, and all the rest – and *they* don't mind taking orders. Why's that, do you think?'

'I . . . well . . . probably because they're farm workers,' said John Roper, unable to keep the dismissive note from his voice.

'And you think that's easy? You want to come out to the races now and help with the branding?'

'No, of course it's not easy,' mumbled John.

'Too right, mate!'

'I just meant . . .'

'Yeah.'

Dave Brookfield took the glass from his wife, and John saw the look they exchanged. He read it clearly, like writing in the sky at an air show. Pommy bastard, it said. It contrasted the ease they both felt within their flesh with his own itchy discomfort, as if his very skin had been transformed into prickly woollen cloth, worn in terrible heat. The split-second complicity he saw between husband and wife made him burn.

The baby looked at him, threw the remains of a soggy biscuit on the floor, and began to grizzle over the soft rock on the radio. Air conditioning hummed like an insect inside his ear.

'No worries,' said Dave Brookfield inexplicably, with a shrug of his massive shoulders. The tone was not as relaxed as the words would imply; the cattleman used the everyday cliché as a dismissal.

John Roper nodded but all the time a high voice inside his head started yelling: *What do you mean? What do you mean?* They all said 'no worries' to fill in spaces in the conversation – but meaning what?

I have no problems.

It's fine.

Nothing to concern yourself about.

That's how it is.

I couldn't give a damn.

Let's change the subject.

Go away.

John passed a hand over his forehead and wiped it on his trousers. Evie Brookfield was looking at him, curiosity mingled with pity.

'You OK? Don't mind Dave – he's just proud of his old farm, aren't you, love?' Dave Brookfield nodded, moved across to the sink, put down his glass, and strode out, calling, 'See ya later,' over his shoulder.

'You feel OK?' she repeated. 'Need some more water?'

'Thank you.'

'No worries . . .'

'Please don't *say* that!'

'What?'

'Damned if I know what it means. Let's be frank, it's one of those things when people usually mean the opposite. Affirmative, not negative.'

'I don't get you,' she said coolly.

'I mean – when people tell me no worries, I know they think there's plenty to worry about. They're saying it's a pretty bad show all round. Can you see that? No worries, he says, your husband, but what he really means is some poor blighter's about to get it in the neck!'

He felt dull satisfaction that he had shocked her out of her complacency – she of the fat plait and the breasts and the brown legs, who thought she would stand there with her husband in their house in the middle of the endless red sand and scrub, and mock him.

Yet he had wanted her to like him . . . to talk to him like last time. To reach past his face with the golden, speckled arm that smelt of apricots, and place the tea tenderly before him. To let him glimpse, just for ten minutes, what life would be

63

like there in the middle of nowhere, with a woman like that to wrap herself around you, body and soul, and love you. For that you would tolerate heat and dust and flies.

He couldn't breathe. The pain in his head clouded the edges of the room. John Roper threw his head back and swigged the water noisily, while Mrs Brookfield watched his exposed pink and white throat.

'It's just an old Aussie expression,' she said flatly.

'Absolutely,' he said blankly.

'Hey – you'll be late.'

'Rightio. I'll be going. Thanks a million for the tea.'

'But I . . .' she began, then stopped.

A heartbeat of drum and guitar whispered in the background, sad but ominous . . . *'Every breath you take . . .'* as Evie Brookfield felt John Roper's eyes fixed on her, and shivered.

'I'll see you next time then,' he barked, turning towards the door.

When he had gone, Evie realized she had forgotten to pass over the letter she had written to her mother in Perth, as well as the bills she and Dave had sat down to do the night before, ready for the mail run. She hit the table with frustration, making her baby jump.

Brookfield Station became a blur on the landscape, and the roar within the cockpit drove out the sound of Dave Brookfield's voice, and Greg Abbott's too.

'No worries,' said John Roper aloud, and the air tossed him upwards, as if in confirmation. Each flight could seem like the first, if you concentrated on each action as if you had just discovered it, as if you were back at the beginning. You had to forget the land below, because it did not matter what was beneath. The air was everywhere.

The first solo flight was a flexing of loneliness, testing that muscle to see if it would sustain you in the future. He remembered the instructor, Len, saying, 'OK, mate – now you can do it on your own,' and the terrifying emptiness of the seat beside him as the aircraft climbed and Len became a dot by the side of the runway. Five hundred feet, and then the ten bank to port, line up a building on the nose, take her up another eighty-five feet . . . then another turn to port took him three miles south-west of the runway, out of sight of Len, and of all the others. Alone. Heart thumping; throttle back to 2,200 revs; trim the plane to the flat horizon; let it fly itself . . .

Up and round, and it was passing too quickly. He knew Len would be timing him. Concentrate on everything, but don't flap, remember the instructor's maxim: 'Don't just do something – *sit* there,' to the rookies who overreacted to stress.

Now the end of the runway slipped past the port wing tip. Carburettor heat on, throttle back to 1,500 revs, hold the nose level. When the speed decays into the white arc, select one notch of flaps, and turn ninety over the buildings, tucking the nose slightly into the wind to correct the drift. Another notch of flaps, then slow, slow, and the nose reassured him by its tilt. Watch the speed, John, watch it . . . Hold seventy knots as the wings straighten; there's the runway straight ahead.

Repeat, *Height is throttle, speed is pitch.*

The last notch of flaps, and he saw the trees rushing by, and the huge white numbers painted on the runway threshold, as he throttled back completely, and eased back the controls. Fight it – wrestle the panic urge to halt this mad progress into the ground. Concentrate, concentrate on the delicate moment when speed bleeds away and you ease the aircraft on to the runway, seeing the nose lift, and feeling that union of earth and sky, as the wheels touch down with a soft bump. Yes!

Ah, he could remember the exquisite release of breath, the triumph. *I'm down, I'm down, I did it alone, I'm a pilot. A real pilot. Oh Nan, if only you could see me now.*

John Roper zigzagged through the day in a trance, delivering mail, not noticing to whom. He imagined shells bursting all around, and 'archie' crackling white among the black puffs of smoke, and then the shrill *wheee* of flying shrapnel . . . *Takatakatakataka* . . .

On and on. Memories and dreams merged seamlessly, like the horizon softened by a haze of heat. The little Cessna crawled through the air beneath the sun, and when at last it banked over the town, the sun low in the sky, John Roper peered down at the savage red swathe that had been carved out of the bush just south of the town, dotted with Dinky Toy diggers.

Down on the ground a man stood near one of the towering diggers, and looked up at the sky. He pushed a filthy hand across his forehead, and then threw his arms into the air behind his head, feeling his sinews stretch. Sunlight flashed on the white wings, and for a second, squinting up, he saw the plane as a living thing in its natural element.

Naturally Eddy did not think of the fellow lodger from Bernie Molloy's house. It was just another plane; all day they droned in the sky while he concentrated on the earth. The bores had been dug; the clubhouse was under construction. Eddy and the other men turned their backs to the sky, their faces shadowed by filthy red-stained cotton hats and their singlets soaking wet. All day they worked to pick up stones the diggers had missed, and spread the soil. The work on the site was proceeding at a pace Eddy had never before witnessed in his jobbing travels.

Today, though, there had been an interruption. Eddy had looked up to see a group of Aranda men, standing on a small hill near where he was working. One of the diggers had been at the point of levelling it when the five men materialized, as if out of the ground itself.

He watched the foreman cross to where they stood, and soon voices were raised. One of the men was shouting, the other four stood impassively, as if what was going on had little to do with them. Curious, Eddy moved nearer. By this time the foreman had stomped off to seek a higher authority, and the five men had descended from their vantage point to stand immediately in front of the little scrubby hill.

'What's wrong?' he asked the one who had been shouting.

Eddy's dusty appearance presented no threat to the visitors. The oldest, a man with white hair and beard and eyes so black they looked like chips of jet, stared at him, then nodded slowly.

'Sacred site,' explained the young man who'd been shouting. 'Put digger in, and . . .' He raised a warning finger.

Eddy looked at the hump in the earth for a long time, narrowing his eyes in appraisal. At last he looked back at the men and asked, 'What is it, then? What's this dreaming?'

Taken aback by the question, the young man opened his mouth as if to reply, but the others shook their heads fiercely. Eddy understood. He preferred to guess anyway, and if, in truth, this was no honey-ant dreaming site, or goanna, or whatever – what did it matter? There was an argument for what he called a Wind-Up Dreaming, if it stopped white Australians in their tracks. They had torn up enough earth on this continent and soon it would be payback time.

The foreman returned with a few men in tow, one of whom Eddy recognized as the architect, another as the site engineer. By now about ten of his fellow workers had gathered round to stare at the black men, some with open hostility.

'OK, break it up, break it up,' the foreman said.

So Eddy was forced to turn his back on the altercation, which seemed to continue for a very long time. At last Eddy glanced up to see the Aranda men filing off in the direction of the works hut after the bosses, who strutted angrily ahead. The digger driver spat on the earth before climbing into his cab to trundle the machine away. There were whistles and catcalls of derision from some of the other labourers. The driver gave them the V sign.

But it was indeed a victory, Eddy thought. The earth on the sacred site would not be flattened. He licked the tip of his dirty forefinger, held it briefly in the air as if testing the wind, and grinned.

It was not long afterwards that he stopped to ease his back, and glanced up to see the little Cessna circling in the sky, until it seemed to fly into the setting sun, and he had to close his eyes against the light.

Ten

It was strange how easily a routine evolved.

Bernie did not see very much of her lodgers. In the morning they'd both leave early, making minimum noise in the kitchen and closing the front door quietly. She'd turn over in her bed and go back to sleep, rising late to idle through her day as usual, unless it was her turn to do a lunchtime shift at the Zoo. Nights when she returned from the bar tired and smelling of beer, she saw the strips of light beneath their doors and instinctively walked on the balls of her feet. She did not ever think of knocking. They were both so quiet, and dishes were always washed up and put away. Bathroom logjams did not materialize, and she could not imagine how they occupied themselves within their small bedrooms.

But sometimes the silence in her house seemed more oppressive because it was shared, as if the strangers breathing behind their doors were a judgment on her own isolation.

'They're both weirdos in their different ways,' she said to Dick Springville, after two weeks.

'Drongos if they ain't tryin to get in your pants yet!' he laughed.

'Jesus, Dick, don't you think of anythin' else?'

'Straight up, Bern – I mean, one of these blokes might do you. What's the Pom like?'

'An oddball. He's done all right for himself out here but he's one of those blokes who looks like he's on another planet half the time.'

'What yer mean?'

'He's got this bee in his bonnet about flying, but we've all known enough pilots round these parts – and this bloke's not like them. It's like they fly the planes, but with this one . . . I dunno . . . maybe the planes are flying *him*. Funny look in his eye.'

'Goin' troppo? You know these Poms – come out here and after ten minutes they're runnin' mad with the flies and the heat, goin' nuts. So – what about the other one?'

'Oh, if his brain was an inkwell he couldn't make a full stop,' she laughed. 'Anyway, he's too young.'

'Nice bit of fresh meat – do you good, Bern! Show him a thing or two, like a good sheila.'

'Oh give me a break, Dick!'

The bar was full of demolition workers. The old town was slowly being knocked down in a barrage of talk of shopping malls and new tourist attractions. The word was that the road south would be sealed, and once the bitumen came, the town would become a mecca. Visionaries talked of cleaning it up, of tours, and new hotels. Bernie couldn't see it. She looked around at the dingy yellow walls of the bar, the wooden counter scored with names, pitted with cigarette burns and slashed for the pleasure of pure destruction, and tried to imagine it turned into a family pub. Stuck to the wall near the door was a collection of photographs of people mooning. When Springing Dick honoured a new regular with an invitation to drop his trousers for the camera, and join the rogues' gallery. No, thought Bernie, it'll take more than a shopping mall to make this town smart.

She slammed the change drawer shut and watched the fat, red-faced Irishman in the middle of the room, playing air guitar to the sound of heavy metal from the screen. Occasionally he would roar unintelligibly, as if remembering a line of his silent song, then return to the head-banging, while his stubby blackened fingers twitched and clutched at vacancy. Nobody took any notice. The faces along the bar bobbed before her eyes, and receded; men called out to her, made the usual cracks, called her 'Bern' and grinned as she served them, not realizing she could not remember any of their names.

Suddenly there was a noise at the door. Big Frank moved across to investigate, but most of the men perched on stools did not turn round. There were always disturbances.

Frank spoke to somebody outside, then announced over his shoulder to no one in particular, 'They've set a tree on fire in the riverbed.'

Bernie looked across at Dick, who was banging glasses down on the drainer.

'Mind if I take a look?'

He shrugged without raising his eyes.

Smoke drifted in the close air. Fragments of ash swirled by on currents of heat. Bernie moved out on to the pavement and stared towards the dry riverbed, where an orange beacon flared in the darkness. A fire wagon roared by. Thin black shapes flitted to and fro, silhouetted against the burning light.

Frank stood with two men, gazing at the fire with malevolence. He lit a cigarette, then offered one to Bernie, who took it. The match flared again.

'Set another tree alight – the bastards,' said one of the men – fat and in his sixties, she guessed.

'Bastards,' nodded the bouncer.

'Tree should fall on 'em and burn 'em,' said the other man, rubbing his hand on the rump of his tight shorts. Red dirt caked his singlet. The flat face was vaguely familiar. Bernie narrowed her eyes against the smoke, and stared at him.

'Yeah, crush 'em to death.'

'Me – I'd tie 'em to the tree and burn 'em to death.'

Suddenly Bernie realized the man in the shorts had been with Skinner that night in the bar, the Night of the Long Turd.

'Be a waste of good rope.'

'Yeah, rope burns . . .'

'Use a chain – that'd do it.'

'Trees are supposed to be fuckin' sacred to them. All this crap about fuckin' sacred sites and so-called fuckin' rights.'

'I'd kill all the bastards,' said Frank, raising a hand to scratch his scar. Turning to Bernie, he added, 'Bloody disgustin' sight, innit?'

'What – the fire?' Bernie asked innocently.

'No – *them*,' he spat with contempt.

'It's like this, Frank,' she said very slowly, giving each word importance to hold his attention. 'I seen plenty of disgusting sights in my time . . .'

'Yeah?'

'. . . and I tell you this for nothing – I'd rather look at a whole room full of aborigines than one white man's stinking turd right in the middle of my bloody pillow.'

The man in shorts shuffled his boots and looked down. There was a brief silence. Then he looked up again, showing his teeth. 'If you didn't like that particular make of sausage, *darlin'*, I reckun Skinno 'ud be ready to do you a favour and give you a taste of another sort?'

Puzzled, Frank Massey looked from one to the other. But in that instant he was rocked back on his heels by the speed of Bernie's attack. Her right fist thumped into the roadworker's stomach and when he doubled up, her left elbow crashed into his face. Then her right palm came back, full force, with a stinging slap that jerked his head forty-five degrees. The man staggered back, fell, and cracked his head against the wall of the Zoo. His mouth opened with pain and astonishment.

'Jesus!' said the fat, older man, taking two steps back.

'Wha . . .?' mumbled the bouncer, looking from Bernie to the man on the floor.

'*Don't* ask, Frank,' said Bernie, brushing her hands together then running them ostentatiously down the sides of her shorts as if she had touched something unpleasant. 'Now, I reckon our boss will be asking why we aren't at work, don't you?'

'Bitch!' hissed the flat-faced roadworker, not choosing to rise.

Bernie stopped for a second and looked down at him. 'And by the way, mate, if you want real trouble, try coming anywhere near my house again. I got a couple of blokes living with me now, and the three of us could chain your mob to trees before you could blink and call for your mammies.'

She heard herself with distaste, the hard voice grating on her own ears, the words familiar yet foreign at the same time. Sometimes it occurred to her that the only hope was that you could inhabit the gutter yet never quite accept its language as your own. But she knew she spoke it too well.

She stalked through to the ladies', wrinkling her nose at the smell, and looked at herself in the mirror. She thought of her mother, as so often these days. In her own face she was beginning to see the features of the woman who would grieve at the crudeness of this daughter who'd learnt to accept the scrapings at the bottom of the barrel as the best the heavens could offer in the way of sustenance. The person in the mirror, hair curling around a thin face which had seen too much, bore little resemblance to sweet Bernadette in her white communion dress, kneeling before Father Mullen and turning at last to see tears rolling down her mother's weatherbeaten cheeks, and her red-faced father fingering the lapel of the unaccustomed suit as they sat in the front row.

'Ah Sean, she looks just like a little angel, so.'

Years later she thought bitterly of her mother's advice on that day, that if she said her Hail Marys regularly, the Blessed Virgin would surely look after her. Hah! The sweet face framed in blue was nowhere to be seen when Bernie needed her. The mother of God had no pity to spare for a small, suffering thing, writhing for sixteen hours on a bed. That day . . .

Bury it . . .

And what was the use of beads and candles when you had steel in your spine and iron in your soul?

The irritation of the aboriginal arson was forgotten; instead the story of what had happened outside flashed round the bar like a real bush fire. No details were required – only the fact that the barmaid had decked a stranger from one of the road gangs. For the rest of the night Bernie laughed off cracks about her muscles, offers to take her on the road as a mud wrestler, theatrical cringing whenever she reached out across the bar to bang down a can, and the covert, hostile stares of the majority, who hated all women, especially those who refused to be afraid. She ignored the man who had the nerve to whisper, 'Fucking lezzy,' a few yards away, confident that if she were to turn sharply he would slink away. Bernie was glad to add to any reputation she already possessed, knowing that any fear she instilled could only be a good thing in this town.

It was forty minutes before closing time when John Roper sidled into the bar, and stood hesitantly by the door for a few minutes, before making his way gingerly through the crowd towards her. Bernie saw how odd he looked, pilot's shirt among the singlets, registered the glances of amusement, curiosity, even hostility, and felt oddly protective of the gauche Englishman.

'What can I get you, John?' she called.

He glanced around nervously.

'This one's on me, mate,' said Bernie, pushing the can towards him with a cheerfulness she did not feel.

'No – it's all right,' he said stiffly, fumbling with coins.

'Suit yourself,' she shrugged, taking the money he offered over the shoulders of the men hunched on stools. One of them, hearing John's accent, slid to the ground and stood there swaying, pointing mockingly at the vacant stool.

'Oh *do* sit down,' he said, in a parody of upper-class English.

Bernie willed her lodger to grin, shake his head and say, 'No worries, mate,' as anybody else would. Instead he looked startled, glanced from right to left like a trapped animal, then climbed awkwardly on the stool. His absurd, artificial accent seemed to cut through the hubbub.

'Oh . . . er . . . thank you very much.'

They'll be in for the kill now, Bernie thought.

'Oehh, theeank yew vairy mach,' said the man, nudging his friend.

'Give it a miss, mate,' said Bernie quietly.

'Friend of yours, eh?' somebody asked in disbelief.

'Garn, Pete, it's her boyfriend! Look at the face on her! Hey, you lucky Pommy bastard, you screwed our Bern and lived to tell the tale!'

'Must have an iron cock, mate!'

Raucous laughter crackled all around John Roper, who looked at Bernie across puddles of beer and soaked cigarette butts, just as a child will look at a passing stranger when the street bullies circle. His face was scarlet. She understood, the man had been there before, so many times throughout his life, baited, and hated too. He wore his difference like a shooting target. There was no hope for him at all, not out here.

'Yeah, he's me new bloke all right – so back off,' she said, enunciating each word to cut through the raucous smoke. People stared. One or two gave suggestive whoops. A small smirk twitched at the corner of John Roper's mouth as he raised the can to his lips, knowing he was safe.

There was a sudden commotion at the opposite end of the bar, as Dick Springville began to lose his temper with a group of five or six men who had just lurched in, and were too drunk to remember that the boss served at his own pace. Frank Massey was already there; the situation looked threatening. Bernie moved along to place herself at Dick's elbow and smiled sweetly at the largest customer.

'Thass more like it,' he slurred.

You have to defuse it; there's no choice. Lift the cheeks into the rictus; swivel the hips, make your body speak as eloquently as any whore's. Anything to avoid the full can crashing on somebody's head, or the glass in the face.

'Go on, Dick – I'll handle this. OK, big guy, what can I give you?' she said, making them laugh.

By the time she had finished, and moved back to her original position, John Roper was deep in talk. The older man now next to him had been outside watching the fire, and witness to her sudden violence. He looked harmless enough; in this town racism was normal. He glanced up warily as she passed, then returned his attention to John Roper.

'Go on then, mate . . .'

''Course, I suppose it was inevitable that I'd choose flying as a career . . . And even if I say so myself, I've done well. Damned well, actually.'

'Too right, mate. RAF, eh? Dambusters and all that!'

'You could say that.'

Head down, Bernie listened as she wiped the bar. She remembered that first conversation, as the three of them sat in her garden, and knew her lodger had never mentioned the RAF. Of course, he would have done, if his story were true. You're a liar, mate, she thought, looking up and meeting his eyes. You know I know it too. You're like all of them who come in here shooting a line – about the tough things they said to the big guy so he backed off, and the size of that fish, and the way the woman made such a racket the neighbours were banging on the wall, but she still went on, gagging for more . . .

Lies. She'd heard them all. They increased in proportion to the beer intake, and sometimes the maudlin tears just before Dick called time were merely an acknowledgment of truth. The bullshitters knew nothing they said stood up, no more than it would if the fantasy were to be real and the woman beside them in the bed. No escape from the truth of the trailer, the grimy room, or the mattress at the back of the cab. Nowhere to hide from the shivering creature with the unformed features of the child your mother bore.

Ah, and don't I know it so, Bernie thought. Lies are just stories, tales of people's own dreamings, which formed them as surely as the aboriginal people think this land was formed. What's the difference between Roper and me, because my stories are different? They take place inside my own head, and I don't know how to talk properly any more. I'm constipated, he's got the runs, and we're both full of shit . . .

'I wondered if you'd give me a lift?' John Roper asked.

'Walked specially, did you?' Bernie mocked, warning him off.

As the Holden rattled away, he cleared his throat and began, 'Thank you for—'

She interrupted. 'You and me, we got to get something understood . . .'

'I mean, thank you for saying *that* – back in there.'

'As long as you don't get any ideas, mate.'

'I don't understand.'

'Yeah you do.'

He said nothing. She drove fast. But as they waited at traffic lights a skinny black figure staggered in front of them, halted, then crumpled, to lie like a heap of rags in the road.

'Can't take their alcohol, can they?' said Roper.

Disliking the superiority in his voice, Bernie jumped out, leaving her door swinging open, and walked over to the man. She knew there'd be those who would happily run over him if she left him there, saying they hadn't seen until too late. It wasn't long ago that somebody put poison in a sherry bottle and left it lying around. It killed five aboriginal people and caused a two-day flurry in the local paper. Most of the whites had hate bred in the bone. No wonder it cut the other way too.

She bent over the man, and inhaled sweat, urine and wood smoke.

74

'Give me a hand, will you?' she yelled over her shoulder, irritated that Roper stayed where he was.

Without waiting for him, she turned the man over. He seemed weightless.

The head lolling back on its stalk as if it might snap; matted hair, grey with dust or age. The shirt gaping over a chest so concave it could have been punched in. His face was broad and lined and wore an expression of puzzled panic.

She bent down and grasped him under the damp armpits. Roper stood by, useless and unwilling. She yelled at him to take the man's legs and help her. Together they moved the unconscious drunk, Roper dropping his burden with alacrity once they reached the side of the road. Bernie knelt and turned the man so he lay on his side, and stood for a second looking down at him, in the gutter.

'Sleep it off, mate,' she whispered.

Then her voice hardened as she turned to Roper. 'Don't really like leaving him there but there's no choice. Know what somebody did last year? Poured paraffin on a bloke like that in the middle of the night and left him burning. Wasn't very pretty for the children to look at on their way to school.'

John Roper shuddered and turned away. Back in the car, he said, 'It's the drink that's the problem, isn't it?'

'It's only a part of the problem,' she replied. 'Cause or effect – you tell me?'

'My nan's teetotal. The one thing she can't bear is the smell of beer. It makes her feel sick.'

'Wouldn't last long out here, then, would she?'

They drove in silence, until they turned into Bernie's road, when she said suddenly, 'I got to ask you. Why let that bloke think you were in the RAF? You didn't tell *us* that. Why did you shoot a line?'

He stayed silent. When she switched off the engine and looked at him, his face was set into an expression of mingled anger and panic. She'd seen it before: the awareness of being found out which could make a man kill the person who knows. Yet it did not occur to Bernie to feel a second's foreboding, because she knew this one was harmless.

'You coming in?' she asked, when he did not move.

'Don't you wish things?' he said, sullenly.

'No point.'

'That people would let you be something.'

'You mean – something *you* think you deserve?'

'Other people can. Other people get it all. Born with a silver spoon, and all that.'

She shrugged. 'No point in having a chip on the shoulder, mate. Ends up weighin' you down so much you can't move.'

'They wouldn't look at me – as a cadet. Bloody toffee noses get it all, don't they? Go in there with a Liverpool accent and they're sitting in a row, and you feel *that* small in front of the table, and all your words come out wrong.'

'You really wanted it and they turned you down . . . It was *that* important to you to join the RAF?'

'Of course it was! All I wanted was to be like my father.'

'And now you get off on telling people what Ma used to call stories.'

'Doesn't do any harm,' he said defensively.

'Who's to know? Maybe it does *you* harm.'

Moths batted the windscreen. Suddenly Bernie had no desire to enter her home. Sitting in the hot darkness with this uneasy man seemed enough, suspending her beyond the rational. It almost seemed possible they might even love each other, in the way of strangers who have nothing. Maybe she should take what she was given? Maybe there would be some peace if she found it within herself to hold someone up? That thin weeping sound inside her head might even cease.

Eleven

A regular sound she did not recognize rasped at the back of Bernie's waking consciousness – to and fro, to and fro, a giant grasshopper rubbing its legs together. What was it?

There came a quick memory of building sites, of Da at work. She and Patrick would take him his tea and watch him in the rubble, face pouring under his greasy old hat and yet gulping the sweet, scalding liquid as if it were water. Patrick would kick his heels, pick up tools, and drop them down, always restless, always wanting to be like the men. One day Sean Molloy handed him a saw and said, 'Well, if you're wanting to be like a man, see how far ye get with that piece of log over there.' Bernie watched the see-saw movement of her brother's thin arm, burnt brown now and shining with sweat. The rasping, harsh to her ears, increased when one labourer guffawed at the boy's puny efforts. Suddenly there was a slither, followed by a moment of silence.

For days her brother had dragged his bandaged leg about the house, enjoying the sound of his parents screaming at each other because of Da's irresponsibility.

A saw. That was the sound.

Bernie watched from the kitchen window. Eddy Carpenter stood facing in her direction, but head down, concentrating on what he was doing. In torn cut-offs, he stood on his right leg, left knee raised to pin a piece of wood across a rough sawhorse, left hand steadying it as he worked. Light gleamed on his golden chest. She watched the vigorous movement of his wiry arm, saw the wood fall, and noticed the speed with which he reached for another plank. The steel rule went down; a stub of pencil from behind his ear made its mark. Then the stork position once more and a mist of fresh sawdust speckled the old planks. Bernie narrowed her eye, the better to see him bend for the piece of wood that fell, study it critically for a moment, then move to compare its length with the verandah floor. Nodding, he laid it to one side, and continued. There was a completeness about the man and his activity that fascinated her. He was at ease within himself and his actions, within the grace of making.

Suddenly he glanced up. His grin was shy, but he waved. She raised a hand then turned away, unable to respond, disconcerted by gratitude. Bernie, whose aim in life was never to need, never to be beholden, realized that somebody was doing something for her.

By the time she'd put the kettle on and looked out again, she saw Eddy joined by John Roper, who stood watching in silence. Arms folded, hugging a book to his chest, his eyes followed Eddy's every action. They seemed companionable, and Bernie realized they must have spent evenings together when she was at work, eaten meals, watched TV. Now the unlikely pair seemed bonded, with no need to talk. It excluded her.

She looked at her watch. It was only eight thirty. Behind the two men the garden lay dappled blue and green in the morning light. The crow cawed and scratched contentedly in the wire cage. She knew instinctively that Eddy had already fed it. Without asking, he had taken over that duty.

It was not all he had taken over.

She looked around her kitchen. There were no plates on the draining board, and its dull stainless steel had been buffed to a shine. Her gaze roamed the small room. No greasy finger-prints on the cupboard doors, a clean dishcloth folded on the edge of the bowl, and the old black and white chequered linoleum cleaner than it had been since Colleen Molloy was laid in the earth.

Pleased but afraid, Bernie took refuge in indignation. The imposition of cleanliness on the kitchen was a comment on the way she had lived, and she felt ashamed. In the bathroom the same magic had been worked. The night before, fuddled with wine, she hadn't noticed. Nothing could improve the ragged yellow shower curtain, but there was no ring around the bath and he'd bleached the tiles and the encrusted grey seal around the edge. She smelt lemons. So, while sweat was running down her face in the Zoo, when the same old loop of filthy mud-wrestling women was provoking the usual cries of lust and derision, while she was wiping cigarette ash mixed into beer slops off the pitted surface and ignoring dirty jokes she'd heard a thousand times – Eddy Carpenter had been *cleaning*. But why should he?

Something stopped her from going outside. It was the flut-tering nervousness she used to feel, at fifteen, before a dance. She glanced into the sitting room and saw that he had tidied, dusted and vacuumed. The cushions were plump and smooth. There were no specks of hair and grit on Ma's old green and brown patterned carpet – the one Bernie vowed to ditch years ago, when Suze said it reminded her of sick. The whole place felt different.

'You bin busy, Eddy,' she said, as laconically as she could manage, leaning at the back door, blowing smoke in his direction.

John Roper was sitting in one of the wicker chairs, reading.

He looked up and nodded at her, then returned to the page. At last, after what seemed like a long time, Eddy Carpenter stopped. He held out the plank towards her.

'That should do it.'

'Do what?'

He gestured towards the place where the timbers caved in like a mouth with broken teeth. The new pieces leaned in a row beneath the kitchen window. There was a clean resinous smell. Eddy dropped his head briefly and ran both hands briskly through his curly hair, releasing a shower of sawdust.

'Where'd you get the stuff?'

'Don't worry. It's free,' he said.

'Nothing's free.'

'Lots of things are free. Didn't you know?'

'No, I didn't.'

He knelt, examining the rotten wood. Bernie stared at the sinews of his long arms, appreciated the spidery grace of his crouching figure – and looked away.

'Lift it from the site, did you?'

He stood to face her.

'Bernie – why don't you just let us fix up the house a bit without letting it bother you?'

'Who's *us*? Doesn't look like he's doing much.'

She jerked a thumb towards John Roper, including him in her embarrassed rage. What business was it of theirs to suggest she was a slut before they came?

'John helped me do some cleaning last night. He's quite good at it.'

Roper looked up again and smiled – making her realize how rarely there was any lightness in that face. 'My nan, she was really house-proud,' he said, with curious pleasure. 'Always cleaning . . .'

'Like my ma!' Bernie interrupted, relaxing suddenly. 'She always said that cleanliness is next to godliness – coming out with it as if she'd invented the thought. No wonder she made me turn into such a crap housewife. They make you so you never want to smell polish ever again in your life.'

'Or bleach,' said John.

'Poor old girls, though, eh? What a life to give yourself,' said Bernie softly.

'Oh – Nan's all right,' said John.

'You write to her?'

He nodded. 'Once a fortnight.'

'Good man. What about you, Eddy, you got family some-where?'

Eddy Carpenter shook his head, keeping it down, staring at the sawhorse. He saw the knots and whorls in the wood, frozen ripples, a dry river – nature overturned, calling his whole life into question. He saw himself confronting a man and a woman he called Mum and Dad, accusing them.

'You knew – and you didn't tell me!'

'I wanted the best for you, son.'

'And so you lied to me, you bastard!'

'We both wanted the best.'

'And you – you're nothing to do with me!'

'Don't talk to your mother like that, Edward.'

'It's the truth. But you wouldn't care about truth, would you?'

'You must have somebody, mate!' she was saying.

'No,' he said shortly, then filled his own ears with energetic sawing, drowning anything else she might say.

Bernie stood for a few seconds, uneasy, sensing something wrong yet unable to guess its source. Used as she was to the dead weight of family memories, she saw no insensitivity in her own question. So the kid had no family? Maybe he was lucky.

At last she blurted, 'I just thought of something . . . I suppose we're all in the same boat in a way. John's nan's back home, and my brother and sisters are all overseas, not that I ever got on with them much anyway, and Eddy's got nobody to speak of . . . OK, then, why don't we do Christmas together? Get a big chook, or maybe a turkey, the full two bob? Do it properly?'

She amazed herself. But the words were out there, uniting them, and could not be snatched back.

John Roper looked up, the most natural smile she'd yet seen lightening that ruddy face. Much later the phrase 'looking almost normal' was to come to her mind, but now she basked for a few seconds in the unaccustomed pleasure of making someone appear so happy through such little effort.

'Roast potatoes and sprouts?' he queried, like a little boy.

'Just like at home, eh?' she grinned. 'That's what Da always insisted on, when Ma complained about the heat. We always did it, the whole works. I haven't eaten a proper Christmas dinner in years. It'll make a change. Mind you, you've both got to help?'

'I used to peel potatoes for Nan,' John said.

Saw in hand, Eddy stared fixedly at the plank he had cut. Bernie bent to pick up the fallen end, and held it out to him. Moisture slicked down the sides of his broad, upturned nose. When he met her eyes, she could not read them.

'You on for a real Christmas this time, then?' she asked.

'What do you usually do?' he countered.

She shrugged. 'In Sydney? Used to hang out with friends. Eat seafood. Go for burn-ups . . . yeah . . . but that was years and years ago. Then when I came back here, after they died, me and Suze used to binge with any old bunch of misfits we could hook up with. All in it together, you know? We'd party night and day and not know where Christmas ended and New Year began. Not much in the way of turkey and mince pies for us.'

'*In* what?' he asked.

She didn't understand.

'You said – all in it together? What do you mean?'

Bernie laughed. 'What kind of a question's that? In the shit, mate, where else? The kind of people we knew just washed up here before shooting through, had nobody, and didn't care too much about that.'

The crow scuttled, with an ineffectual flurry of feathers. Both of them glanced towards the cage. John Roper's eyes had returned to his book. Eddy wanted to tell her that the rough act did not convince him, that he heard the loneliness and self-disgust behind her words and knew nothing was irretrievable. He wanted to tell her that, but kept his counsel because it was too soon. Besides, he was afraid of her. Even when he was cleaning up her house, he did so in the suspicion that little that might help could be done for this woman, unless it were possible for her to seek the grace that he himself had ceased to believe in at the age of seventeen. And who was he to demand miracles?

The energy seeped from him, and his shoulders sagged. Bernie saw it, and wondered. The garden threatened them with its rustlings and trillings, as heat balled up in the white sky, ready to roll and flatten all in its way. Next door a small child began to cry, and as if in answer the stricken bird spread its broken wing fruitlessly again and let out a savage caw. Both sounds made Bernie shudder.

81

Roper turned a page, then looked up, curious, at the silence of the two people who stood frowning at each other at each end of the rough sawhorse.

'There's someone walking over your graves,' he said.

'No – *yours*, mate!' she countered, shaking herself, and attempting a grin.

'I thought it was – an angel passing?' said Eddy, picking up her tone.

'You're right – quiet means an angel passing. Ma always said that.'

'Could be it's her going past?' said Eddy softly.

Bernie looked at him sharply, looking for mockery, but found none. Lightly she said, 'Don't wish that on me, mate! I got into enough trouble when the old girl was alive, so the thought of her fluttering about on her little wings and watching freaks me out.'

'Except – you're being quite good at the moment,' he said mischievously. Delighted at the shift in his tone, she grinned back.

'Yeah, and with you cleaning up the house like she used to have it . . . Hey, maybe *you're* the bloody angel, sent along by Colleen Molloy, now sitting on the right hand of God the Father . . .'

'With a pair of feather dusters for wings!' added John.

Their laughter rose to cobweb strings, dust and husks of insects beneath the verandah beams. Tears of mirth filled Bernie's eyes. Suddenly the thought of her mother's spirit looking down did not fill her with dread. She had been a good woman, if a martyr, and it was inevitable, wasn't it, that you disappointed them? Mothers always keep their claws in you, even after they've gone . . .

She said so, still laughing. But the two men went quiet and too late she remembered John Roper's story. Now the sad little suicide – the young mother whose love smashed to earth somewhere in Minnesota – stalked the boards between them, and Roper stared blankly into space.

Bernie wanted to hit herself. As usual she had put her big foot in it; she should have learned by now that mentioning mothers is often dangerous. Yet she was perplexed by Eddy. The wide grin had gone. He looked abstracted, almost angry, and made savage little chopping motions with the saw. A large splinter fell to the ground. She wondered if her words had sliced a wound in his history too.

'Yeah . . . well . . . Christmas?' she offered.

'Be good,' Eddy muttered, grudgingly.

John flopped down, and took up his book again. Bernie glimpsed a bright jacket, showing an airman in goggles and flying helmet, reminding her of Patrick's comics. Then his head was bent again.

'Do you ever read books, Eddy?' she asked.

'Oh, sometimes,' he replied, dryly. 'You?'

She shook her head. 'Not now – no time. When I was a little girl I was forever in the library. I remember when it opened. The woman there was called Miss Fitzgerald and I loved her. She had those upswept glasses, you know? She looked like a strict old stick, kind of sexless spinster type – but man, did she love those books! She knew everything – all the stories, all the writers, and she could point you in the direction of things – just like somebody who knows a special bit of country, knows all the tracks. You know?'

He did.

'Anyways, I read all the usual stories – those fairy tales like Hans Anderson and the other blokes . . . and I liked the one about the Ugly Duckling best. Because that was how I felt.'

'Not fitting in?' Eddy said.

She looked at him in surprise. 'That's right! But he did in the end. I liked that. Kind of gave us all something to hope for, or something like that. A bit like Snow White, my favourite, when she sings '*Some day my prince will come.*' When you get a bit older, and know the score, you want to say, don't you believe it, babe! 'Cos you know he won't – or if he does, he'll be a real bastard! And you reckon the ugly duckling would of ended up in some mucky bedsit in the city all on his own, just because nobody ever found him and told him what he really was . . . But you don't know any of that stuff when you're little, eh?'

'No, you don't,' he nodded.

She sighed.

'Do you still think all that, then?' he asked.

'All what?'

'About the prince being a bastard?'

Bernie threw back her head and laughed again, with real merriment. ''Course I do – *bo–oy*' (she drew the word out in a parody of the American south) '– but I can't say it bothers me any more. I went into a ladies' toilet once, out of town, when me and Zippo were riding, and the place was full of little green frogs, all looking at me with their boggly eyes, hopping all over the floor, the walls, and inside the toilets. I mean, how could you pee on them? At first I thought *yuk*, and then I wanted to laugh my head off, because I thought of all those fairy tales and realized this could be my chance – a room full of princes, if only I knew which one to pick! A frog lottery. Then I thought of all the gunk you'd have to get round your mouth while you was trying, and it didn't seem worth it. So I left all the little princes croaking there and went off to pee in the bushes. See! Wasted me chance! But at least I didn't run the risk of finding out if I was right.'

'Maybe you'll meet some ugly duckling kind of guy, and find out he's a prince, and a bastard only in name,' he said. There was no trace of a smile.

'Yeah – and I'll dress like the Queen of bloody Sheba too, and ride round town in a Rolls Royce with you and him as outriders!'

Bernie ran a hand through her hair, tousling it still further, and bent to look at his work.

'I'll give you the money – for the stuff.'

'It's free. I told you.'

'Paint then?'

'OK – give me the money and I'll get it.'

'Maybe . . . I could help you. Haven't done that for years.'

He shrugged. 'Two makes the going quicker. But only if you want . . .'

'Maybe, after that, we could do the inside of the house.'

'That's a winter job.'

''Course, you might not be here. You might of . . . shot through.'

'Been travelling since I was seventeen, so . . .'

'That's how long?'

'Seven years.'

She was wrong. She'd put him at twenty-five but he was a year younger.

'Where've you been?'

'All over.'

'Maybe the seven year itch'll work in reverse with you, an' you'll stay put,' she said.

It was impossible to tell anything from his face.

'Give you time to fix the place up?'

'Maybe.'

He turned to get on with his work, turning his back on all her questions. She stood watching him for a short time, but he seemed oblivious to her presence, mouth full of nails, driving her off with hammer blows.

Twelve

Biggles landed, taxied in, and sat for a moment or two on the 'hump' of his Camel in front of the hangars. Then he yawned, switched off and climbed stiffly to the ground.

'Is she flying all right, sir?' asked Smyth, his flight-sergeant, running up.

'She's inclined to be a bit heavy on right rudder – nothing very much, but you might have a look at her.'

John Roper is reading the story for what must be the tenth time. At the edge of his mind, he hears the woman and the other man talking, but their voices are receding now, and instead he can hear the buzz of the mess as the chaps lark about. Then the voice of the CO talking just to him. Heels click in unison along the corridor, then the colonel is standing there. He has sought him out especially for this vital mission. He will find out and destroy the enemy camera.

The steady hum of insects in the garden becomes the distant drone of aircraft, safely returned from dogfights with the Hun. Algy's back. And Wilks. And Ginger. Phew.

The airfield buzzes with activity out there, but in here the colonel is looking at him expectantly, knowing it is only he who is capable of accomplishing this task.

'We're counting on you, Roper,' he says . . .

Roper feels the ascent through his backbone, the cold increasing. Pulls the sheepskin tighter around his throat. Should have remembered his scarf. He adjusts his goggles, breathing deeply. Nineteen thousand feet effortlessly; only three or four thousand more to go. But the air is thin; the enemy will be carrying oxygen equipment. Should have thought of that. Too late. But now he sees the Hun up ahead and gets him in his sights . . .

Rat-tat-tat-tat . . .

'No, you don't!', snarled Biggles. 'You can't get away with that!'

The Hun turned slowly over on its back, and, with the tell-tale streamers still fluttering in the slipstream, roared earthwards, black smoke pouring from its engine.

John knows the endings by heart. Biggles will always outwit them, always prevail. And John swings out of the cockpit with him, strides towards the hangar, barks his orders to the flight-sergeant. He smells the slightly oily aroma of his sheepskin jacket as he pulls it off and hangs it on the peg. Then Algy's there, and Ginger, and the usual crowd. They lounge in the mess and plan some japes for Christmas.

'Johnny's the best pilot in the squadron,' says Biggles, clapping him on the shoulder.

'For he's a jolly good fellow' takes John Roper to heights no man has ever reached.

And on the other side of the world Lily Roper opens the bedroom door to look up at the Spitfire hanging still in the centre of the room. The solemnity of ritual, this moment of communion with John, in the cold little bedroom where her white breath rises to the plane and starts the movement. Round and round, so slowly, on a fine black thread, plastic suspended between flaking plaster and threadbare rug, then turning back again.

Back in time, you might have done things differently. If only you could. Wash it all away like you wash the kitchen floor, making it clean again. And all the trophies of his life surround her, except the shelf of flying books he carried away with him.

'*You're doing well for yourself, our John,*' whispers Lily. '*And I always knew you would.*'

She reaches out a finger and runs it along the veneer of the drawers, holding it up to her eyes, frowning at the dust. Then she heaves herself across to the shelf of planes, poised at different angles on their plastic stands, and touches one of them, disturbing a strand of spider's web. Old woman's cloud-breath into dust of memory . . .

*   *   *

86

Bernie called him. The eyes John Roper turned up were vacant, yet hostile, a combination Bernie had only seen before in drunks. He hunched in the chair, left shoulder higher than the other, as if she had asked him something intrusive, instead of just the name of his book. He looked so affronted she was tempted to back off, palms turned up to face him, saying, 'No worries, mate, I don't want to know.'

Yet that was not Bernie Molloy's style. Eddy hammered a few yards away, so she raised her voice a fraction above the noise to repeat, 'Just wondering what you got your nose so stuck in?'

He flipped the book over so she could see the jacket. She looked down at an action illustration of two pilots in biplanes, guns streaming orange and yellow flame, the flier in the foreground in leather helmet and goggles, an expression of determination on his craggy face. Below him a tiny grey shadow of a plane was plunging to earth, trailing clouds of dark smoke.

'Biggles of 266,' she read aloud.

There was a pause. She saw his eyes come back from whatever skies they had been surveying, and drop to the ground.

'Good?'

'I've read it before.'

'Must be good then! I used to read *Winnie the Pooh* again and again. Like eating burgers. You know – comfort food?'

He nodded.

'Must mean a lot to you, all that stuff – I mean, to lug all those books out here?'

John Roper's chest rose and fell, as if summoning the oxygen to clear his head and plunge towards her.

'It was my collection. That and the model planes. Nan bought them for me – not that she had much money, she only worked in the biscuit factory and then as a dinner lady, and she cleaned too – but she always bought me books. She said it wasn't the same getting them from the library; nothing like seeing them lined up on the shelf.'

Bernie squatted down beside him, one brown leg outstretched for balance. She looked from the book jacket to his face, and was surprised by tenderness.

'So what's with this Biggles bloke?' she asked gently.

'Haven't you heard of him?'

'Oh yeah, I think Patrick – he's my brother – read him at one time. Big hero, is he?'

Roper glanced up sharply, looking for mockery in those clear blue-grey eyes, but found none. Shyly he explained, 'You could say that . . . yes. I always thought he was everything it means to be . . . to be . . . British, I suppose. He's the one I . . .'

'Wanted to be like, eh?'

He nodded. Like a little boy, she thought.

'And maybe . . . like you think of your dad too? Right?'

This nod had fierce emphasis, as if he did not trust himself to speak. The book slipped and fell to the ground, and Bernie picked it up, replacing it gently on his knee. One if his hands held it steady, the other returned to tracing the shapes on the jacket, but faster now.

'I do more than imagine,' he said at last. 'It's as if – sort of – I *know*. It sounds daft but when I read, I feel I'm up there with him,' (jabbing the goggled face of Biggles), 'but then I'm with *him* too. Feels a bit different in a Fortress, mind! And my dad's just like Biggles, he even talks like him in my head. Anyway, sometimes we're all up there together and we climb higher and higher, and them telling me I'm good, as good *as* them – and I could go on forever, never coming back down to earth.'

Bernie stood up. 'Reckon we all have to come down to earth in the end, mate.'

The crow scratched and the bushes hummed.

'But you don't want to,' said John. 'Nobody does, do they?'

'Oh, I dunno,' she replied lazily.

Eddy had ceased his angry hammering and stood at the edge of the verandah, listening. His eyes travelled from John back to Bernie, and remained on her face.

'What d' *you* dream about, Bernie?' he prompted. Like a challenge.

Bernie's laugh rang out. 'Jeez! OK – we'll start with me wanting to stay where I was born, back home in Cork, where the rain hits you so hard the dirt can't stick. And wouldn't that be grand? Bernie Molloy going through the *oirish* laundry and coming out squeaky clean!'

They looked unsettled by the harshness behind her mirth. Yet her laughter continued, its tone shifting into real amusement, as if she knew a joke they had not heard. At last she stopped, and grinned at them, catching her breath.

'Honest – it *is* funny – if you knew,' she assured them.

'You gorra laff,' said John, broadening his accent.

'Laughing's better than talking,' grunted Eddy. 'Talking of which – why don't we get on with this bit of building? If I show you what to do, John?'

The old chair creaked as he rose with alacrity.

'So,' said Bernie, 'that's decided then? We're going to do Christmas? All chip in together?'

The word 'together' chimed oddly. None of them claimed it for their own. It belonged in the lexicon of another land, where other sorts of people were drawn to nest in rows. Yet they liked it. And when their individual tongues slipped out to moisten dry lips as the sun rose higher and higher, they accidentally licked up a little of that word as it hung in the still air – and drew it into their separate lives.

Thirteen

The old bungalow went on changing. Confused by delight, Bernie telephoned Suzanne for her opinion. How could this man pitch up out of nowhere and make such a difference? The tap that had dripped for ten years now kept itself as tight as Eddy's own mouth. The bathroom window closed properly. The verandah no longer sagged, the roof was whole. It was as if Sean Molloy had come back from the dead, tool box in hand, to make the place like new once more.

'Maybe . . . maybe . . . this bloke's trying to turn it into the kind of place he wants to stay in,' Suze suggested, her voice sounding even further away than usual.

'Good enough for us all that time,' said Bernie defensively.

'Yeah, but . . . we got grown-up, all of a sudden, didn't we? Don't know about you, but I'm sick of living in a pigsty. Maybe this is your new life, Bern.'

'What is?'

'Oh, I dunno.'

'Anyway, who said I want the bloke to stay?'

'I reckoned you did.'

That's the trouble with old friends, Bernie thought. When you don't see them they forget what you're really like, and make mistakes. But Bernie was no longer sure what she wanted. She found herself watching Eddy Carpenter at odd moments, admiring the wiry elegance of his movements, and marvelling to recall that at first she'd thought him awkward, like a puppet. Sometimes, at night, as the bar noises raged as usual, she took refuge in wondering what he was up to at that minute. He'd asked her for four dollars, which she handed over without question. Two nights later the kitchen was pale yellow. She found herself becoming excited when she drove home, in case her lodger had achieved something new. Yet still she tiptoed past the strip of light beneath his door. Sometimes the need to knock overwhelmed her, but she never did. It was, she told herself, only curiosity. With John Roper present she found it easy to talk to Eddy, but if the pilot was out, or asleep, she avoided him.

Some evenings she found both lodgers still watching television in the lounge room, sprawled, not speaking, eyes fixed on the screen. Then she would offer tea or coffee, easing herself into this new role of considering people, even looking after them. These glimmerings of new concern puzzled her, but old habits warned her they should be resisted.

As Christmas approached, the Zoo rocked more desperately than ever. The drinking was frenetic, the aggression even worse than usual. Occasionally a couple broke into spontaneous dancing in the middle of the floor, the awkward movements of people who did not know each others' rhythms yet hoped to learn through quick sex later on that night.

But those were the better moments. The people whose sweat rubbed off on each other as they jostled for service would remain strangers bonded only by beer. Mates on construction gangs knew that when the job was done they would never see each other again; *just shootin' through* became a metaphor, a philosophy even, that nobody could contradict. At Christmas these truths were painful, even to the most hardened ringer.

90

Two thickset men in their early forties, with moustaches and dark shoulder-length hair, blew in briefly for a couple of cans. Bernie recognized bikies even before she saw the *Live to Ride, Ride to Live* motto tattooed on an upper arm. One of them wore a red bandanna; their denim vests were crusted white under the arms. The drinkers gave them space. They drank for thirty minutes without speaking, and as they rose to leave, one of them offered Bernie a drink for herself. His face was hard, but she smiled for the first time that evening.

'You ridin' Harleys?'

They nodded, appraising her.

'Used to be a bikie, years ago, living at Bondi. Me an' this bloke – Zippo . . . yeah . . . his friend had a Shovelhead, but Zippo liked British bikes. Rode a beautiful pre-unit Bonnie. He was like you two – cool – you know what I mean?'

They did, although they did not speak, merely nodded approval of the woman behind the bar, who tried to resist the impulse to clutch a hairy, tattooed arm and impose her tale. '. . . Yeah . . . we hung out. Had some good times. 'Til he wiped out. You know?' She stroked her little butterfly, and looked down with a shrug.

They nodded again. One of them shook his head. The other one muttered, 'Fuck,' in sympathy.

'Ride safe,' she whispered, as they moved slowly towards the door.

Bernie heard the puttering rumble, then the pulsing roar, and felt her loss as it thinned into distance. She remembered how her head snapped back at the thrust, how the wind screamed, how the road vibrated through metal and up the length of her spine, like they were all part of a whole. And how from that point onward the pain tossed her on to the shore, pulverizing her into the finest grains.

The bikies had gone. Ah, she thought – to be stuck forever in this town, instead of being able to move on like them, to know it would go on and on, just the same. The night began to crush her. Driven to accept every drink the saddest loser offered her, she even went outside for a couple of long drags on somebody's joint, although she knew Dick would be angry if he saw. Again and again her head sang its chorus, *Who gives a shit? Who?*

By the end of the evening she could barely stand.

'Look at the state of you, Bern! Leave your old crate here and I'll take you home,' said Dick. Out of habit, he added, 'Maybe you'll ask me in and do us both a favour.'

'Lishen Dick, you know I w-w-wouldn't mesh with Joanie,' she giggled.

The hall was dark when, at the fifth attempt, she managed to turn her key in the lock and stumble inside. It was just before midnight. The house was silent. John's room was in darkness; the pilot went to bed very early because of his dawn starts. But Eddy's threshold was a sliver of light.

She stood swaying slightly. He might pretend not to hear her knock. He always made it clear he did not welcome questions or even conversation. It was as if he was content to be a glorified cleaner and handyman, and nothing more. Well, she wasn't going to play it that way. Not at all. It was her house.

First she went to the kitchen, and made a mug of sweet black coffee. The lemon walls were somebody's vision of how fresh life could be. The coffee hurt her mouth, but she guessed there was no time to lose. He might go to bed. After a pause, she grabbed the bottle of scotch and upended the dregs into her mug. Thus fortified, she padded back along the hall, carrying the mug. After a quick knock she turned the handle.

Eddy Carpenter sat hunched over the small wooden table that served as a nightstand. At first she could not see what he was doing. Startled, he turned, half rose, and something crashed to the floor.

'What . . .?'

The jam jar had not smashed, but dirty orange liquid was spreading in a pool, snaking across the lino to soak into the edge of the old grey and blue rug in the middle of the room. Both of them stared at it, not moving.

'Sh—orry I gave you a f–f–right,' said Bernie, slopping coffee to the floor as well.

She saw that he had a piece of stick in his hand, and a few large tubes of paint lay scattered on the table. A small square of wood served as a palette, blobs of acrylic laid out in a line. Just five colours: ochre, rust, yellow, black and white. A larger piece of thin board was in the centre, primed white and half patterned with dots dabbed close together. She walked over and looked down at it. He stared at her, oblivious to the water lapping his bare feet.

Then she began to laugh, snorting and swaying like a madwoman.

Still he did not speak.

Spluttering, Bernie put her mug down on the table, and bent to look closely at the painting. The dots swirled in patterns that were becoming familiar to any tourist who visited the town: circles, wavy lines, zig-zags all mimicking patterns once marked out with a finger in sand, to represent the creation stories of the first inhabitants of the land. Now they danced before her eyes as she blinked, trying to focus.

'My God, Eddy! What *you* doing – painting like *this*?'

Abruptly he threw down the stick, walked across to a pile of clothes at the foot of his bed, picked up a T-shirt and started mopping up the paint water with angry movements. Bernie picked up the stick, examined it, then dabbed it in the yellow paint. Her hand wavering, still laughing to herself, she bent as if to put her own dot on the board. But Eddy snatched it from her hand.

'Don't do that – you'll spoil it,' he snapped.

'Oh, c'mon, Eddy, give me a break. You can't be serioush about this?'

'Mind your own business.'

'Ouuuuh,' she mocked, 'getting angry, is it? C'mon, Leonardo, lesh have a go . . .'

She made a grab for the paint stick, but he held on firmly. Bernie burst out laughing again as they wrestled for control, hooting with derision as she struggled for balance. At last Eddy managed to dislodge her grip, but only by causing her to fall against him.

'You're drunk,' he said, with distaste – holding her back at arms' length.

Bernie sucked her finger resentfully. 'Ow, I think you've put a splinter in it,' she mumbled. 'An I only wanted to have a go at being a *real painter* . . .' Suddenly feeling a little more sober, she frowned at him. 'So this is how you pay your rent, is it? Nice little game, Eddy! Wassh this going to be, then?' She waved a hand at the painting on the table. 'Honey-ant dreaming? Wild-potato dreaming? Or old-fuckin'-fraud-Eddy dreaming? Make it up as you go along, do you?'

'I was taught,' he said, defensively.

'Who by?'

'Never mind.'

'So. Doesn't make it real, does it?'

'What's real, for God's sake?'

She made an effort to concentrate. 'Those people up at Papu-whassit-called – them painting their own stuff, that's what's real! It's like – you're rippin' them off, doing this! What gives you the right?'

The passion of her speech was diminished by a small belch.

'Got more right than you think,' he muttered, turning away to sit in the chair, his back to her. 'What the fuck do you know?'

'You do boomerangs too?'

'Sometimes – yeah, I do!'

Bernie moved across to sprawl on one elbow on his bed. For a few minutes she said nothing, watching the sag of his shoulders. He looked dejected, and she felt sorry for him. But she was still shocked and amused at once by his game. The tourist shops had become more and more dependent on paintings and artifacts marketed as 'the art of the first Australians', and already the designs were being used on ashtrays and scarves. Once Bernie saw an elderly aboriginal man enter one of the smarter shops, a single painted board under his arm. It must have been rejected, because she saw him leave a few minutes later, put it down, look back at the shop, then deliberately urinate in the flower bed outside.

On another occasion, about four months earlier, she was killing time in one of the new galleries when a young man came in, dressed in a lime-green nylon shirt and white flares, carrying a long roll under one arm. He unrolled five large tarpaulin paintings on the floor. The elderly lady who ran the shop examined them carefully.

'What's this one, Barney?' she asked, in a nursery-teacher voice.

The man explained the dreaming in the painting, mumbling so that Bernie could hardly hear. 'This waterhole . . . and emu . . . this one emu wife . . . blackfellas huntin' . . . come back . . .'

The woman nodded. 'Yes, but I didn't think the emu was your totem, Barney?' The man mumbled something and she nodded, apparently satisfied. It went on, questions and explanations, until at last she said, 'I want you to do me more black-snake dreamings. Your own dreaming. People like black snakes. You understand? Big important dreaming, eh, Barney? Like this one. This is the best one.'

'Mind if I take a look?' Bernie said.

'There – beautiful!' said the woman.

She patted the artist on his shoulder and smiled up at Bernie, who immediately changed her mind about her. Patronizing she might sound, yet she was kind. And it was clear, from the way her hand moved caressingly across the tarp, she cared about this work.

'Barney actually cut up his tent, he's got so much to say,' she said.

Even Bernie could see that the painting on top of the pile was magnificent. It measured about four foot by three, and the whole background was stippled brown and green with traces of yellow: the colours of the desert after rain. The snake was not black at all but barred with wide brown and dark green stripes, delineated by yellow dots. His coils wound around two black circles the size of tennis balls, each surrounded by white dots and with a white dot in the centre as well.

'They're the waterholes,' said the woman, 'and what's interesting is – that the same symbol is a woman's breast. Life-giving you see? Milk, and water . . .'

The snake was surrounded by little curved lozenges in rust-red, and at each side of the picture was a row of four of these, coloured black.

'So what's happening here?' Bernie asked diffidently, nervous they both might think her stupid.

'Tell her, Barney,' encouraged the woman.

'Black snake my totem, passed on by my father, Tjapaljarri. Dreamtime ancestor. They came when the earth was dark, and went all across the land. This how the earth was made, and everything have its name. This was the Tjukurrpa – the dream-time?'

Bernie met his eyes. She once borrowed a book about the legends, and decided it was all just as good as God creating the earth in seven days, as the nuns had taught them. Dividing the light from the darkness, creating the oceans, naming all the animals . . . and doing it all in seven days too. Good old God. But these others, they did it differently – they slithered and

95

stalked about the land, resting here and there and naming all the parts. Bernie liked to close her eyes and imagine the undulating green of home transforming itself into a great reptile, hunching its back against the elements, or burrowing to hide. It pleased her. After all, they said Ireland was full of sacred sites. Who was to say what was sacred?

She had heard the artist explaining that the black shapes represented the men the serpent had killed, but the other ones were the hunters coming to take their vengeance as the great ancestral being wound his way from waterhole to waterhole. She heard his story and knew that the core of his narrative was the idea of belonging – the oneness with the world around that was forever lost to her in exile. She knew that the man Barney was speaking of her own being as well as his own. Yet the evidence of the tarpaulins spread out, patterned with their iconography of acrylic dots, showed that he was far more fortunate than she. Tears filled her eyes.

He saw – and glanced away.

'You reckon the snake'll get caught?' she asked.

Still looking down he shook his head, then shrugged as if to say it did not matter anyway, because the creature was eternal, and his story would go on being remade as it was retold. It would outlive them all.

'Great picture,' she said.

He looked up at her once more, then inclined his head with the dignity of a very old man, because he knew she was right.

Now, despite her drunken state, Bernie recalled that painter clearly, and compared his pride to the humiliation of the one before her, caught out in his little imitation game. She looked around the room. Leaning in the corner behind the door was the long woven cloth case he'd slung on his shoulder when he arrived.

'You play didge?'

He shook his head.

'Why you carrying it around then?'

'Yidaki.'

'You what?' She started to giggle.

'They call it yidaki – in Arnhemland. That's where I learnt, when I was travelling. A friend made it for me, but I don't play it any more – if it's any business . . .' He turned to face her, mouth tense, defiant. 'I'll tell you something though. I'm gonna start doing nice bright didgeridoos, making them, painting them – the lot. Small ones at first. Precious original aboriginal artifacts, yeah? Tourists love them – take one home slung on your rucksack and think you're really cool. Bit of native art – the real thing. Guy I supply – he's telling me to get cracking. Beats digging holes, any day. That all right with you?'

'OK, OK – who gives a shit?' said Bernie, leaning back and watching the room shift. The centre light in its paper shade doubled and quadrupled itself and circled her head. Constellations danced at the edges of her eyes. When she closed them her skull rollercoastered, making her grip the edge of the bed and groan. This seemed to go on for a very long time. She struggled for control, but failed.

'You should get to your own room,' Eddy was saying coldly, looming over her, yet thousands of miles away.

'Too nishe . . . here,' she murmured, turning her face sideways on his pillow. Dimly conscious of the smell of it, warm, earthy and seductive. She wanted to lie there forever.

'Come on.' He took her hand, but she pulled it back in sudden panic.

'Reckon . . . I'm going to be sick.'

'Oh God – not here. Come *on* . . .'

She was aware of being helped to her feet, which gave way at the last minute. Eddy cursed her, then supported her weight. She closed her eyes again, to a universe whirling in colours of red and green which merged to muddy chaos. Somebody was taking her somewhere. Bernie knew nothing except she wanted to be supported by this strength that was holding her up. It was so pleasant to be half carried. Voluptuously she leaned into the experience, smelling that earthy smell once more, wanting to bury herself there, whatever the cost, even if it meant dying . . .

She heard a voice mumble, 'Oh you stupid bloody woman.' And yet she did not feel it was unkind.

Bernie woke to a room filled with sunlight and the faint odour of disinfectant. She groaned and pulled the pillow over her head. Here I am again, she thought, with the hangover to end them all. How many years have I been doing this?

She rolled over on to her stomach and realized two things

simultaneously. The first was that her pillow smelt faintly of flowers and the bedclothes were all clean. The second was that she was naked. Confused, she screwed her eyes tightly shut in a vain effort to banish the light – and also to remember what she had been wearing last night. It was an old Indian cotton top with a drawstring neck, over cut-offs . . .

Yes.

Then Bernie groaned again as memory filtered through.

'Oh fuck!' she said aloud.

Eddy Carpenter had been in his room, she had disturbed him painting, caught him out in his tatty little forgeries . . . They'd argued and he had helped her from his room. And now she was lying in bed, naked, in a bedroom smelling suspiciously fresh, even clinical.

She ground at her eyes with her fists, as if the pain might drive away the unavoidable image of her lodger undressing her before putting her to bed. But what else had happened? Supposing they'd had sex? But no, she knew that was not possible. Eddy wasn't the type to take advantage of a drunk, and in any case (she reasoned, in a state approaching panic) she must have looked so vile nobody in his right mind would have wanted to.

She pulled the sheet over her head like a child who wants to be invisible. What do you say to a young man who has struggled to get your dead-drunk legs out of knickers? *Er – thank you, Eddy, but why didn't you leave them on?* Whatever she said, she would have to apologize and that went against her grain.

'Oh God, oh God,' she mumbled, face pressed into the mattress.

Then somebody was standing by the bed, and a hand was laid on her shoulder for a second, so lightly it might have been an illusion.

'Are you awake?' he asked.

She groaned again.

'Feel sick?'

'Go away.'

'I brought you sweet tea. Come on – it's what you need.'

There was no avoiding the confrontation. She turned over and poked her head up over the sheet, once again smelling the fragrance.

98

Eddy stood by the bed, looking down at her, a mug in his hand. He held it out to her, with the faintest of smiles. She cringed. The knowledge that she must find out exactly what had happened was additional poison in her system.

'Do you feel sick?'

She shook her head, saying nothing. His smile widened a fraction as he held the mug closer to her face. 'Well, I reckon that with all the stuff that came out of you last night, there can't be much left.'

'Jesus, Eddy, I'm . . .'

'Don't say you're sorry, Bernie. Drunks should always face it out, I reckon. Anyway, it was a – what shall I say – *interesting* experience.'

Hot and angry, Bernie clutched the sheet to her chest and sat up. 'Look, mate, just because you saw me at me worst, doesn't give you the right to take the piss, OK? I made a complete fool of myself, but so what? Wasn't the first time, and I reckon it won't be the last. Thanks – for the tea.'

She swallowed, burning her mouth. Eddy stood watching her, hands hanging loosely by his sides in that old puppet stance she used to find faintly comical. But now he was in control.

'Haven't you got a job to go to?' she asked at last.

'I pulled a sickie.'

'Why?'

'Reckoned you might need looking after.'

Bernie looked quickly down at the tea, afraid her expression would reveal too much. Nobody looked after her, not since Zippo, and if the truth were told, he wasn't very good at that either – if you count 'looking after' as bringing cups and clearing up. So, nobody since she left home, and certainly nobody through the worst of times. Falling back against the pillows, Bernie closed her eyes and had an instant vision of herself on a hospital bed, a small writhing creature, put through a torture she could never have imagined. Nobody there then, or afterwards. Why would you expect anything else?

'Used to lookin' after myself,' she muttered.

He said nothing, knowing silence would force her to look at him. Then he stared pointedly at an old navy-blue jacket, her one attempt at 'smart' clothes, which was suspended from the picture rail with all the other tattered remnants of her life.

'Don't make much of a job of it, do you, Bernie?'

'I do all right,' she said, defiant and close to tears.

'Last night . . .' he began.

'Don't talk about it. I'm sorry, all right? Leave it at that – OK?'

'Don't try so hard, Bernie. As I was saying, last night . . . you told me something strange . . .'

'Drunks always talk strange. I wouldn't take any notice, mate.'

'No, it was more than that. You were sick on the floor and all over everything you were wearing . . .' Bernie covered her eyes again, and groaned softly. 'And so, I'm sorry . . . but I had to . . .'

'OK, OK, you managed to get me clothes off. So let's both be embarrassed and get it over with. End of story.'

'Well, no, it was after that. I put you into bed, and you started to cry. You were staring over there –' he gestured towards the old wardrobe – 'and when I asked you why you hung all your clothes from the rail when you've got a wardrobe, you told me . . . you said . . . you couldn't open it any more because there was a *body* in it. You said you'd killed somebody, Bernie!'

She did not speak.

'When I asked what you meant, you cried even more, and it was hard to understand you, but all I could make out was . . . you said, "It was my fault, and that means I killed him." You were choking by then, crying like I've never seen anybody cry, and . . . hey, what was all that about?'

'Nothing.'

'You must—'

'So what happened then?' she asked abruptly.

'You passed out. *Zonk* – like that. I put you on your side, and then went and got the bucket to clear up.'

'Pleasant for you.'

'Seen and done worse.'

'Me too.'

'Aren't you goin' to tell me then?'

'What?'

Eddy was impatient now. 'You know what! Listen, I'm living in your house, and last night you found out something about me – like now you know I'm a con-merchant who'll do anything for a few dollars. Then I put you to bed because you're pissed out of your skull, and you throw up everywhere, and I take forever getting your clothes off – for God's sake! – because you're covered in the stuff, even soaked through to your undies. Then you say the weirdest thing I ever heard, and it's like you're crying for everybody and everything in the world. I could hardly stand it. And now you're telling me it's nothing – oh, come on!'

'You don't give much away yourself, so why should I? John – he's told me plenty about where he's from and—'

'Don't get off the subject,' Eddy said, clicking his fingers in exasperation.

He watched her. She raised a hand and put it to her head, letting it drop down again as if her own flesh was too heavy to bear. Without speaking, Eddy turned and went to the bathroom, returning with a washcloth wrung out in cold water and shaped into a pad. Gently he placed it on her forehead and heard an involuntary murmur of pleasure. Then he fished a small brown bottle from his pocket and unscrewed the lid.

'There,' he said quietly, like a parent settling a child.

Bernie felt the movement as he dabbed a finger on the pillow around her head; then the sweet smell drifted into her nostrils, combining with the soothing cold on her forehead to make her feel at peace.

'What is it?' she whispered.

'Jasmine oil. Do you like it?'

Her voice was fainter now. 'Smells of flowers.'

He stood watching her long after she had already drifted back into sleep. Rats' tails on her pillow, unhealthy pallor beneath the tan, the panda smudges of mascara beneath her eyes – for once Bernie Molloy looked her age, ravaged and plain, and yet he did not mind.

Last night she'd clutched him, gulping for breath through savage tears. Her hands scrabbled at his arms and she choked out the words, 'Help me!' And Eddy found he wanted to help her, although he did not understand why. He turned to contemplate his own reflection in the smeary glass of the old wardrobe which held some terror for her. A spectre grimaced back at him, so that he too was afraid for a second, and wanted to avert his gaze.

How could she have killed somebody? It was fantasy of course, and yet it haunted her. He would find out. But for now he stepped towards the bed and rested a finger for a second on the tiny butterfly tattoo revealed on the one shoulder. Then turned away to go and switch on the washing machine.

Fourteen

On Christmas Eve morning Bernie and John went shopping for food. She was conscious of him pushing the trolley behind her, wearing his pleasure like a badge. It was as if they were a married couple, she thought wryly, and this was what he wanted – apart from the flying, of course. He wanted them to seem enclosed in that sacred ritual of domesticity which can turn an ordinary man and a woman in supermarket aisles into priests.

Yet it did not annoy her. Something had shifted.

It occurred to her that they might change him, that she and Eddy Carpenter could do this Pom good. If she left him to fantasize about a new role, it might make his life easier, pull the edges into a new shape.

'Are we having Christmas pudding?' he asked.

'I hate it, meself – but we'll have it if you want it.'

'Nan always put a sixpence in, for me to find.'

'Da was crazy about the stuff, and Ma made proper brandy butter . . .'

'Are *we* having that?'

'Too much like hard work, mate. You'll have to make do with ice cream.'

'No worries.'

She stopped, and he ran the trolley into her leg, making her grimace in pain.

'*What* did you say?' she asked.

His cheeks flamed, and she gave him a light punch on the chest.

'It just came out,' he said sheepishly.

'Strikes me you're going native!' She smiled.

'You have to try – to fit in,' he said dubiously.

102

Something in his face – a line at the corner of his mouth, a wistfulness behind the eyes – made Bernie realize how serious it was.

'Yeah,' she said softly. 'Always found it hard myself. Still do. Just wanted to go home. But I reckon you have to settle for what you've got. Have to say, "This is the only hand I'm going to be dealt, so I might as well play it to win" – right?'

John bent to make an unnecessary fuss of rearranging things in the trolley, hiding his face. Bernie saw that his hands shook slightly. She turned and walked on, leaving him to follow, until she reached the eggs and turned brightly to ask him if he thought a dozen would be enough.

At the bungalow they found Eddy putting the finishing touches to decorations in the sitting room. He had sprayed a few branches silver to construct the most artistic 'tree' Bernie had ever seen – one which John (reared on the dusty green artificial tree Lily Roper retrieved from the loft each year) thought looked like a silly bundle of twigs, no more nor less. But he did not say so. Eddy's creation was adorned with red and silver baubles; the pot it stood in covered with silver foil, and placed on a square of red crêpe paper. He'd pinned red, green and silver tinsel in loops around the picture rail.

They stood admiring his handiwork. Then Bernie asked, 'Did you use to get a Christmas stocking, John?'

'Yes – of course,' he said, far away.

She waited, and he went on, 'It was made from a sort of net, so you could see the colours of what was inside, and Nan always filled it so the toys fell out the top. There'd always be sweets of course, and a sugar mouse – pink, and those gold chocolate coins, and things like a helicopter you made work with an elastic band, and a trumpet, and a yo-yo maybe, and, and . . . things like that. There'd always be a tangerine in silver foil in the foot, and at the very bottom a potato – sometimes.'

'A potato?'

'Yes, don't you know about that? You get a potato for the times you've been badly behaved.'

Bernie whistled. 'Good job Ma didn't know that one; I'd have found oirish sackfuls at the foot of the bloody bed! We always—'

'Nan didn't give me one very often.'

103

'Yeah, yeah, I know, John, you were top of the class, flying hero number one – and all the rest of it!'

Bernie could not keep the edge out of her voice. Nobody else's story mattered to him and it annoyed her.

'I didn't say I was top of the class,' he said sullenly, turning away.

'OK, OK, no worries – as you'd say.'

Then Eddy frowned at her. 'Anyway – it's Christmas,' he said. Nobody replied.

Christmas Eve was the time for the ceremony Colleen Molloy brought with her from home in Skibbereen. A precious part of her childhood, it became part of theirs and Bernie knew her mother cherished the belief that these things would go on forever, that one day she would surely see grandchildren on tiptoe to light the holy Christmas candle. One of Bernie's first memories was of the hush of the moment on Christmas Eve when they clustered around the Bible and read the Christmas story. The children couldn't read, of course, so Da and Ma alternated the verses, and later Patrick joined them, then Bernie, then Siobhan and Louisa – all taking their turns to read Luke 2 aloud. Bernie hustled for her favourite verses, which Patrick wanted to read only because he knew it would annoy her.

Two minutes later they'd be wearing their Sunday faces and reading like angels, as their mother said. They told themselves and each other that they only did it to please her, while all the time the need for the words ran deep in their veins. Bernie's finger followed the lines, although she knew the verses by heart:

And so it was that, while they were there, the days were accomplished that she should be delivered.

And she brought forth her firstborn son, and wrapped him in swaddling clothes and laid him in a manger; because there was no room for them at the inn.

The readings done, the black Bible closed reverentially and placed on the sideboard, Sean took a box of matches from his pocket. It was time for the candle. Year after year the fat church candle, in the cupboard as long as Bernie could remember, was brought out, put on a plate and placed at the end of the mantelpiece. Each of the four children was allowed to strike a match; Ma said, 'Quick now!' and Da said, 'Be careful!' and the four of them lit it together as Ma whispered, 'God bless us all.' They watched as the flame lengthened, the light soft on their faces, holding them there, before they grew older.

It was inevitable that the growing Molloys would need to smash the ritual that travelled with them from the brainwashed country. So Patrick would snigger and say 'socks' instead of 'flock', and Siobhan would giggle at the way Bernie said 'delivered' and probably at its meaning too; Lou would join in, and Bernie would push and shove her three siblings, telling them to shut up. One year Colleen Molloy burst into tears because it was not as it was, and Sean stormed out to fetch a beer. Later still, Patrick refused to read at all, and the others performed the Christmas ritual in the full knowledge that its days were numbered.

One year, when Bernie was about fifteen, without anything being said, nothing happened at all. It vanished like the candle being blown out for another year. Colleen sat in her cane chair at the time she should have been opening the Bible at Luke, and stared into the oppressive shadows as if hoping something might materialize above the waxy blossoms to reassure her the past could not be killed. Bernie could not bear the look of reproach in her father's eyes, and knew she could not stay there long.

Each Christmas, immersed in such a different life far away, she had thought of those readings, and the memory softened like candlelight until the bad moments became unfocussed. But later, words and meanings proved unbearable, and the image of the baby in the manger was the spectre which would not depart.

Oh, how can I bury it?

'What did *you* do?' Eddy was asking.

'About what?'

'Christmas stockings and all that stuff?'

'Oh, before we went to bed we'd blow out the candle we'd all lit earlier, and read something from the Bible, and then we hung up a sock each – only a sock mind, one of Dad's – from the mantelpiece. There wasn't much money, so there'd not be much in it: a few sweets, a toy, the usual things. But it felt heavy when you woke up, even though it was quite small. Rustled on your foot . . .'

A fly buzzed in the heat of the small kitchen where the three of them seemed frozen for a second, Eddy leaning on the door frame, Bernie gazing at the Calibre wine boxes she'd bought on special at a dollar off, John watching the kettle boil for the tea he drank in quantities Bernie hadn't seen in years. The shopping still waiting to be put away evoked Christmas plans made keenly, but which had suddenly died for each of them.

John ached to be back with Nan. He could smell the slight whiff of damp mingled with fried food in the narrow hall she used to repaper each year. He wondered if she would get out the tree. No, with him away she wouldn't bother . . . He visualized her opening the parcel he'd sent and wishing he was there. He thought of the small coal fire, and his eyes filmed. His bones cracked with longing for the slush, the hail, the blast of wind off the Mersey.

'You crook, mate?' Eddy asked.

'Why are you asking me? I'm fine . . .'

He shoved past them. They heard his door slam. Meeting Eddy's stare, Bernie raised her eyebrows. 'What did we say?'

'Not *we*,' he replied.

'Me?'

'Yes, I heard. You put him down – but he can't take it, Bernie. He's not like you . . .'

'That's for sure!'

'No, listen. I talk to him. We're thrown together. Sometimes it's like I'm the first person he's met over here who takes any notice. OK, so he goes on and on about his father, and the flying – poor bugger. But he's harmless enough. Nice, really.'

'You think he's a bit nuts?'

He sighed. 'I reckon you could be a bit more subtle, Bernie.'

She looked down, wondering what to say. His bare feet were thin, the toenails cracked and grimy, the hard skin like a leather sole along the sides. Yet Bernie was rocked by a sudden need to hold them between the palms of her hands, and stroke away the tiredness from travelling she knew lay beneath those calloused surfaces. When she raised her face to meet his steady, grey gaze, he was smiling. She felt she'd suddenly been given a gift.

'I should get him a present, maybe?' she said slowly.

'Be a nice thing to do.'

'I didn't know . . . if we were doing presents, Eddy.'

'We do what we feel like. No landlady's rules, are there?'

'I'll have to go out again . . . OK – so what do *you* feel like?'

'That's my secret.'

'Like everything else about you, mate! You never talk about yourself, do you?'

'Why should I?'

'Because of what you just said. We're all living here – so it's natural to let the odd thing drop. But you never do. Say I asked you something . . . something easy . . . say I asked if *you* had a Christmas stocking when you were a kid. What would you say?'

Eddy took two steps past her, put a teabag from the packet into a mug, and poured the boiling water. He pushed the bag around so some of the liquid splashed on the formica, then added two heaped teaspoons of sugar. The fridge door clunked shut on the milk before he spoke.

'I'll take this to John.'

'Oh, come on, Eddy! Can't be that hard, for Chrissake!'

He picked up the mug and walked past her, only stopping to turn briefly in the doorway. No vestige of a smile now. His expression was bleak.

'Well – it wasn't a stocking, it was a dirty great pillow-case,' he said, with an odd, bitter emphasis, 'and it was full of stuff. Too much stuff. Much more than the kids at school got. But you see, *he* had a lot to make up for.'

That night, when big Frank was arm-locking somebody out of the door, she remembered the expression on Eddy's face. In a dream, she took orders, pulled and poured, slammed the till shut, and even uttered vague pleasantries and precise banter – all the time recalling how its contours became as harsh as rock split in an ancient seismic upheaval. And when she drove home – sounds of drunken Christmas greetings echoing in her ears – the reflections in her windscreen danced like the unnatural brightness in his eyes.

The house was silent. A scent of sandalwood joss stick lent an unaccustomed air of calm. When Bernie crept past the two doors of her lodgers' rooms she held her breath, dreading their sudden appearance. Yet she was glad they were there. It was

107

that knowledge, and the sense that something had changed and would change still further, that made her afraid to breathe. And all the more so when she closed the door of her own room behind her.

The bed was made. Needless to say, she had not left it that way. Dazed, she heard her own voice let out a squeak at the sight of something on her pillow, where the faeces had lain just eight weeks before. It sagged between her finger and thumb, and felt heavy in her hand. Small objects rustled in tissue. In wonder, she brought the other one up to cup the lumpy sock.

For a long time Bernie stood without moving, looking down at this misshapen little object of ineffable beauty. She noticed the small hole in the heel, through which some green tissue poked. Hesitantly she moved her fingers to make it whisper, then allowed them to squeeze a little, as a blind person will trace identity through shape.

She looked at her watch. It was already Christmas Day, but she did not want to unpack the stocking until morning. She needed it to exist for a while longer, with all its promise intact. Unwilling to be parted from it for a moment, Bernie carried it to the bathroom, and laid it down on the tiles while she showered. Then she cradled it in both hands, pulled back the sheet and put it in the bed beside her. She lay, tracing its contours as if it were a beloved body, and when she fell asleep it gave her comfort which radiated into her dreams.

Fifteen

There was nothing at the bottom of his bed. Yet for a second he imagined a weight, moving his foot and waiting for the creaking rustle that did not come.

Did you forget this time, Nan?

A sugar mouse, a plastic helicopter driven by elastic, a

magic painting book, a pencil sharpener, a packet of crayons, a net of chocolate coins, a rubber ball like plasticine marled together . . .

You wouldn't forget.

'Course I wouldn't, love.

It's me own fault, for being in the wrong place.

Don't you be so daft, our Johnny, nothing's your fault.

Whose is it then?

Something went wrong.

Whose fault is it then?

My fault, our Johnny.

A potato then, eh?

It was so hot already. How could they exist for so long without rain?

The weight of the air was a great invisible hand pushing him down into the damp pillow; death by suffocation in feathers and fabric. Then – worse – burial in sand and soil mixed: damp flesh coated, veins silted, eyeballs rolled in a sugaring of quartz as you struggled for breath and the sand poured in down your throat . . .

The blood boils under this pitiless sky.

A woman laughed at me, once, right in my face. I bought her, so she had no right. But they're like that here, they laugh at your accent, your white skin, the way you . . . She was a bitch! She could have helped, instead of just laughing her head off, smelling of beer. Nan hates the smell of beer.

'John!'

No, Nan, it's too early.

'John!'

Sometimes you look down and it's all so red – you're hanging over frozen fire, the flames stuck there forever, like hell, never changing, tormenting you because they never burn you up, just go on. It's insane, down there, you'd die if you had to ditch in that burning sand. And the air – only the air, where you feel free – is all that keeps you from it, bouncing you up on the thermals. Heat, thirst, flies. Blinding and burning in the silence. What chance do you have in a furnace? Incineration when you fall to the earth. Cremation – a quick collapse into white ash.

It's not time yet, Nan.

Eddy looked down at him, and repeated, 'John!' Sleep-encrusted eyes opened at last and fixed on him a gaze of dark bewilderment, as if John Roper had no idea who he was.

'Come on, mate! I've got the tea on!'

'Nothing to get up for,' said John, his voice dead.

'It's Christmas Day.'

'So what?'

Eddy shrugged and turned away, calling over his shoulder, 'Well, I did get you a present, but it's all the same to me.'

'A present?'

'Yeah, mate – an old Christmas custom, remember?'

John sat up. 'I got you one too.'

Eddy left him to dress, and crept along to the kitchen. Passing her door, he stopped for a second, hoping to hear the sound of paper, even a small laugh, but there was nothing. Knowing her, she'd have opened it last night, greedily unpacked all its little secrets. She'd have been pleased, but feel embarrassed this morning, and need to seem hard-boiled. That's what she was like. Each day she had to put on her carapace like other women wear make-up. Tough old Bernie Molloy . . . afraid.

Imagining the sun falling across her bed, hair spread on the pillow, he smiled again. He remembered her body, flopping about in his hands as he struggled with her clothes and felt the smoothness of her tanned skin. He could picture the brownness of her nipples, and the triangle of curly red-brown hair under the curve of her belly. Eddy closed his eyes. She would wake soon.

In the kitchen he opened the fridge, took out the box, and poked about amongst the rank meat. The crow was his duty now, like so many other things in the bungalow in Dean Street. That first day he talked to it, the ugly old bird knew him. All wild things recognized him, and he clutched that private knowledge to himself with the rest of his secrets. He heard it in the squawk of the galah, the fluting of the butcherbird, and now in the gentle *uk, uk, uk* that greeted him as he walked from the back door.

'Hey–ey, you'd be a savage old thing if you'd half the chance, wouldn't you?'

'*Kruuuuk-uk-uk!*'

'Like her, Crow. Locked up and can't fly, yet you got to snap and scratch and pretend you're mean, hey?'

The bird pulled at the gobbet of meat Eddy refused to relinquish. He enjoyed the way the thin black head bobbed and weaved, and the hard little eyes swivelled from him to the food, as the beak jerked at it with surprising strength.

They understood each other. The monosyllabic grunts he'd heard that night in her Zoo, the short barks of the men on site – none of it was superior communication to the range of sounds that came from this injured creature. He could identify its greetings, its hunger, its irritation, its sleepiness, and the deep frustration at its core when it looked beyond bars to the sky. Each day he talked to it, and when the bird cocked its shiny head he convinced himself it understood. So many years of near silence, but now Eddy was becoming aware that he had to learn to communicate again, and the half-articulate croonings he made to the injured bird were a part of that process.

It was like the softening in Bernie Molloy. He saw it. She would start to speak too, he hoped. He trusted. But he knew that both of them must learn a language that would build on the grunts and the barks which had become the habit. You could never unlearn the silences.

Bernie woke to find herself hugging the little sock as though it were her teddy bear and she was a child again. Under the same roof. With everything ahead – to be changed, discovered, made new again.

'Happy Christmas, Bernadette,' she said aloud.

She sat up quickly, placing the sock in the concave of sheet over her thighs. A small bird beat against her ribs, chirping a message she did not fully understand. She hadn't felt so excited for years and years. Very slowly she unpacked the Christmas stocking, taking trouble over each small parcel. No need to rush.

He'd used tissue in two shades of green. Small slivers of sticky tape held it in place. Trouble had been taken. She imagined his head bent over the task, those long fingers laboriously folding and cutting, and then pushing the parcels down into the sad old sock, so that everything fitted. The thought was like a window opening and the fresh air gave her strength.

She unwrapped a bar of rose-scented soap, a tube of lemon lollies, a strawberry-flavoured lip gloss, a biro with a tiny plastic Ayers Rock floating around inside the clear stem, a small lump of sparkling gold-coloured mineral, a tiny bottle of the jasmine oil he'd used on her pillow, a miniature Hohner mouth-organ engraved 'Little Lady', and a skeletal fragment

111

that had once been the interior of a large shell, holding infinity within its whorls. She spread the presents out on the sheet and stared.

There was one parcel left in the foot, but she wanted to wait. She traced the spiral of the inner shell with her finger, round and round, feeling its smoothness, fascinated by its beauty. She unscrewed the lid of the lip gloss, dipped her finger in the pot, and smoothed it across her mouth, tasting perfumed sweetness. The tiny harmonica made a tinny insistent sound which made her laugh aloud. It reminded her of herself as a small girl, back home, stamping her foot in protest against some long-forgotten injury, shouting 'Don't you dare!' at the universe. So little to make such a big noise . . .

Nothing threatening in this room just now. Only the light, and the sound of birds outside. She reached into the sock again. Her stubby nails and the rough skin on one fingertip snagged on the nylon mix as she pulled out the last small package.

He had carved a cube of wood about two inches square. Five sides were engraved with stems and leaves, twisting all over like the pattern on a medieval manuscript. Into the face of the cube he had chiselled a 'B', cutting the wood away so that it stood in relief, like the four stylized leaves at each of its corners. The leaves themselves had veins inscribed, and the initial was similarly decorated with a light scratching of little flowers.

Bernie lay back on the pillow, holding it in her hand. She wanted to gather up all her presents and press them to her face, smelling them as a bouquet. Fragrance of rose, jasmine and strawberries. Glitter of fools' gold. A rock that floated in liquid, the sacred contained within silliness. Plaintive echoes of rhythm and blues in the palm of her hand. The ghost of a shell singing of the fabled inland sea men sought but never found. Lemons sweet-sour, yet fresh. And a carving that whittled away at her heart, letting shavings of sadness fall to the earth.

Why did he?

Intoxicated, she felt her face flame. The thought of opening the door and facing Eddy Carpenter terrified her. She had no language to cope with this.

*   *   *

It was noon by the time she appeared. They were sitting on the verandah, each with a mug of tea. Bernie had dressed carefully in a clean denim skirt and a scarlet sleeveless blouse, rolled up and knotted under her breasts. Droplets of water still clung to the hair she had hastily towel-dried. Her smile dazzled them both, as she intended – knowing that unless she took control she would be lost. She threw out her hands, striking a pose.

'Happy Christmas, house mates!' she said.

'And the same to you,' said John, formally.

Eddy stared, then allowed himself the slightest of nods, as if acknowledging a secret between them. Bernie guessed she should not mention the stocking in front of John, and so she felt relieved at his presence.

'When I was little it always seemed to rain on Christmas day,' Bernie said, taking her mother's old chair. 'There'd be sheets of it, and if we'd got something to play with outside, you know – bats and balls and things like that – we always went out even though we'd be soaked in a few minutes. You never minded. Ma 'ud be glad to see the back of us while she cooked. And then we'd come in, the rain running off our hoods like off seals, and there'd be that smell of wet gabardine . . . You know?'

Puzzled, Eddy shook his head. '*Gabardine?*'

'*Uk-uk-uk.*'

'Old bastard crow,' Bernie said.

'Wants something he can't get,' said Eddy.

'Don't we all,' muttered John.

'What's that then, Eddy?' Bernie challenged.

'Somebody to open the door of that cage – but he'd need to be made better too. He'd need his wing back.'

'Yeah, so he wants a miracle,' snorted Bernie.

'Don't we all?' John repeated.

'*Uk–uk–crrrrk.*'

The sound was contented. The three of them looked over at the creature of the air who shuttled to and fro on his perch, occasionally swivelling his head to stare at them coldly.

'Or maybe . . .' Eddy began.

'What?'

'Maybe there's another thing. Somebody – I mean, something – could open that door and get in there with him. So he wouldn't be on his own.'

113

Bernie looked at him in amazement, then laughed. 'Man, are you talkative today! I reckon he'd realize that was a con!'

'You reckon?'

'Can't change a bird's nature, mate. He wants to fly.'

'Like me!' said John. He required a hearing.

'Mmm, but things can get used to new ways of surviving. No choice really.'

'So you stick with the perch, and forget the wings?'

Eddy nodded. 'Maybe the perch gets to seem like the safest place. In the end.'

She shook her head. 'I always wanted to rattle the bars of me cage.'

'Yeah, but . . . doesn't it make you tired?'

She laughed as if he had made a joke. John Roper looked from one to the other as if he had heard something new, and disliked it without understanding why.

He said, 'You look . . . er . . . very nice today, Bernie.'

She laughed and touched her blouse. 'Red for Mother Christmas.'

'I got you both a present,' said Eddy.

'But you al—'

He caught her eye and she saw the infinitesimal shake of the head. Bernie looked down.She took pleasure in the tanned legs stretched out before her, knowing his gaze followed hers, and that she had been right about his wishes.

'OK – and I got you presents too,' she said brusquely. 'Let's go.'

Beneath Eddy's silver twig tree was a small array of parcels. Even Bernie had taken the trouble to use Christmas paper, although she'd argued to herself that it was against her principles. My word, she thought, even Ma would approve of me. I'm slipping . . .

They were shy like children who don't know each other very well, wondering who will start to play. Bernie experienced an instant of panic, wondering whether her presents were paltry. *This is weird*, said the voice in her head – three beached people in a room, pretending they belong together.

'Ma used to make us sit down, and then she'd bring the presents to us,' she announced. 'So, Eddy, you take the lounge and, John, you sit in that chair, and I'll do the honours.'

Eddy read the tag on the first one. It said, *Maybe this will get you going! Love, Bernie.* Expecting a joke, he unwrapped a sketchbook, four pencils, a small box of pastels and a rubber. He looked up at her. She was anxious.

'I reckon you could do your *own* stuff, Eddy.'

'Oh – I could,' he said slowly.

'What stuff?' asked John.

'Drawings,' Eddy said.

John thrust his own present forward, and Eddy unwrapped a small bottle of Old Spice aftershave lotion.

'That's great, John – anything to improve the way I smell,' he said.

'It's a *good* one . . .' John began.

'What I need,' Eddy said, with a grin.

'Nice,' Bernie said unconvincingly, staring at the red box. 'Now it's your turn, John. Here's a big 'un.'

He read aloud, 'To John – Happy Christmas and hope this makes you feel at home. Love, Bernie.' In his hands he held a beige canvas hat, with six corks suspended on strings at the front. He examined it carefully, turned it around in his hand, saying nothing.

'You can cut the corks off, they're just a joke really, that old cliché, you know? But you should shade your face, mate, you really should – and if you wear this you'll look like a real Aussie.'

'I like it,' he said, seriously.

'Open mine now, mate,' said Eddy.

Eddy had bought him a small red penknife-tool, and leaned across to show how the tiny scissors slid out, and where the toothpick fitted, and the other small implements too. Bernie fixed her eyes on the angle of his shoulders, all bone, carved as the wind shapes dunes. A lean, desert creature. The Englishman looked heavy in comparison.

'You can get huge ones, but this is all . . .' He shrugged.

'It's . . . I never had one. Thanks, Eddy,' said John, still serious, as if the effort of receiving took all his concentration.

'I'll go get us a beer,' Bernie said, because she was touched, despite herself.

'Not before you've had *your* presents,' said Eddy. 'Sit here.'

The first label said, *Bernie from John Roper*, in spidery script, sloping so far backwards it looked as if it might topple over. She ripped at paper patterned with sleighs, to reveal a

115

bath set. Talcum powder, soap and bath salts, lavender-scented, the smell she associated with her mother. She stared at it, then across the room to where the Englishman sat, looking worried.

'I hope it's what you like,' he said, hesitantly.

'My favourite!' she said loudly.

Eddy smiled. 'Make us all smell good, eh, John?'

John looked pleased, comical in the hat, leaning back in the sagging armchair, holding his penknife, watching them. The little corks bobbed before his eyes.

Bernie read the label on the other parcel, wrapped in green tissue. Eddy's handwriting was large and round, rather like her own. She read, 'Happy Christmas, landlady! Best wishes, Eddy,' and felt a second's disappointment that there was no more to the message.

Beneath the tissue was a small silver cardboard box. She removed the lid to see a necklace of liquid silver, with a single tooth of coral in the middle, flanked by two small freshwater pearls. She took it out and held it in her hand.

'I can't see it,' John complained from across the room.

She held it between finger and thumb.

'It's a necklace. It's . . .'

She could not look at him. She stared at what she held between finger and thumb, so pretty it hurt. When at last she turned to him, something like accusation swam in her eyes.

'You . . . hey, this is like a *proper* present. Not that . . .' In confusion she laid a hand on John's bath set, as if to protect it, then shook her head.

'It wasn't expensive,' he reassured her.

'When did that ever matter? It's . . . a beautiful thing.'

Without speaking, Bernie rose, crossed to the mirror over the mantelpiece and fastened the necklace. The coral went with her blouse. She saw her own reflection, as if for the first time, and realized how beauty was always a hair's breadth away, waiting to be caught and fastened in a little hoop of silver. But perhaps she had never fully recognized it before.

John Roper rose and stood behind her, and it was then she remembered the parcel that had arrived from England. Clapping a hand over her mouth, she ran to her room to get it. 'Look, John, this came. I nearly forgot! It says to save till the twenty-fifth, so I put it away in case you were tempted to open it. Must be from your gran?'

'I told her not to send anything,' he said glumly.

'She'd want to – it's Christmas!' said Bernie.

'I wrote and told her not to,' he repeated.

'Well, it's here, mate, so you'd better open it,' said Eddy.

Lily Roper had sent a wallet. It was light tan plastic with an embossed decoration of fleur de lys. John peered into the pocket, pulled out two ten-pound notes, stared at the image of Queen Elizabeth, then replaced them. At last he looked up.

'She's sent me a wallet and some money,' he said, unnecessarily.

Bernie wanted to cry. Instead she turned away and called over her shoulder that she'd bring three beers. She left Eddy holding out a hand to take the wallet. He would look and admire, make all the right sounds, because that's what he was like.

'Oh Jesus, I hate Christmas,' she muttered, opening the fridge.

But she fingered her necklace and thought of the little treasures in her room, bringing Ma's old dressing table back to life – and knew she did not. It was the anguish of the unwanted she hated. Presents that were so carefully chosen, and squatted amongst the debris of paper like unloved children – ugly, stupid, yet needing attention nevertheless.

When she returned to the lounge room, Eddy was alone. He was picking up the scattered Christmas paper from the floor. When he saw her in the doorway, he spread his arms out in a gesture of defeat.

'Poor guy's homesick,' he said simply.

'I know.'

'I don't know why he hates it here so much. I mean – if he hadn't come, he wouldn't have got his dream, would he? This country has delivered.'

'Sometimes people get dreams and find out they're not all they're cracked up to be,' she said, shaking her head.

'You reckon? Me – I never had any.'

'I don't believe that, Eddy.'

When they were sitting on the verandah, he asked if she thought he should go and knock on John's door.

'No – leave him for a bit. What did he say, anyway?'

'That he was just going to make his bed and tidy up.'

She shook her head. 'On Christmas Day? God, Eddy . . . Oh yeah, I know. He wanted to be there on his own with his Biggles books, and whatever. You know, one time, some guy came in the bar – English. He'd had a kind of vision back home that he wanted to come out to do good, teach the aboriginals – all that stuff. That was his dream, he said. Ha! He'd been here for ten years and he told me his new dream. You know what it was? To go home to bloody Birmingham. It's all he thought of. He found out it's not so easy to do good if the people don't particularly want your efforts. He was disappointed by them. By everything. So his dream just dried up. That's what's happened to John – yeah?'

Eddy nodded.

'Pyrite,' he said abruptly, after a pause.

'What?'

'That stone I gave you – the one in your room – in the sock. It's pyrite, or fools' gold. The prospectors would find it and think they'd struck it rich. Same idea. Digging in the earth and turning up this stuff that looks real, then finding it's not.'

'Eddy?'

'Yeah?'

'No easy way to say this – but thanks. For all the presents. I . . .'

'No easy way to say a lot of things, Bernie.'

'I know. Or at least, I'm finding out.'

'Is Bernie short for what I think?'

'Bernadette – of course.'

He swivelled and leaned forward in his chair so that he was facing her. The swift grin curved across his face and made her giddy.

'*Bern–a–dette,*' he said, drawing the word out with singing softness, the final letter clicking gently off his tongue. '*Bern–a–dette.* That's nice.'

'Yeah, when you say it like that,' she said nervously, 'but you can't imagine them saying it like that in the Zoo, eh?'

'I might just start calling you Bernadette,' he said.

'Bit of a mouthful.'

'I'll be able to manage.'

'That a threat or a promise?' she laughed.

The humming and rustling and scratching and twittering seemed magnified, and somewhere down the street a child cried out with excitement while adults laughed and music floated from next door's radio – soft rock she could not identify. The air was heavy with flowers and food.

118

They sat in silence as the minutes hung in the still air like prayer flags. Dreamily Bernie touched her necklace and thought of coral and pearls in azure depths, shoals of coloured fish. She imagined herself floating weightless, hair ribboning around her head. What would it be like? Here – surrounded by the endless red sea, all sand and rock and scrub, you yearned for water. Yet waves broke within her now, in the textures she touched, and Bernie remembered that she hardly knew how to swim.

'That suits you,' Eddy said, reaching out to touch the necklace he'd taken so long choosing.

John Roper stood at the kitchen window and watched the backs of their heads, envious of their stillness. The garden was pale and dusty, their heads haloed in a haze of heat. Those two – they belonged, and the need to be like them made him sweat all the more, in panic. He wanted to hate them too, and yet he did not. They were kind – the good-looking woman with the rough tongue and the young man with the wide smile and limbs like a sapling. In this stony wasteland they'd been kind to *him*.

Yet kindness can break the heart.

He turned from the window and put his head under the cold tap. Water splashed down his neck and brought relief.

The three of them peeled potatoes, prepared sprouts and carrots as the afternoon temperature rose with the level of empty beer cans in the bin. Eddy watched as Bernie shook packet stuffing into a bowl and added hot water, too quickly, so some of the mixture spilt. She cracked in an egg, laughing that it was her effort at haute cuisine.

In turn she watched as his long fingers pushed the gooey mix into the cavity of the small turkey, and laid lemon slices and rashers of bacon in rows across the breast. Everything he did was precise, as if even the action of wiping the surface she had dirtied in her carelessness mattered.

She had asked John Roper to lay the table on the verandah, telling him where to find the plates which dated from Colleen Molloy's reign in the bungalow on Dean Street. 'We might as well use Ma's best stuff, eh? Make it special.'

John knelt by the sideboard in the lounge room and inhaled his own home. Nan's sideboard of wartime veneer. The things kept for best that were never used because no 'best' ever appeared on the horizon. What was that smell? Old polish on tired wood. Old crumbs caught in crevices. Dust in corners, and the dried remains of woodlice. The residual stickiness of the bottle of sweet sherry that had finally been thrown away, half drunk, but left its circular trace in a corner. He remembered her opening one of the drawers with the brass handles like hanging tassels, to show him ration books spotted with grease. They lay among skeins of looped string and brown paper bags kept for their promise of usefulness. He remembered the frugality, the making-do and mending that wrenched his heart, carried as it was across the world within a plastic wallet and two ten-pound notes.

The Molloy sideboard had the same smell. He knelt and picked up china plates patterned with pink roses. A curly gravy boat and a vegetable dish with a china rose as handle on the gilded lid. None of this stuff spoke to him of Bernie; it belonged to her mother's world, and Lily Roper's. Yet it was his too. He yearned to become small enough to climb inside the sideboard and be transported back to where he came from, and where (maybe) he might find that mother too, the vision with the padded shoulders and roll of hair, who might surely have laid a hand on her mother Lily's sideboard and left a mark for him to find.

'You OK, John? You got the stuff?' came a call from the kitchen.

'Just sorting it out!' he shouted back.

Carefully, he took out three china plates, side plates, the gravy boat and two vegetable dishes and carried them through to the kitchen.

'Just look at Ma's stuff! Not exactly my taste, but . . .'

'It's just fine,' said Eddy.

He returned to explore the three drawers. The linen was folded in little piles. There were napkins, and embroidered tray cloths, and little crocheted circlets weighed with beads to put over jugs to keep the flies off. Nan had those too. He lifted the corners of tablecloths, and chose one patterned with pink-tipped daisies around the edge.

'Ma embroidered the flowers,' said a soft voice behind him.

'My grandmother did that kind of thing too, before her fingers got so bad.'

'Poor Ma, she brought most of this stuff with her and never used it out here. Nobody bothered. You wouldn't, would you – living in a tin shack with those O'Donnells and the dunny stinking to high heaven?'

'I . . . Nan always says you have to keep up appearances,' said John.

'Same as Ma,' said Bernie.

She surprised them by changing into a short black sundress for dinner. Admiration settled on her bare shoulders, as she brought a jug of white wine decanted from the cask, and glasses on a tray. This is how you could live your life, she thought. Properly.

The three of them drank on the dusky verandah, next to the rickety table now covered in white and set with bone cutlery and pink, gold and white china. Naturally Eddy had thought to buy a box of six crackers, and laid two at each place. Moths jitterbugged around the candles, occasionally zipping to oblivion. Crickets rasped a hidden chorus. Savoury smells drifted from the kitchen as Bernie told them tales of her teenage years in the town, making them laugh.

'You were quite a wild one,' said Eddy admiringly.

'Had my moments,' she grinned, blowing smoke high.

'I sometimes wish I'd come out here sooner,' said John. 'Then you'd get used to it, wouldn't you? Like you did?'

'I'm not sure I ever did,' she said. 'What's getting used to a place mean?'

'Depends who you're with,' Eddy replied.

When at last they all piled into the kitchen to dish up the meal, Bernie felt more satisfied than she thought possible. It would be hard for the men to understand – that this time her gravy was as good as Ma's. No – better, and the potatoes cooked perfectly. She could do things like this! As Eddy hacked inexpertly at the bird, she dotted butter on the vegetables just as her mother used to do – even when there was hardly money for clothes.

Eddy and John instructed her to sit down while they carried everything outside. Eddy brought the carved meat and piles of stuffing and chipolatas on a platter and John took the vegetables in two dishes. They spooned cranberry sauce straight from the jar, but that did not lessen the odd, precious formality of this occasion.

Bernie looked down at her plate and saw tawny potatoes, wine-dark gravy, moist taupe meat, clusters of nut-brown stuffing, sauces ruby and white, crisp toasty sausages, carrots like a pile of copper coins and the viridian spheres of brussels sprouts. How come she had never appreciated such things before? She gaped at the sensual beauty of the world, encapsulated in the subtle hues arrayed on china before her eyes.

'It'll go cold,' Eddy warned, motioning to her to eat.

The textures! The moment of ecstasy when teeth break through a salty roasted crust into the steaming white fluffiness of what Da always called praties. Or the perfect smoothness of sweet carrots saved from blandness by the grit of pepper. Sausage and stuffing disintegrated in her mouth in a landslide of little nubbly nodes. Gravy and juices rolled, viscous and pungent, on her tongue.

'Never tasted so good,' she mumbled.

Their conversation, such as it was, was mundane during that meal. Speech was less important than the tiny, involuntary sounds of contentment as the plates emptied. The lack of words did not reduce them. They shared what Bernie came to think of – much later – as a sacrament more precious than those of her youth, with Father Mullen frowning down at her as she took the wafer and tried not to gag.

'Let's pull a cracker,' said John, eagerly.

At last, still wearing the paper hats, they rose to clear the plates, then John carried out the small pudding, flaming with brandy. Bernie watched him. His face, habitually haunted, red and almost sullen in repose, was briefly transformed by the flickering blue light into a mask of wonder, beneath a yellow paper hat. She thought of his dead parents, and his old grandmother waiting at home, the lonely passion for flying that had brought him across the world, and her heart contracted. You could even get to love somebody with so many needs, she thought.

Eddy met her eyes and understood their brightness.

'Nan always said we had to make a wish,' John said, as the flames died away.

'I already did,' Eddy said.

'Me too,' whispered Bernie, gazing into the dark bushes.

'Make yours then, mate!' said Eddy.

John Roper still stood, awkward now the light had gone, a

clumsy man with a plate bearing a small, unprepossessing, sticky brown mound none of them truly wanted to eat. He appeared deep in thought, as if concentration might summon up a simple wish from his depths.

'Wouldn't work anyway,' he said quietly.

'C'mon, man!' Bernie chimed. 'You have to believe in stuff! You have to go out there saying anything's possible! Look at you – if you hadn't believed you could be a pilot, you wouldn't have got yourself out here and learned to fly, would you?'

'I don't think I did it for *me*,' he said slowly. 'For my dad. As if he was telling me what to do. I used to think . . . I could hear him. I know it sounds daft . . .'

'No, we've all got our ghosts,' Bernie said.

'Too right,' said Eddy.

Bernie turned her gaze on him. 'You too?'

He nodded, meeting her eyes.

'Well, that's something you've given away for a change, Eddy Carpenter! One a these days, maybe you'll tell me and John the story of your life – so far.'

'Maybe,' he said calmly, 'but then again, maybe not.'

They picked at the pudding then pushed their plates away, sloshing down wine cold from the cask in the fridge. Bernie felt her senses were dangling on strings.

She was aware of Eddy's shape to her left, but would not allow herself to look. It was impossible to tell if the light astringent smell came from him, or from a plant she could not name, out there in the gloom. The candle guttered.

John Roper stirred. 'I feel like watching some TV,' he said. 'Nan and I always watched TV on Christmas night. She'd watch anything, really.'

'Same with Ma,' Bernie said, too loud.

Eddy stirred, folding his legs under the chair.

Don't go in, don't go in, she thought.

The sound of the television drifted out to them, canned laughter echoing the sound in Bernie's head. She waited for Eddy to speak but the air between them was so clotted with warmth, sounds and smells, that words could not struggle to the surface and be heard.

Eddy sighed. Bernie turned her head and nodded at him, acknowledging his contentment, then immediately turning her face back to the garden. After another long silence, during which a star fell through the sky, and the crow scratched his perch in sleep, he threw back his head and sighed again. 'We–ell . . . Bernadette.'

It was a statement, not a question.

She could not breathe. When her voice came out at last, despite herself, the words squeaked foolishly. 'Well what?'

'We did good,' he said.

'The food was good,' she replied.

'Everything.'

'Yes.'

'And now . . .'

'I wanted John to go in,' she blurted, in a whisper, 'so . . .'

'Shhhh.'

'You bought me all those things. Lovely things. I don't understand why – how you know . . . I wish you'd bloody well say something!'

'I'm not much of a one for talking, Bernadette. You could say I'm just manual,' he said, self-mocking but nervous too. She heard it, and plunged.

'Well, that sounds just *fine* to me.'

Eddy turned to her, looked as if he was about to speak, then rose quickly.

'Maybe we should start taking this stuff in,' he said.

She heard her mistake echoing back – the pushiness, the innuendo – and cringed. Oh Jesus, why do I always have to open my mouth? Why always have to spoil things?'

Bernie stacked the dried best plates, aware as she did so that all her instincts would have been to leave the pile festering in grease and rancid cream until morning, while she got drunk. But Eddy Carpenter was calling the shots, whether she liked it or not, and so she did the proper thing. Once he looked at her, handing a dish there was no room for on the crowded drainer, and said, 'Thanks, Bernadette,' so quietly she might have imagined it. She felt grateful.

Taking the clean plates through on a tray, she called, 'Hey, John – it's Christmas! Turn that thing off and have a nightcap!' Eddy followed her with a bottle of scotch and three glasses.

Then Bernie took a quick shot and danced around the room as Mick Jagger snarled. She whipped her own cheeks with her hair, and flexed her stomach muscles, pumping in time to the mean bass, rolling her shoulders, gyrating around that square room where Colleen Molloy had sat with her knitting, and later Suze had tripped out, screaming and crying that they were coming in through the window to get her – so Bernie had to hold her down and croon *Shhh shushdi, darlin', shhh shushdi* – like a mother.

Ash dropped from her cigarette as she danced.

At last Eddy rose, murmuring that he was tired. Bernie laughed, shouted that he was lame and clicked her fingers, so he would not guess how her gut sank in disappointment. Not long afterwards John downed the dregs of his scotch and rose unsteadily. Christmas was over.

'Let me tell you something,' he slurred, holding her arm.

'Happy Christmas, babe!' she trilled.

'No – no – I mean it seriously. This . . . today . . . has been . . . this is . . .'

'Leave it, John!'

'But I want to tell you . . .'

Bernie pressed her lips briefly to his cheek, feeling the burning skin. 'Look, mate, we had a great day. Now you bloody well wear that hat to keep the sun off your face, OK?'

She danced on in the empty room, but felt flat without the audience. After ten minutes more, she gave up, leaving the dirty glasses where they were, knowing that Eddy would rise early and clear them. He could be trusted, that guy. It was a fact you could grow to depend on, and that was dangerous.

No guy scares me, thought Bernie, as she undressed. Elated, not tired, she climbed into bed and stroked her own body, naked but for the necklace Eddy had given her. She could not take it off. She wanted him to come and knock on her door, even if it were just to talk. She fantasized about the night she had been drunk and disgusting and he had undressed her . . . what if she had not been drunk? Yet if she had not been in such a state, he wouldn't have put her to bed.

Bernie was slipping into sleep, the scotch doing its work at last, when she heard her door click open. She held her breath and listened to the tiny adhesive sound of bare feet on lino and the suggestion of a snuffle. Filled with wild joy and trepidation mixed, she knew it was time. He had come to her. She tensed to raise herself on one elbow and was on the point of calling his name when the person in the room sighed heavily. She released her own breath. This wasn't right. It was the wrong sound.

'Hey?' she whispered.

'It's me,' said John Roper.

Bernie snapped her bedside light on and sat up, heaving the sheet up around her neck. He stood about a metre from the bed, a stocky pale figure in white underpants, one hand held out as if in supplication.

'Now – listen, John,' she began.

'Please,' he said.

'I reckon you've got the wrong . . .'

He moved forward to stand right next to her, and she inhaled his sharp, animal fear. She contemplated the line of demarcation where the sun had roasted his neck, arms and face.

'Bernie, please . . .' he repeated.

'Sit down,' she said sternly, patting the bed.

He obeyed, paused for a second, then lurched towards her in a clumsy attempt at a kiss. Bernie's instinct was to push him, but she knew she would hurt him enough, without that. She held him at bay.

'You and me need to do some talking.'

'All I want . . . please . . . let me stay here with you.'

'You off your rocker?'

'You were dancing, and the way you were looking at me before. I thought . . . You do like me, don't you? You looked at me, so . . . And you must know I love you, Bernie. Ever since I moved here.'

She shook her head. 'No, you don't, John. That's a bloody fantasy. I'm just a tough old barmaid pushing forty and one day you'll meet yourself a nice young girl who'll think you're the bee's knees. You're a nice-looking bloke, especially if you lose the 'tache and get a tan. But hey . . . if it's just sex you want . . . well, I've been known to show the kindness of my heart . . .?' She cocked her head, quizzical and mocking, knowing how he would respond.

He shook his head. There were tears in his eyes. 'Don't talk like that. Why do you make yourself sound so . . .?'

'But that's what I thought you were askin' for! Why'd you walk in here like that?'

He hung his head and started to tremble.

'I . . . I . . . just want you to . . . Please.'

'Go back to your own bed, John, and sleep it off – go on now, go on,' she crooned, giving him a little shove. 'And we'll forget this ever happened. Go on, mate!'

She watched him stumble to the door then turn with a last pleading look. Bernie knew he was asking all the women he'd ever known to see him and like what they saw. For a reckless moment she thought – I could have let him come in my bed, and held him. Held the poor bastard for about half an hour, then chucked him out, what harm would it have done? What harm would it do to call him back now, to show mercy – like she did to Springing Dick all those years ago? But she couldn't. Not with Eddy breathing so near. Maybe he wasn't asleep. Maybe he could hear . . .

Bloody Eddy, she thought, bloody John, bloody Christmas.

She looked at John, hesitating at her door, and shook her head firmly, just as a mother warns a small boy he mustn't do it ever again.

Sixteen

Eddy squatted by the verandah, balancing on one outstretched leg. He narrowed his eyes, and looked around. The path was stippled grey and lilac. It was so early, the moon's ghost still hung in the sky, but golden light gathered at the edges like a shower of coins ready to drop into the lap of the world. The air smelt of earth and flowers. He inhaled it purposefully in long, slow breaths, until he was lightheaded with the peace, the emptiness of the hour.

The subject is here, he thought, but how did you know how to begin?

He peered from right to left, unsure of what he was looking for but knowing he would recognize it, before committing it to the paper she had bought. Eddy Carpenter balanced the sketch book on his knee, and smiled to think of her choosing it well. He loved the mystery that a woman hard enough to handle the drunks in the Zoo still knew about soft pencils.

Where to start?

He felt afraid, as if the act of making the smallest mark on the blank sheet would give things away. Perhaps she would come and look over his shoulder and be disappointed. He wanted to please her, and, more strong than his fear of the challenging emptiness of paper was an uneasiness at what that need implied. He did not understand how it could happen so quickly – that the air around you could shiver with waiting, and only become still when that person entered the space. Eddy didn't like it.

He put the pad on the ground, where he had already laid the pencils, rubber and pastels, and rose, stretching his arms above his head. He felt weightless, and yet rooted there in Bernie Molloy's garden, bending his body backwards like a gum in a dry breeze off the desert.

He couldn't see anything to draw near the house, so wandered down the path which curved away into shadows, which were lightening by the minute.When he reached the high fence at the rear perimeter, he sat down, looking back at the bungalow through a veil of leaves and grass. Soon ants were moving in formation over his bare feet, picking up minute particles of his skin along with the dust, and carrying him away to become a part of their lives whether he liked it or not.

But he did like it, and as the persistent sun hit his foot and gilded even the dirty ridges of his toenails, Eddy smiled. He looked down and watched the ants navigating the blue rivers of his veins and felt that loosening deep within him – the involuntary blessing he had first experienced in Arnhemland when he was twenty, and one evening in the wet season showed him, simultaneously, the sun setting behind him, the moon rising in front, and distant lightening storms on both sides. Surrounded thus by miracles, he had started to come to terms with what he had discovered, which had driven him from the place he'd called home.

Come to terms – but not forgive.

Would Bernie Molloy understand that?

Over and over again in his mind Eddy Carpenter told her the story of his life, as he had told nobody up until now. He knew the moment was approaching, and the revelation could not be avoided. She would bend to him, with no sharp or crude words as barriers between them. Against his will, he thought of her arms enfolding him, like never before. Yes, Bernie, he thought, I will talk, I will.

He turned his head to contemplate the mulga on his right. This garden of hers was unkempt, but he liked it. In time he could make it better, as he had already started to improve the house. But, holding the drawing block, he reminded himself that it's always a mistake to wait for beauty, for inspiration. You have to reach for the nearest thing and make the best of it, knowing you may not get another shot. And if it happens to be common or dirty, if it turns out you never move beyond its straggly edges, no matter. You will turn to it again and again, and observe the unlikely radiance at its core.

Eddy shifted along a couple of feet, so that a scraggy, dipping branch was almost in front of his nose. Then he took the sharp B, narrowed his eyes and began to delineate the twig in short precise strokes, building the outline of something he knew well but was looking at afresh. The tiny grey-green leaves pointed upwards like needles, designed to make the most of whatever rain might fall, channelling it from leaf to branch, from trunk to root zone, to penetrate deeply and ensure survival even when drought crisped the land. Painstakingly he dotted shade, remembering those bright acrylic dot-daubs and her drunken mockery.

Then, as if on cue, she was moving along the path towards him. He fought to control panic at this invasion of his privacy and remain still, though his instinct was to snap the sketchbook shut. The sunlight lit her tawny hair, but as she drew nearer he saw with a kind of melancholy that she was frowsty in the morning light, dark shadows of hangover and mascara beneath her eyes. Yet it was impossible for her not to look beautiful, he thought: the wild creature, the broken thing in a cage.

Bernie stopped about four paces away, and folded her arms. Her feet were bare; she wore an oversized Beach Boys T-shirt with the neck slashed wider with scissors and the sleeves torn off. For a second he found himself speculating whether she was wearing anything beneath it, but shoved the thought away. He looked at her legs, then let his gaze move up to where her forearms flattened against each other and the light caught the down of golden hair on her skin. She wore the necklace he had given her, and the sight made something call within him like the galah that flashed over her head, followed by four more, shrieking in the brilliant air.

'Up early?' he said at last.

'You too.'

'How're you feeling?'

'Same as usual . . .' She grinned in rueful recognition.

'You need sweet tea.'

'Need a new head, Eddy.'

He said, 'I like the one you've got,' – to be rewarded by a slight headshake of disbelief, the faintest of flushes. Her arms dropped to her sides.

'You're using the stuff I gave you. That's nice.'

'Didn't know what to do at first. What to try. Your mind goes blank, like the page.'

'Have to try what you can, I reckon.'

'That's what I decided.'

'Did you like art and stuff like that – at school?'

'Yeah. That and biology were my best subjects. Not that I was brilliant or anything . . .'

'Can I take a look?'

'I'd rather you didn't. It's . . .'

'No good?'

He nodded, and looked down at the pad. A fly walked over his light version of the mulga twig, making a tiny travelling shadow on the page.

'So what? What's *good* mean, anyway? Some of this modern art you see . . . pile of shite. You'd be better than that. At least you're *doing* it, least you're having a go . . .'

'Yeah. Thanks to you.'

She attempted to shrug, but it was too late to stem the small laugh of pleasure that escaped her lips. She took a stride, paused as if unsure, then carefully sat down about three feet away from him, pulling the T-shirt down. Back against the fence, she looked sideways and grinned.

'No more bloody sad fake dots?'

'Needed the money . . . but . . .' He grinned. 'The boomerangs were the worst!'

They both laughed.

He looked down and watched the fly's progress. She was

still staring at him, and now it was his turn to feel embarrassed. At last he turned his head too, facing her across a small
void of dust, dirt and leaves.

'Yesterday worked?' she said at last, sounding less than
convincing to herself because of the way the night had ended.
But Eddy did not know that.

'Yeah – good we made the effort.'

'Cold turkey today,' she said, 'and the way I'm feeling . . .'

He put the sketchbook on the ground beside him and drew
up his knees, letting his hands dangle loosely between them.

'Don't want to interrupt,' she said.

'No worries. I reckon I'd done all I was going to. Maybe
I'll get back to it later.'

'Try the chalks?'

'Yeah, maybe tonight – for shadows.'

Bernie sighed, resting her head back to stare at the sky. 'I
like shadows too. I've got this thing in my mind . . . where
I grew up, and everything was all grey and green, all soft at
the edges, blue too, under trees, fuschia hedges . . . Mother
of God – was it beautiful! We left when I was nearly twelve,
but I can see it like I was there yesterday.'

'See what?'

'Like I said, all the shadows. And light breaking through
the clouds, pearly like you could touch it. Like you could
reach out, and find the clouds fallen down on the ground, with
this . . . ribbon of light above them . . . Then it'd clear like
a mirror, like the sea. And rain over the hills – like you see
fields of wheat moving in the wind, you know? A kind of
ripple – but of rain. We'd a cottage just outside the town,
pretty broken-down really cos Da was always too busy fixing
up other people's, and the path was always all puddles cos of
the holes, and Patrick and me, we'd try to wrestle each other
into them, til Ma came out yelling at us cos of the mud . . .
Oh, ye'd have the stuff up to your armpits, and all the mist
caught in your hair like little jewels . . .'

Eddy listened to her soft sing-song, barely daring to breathe
in case he should break the spell and return her to the metallic
clang of the present. The crow called to them, ugly and discordant, but she did not appear to hear. He studied her profile –
the straight nose, the tumble of unbrushed hair, the lips slightly
apart with a bead of moisture on the lower fullness, as if she

131

had just tasted something delicious and did not want to let the flavour go.

'You never talk about yourself,' she said at last, still surveying the sky.

'More interesting to hear about you,' he said.

'One way's no conversation,' Bernie smiled, swivelling to face him again. She adopted the exaggerated diction of the nursery teacher and explained, 'I told *you* stuff, and now you have to tell *me* stuff. That's the way it *works*, bo–oy. That's the way we play the *game*.'

Eddy was silent. He looked down at his own hands and realized how ill-equipped they were to reach out and grasp any opportunity. They were rough; they could fix and mend and make, but for anything else . . .? Hopeless.

'Go on, Eddy, push the boat out! Tell me the story of your life!'

'I . . . can't.' Something caught in his throat. 'No.'

Bernie heard, and was overcome by the desire to hold him until he felt he could tell, until he no longer felt ashamed of the tedium of his young life. For it must be so, she thought, it must be so ordinary he did not want to bore her. That, or else he'd been a real villain, but that simply wasn't believable.

'Where're your folks, Eddy?'

'Adelaide.' His tone was almost sullen.

'Yeah, and . . .? So when did you leave? How come you fetched up here?'

'A long journey, Bernie.'

She sensed it would be fatal for her to fill the silence with her usual banter, the rough noises she created all her waking hours to drown out the secret sounds of her heart. Eddy might tell her things he'd told nobody else, and if he did, she would have to reciprocate. She leaned back on the fence for stability.

'It's going to happen,' said a voice aloud, and it was hers, but with a new sound.

He murmured, 'It isn't easy.'

'Talking?'

'Yeah, giving it away. I'm not used to it. Never have been. Reckon I stopped talking when I was seventeen . . .'

'What happened then? To make you?'

'I . . . uh . . . ran away from home.'

132

'Me too! Only I waited till I was nearly nineteen. You were braver than me, mate! Gets you, though, don't it – the guilt?'

There you go again . . . Bernie cursed herself for the chiming incontinence of her own voice and dug her nails hard into the back of her hand. She had to make herself keep quiet. She must be patient, absolutely still, or he would escape her.

'I wasn't guilty,' he said flatly.

'No?'

'No, it was him. My dad. So-called father . . .' He hauled breath in, as if it might be his last. 'Y'see . . . I found something out. I found out my whole life had been a sort of lie. Funnily enough, I was thinking of it – just before, when I was drawing, just before you came. I was remembering. I don't know why it came into my head.'

'Maybe you was practising for telling me, Eddy.'

She watched as he dropped his head, cradling it. His long tanned fingers played in the sandy springs of hair, pulling and letting go, then pulling harder, as if he wanted to give himself pain. He was all angles – the joints of ankles, elbows and wrists so spiky, you could catch yourself on them, she thought, and do yourself an injury if you got too close. Ah, but there you go again, she caught herself . . . why would you be afraid of getting hurt, Bernie Molloy? Nothing can hurt *you* any more, it's all been done. But this one, this boy – he'd snap if he fell over. You have to stop him falling and breaking himself, Bernie. Or else, you have to catch him when he does.

'What did you remember?' she prompted, in a whisper.

He shook the head that still rested in his hands. 'All of it. Not that I ever forgot, but when I was moving around, just drifting on from place to place, I could stop thinking of it – doing other things, learning things. Once I left home – no left *them* – I . . . I . . . didn't know who I was any more, because of the lie, and so I had to start finding it out.'

'And did you?'

'In the end. A bit.'

She allowed the sounds of the garden to prevail, then felt afraid that the silence would stretch such a distance between them they would lose sight of each other. 'What was it you found out, Ed?' she prompted.

'The real story,' he said, looking across at her. 'My story – such as it was.'

133

'Tell me, go on.'

He'd never heard that voice so cajoling, so sweet, as if the woman who inhabited the bungalow had gone, leaving this new person next to him – a creature of rain and mist and infinite gentleness. He felt his eyes fill.

'Where'd you start? I overheard something one night . . . I was just a schoolboy but I guessed something was wrong.'

He described a time when suspicion accumulated so slowly – oozing into the spaces of his life, coagulating in its corners, dropping its debris into the channels, until at last nothing could move. Hints and whispers, missing links in time and place, papers in locked drawers, dates that didn't add up, a murmur of talk in the distance suddenly silenced . . . and one day the truth was there, and everything was over.

That's how it was, Eddy told her, speaking in a voice as creaky as a hinge unoiled for years. He could not remember when it began, but at seventeen his questions became more real. It was the mirror that began it. The image that confronted him each day, as he examined his spots and fingered the fuzz on his chin – that visage belonged to a stranger and it did not fit within the long white bungalow owned by Vernon and Pam Carpenter. It was the face of an outsider.

Each morning his father went to the school, to keep order among staff and pupils alike – the respected head teacher, the pillar of society, the man of committees and fundraising events. At the same time his mother left for the mall to sell tourists books about the outback, the stars, the wildlife, the plants, and guide her husband's pupils to the shelves where they would find help with their homework. At night they would all return, and the smell of lamb and potatoes would fill the house, or seafood and salad would be piled on platters she carried out to the verandah. It was a good life . . . there was no denying it. Later the parents would sit on the green velvet lounge and watch TV movies, while Eddy moped over homework in his bedroom, surrounded by the objects that told him who he was. But still sensing more and more that he did not belong with them.

No – he did not know why, he said, in response to Bernie's whispered question. It was just that he sat at the table, eating steak, between the tall fair man, and the woman with dark brown hair caught up in an untidy nest on the top of her head, and felt their language, their small talk, was not his own.

'How can you explain – when you know you don't fit?' he asked.

'Oh, I know about that,' she said.

The revelation, when it came, was swift. It would be satisfying to be able to boast of clever detective work, he told her – a painstaking unravelling of the mystery within his own face. But all he did was ask the wrong questions, and noticed how his father became unsettled. Then he started to listen at doors, until one night he heard Vern murmur, 'We've got to tell him one day.'

'For God's sake – why, Vern?'

'Because he'll find out soon enough, and then . . .'

'How can he find out? Oh don't, Vern, please – for me, please don't spoil everything! What good will it do?'

And Eddy creeps away from the door and wonders. Next time they're both out, he starts to search his father's desk, not knowing what he is looking for, but hoping for some letter, some clue. He doesn't know Vernon has forgotten his wallet. Eddy looks up from his fruitless rummaging to see his father in the doorway, looking angry and afraid.

'What d'you think you're doing, Eddy?

'Nothing.'

'Better tell me!'

'I heard you and Mum talking. I heard you say I'd have to find something out sooner or later. What, Dad? What're you hiding from me? I need to know!'

Vernon shakes his head, then sits down heavily in the leatherette desk chair, making it rock violently from side to side.

'Christ, son, I . . .'

'You can't *not* tell me now. There's something wrong – and whatever it is, I'll find out . . .'

His face scarlet and shiny, Vern Carpenter slumps. Then at last he looks up with watery grey eyes, and croaks, 'It's not like it seems.'

'*What?* Are you trying to tell me I'm . . . I'm . . . adopted or something?

'Sort of. That's about the sum of it.'

'So you're not – my *parents*?'

'I didn't say that, did I? Oh Christ, if you knew how complicated it is, you wouldn't . . . You'd see . . .'

'Try me, Dad. Try me!'

Reluctantly Vernon Carpenter tells his son the story of his life, and of lives before him, the little that he knows for sure, which is enough. And the roof peels off the world, like skin off a face in a horror movie, revealing the ugly, the alien – as Eddy hears the story of his real mother.

Halfway through the stumbling account, Pam Carpenter comes in, hand to her mouth. Held within each other's gaze, neither of them speaks to her. All the pale woman can do is slump in a chair, in the autumn chill of the room. At one point her husband, Eddy's father, reaches out and takes her hand in silence. Neither of them can know that this is the beginning of the end for their son, although Vernon had guessed nothing would be the same again. The seventeen-year-old stares wildly at them, shock yellowing his face. Then the shouting begins.

Eddy stopped talking, and Bernie waited. For a long time she watched his fingers pulling sharply at the spirals of his hair, then whispered, 'Go on, Eddy. I'm not with you – yet. What was it he told you?'

He raised his head, threw it back sharply against the fence with a dull clunk, then turned to face her again. 'I was adopted all right but Vern *was* my real father. I was born in 1958, Bernie, and he was my dad all right, but my mother – my real mother – was called May. He said all the usual stuff, he said he thought he wanted to marry her, but he didn't really. None of them do. They just use them – you know?'

She nodded.

'Talking to him was like getting blood out of a stone. But I got it out in the end. Maybe it was cos he was a teacher, he always wanted the facts, so he could tell me more than you'd expect . . .'

'Tell what?' she breathed.

'I'm . . . *black*, Bernie.'

'What you talking about?'

'I *am*. A part of me, anyway. OK, not *his* part, but enough. You ever heard the word "octoroon"?'

She shook her head. A hyena laugh, brief and shocking, escaped him, and the crow cawed harshly in response at the other end of the garden. 'Well, that's what I am. Good there's a word for it, eh? It was the term they used to describe people

136

like me, in something called the Bleakley Report – you won't know what that is either? It was . . . oh, never mind that for now. It means one eighth aboriginal blood. Just one eighth. Not very much really!'

Again that terrible bark of a laugh rang out, and she remained silent. 'I'll give you the whole thing quickly, although there's gaps, and I did try a couple of years ago to fill them in . . . when I was travelling about. I even went to the mission, tried to find records. Research, yeah? Ah, what the hell, Bernie, what's it matter? My mother May, she was only eighteen and she wanted to be a nurse when she fell for him, and he told me he did love her. That's what he says. He was twenty-four. But he was already going out with Pam then – the two-timing bastard – and when May had me in '58, he had no intention of marrying her. No way! Not when he had his nice white woman lined up! May was living in a hostel, he said, and started to use drugs. No wonder, eh? He wouldn't say much about all this, so I'm hazy on the timing. About one year after I was born he married Pam, but she told him she couldn't ever have children. Something wrong with her tubes, or something.'

Bernie felt sweat break and drop from armpit to hip, striking it cold.

'So, because May was all strung out, he took the thing to court and said she was inadequate and I should be taken away from her, and given to them. So I was. Just like that. It was so fucking easy for him to get what he wanted – what chance did she have, half-caste loser against the brave white professional guy? The point is, it was just repeating the whole saga . . . the whole bloody thing.'

'What saga?'

'Seems May was actually a quarter-blood. Her grandmother – that's my great-grandmother was Walbiri people. She had a daughter by some white man – stockman or something I reckon – and then, in the late twenties, after this Bleakley Report, that baby was taken away from her, and raised in an orphanage. That's what they did, you know? They actually stole the babies . . .'

'I knew that,' Bernie whispered.

'According to Vern, May told him that *her* mother, my grandmother – the one they put in the orphanage – was raped herself at the age of fifteen – by some white man who came

137

to the place to do a job – something like that – and she had a baby. That was May, see, my mother, and she was brought up on a mission. So then she met my father – yet another fucking white man, doing the same things – and had me.'

'What happened to her, to May?'

'God knows – because sure as hell *he* didn't know. They got custody of me, and she disappeared. Just like that. In the night. Never seen or heard of again. He reckoned she must've died, because of the stuff she was pumping into herself. I reckon she died of a broken heart, as much as anything, and all the junk was just the icing on the cake. 'Cause she'd lost him and then she lost me, and it was all just a repeat, she knew, of everything that had happened before. Her grandmother, her mother and now her. She must have felt so worthless, Bernie!'

The words choked in his throat and he dropped his head into his hands once more, the bony fingers pulling his hair to inflict real pain. She watched, understanding his strangeness at last – that sandy ochre desert of skin, the scribbles of his hair, the whiplash leanness of him, and the pale, drifting emptiness of his icy eyes. Ah, but he is beautiful, she thought suddenly, more beautiful than anyone.

'Yeah, she must,' she said at last, 'the poor woman.'

'She must've felt there's nothing can be done to break the chain. Well – I had to break it, Bernie! I left them there in their *nice* big bungalow with all their lies! I got the hell out, in the night, just like she did. Seven years and I've never been back.'

'Where did you go?'

'Headed round the coast. I can't remember what I was thinking at the time, I was all messed up. I had this fantasy that I'd find her, I'd see some bundle of bones one day and it would be her. She'd recognize me. I'd be able to help her at last . . . as if!'

He was panting, and paused to calm himself. 'I've done such a lot of stuff, Bernie – slept rough, worked rough too, always running away from the white bit of me, until I realized it was bigger than the other bit, and I couldn't hide that. But I couldn't fit in anywhere – except out there . . . in the land. I could spend days telling you what I did. Anyway, up in Arnhemland I met this bloke, an old Wangurri guy, and he showed me how to work with wood. I'd been sick but this

Tommo, he took me under his wing, taught me the skills, everything I know, taught me yidaki too . . . He was brilliant. Like a father to me. But I never stayed long with people I liked, and he understood that. I had to shoot through. I always move on, Bernie.'

'Still?'

'You can see why, can't you?'

'I can, Eddy. But sometimes, to be sure, you have to break patterns.'

He wasn't listening. 'Some bundle of bones,' he said in a faraway voice, 'and it's her, my mother May, and I put out my hand and she takes it and gets up and leans on me. She's thinking she can trust somebody at last. And it's me. And we . . . know each other. We've found each other at last – no worries.' He bent his head, and she heard the rivers in his voice. 'But it never happened. If it had, I wouldn't have moved on. You have to give up dreaming about something in the end, don't you?'

Bernie reached out to rest her hand on his forearm. Curled forward, head in hands, Eddy made no response, so she eased herself across the small patch of dirt until she was next to him, then awkwardly snaked an arm around his thin shoulders and pulled him to her, meeting no resistance. As she smelt the vegetal scent of his hair and skin, Bernie felt his shaking grow still.

'Shh–sssssh, it's all right, lovey, it's all right,' she crooned, marvelling at the stirring within her womb, at her own nursery sound, and the nestling weight of his head on her shoulder.

She closed her eyes. Bernie felt suspended in a silence punctuated only by their twin heartbeats, then her own lilting voice: 'Once, I didn't believe anything could ever be better again, Ed. I didn't – *believe me*. But that was then. Now it's different . . . partly because you came to live here, you know that? You mended things, and now I'm going to mend things as well, if you let me.' Her voice soothed them both. 'It'll be as good as anything can be, you see. I'll help you, I promise, Eddy.'

Still he did not move or speak. Gradually the sounds of the garden returned, the crow's insistent hungry cawing an unavoidable reminder of need, and duty. Pins and needles daggered along her legs and arms as Eddy shifted away, pulling himself upright with a slight shake, like someone waking from a long sleep. Both of them eased away from the awkward stickiness of their flesh.

Bernie sighed because she did not want it to be over. At first the glare was almost unbearable and red spots sailed across her vision. When they faded she found herself staring back at the house, where a figure stood on the edge of the verandah, peering into the garden as if unsure of what he saw. John Roper wore the hat she had given him, and the silly corks were dancing before his shadowed face.

Seventeen

December 25th
Dear John,

Happy Christmas to you, love!

I hope this finds you well – I havnt been feeling too good myself just lately but I think its the weather. The stairs get me down too but thats because I need to lose some wait! This morning I went in your old room and said happy christmas and god bless. Did you get the wallett I sent you? Buy yourself something useful you need, like some socks or hankies, you can never have too many.

Your parcel came in time, and it was good of you to remember your old Nan but you shouldnt of gone to the trouble because I didnt expect anything and I think things are dear over there. But it was nice to hear the postman knock on the door for a change, and he stopped for a couple of minutes to. I like the picture's in the book you sent, of course I knew what it looks like from the poscards, but it was nice to see more. I showed Hilda. We could do with some of your weather over here! Is the soil realy that colour red? The soap is nice to, I'll save it in my special drawer.

I tidyed all round this morning and this afternoon I watched the Queen. She gave a nice talk – but it made me fill up, maybe its because I think of the war and all that. Then I went down to Hilda for a drink of tea and a piece of her cake.

Oh well John Id better go and start making my meal. I've got a nice chicken leg. Write when youve got time and tell me about your new friends. I'm glad you've met nice people and I told Hilda how well your doing in your job. It just goes to show I told her – you can always get what you want in this life if you try hard enough. You deserve to have a good life out there.

God bless you John, and keep happy –
and best love – from your loving Nan

25/12/81
Dear Nan,

I hope you are well and looking after yourself. Thank you for the wallet and money but you shouldn't have. I am on a good salary now and my new boss Greg Abbott, who's the son of the man who started the company, said I will be promoted in the new year. He said I won't be on the Mail Run very long because I'm such a good pilot they need men like me in positions of Seniority. His father is called Ace Abbott and he's a famous pilot in these parts, or at least he was, because he's retired now and Greg is in charge. Anyway, I told Greg all about my father. I think Greg and I will get to be good friends.

I like where I am living now. It's a big bungalow, modern, with nice rooms and furniture, and the woman who owns it is called Bernie. She's very pretty with long curly red hair and works in the local library. She's an educated person and understands about flying, because she's read lots of books about it. She's very smart too, you'd like her dresses – and she keeps the house nice, just like you do. Tell you a secret, I think she likes me a lot. The other day I was wearing my uniform and she said I look handsome!

Tomorrow night (Boxing Day) we're going to the best restaurant in town for a tip-top meal, with wine – all the trimmings. She said she likes romantic meals, with candles and dancing. Your wish is my command, I said!

141

Bernie gave me a real Australian hat for Christmas (to keep the sun off, she knows I hate the heat) and a new white shirt and some cufflinks, as well as this really great penknife with lots of blades and scissors and things like that. I gave her a really expensive necklace made of silver and coral and pearls as well as some soap and things like that. So you can see we're getting on very well!!!!!!!!

I'm writing this in my room, because we've just had our presents and Bernie wants to get on with the dinner. She's a good cook too, a real housewife like you used to say – so I'm looking forward to the turkey. The bloke that lives here too is helping her.

Well I'd better stop now because I want to read this book on navigation that Greg gave me, because he said next year I could sit the exam for an instructor's qualification. So I thought I'd better start swotting early because it's good to be ahead of the game.

Must go now because the old books are calling!

Love from – your affectionate grandson,
John

Eighteen

Each Boxing Day, Dick and Joan Springville threw their place open for a lunchtime barbecue that stretched into early evening, at which point, knowing his wife needed to sleep it off, Dick would suggest the crowd moved to the Zoo. Beaten-up cars would barrel through the streets, and the drinkers would overflow on to the pavement, and only the most hardened would manage to see it through to the final, riotous lock-in. Couples would slink off to hump drunkenly in the darkness, while men without the luck of such distractions would deliver bloody noses and black eyes to each other, followed later by a jovial thump on the shoulder and a reassuring, 'No worries, mate!'

Bernie was used to the annual blow-out. She and Suze used to yell and laugh with the rest, boasting they could drink all the men under the table. They were terrible, destructive days, she realized now, cradling coffee in her hands and watching John and Eddy poke slivers of meat through the bars of Crow's cage. Their heads were close together, one shaded by the hat, the other untroubled by the sun.

'See? He's not afraid of anybody,' Eddy said.

'He took it from me!' John exclaimed. 'He doesn't scuttle away any more.'

'That's cos the greedy bugger's desperate,' Bernie murmured, unheard.

Eddy grinned at his pupil. 'You could feed him every day, mate. He'd get used to you then – be like he is with me. Animals and birds – they get to know you quick. You only have to breathe their air and say the right things to them.'

'Nan never let me have a pet. She said they made too much mess . . .' John paused, staring at the creature, which suddenly ruffled its neck feathers.

Kraa . . . kraaa . . . kraaak.

'Looking at him . . . I feel sorry for him,' John said.

'Because he can't fly?'

'He should be up there in the sky. We should be watching him – up there.' John flailed an arm in the direction of the sun.

Bernie could not bear it. 'He's only ever known the cage really,' she called. 'And it's better'n bein' dead.'

'*Is* it?' John queried, looking up with a challenge.

'Poor crow's grounded forever,' shrugged Eddy, turning from the cage.

His expression was opaque. There was no flicker to indicate that she'd been given the privilege of hearing his story; no sense, in the angle of those thin shoulders, that her arm had enfolded them. His eyes slid away from hers as he informed her matter-of-factly that one of the bathroom taps was dripping and he would fix it.

Bernie wanted to scream at him: 'What the hell are you talking about taps for?' Instead she clapped her hands together, as if she had only just thought of what she proposed.

'Hey – you fellas want to come to Dick's place with me? He won't mind – and the barbie's always terrific. Let's go out and have a party!'

143

She explained about the annual event, not looking at John but at Eddy, surprised by her need for him to accompany her. Just to walk around in the same air seemed enough, even if it was at the Springvilles'.

'I go every year – wouldn't miss it! Go on – it's a free meal, free booze and you'll have a great time,' she said persuasively. 'Might as well, if you're not doing anything else. An' if you can tear yourself away from the taps, Eddy!'

Remembering in time, she switched her gaze to John Roper, whose head was flung back, eyes closed. 'What say, Biggles?' she called mischievously.

The pilot jerked himself upright, and the face he turned to her was totally different to that which she'd last seen: the mask ripped off to reveal an enthusiastic schoolboy. 'Yes, I'll come. Might as well.'

'Eddy?'

He shook his head.

'Why not?'

'Don't feel like being with a bunch of strangers. Talking.'

'They play music. You can just sit in the corner under a tree with a beer,' she babbled. 'You can jump in the pool to cool off, then just watch and listen. You won't have to talk . . .'

'No, I'll stay here. I'd rather try to do another drawing. I need to practise. In fact, if I had all the stuff, I *would* rather do the taps.'

'Bugger the bloody taps! Come on, Eddy – it's Boxing Day!'

'So what?'

'So use your holiday to come out and have a good time.'

'Your idea of a good time and mine's probably different.'

'You reckon?'

'I reckon.'

The shuttered face turned away again. A small wild creature inside her gnawed through into Bernie's heart and began carefully chewing its way through ventricle and aorta, causing her precise and exquisite pain. You couldn't go down on your knees and beg and plead, she thought. You had to shrug as if nothing mattered in the whole godforsaken world.

But John Roper rose with alacrity and said it was all right, he would be with her, they'd have a good time. Eager, his accent veering alarmingly between Biggles and Barry

144

Mackenzie, he asked whether he should change his clothes, when they would leave, if she thought she should ring the Springvilles to tell them he was coming, how long it would last . . .

'You never been to a party before, mate?' she asked coldly.

John stopped his flow, mouth open like a fish, arms hanging limply at his sides – as if he'd been sluiced with icy water. Eddy looked across and she read the disapproval in his eyes. *Fuck you, you bastard, and it's all your fault,* she thought. But altered her tone to please him. 'Listen, John, we'll have a great time an' it's really cool you're coming,' she said, 'but I don't want you to *worry* about it, OK? That's all I'm meaning.' She injected all the warmth she could muster into her voice.

'But . . .?' He tweaked at his shirt, almost shyly.

As she contemplated her fate, Bernie allowed a sigh to escape into the strip of air that lay between her and Eddy, knowing he would hear it and understand that her kindness to Roper was only for him. No, for all their sakes.

'OK, John – between us we'll find you something else to wear, won't we, Eddy?'

When they climbed into the Holden a couple of hours later, John Roper was wearing a big black T-shirt of Bernie's and a pair of rather baggy blue jeans he produced with a flourish for her approval, but which he had never worn in all the weeks he had lived in her house. Once Bernie had made him lose the grey socks he'd put on beneath the brown sandals, she felt she could appear with him without losing too much face.

The Springvilles lived in a white bungalow on the edge of town, near the site where Eddy worked. Their road loitered towards the distant ranges and ended in a half-dug foundation, overgrown with scrub – as if years ago some builder went bust, leaving the desert to rasp its relief into the burning air.

Sometimes Bernie enjoyed imagining some catastrophe, the people all gone, the town abandoned to its fate. She pictured the swift destruction of everything her parents' generation had built on their proud plots of land, each home vying with the next in individualistic whim. For it would not take long before the patchwork houses fell, and the orange soil invaded this town they had built, crusting over cookers in modern kitchens, leaving lounge rooms to lizards and scorpions, banking up in bedrooms where love, lust or sheer exhaustion had sweated endless nights. Asserting forever the brutal potency of the earth itself, which would triumph despite human dreamings of hotels, golf course, new roads, and shopping malls. She held the word 'deserted' on lips dry with sand carried on the blast from outside.

'Hotter than ever today,' she said, as she parked in a street already littered with cars and pickups, nose to tail. 'You gonna survive, Biggles?'

'It makes my head ache,' he said.

'You didn't bring your hat, mate!' she said, without solicitude.

The strains of rock 'n' roll bounced over the Springvilles' low roof and shimmied along the path towards them.

'Joanie's crazy over Elvis,' Bernie said, as they walked up the path to the open door at the side of which was a polished wooden plaque bearing the words JORICH SPRINGS in elaborately curving ironwork. John paused to look at this.

'Joan plus Richard – see? With two of them Springvilles making Springs,' Bernie explained.

'That's clever,' he said.

'Oh yeah, big intellectual is Springing Dick.'

Joan Springville greeted Bernie with an open-armed shriek that indicated she'd broached a cask of Calibre at least an hour ago. She was a short, leathery woman in her fifties whose voluptuous form was crammed into skintight capri pants and matching sleeveless blouse in a lurid lime and flame tropical print, which showed the top half of enormous breasts. Golden hoops banged against her cheeks as she talked, bracelets clattered, and a sprig of frangipani nodded in her backcombed brass-blonde chignon. Bernie smiled inwardly as she recalled what Joan looked like back when she'd at last managed to snare the notorious owner of the Zoo. The plump housewife with short brown hair, who knew her first duty was to give her bloke steak and eggs nearly every meal, had transformed herself into a siren who quickly caught on that her second was to give him whatever else he needed.

'G'day, Bern – how's it going? We thought you wasn't coming! Who's your friend? You two an item, then? Go on, give us the goss!' rattled Joan Springville, branding Bernie's cheek with fuschia lipstick.

146

Bernie caught the tightening of John's jaw and squaring of shoulders which is the male's instinctive response to a suggestion that flatters him.

'This is . . . uh . . . John Roper, Joanie. He's from England – and he's my lodger,' she said coolly, to be rewarded by a suggestive cackle and a dig in the ribs, mercifully neutralized by the flesh which padded even Mrs Springville's elbows.

'You know what they say about lodgers, girl!'

'Can't say I do, Joan.'

Their hostess directed her parroty scream at a new group of arrivals. Names flew into the air. Women laughed. Men yelled their 'G'day mates' as if communicating across a canyon. The hubbub rose all around, tightening about John Roper's forehead, and scraping down the walls of Bernie's mind like fingernails down a school blackboard.

'See you later,' she said in Joan's direction, then jerked her head at John, who followed, as 'You ain't never caught a rabbit and you ain't no friend of mine' blared in his ears like a personal reproach.

On the wide verandah, people lounged in wicker chairs, all in various stages of undress. The men wore shorts and singlets but the women . . , John stared at bikini tops, halter necks, tiny skirts and shorts that parted buttocks like a cleaver. At the side of the pool, girls lay topless – shiny golden breasts lolling towards their outstretched arms, coppery nipples in all sizes of well-handled coinage.

'I don't know where to look,' he muttered in Bernie's ear, with a nervous cough.

She glanced at him in astonishment. 'I'd look for a beer if I were you – and get me one while you're about it.'

'W–where do I go?' he stuttered.

She sighed. 'There's an eskie each end of the verandah and you'll find them all over the house, and poolside too. Make your way over there and give yourself another eyeful!'

'Aren't you coming with me?'

Bernie recognized the fear in his voice. Suddenly she remembered a party her mother had insisted she go to, in 1955, six months after they'd arrived on the ten-pound fare. One of her classmates was Adele Simons, whose father was big in the town – a strutting rectangle of a man whose sister was married to Ace Abbott.

Jim and Nola Simons decided to celebrate Adele's twelfth birthday by inviting every single classmate to a 'slap-up sports day' and barbecue at their large home a couple of blocks from the new library. Adele boasted of the prizes there would be, the food, the music. Word of Jim Simons's largesse spread through the streets and homes of the developing town – as he knew it would.

'I don't want to go, Ma.'

'Sure an' you do so.'

'I hate her and they all hate me.'

Standing in her knickers, Bernie was scrubbed under a perforated bucket outside the tin shack, holding her arms across her tiny breasts, whilst the Doyle children sniggered. Colleen had stayed up late sewing her a new skirt of heavy turquoise cotton, patterned with yellow horses with red saddles, and gathered into fullness that bunched over her hips. She'd cut out two horses and appliquéd them on to the bodice of one of her own white blouses, cut down to fit snugly and with the fabric starched so stiffly the Peter-Pan collar chafed Bernie's neck. Then red and yellow bars of plastic dragged back Bernie's hair each side of her moon-like forehead. When it was done, and she squinted at herself in the mirror, she realized the two carefully appliquéd horses were placed so that they exactly covered her developing breasts, flagging the swellings with yellow and red blobs.

Bernie cringed to remember her father's fawning handshake when Jim Simons opened the large glass-paned door. The other girls' pastel party dresses. The boys' nudges and sniggers. Then the sports, when Mrs Simons announced they would all go and change into their shorts.

'Mrs Simons, I haven't got . . .'

'What – oh, didn't Adele . . .?'

'No.'

'No worries! You can run in your knickers and vest?'

'No.'

'No worries! Your dress then?'

Horror increased with the heat. Bernie waited on the side as Adele and her best friend Noreen chose their teams for rounders, and knew she would be the one nobody wanted. With good reason. She flailed the bat in the direction of a fast ball that was caught with a triumphant smack behind her. She dropped the easiest of catches as the rest of her team groaned aloud. She tumbled between first and second bases, and felt her skirt fly up over her navy-blue knickers. Dust on her tongue, laughter in her ears. She sweated through repeated walking, hopping and running races, patches of sweat staining her blouse.

Winners were allowed to plunge their hands into a bran tub and retrieve a prize. In the melee Bernie found herself flanked by Pete Smith and Billy Wilson, the biggest, toughest boys in the class.

Now Pete flicked a finger and thumb at the horse projecting from her right breast, making her recoil. At the same time Billy was sniffing the air above her shoulder with the exaggerated pose of the Bisto Kids.

'I bet I could ride that nag pretty good.'

'Wouldya want to, Pete?'

'I dunno, I reckun she'd mount easy, maybe buck about a bit, but I'd stay on.'

'I reckun it's in a lather, needs a good rub down.'

'Yeah, Billy, but your Oirish nags go real fast, famous for it.'

'S'all the spuds they feed 'em, Pete – go straight to the armpits, right?'

'Reckun if you stuck your finger in it'd come out smellun of chips?'

Bernie heard the snorts all round her and stumbled backwards, wanting to die. But neither that nor any other escape was on offer, and she knew then it never would be. All she could do was endure.

Nola Simons clapped her hands again and announced that if the children would like to go back to the rooms, with no pushing mind, they could change into their 'bathers' and cool off before the barbie.

'Mrs Simons . . .'

'No worries! We can find an old one of Adele's?'

'No.'

'Yes, de-ah, don't be silly now? We want all Adele's friends to be comfortable? And we don't want to spoil the party by not joining in, do we?

No resisting the steel in that voice. Bernie was led upstairs with the others and waited in the sugar-pink bedroom while Adele sulkily produced an old yellow knitted cotton swimsuit

Bernie knew would only just fit. When at last she went downstairs, she wore the hateful sweaty blouse on top of the swimming costume, which, yanked up as best she could, came to rest only just over the protuberances which, in her mind, stuck out like balled socks. At the other end it seemed to cut her in half, so her stomach melted at the thought of those boys seeing her bottom.

When the time came to change back into party clothes and dance to Bill Haley on the brand new Dansette record player Jim Simons carried on to the verandah, Bernie retreated to the bathroom, locked the door, and vomited.

When at last it was over, and the parents lined up outside, she saw with fresh anguish that this time Ma and Da had both come to meet her – an unfortunate welcoming committee standing with visible eagerness by their battered old pickup.

Hours passed before she could even be persuaded by her worried mother to look at the going-home bag Nola Simons had distributed at the front door, different ones for girls and for boys. It contained a rubber, a pencil, a notebook, a tube of sweets, a small mirror and two large hairslides of pearlized pink plastic, each one bearing three flowers in a slightly darker pink, which were far superior to the ones she had lost. Her parents could not understand her hysterical tears.

Five years after Adele Simons' party, when the Molloys had their own place, and Bernie had learned to stalk through school challenging anybody to stand in her way, Pete Smith drove her out of town. She allowed him to remove the few clothes she wore and drove him crazy with her hands, her mouth, her pliancy, until at last, groaning, shorts round his ankles, he prepared to roll on top of her, only to be stopped by a fast manoeuvre which had him on his back, wrists pionioned each side. He looked up at her face, hard above him, and felt his erection wilt like a flower in the heat. Bernie seized his right hand, the one that had been fingering her, and jammed the fingers roughly under his nose.

'Can you smell them then, Pete, the chips? Eh? Can you?'

'Wha . . .?'

'Don't you remember?'

'Wha . . .?'

'When we was twelve, years back, at Adele's party? Now drive me back to town and if you do it fast, I won't spread it

150

*around that your prick's the size of a witchetty grub and just
as soft – all right?'*

Looking back, Bernie knew something important happened
to her at Adele's party. Iron in the soul, steel in the spine . . .
all the clichés began to fit her then. And should she be glad
of that? Perhaps . . . for at least now it helped her understand
John Roper's panic. She'd been there.

'Ah – I'll come with you,' she said. 'Not fair on a bloke to
make him find his own beer when he doesn't know the place.'

She lit a cigarette and led John across the garden.There
were always people at this gathering Bernie had no wish to
see – men who she'd treated like Pete Smith, women whose
men had fancied her, one-time friends who bored her now
and couldn't understand why she had withdrawn, men who
drank in the Zoo and avoided her eyes when she met them
with their wives, because they knew she had seen them at
their worst – and hated her for possessing that knowledge.
Usually none of it mattered. She would get drunk as fast as
possible, knowing everybody else was doing the same, until
that shared state neutralized old enmities and made the tired
jokes sound funny once more.

She bent to rummage in the eskie, and handed John a blue
can, before lifting the cask to squirt white wine into a plastic
tumbler. She felt his eyes on her, and knew this was all a
terrible mistake, she should never have mentioned the party
to the two lodgers, she should have come on her own. John
Roper's expression – mingling doggy devotion and naked
gratitude – was hard to bear.

Bernie was at the point of telling him not to get it wrong,
when she was seized from behind in a moist bear-hug, and a
kiss was pressed on her neck. Without turning she said, 'G'day,
boss,' and grinned.

'How'd you know it was me, Bern?'

'You smell of the barbie, Dick! Quite apart from your natural
masculine odour and muscles.'

He leaned towards her and winked. 'Who's yer friend?'

John had been watching the exchange with a set face. He
saw the grey-haired man, with a look of barbed wire about
him, drape a tattooed arm across Bernie's shoulders, and
absentmindedly allow his index finger to make little circular
rubbing movements on the tiny butterfly above her left breast.

151

He witnessed how she leaned into him lazily instead of pulling away, and dragged on her cigarette before turning to puff into his face through flirtatiously puckered lips.

'This is John Roper, he's my Pommy lodger. John – meet my boss, Dick, otherwise known as your host, Richard Springville.'

'Pleased to meet you, I'm . . .' said John.

'Goodonya!' was the reply. 'You the one who's a pilot?'

At that, John Roper leaned forward eagerly, seizing Dick's hand as an afterthought and pumping it up and down. 'Yes. I'm on the mail run – temporarily, you see, because it's quite a junior job, but I'm expecting to move on to be . . .'

Shut up, for Chissake, Bernie thought, as Dick interrupted. 'Goodonya! Bit of luck, that, mate – because there's a sheila by the barbie you must know. Friend of my Joanie's girl, and never been here before, so you two can talk shop.'

They followed their host, skirting the pool, to the corner of the garden where smoke wafted from a large brick-built barbecue. Smells of chicken, pork, steak and lamb, spitting fat and caramelized marinade, shimmered in waves towards them.

Two girls were lolling in plastic loungers just to the left, out of reach of the smoke. Bernie recognized their faces; you saw everybody in this town sooner or later. The tall one – sultry in white halter a size too small, and tight scarlet shorts – looked as if she knew the way of the world. Her blonde hair was bundled up into a rough bun, and the wisps that fell down only served to enhance her easy availability.

In contrast, the friend was smaller and prettier, with dark hair hanging in shining sheets to just below her jawbone and a pale, freckled face. She wore a knee-length sundress in pink and white checked cotton, which touched Bernie with its innocence: all ironed, fresh and sweet, like an idealized teenager from the fifties. The girl looked as out of place at Dick's party as Bernie herself would in a nunnery garden.

'Hello, John,' said Hazel Cartwright, scrambling to her feet.

Dick was rattling on, 'This is Joan's Leanne, Bernie – best looker in town, aincha, my girl? Not long come back from Victoria. This is Bernie Molloy, Leanne – the backbone of my pub. Keeps the peace in the fuckin' place.'

'Thanks, Dick.'

'And this here's . . . er . . .'

'Hazel. She works for the boss, Greg Abbott? At the airport. Me, I'm in bookings?' explained Leanne, her questioning staccato.

'Good to meet you,' Bernie said generally, wishing she was on her own verandah, mended by Eddy, outside the kitchen painted by Eddy, just watching his delicate long fingers offer little shreds of kangaroo meat to the crow, mimicking its sounds in a soothing guttural. You could be so happy, she thought, being quiet like that. You could get to expect it. You could want it to last.

Heat blasted from the barbecue.

'Joanie says there ain't a woman in town wouldn't lie down with her paws in the air for Greg Abbott – that right, Leanne?'

'Too ri–ight, mate – and I told Mum she's too old to be having dirty thoughts like that about a bloke young enough to be her son, or as good as.'

'Age got nothing to do with dirty thoughts, girl, and never has had,' grinned Dick, snaking an arm around his step-daughter's shoulders and squeezing hard as he planted a sloppy kiss on her brown shoulder.

She frowned and wriggled free, giving him the slightest of pushes as she did so. 'Get your paws off, Dick.'

He frowned too.

'Wouldn't say that to Greg Abbott, would you?'

'Too right, but there's a small matter of him being the best looking bloke in town, you know? 'Fraid you old blokes can't compete, *Pa.*'

Dick looked at her meanly. 'From what I hear, Leanne, you're none too choosy when you've got a few wines down you. Blokes talk in the bar, y'know.'

Without another word, Leanne stalked off into the crowd, her swaying buttocks watched in silence by Dick Springville and John Roper. 'She's a goer,' was all Dick said by way of explanation, as if daring Bernie to tell him what she thought of his behaviour.

Bernie felt sorry for the young girl who had observed the exchange with pink cheeks and a look of mounting anxiety. John Roper was standing in silence.

'You see much of each other in work?' she asked, as Dick sloped off to the barbecue without another word.

'Only if I'm summoned to an audience with God,' he said.

'Yes, but I sometimes see you in the morning, or after work,' said Hazel eagerly. 'In the car park, and things like that. John's not one to waste time,' she explained to Bernie, 'so he doesn't mix much.'

'I mix just as much as I want to,' he said flatly.

Hazel looked so crestfallen that Bernie wanted to punch her lodger for his rudeness. Yet, despite herself, her irritation was tempered by pity. She thought of his Christmas presents to them, and recalled the elation on his face when he'd carried in the pudding. He'd been equally excited at the prospect of this party, but so nervous of everybody, so afraid of what they might say . . .

Eddy was kind to John, as he was kind to most things, and you had to learn from that, she thought. Like opening a present somebody had left at the end of the bed.

So Bernie chose to embrace the ill-matched pair with a smile so wide it soothed them without knowing. She settled them in chairs and went to fetch food from the barbecue, joking that a barmaid is used to having to serve.

Nineteen

'Blood pressure again, I'm afraid, Mrs Roper.'

'Look at me ankles! I look down there and think it's Dumbo.'

Lily forced a laugh, but the person opposite her did not smile in response. Her brow was furrowed as she gazed at Lily's sparse notes. Dr Attra was a pleasant young woman, Lily and Hilda agreed, even if she was brown, because she couldn't help that, and it was better than having a man doctor if . . . well . . . you might have ladies' troubles. But you expect a doctor to be a man, don't you? You can't help it. It wasn't like it used to be when old Dr Fitzgerald sat there in his three-piece suit and peered at you (sitting there in your best clothes for the doctor) over his glasses.

'I was wondering . . . do you suffer from depression at all? Things get you down?'

'We never had time for things like that. Just got to soldier on, haven't you?'

'Yes, but – you're living on your own and . . .'

'Some new tablets, that's what I need. They'll put me right.'

'Yes, well, I can do that, of course . . . but . . .'

'I'll keep on taking them, this time.'

'Mrs Roper, your general health is very low, and it worries me that you don't seem to take care of yourself. Are you eating well?'

'I said to Hilda, the trouble with being on your own is, you set one knife, one fork, one plate, one cup and saucer, and it seems to take so long to clear them away. But I do all right. I'm partial to a nice bit of cheese.'

Dr Attra sighed. 'Cheese is good, but in weather like this you need hot food. Even soup – that's easy.'

'You must find it hard – this cold. After coming from . . . you know. Over there.'

The doctor smiled. 'Oh, I was born in London, Mrs Roper, so British weather is all I've ever known. Except for family holidays in France when I was younger. And my husband and I had a honeymoon in Bermuda. That was lovely weather.'

It was Lily's turn to frown. It was all so puzzling. Nothing was like you thought it would be.

'Talking of the weather, have you heard from your grandson recently? I shouldn't think he's suffering from cold!' asked the doctor, as she started to scribble a prescription.

'He keeps in touch, he's a good boy, our John. Got a good job, with some promotion coming up soon, he said . . .'

'That's good news, Mrs Roper. Now, look – what I'd really like to do is send you along to the hospital, for one or two tests.'

'I don't want to go to no hospital. There's no call. Nothing wrong with me some new tablets won't put right. If they get you into hospital you don't know what they'll do. They ask you a lot of questions, and get you all in a muddle . . .'

'Don't upset yourself, please. Here, take a tissue, Mrs Roper. We can postpone the hospital for a while, though I do think . . .'

'Sometimes it all builds up inside you.'

155

'What sort of things, Mrs Roper?'

The voice in her ears was as soft as a pillow. You could bury your face in it, until you no longer wanted to breathe, nestling, knowing the softness would envelop you, forever. Lily Roper stared at Dr Attra as if not seeing her. From a distance she heard her prompt once more.

'If there are things you'd like to talk about . . .?'

Lily shook her head.

'I'll always make the time, you know.'

Lily just held out a quivering hand for the prescription. Dr Attra watched her stuff it into her coat pocket as if it did not matter, then lean heavily on the table to push herself to her feet. 'Come back in a week's time?' the doctor said, with a smile.

The waiting room was full. Hostile eyes watched Lily's lumbering progress towards the door, blaming her for their wait. A toddler raced in front of her, so that she stopped and swayed, before regaining her balance and tottering on. The young mother said nothing; she slumped in her seat and glowered at Lily as if it were her fault, whilst the child bashed into chairs and shrieked at the room.

'Do you need to make another appointment, Mrs Roper?' the receptionist asked.

Lily shook her head, and rolled out into the street. Razors of sleet made her stop. She fumbled with her top button and turned her collar up, pulling the woolly hat down to meet it. She had forgotten her gloves; already her hands were numb. The bitter wind, howling through the city streets from the river, blew a sheet of newspaper around her legs, making her stop in a sudden terror of falling. But another gust whirled the paper on, with sweet wrappers, plastic bags and fragments of polystyrene, like flocks of dirty birds tossed on a storm.

Lily felt the cold penetrate her soul. She turned to walk, shoving her hands deep into her pockets and crumpling Dr Attra's prescription in one fist as she shuffled, head down, straight past the chemist.

Twenty

Somebody she did not recognize offered a drooping joint. 'Care for a smoke?'

Bernie held out two fingers and accepted out of habit. She looked down. The cigarette wasn't well rolled and the end was wet with saliva. As she raised it slowly towards her mouth she could smell the herby aroma. She examined the strands of tobacco poking from the wet end, turning it before her face.

'You're supposed to take a drag, not a look, girl!' said the man.

She scrutinized him. Blue denim short-sleeved shirt, beige shorts, two-day stubble on a wide, tanned face. His eyes were the colour of the shirt; he was about forty, she guessed, and muscular. Not bad. His teeth were even. She decided to smile back.

'You a friend of Dick's?'

'Just moved here from Katherine. Water's my business, so I'm giving them the benefit of my expertise over there.' He jerked his head roughly in the direction of the golf-course development. 'The name's Tony. What's yours?'

'Bernie Molloy.'

He took the joint back from her and took a long drag, closing his eyes for a few seconds. Bernie watched, almost experiencing the sensation. She could make herself shiver, remembering. Yet, as if through the wrong end of a telescope, she watched herself at this same party, so many times past, smoking and drinking herself into oblivion. Now she did not want it. And yet *that* person, that old blueprint, was all she knew, so where was there to go?

The man was talking. He told her all about the Artesian Basin, and the three pumps that would draw water from it, to keep the golf club green. The bores would go down between sixty and a hundred and twenty metres he said, and that was where he came in. It would be a sweet little piece of engineering . . .

Bores is about right, Bernie thought. But she nodded and smiled.

'It makes a change to meet a bloke who likes what he does,' she said.

His grin widened.

'You're the best-looking woman here, Bernie Molloy. I've been watching you.'

'Forget it, Tony.'

'You got a bloke?'

'Yeah, I got a bloke.' She hoped he did not identify the hesitation in her voice.

'The one you came with?'

Bernie denied John Roper with alacrity. She knew she should go and find him, rescue him from people who'd be bound to judge him harshly. She had left him sitting on the lounger, a plate of food in one hand and a beer in the other, talking about his ATS training in Liverpool to the sweet young girl, who was actually bothering to look interested. But how long ago was that? With plenty of white wine inside her, dazed by passing banter, faintly sickened by heat, nicotine and noise, Bernie had lost all sense of time.

'Sorry, Tony – it was nice to meet you, but I got to go,' she said, moving away from his expression of disappointment.

So it went, she thought. There'd been many blokes over the years she might have bothered to love, but the memory of Zippo was an excuse, long after she had started to forget the detail of his face. She had read somewhere that in Mexico, on October 31st, they set the table for a special dinner, laying places for their beloved dead, whose spirits come and take the essence of the food. She liked that idea. There were times in the last couple of years when Bernie thought it would have been more real for her to sit there at home every night with the table set for five – to preside over the empty feast and try to make amends – than to dare allow anybody living into her life.

And then Eddy Carpenter and John Roper arrived.

She passed Joan and Dick arguing, and heard the name 'Leanne'. Then she spotted Leanne herself, leaning against the side of the bungalow, her arms around a man whose face ground slowly into hers. People were chucking each other into the pool; screams of laughter mingled with an increased volume of the Supremes.

The barbecue was finished now, the seats nearby empty. Bernie looked around but could not see John Roper anywhere.

Bernie cursed herself, and Roper, because she'd begun to feel protective, and the music intensified her melancholy. Jesus, she thought, I feel bloody sorry for myself as well as him, and for Eddy too, who ran away with nothing to run towards, just like the rest of us.

You came into my house, baby, baby . . .

Hazel Cartwright was walking across the garden, carrying a tumbler of cola. The girl's brow crinkled; she tossed her hair back with a look almost like guilt on her face. 'I wish I could have stopped it, but . . . he got a bit upset, you know? Went off in a temper, but between you and me, Bernie, I reckon he was more weepy than mad, if you know what I mean?'

She explained that they had been sitting talking, and John had told her the story of his life. 'Isn't it such a *tragic* story? Makes you think, doesn't it? How some people are – sort of – born into sad lives?'

Bernie nodded.

'Then he said all about passing his flying exams . . . Was that at home, or over here? I got a bit mixed up . . .'

'OK, I know all that stuff. Where'd he go?'

The girl looked even more distressed. 'It's such a shame – suddenly this man behind us starts talking about "Roper-the-Hoper".' She lowered her voice. 'That's what they call him, you see, at work. It's sort of sarcastic, you know? They don't like him much, not even my boss. No reason I can see, except he's . . . sort of . . . different. It's not fair, really, but you know what men are like . . .'

Bernie sighed.

'I whispered not to take any notice, but he went all red. It was horrible, the things they were saying. I think one of them's a mechanic . . . Anyway, in the end he gets up and asks if they're talking about him – which was a bit silly really, cos it was obvious, and the way it came out, in that lah-di-dah accent – it sounded worse. So one thing leads to another, and they call him a Pommy bastard, and next thing somebody gives him a shove, and he's on the ground.'

159

Within Bernie's rage was sheer astonishment that it should matter to her at all. Yet it did.

'Hazel, did you see where he went?'

'He walked off in that way people do when they're making out they know where they're going, you know? But they don't?'

Bernie walked back to the house, and was just about to mount the verandah steps when Dick Springville grabbed her hand. He was grinning in that wolfish way she knew to distrust.

'My word, Bern, your Pommy mate can't hold his juice.'

'Where is he?'

'I left him with what was left of the whisky bottle, and the last anybody sees of him he's heading for the back dunny lookin' a bit crook.'

There was a small queue of women outside the small guest lavatory, just inside the corridor by the garden door. Joan Springville was at the head, at that cusp of mood where the giggles will soon turn to anger. She thumped on the wood.

'Listen, mate, there's a mob of sheilas out here who'll take you apart if that door's not opened in three seconds. It's all right for you blokes, you can piss in the bushes, but us girls need a sit down . . . You ready? One . . . Two . . .'

Before the count of three, Bernie pushed through and told Joan she'd handle it. A knowing curiosity flickered in the woman's eyes as she stepped back. Mouth against the wood, Bernie spoke very gently and firmly, as if to a child.

'John? It's Bernie – can you hear me? Listen to me, John. I want you to open this door now, and I'll take you home, and it'll all be OK. You hear me? Now – open the door, John. Open the door for me.'

There was a pause. Then came the small click of the lock, accompanied by a faint groan. Bernie tried to push the door open, but he was in the way. So she applied more force, to create a space big enough to squeeze through – treading, as she did so, on one of the legs of the man who cradled the toilet bowl.

'Oh, come on, mate,' she whispered. 'Don't let 'em see you like this! We'll get you out of here and home soon as I can get the toilet clean.'

With difficulty she hauled him to his feet, and held him upright with one hand, pressing him back against the wall, while she poured cleaner into the bowl and attacked it vigorously with the brush.

'Lucky I'm used to it,' she muttered as she worked.

Then she took a corner of the pink towel, wet it under the tap, and rubbed it around his face as if he were her child.

They let her through, but nobody offered to help. Bernie yelled back thanks for the party – managing pleasantries she did not mean, as she slung John Roper's right arm around her shoulders, and guided his rubbery legs in the direction of the front door.

Every bump in the road sent John's head lolling and swaying and bumping against the side window. It was five o'clock already, and the town slumbered in the close, dreary Boxing Day afternoon. There was no air. A light veil of cloud had covered the sun in the last half hour, and massed like a bruise on the horizon.

'Might get a storm,' she said aloud, then glanced sideways.

John's mouth gaped. He looked pathetic, slumped beside her in her dirty old car. Bernie tried to imagine him in the cockpit of a Cessna, lent grace by the machine, transformed by the act of flying, the brief mastery of air. But she could not. She could see no connection between the swashbuckling pilot of all those dreams and boasts, and the sick drunk beside her.

'What'd it be like, flying straight into a storm?' she asked as if he could hear. 'Would you head straight for it, and feel it crashing all round, and have to fight the plane, like a bucking bronco? What'd that feel like, John? Don't you ever dream of doing that, man? Don't you ever just want to head for the dead centre, the still bit, and go wheeeee . . . and that'd be it? I do . . . *So* I do.'

As she drove over a bump in the road, a snore jolted from his crusted mouth.

'That's right, Biggles. I knew you felt that way too. Maybe one day I'll go up with you – see what it's like up there. What I'd like is . . . fly up in a rainstorm and see if you'd go right through a rainbow. Would that happen, you reckon? Ah, it'd be great to be soaked in all those *colours*, mate! That'd be right.'

She pulled up outside her house and ran in to find Eddy. He was on the verandah, asleep, and she allowed herself to pause for a second and take in the planes of his face, with the full mouth almost out of proportion. There was no peace in his face, she thought. Bernie experienced an acute need to brush his hair.

He opened his eyes wide, looked up at her, but said nothing. Bernie shrank before the milky vacancy of his gaze, yet she would not let him know. No, not ever.

So she told him to help her get John Roper into the house, because the man was a dead weight, and the stupid Pom couldn't hold his booze . . .

'You should have stopped him drinking,' Eddy said flatly.

'I'm not his keeper!' she snapped.

Eddy took one side, Bernie the other, and they hauled John into his bedroom. 'Put him on his side. I'll get the washing-up bowl in case. Take his sandals off,' said Eddy, 'and get that T-shirt off him if you can, it stinks.'

Eddy held John up as she struggled to drag the garment over the lolling head. He opened his eyes for a moment.

'Hot . . .' he moaned.

Yet he was shivering.

'I . . . I'm shorry . . . I . . .'

'That's all right, mate. You get a rest now,' Eddy said, gently. Then he murmured, 'I think he might have a temperature. It's probably the heat as well as the booze . . .'

When Bernie told him Hazel's story, he shook his head sadly. 'Those guys – why didn't they just leave him alone? Poor bloke don't do any harm . . .'

She shook her head. 'No, he just tells everybody the wrong story. They take one look at him, and get an earful of that stupid accent he puts on – and that's it. People aren't stupid – they know he hasn't got a bloody idea who he is, but he craps on, full of bullshit . . .'

'A bit like you. No, *just* like you,' he said.

She jerked her head up. He saw panic turn to hostility in a second.

'Yes – what you just said about him's just as true of you, *Bernadette*,' he said quietly, pulling the single sheet up over John. 'If you knew how *your* voice changes, you wouldn't be so quick to take the piss out of John.'

'Oh, don't be so bloody stupid!' she yelled, crashing out of the room.

Eddy heard her bedroom door slam, and waited. John was

breathing heavily now; he would not wake for a long time. So Eddy moved to the door of the room, and stood staring at Bernie's door, waiting for her to emerge clutching the drawing he had made for her. He'd put, *To Bernadette with best wishes from Eddy* on the bottom of a sketch of the crow in his cage, and added the date. He imagined her being so pleased she wouldn't know what to say, and her silence would meet his own, face to face.

But there was no sound and she did not appear. After waiting a few more moments, leaning on the doorpost and straining his ears, Eddy shrugged and walked out into the garden once more.

Clouds mobbed overhead. The air was almost as stale and heavy as in John Roper's room, as if a vast invisible glass dome was upended over them all, so you could imagine the oxygen running out, the world drifting into an endless sleep. Nothing moved. The crow was poised at the side of the perch, its head tucked into its shoulder like a miniature hunchback. Apart from one or two squawks overhead as a galah sought its flock, the birds were quiet, waiting for the storm to break. Even the insect hum had ceased.

Eddy realized he too was holding his breath. He let it out in a gust, then dragged in more air, pressing his hands on his chest to feel it expand. There was a fluttering inside him, a nervous, sick movement of heart and stomach. He wondered if she had torn his drawing to shreds. In his imagination the fragments rose like birds, wings beating against his head.

He'd been sitting for about an hour, chin resting on his clasped hands, staring into the mauve of the garden, when at last he heard the faint suction of bare feet approaching. He knew she'd showered and sensed the fresh dampness of her, the minute rivulets trickling down from tendrils of hair, as she hesitated for a second, then slid into the other chair. Dry cane wheezed beneath her weight.

Neither of them spoke. The air thickened. Then the sky groaned – the faintest sound, too timid to be called thunder, yet.

'I like storms,' Bernie said.

'Me too . . . A couple of years ago . . .' He stopped.

'What?'

'Don't you hate people always yarning about their lives, as if it mattered?'

163

'Depends who – so go on.'

'I was in Arnhemland – right up near the coast. Been moving around and I ended up there. I'd met this old guy, Tommo – I told you about him. He'd teach me stuff – the names of things, how to fish, how to play yidaki, just about everything. He called me good Balandra . . .

'Which is . . .?'

'White people.'

'How'd you meet him?'

'He gave me a lift – in his Toyota.'

She laughed.

'Anyway, we were in his flat-bottomed boat, poking around a lagoon. The sea was only about four hundred metres away. You could hear it, but only just. We'd been there all day. I remember the flying foxes raising hell, and the black cockatoos screaming overhead, and he shows me how to tell the whistle of the oriel in all this noise, and the frogs are croaking – incredible! We're sliding through mangroves and stringybarks, and the trunks of the melaleucas are like ghosts. All the birds are trying to get home, because they've picked the storm before us. Like now. Tommo and me sit there for God knows how long. I reckon that was the first time I . . . oh, never mind.'

'What?'

'Nothing. Anyway, it was like we were in a ringside seat at some great show in the sky. The sun went down and at the same time a pale full moon was rising on the other side, with a haze, a halo round it. The rocks were glowing like they were on fire. And over in the distance the horizon flashed with great sheets of lightning –' (he clapped his hands) – '*one* . . . *two* . . . *three* . . . Like that. We just sat and watched. There was a rumbling from way over too, but a stillness round us. At last, when it was nearly dark, we headed back. And there were so many stars overhead, and the moon in front of us, and the streaky, wild ends of sunset behind us, and all the time the storm flashing over in the south like fire in the sky. And because they sensed the storm wouldn't reach us, there was this chorus of *relief* in the darkness. Things rustling, and splashing, and plopping. It was like being in the middle of . . . a sort of *miracle.* Only a way of saying it, Bernie – what we saw.'

Eddy's head was thrown back against the chair, and his eyes were closed, as if with the effort of the longest speech he had ever made. Bernie followed the ski-jump contour of his nose in profile, and the length of his neck. Then she whispered, 'What was it you were going to say? Something about the first time?'

He said nothing for a while, then drew in his breath.

'It's to do with . . . what I told you. There was all that beauty round me, and suddenly I felt it didn't matter – all the lies. Oh, what had happened to *her* – my real mother – mattered, of course it did. And her mother too. Nothing could ever make that OK. But *me* and *them* – Vern and Pam – I just realized then I couldn't go on letting it fester like I had. I mean, I knew my life was a mess, I had to accept that – but at least I could try to live it the best I could. You know, I mean *live* it. That doesn't leave room for all the other crap.'

'I wish I knew how,' she said, so softly he could hardly hear.

Eddy knew there was nothing to say to that.

'Anyway,' she went on, in a louder voice, 'you say your life's fucked up, Eddy, but you don't know that. Things can change, can't they? Man, if you thought that was impossible, you'd kill yourself!'

'I never wanted to do that, did you?'

The rumbles in the distance were stronger now. A vivid yellow light streaked the mauve of the sky; every leaf on the trees drooped with the weight of its own dust.

Bernie coughed. 'Yeah, I did. For quite a while.'

'Why?'

She was silent. Then asked, 'What happened to Tommo?'

'Oh, I reckon he's still there. He'd a big family.'

'Why'd he look after you?'

'He gave me a lift and I told him stuff. It was a long ride. I was bumming around . . . It's like that when you're running.'

'I know.'

'So I spent time with him, and it got longer, that's all. He'd had a son my age who died. There were three others but they were away, one was in prison and one of the other two an alcoholic. But his four girls were great, and so was Miwura, his wife. Sometimes when I was with Tommo I thought I'd be right again. I had this fantasy I could – sort of – listen to that little bit of my blood, and fit in. But it wouldn't work. I had to leave in the end.'

'Don't you mind – leaving people behind all the time?'

165

'Yolnu – that's the people – believe the appearance of Wulma, the thunderclouds, tell you it's time to move camp. So . . .'

'So – what?'

'That's the way it has to be.'

'Always?'

'I reckon.'

Agitated, Bernie shifted in the chair. She felt she could drown, and nobody would reach out a hand to pull her to safety. Not this man anyway. She was stupid to have imagined.

'Suit yourself,' she said sharply. 'Only, seeing I'll have to put an ad in, give me a bit of notice, won't you?'

'Ah, Bernadette – there you go again,' he said, shaking his head, 'in that voice I was telling you about. There's no *need*. I didn't say I was leaving here, did I?'

'No, but there's a big mob of thunderclouds up there, right? And . . . I . . . Oh, Eddy!' She stopped, as if she was having difficulty breathing.

'What?'

'I . . . I . . . just loved the drawing. Couldn't believe you'd done it for me. An' I can't help it – I'd like to think you'd stay a while, and do more. That's all I'm trying to say.'

He smiled. 'Funny way round it.'

'Most ways are,' she said, smiling back.

'It's not too bad, is it? I'll do better though. I reckon I need bigger paper.'

'Bloody brilliant, Eddy! Gets him just perfect. I reckon he was posing – rewarding you for all that kangaroo you've shoved down his throat! You glad I took the piss out of you for that forging?'

He shrugged. 'Yeah. I knew it was cheap and nasty and I felt guilty all the time. Thinking of Tommo. But I reckoned he wouldn't know, and I had the technique and there was money in it. People do all sorts of stuff to make a living.'

'I've been thinking, after what you told me, it doesn't seem quite so bad. Least a bit – a small part – of you had the *right* to steal their ideas and style and everything.'

Eddy laughed. 'To make money for some tourist shops? That's kind of you, Bernie, but I don't think so.'

The atmosphere had eased. They sat without talking, watching the sky darken. Bernie wanted to reach across the void between them, to press his hand to her face and leave it there.

'I wish it would rain,' she said at last.

'It won't,' he said.

'I hate the dry so much. It gets in your nose and throat.'

'Shall I get you a beer?'

When she heard him moving in the kitchen she rose and followed. The sudden light in the yellow room made her blink. She knew it must illuminate all the flaws on her tired face. So took the ice tray out and turned to the sink, murmuring it was water she needed, not beer.

She filled a tumbler. He was watching, heat between them in the tiny room. Bernie passed an ice cube over her forehead, then drank deeply from the glass. The tap dripped. Eddy reached past her to apply more pressure, then tutted.

'See?'

'Sure.'

'It's a pain, wasting water like that. I'll pick up a mixer the day after tomorrow.'

He was standing next to her, staring at the tap, his brow furrowed. She saw the freckles on his wiry arms, smelt his skin and couldn't stop herself. 'Oh, *stop* talking about bloody *taps*, Eddy! Can't you see I'm crazy about you?'

His eyes widened. He jabbed his own chest and gasped, '*Me?*'

All Bernie could do was nod her head. Her expression of disbelief matched his. They stood staring at each other, listening to the tiny, insistent percussion from the sink. That small tattoo slowed the universe and took the heart back to its beginnings. Then Bernie held out her arms and murmured, 'Oh, come on, Eddy – come here.'

He raised a hand as if to ward her off, then stepped into the circle of her embrace. Exhausted, Bernie rested her head against his chest, leaning back against the sink unit, her arms around his waist, his locked across the small of her back in perfect symmetry.They were both trembling. After a few seconds their hold tightened, as if, having travelled this impossible distance, they feared whatever circumstance or mood might prise them apart.

Eddy's face was in her hair, so that she could barely hear his thick whisper. 'I don't think this is happening.' He was shivering.

Then she shushed him, soothing, repeating the sound as if he were a baby. Her breath vibrated through his chest. 'It is happening, Eddy,' she murmured at last, 'but neither of us thought it ever would.'

She felt him nod agreement, then they stood motionless until all sensation disappeared – the physical pressure of her spine on the steel sink, hands clasped, stiffness settling in joints – and a great calm descended which awed them both with its strangeness.

At last Bernie pulled her head back and raised her face – waiting for that wide mouth to grind down on hers, as mouths do, lips and tongues she had encountered so many times, in those other lives. Waiting for that familiar greed, she was astonished to find herself shy, even afraid. Yet nothing happened. Eddy made no move. He simply stared as if seeing her for the first time, holding her out and away from him as if surveying a vision that made him move his head from side to side again, in wonder and disbelief.

'How could you want *me*? You're beautiful.'

'I'm getting old. Much older than you.' She sighed and dropped her head again, so he could no longer see her face.

'What's that got to do with anything?'

'At this moment? Nothing.'

'Let's go back outside.'

He took her hand, and led her into the passage. John's door was ajar, and they both stopped short, guilty for forgetting about him.

'Better go check he's OK,' Eddy whispered.

The room smelt of sweat, with a faint overlay of sick. They stood by his bed, still holding hands, until Bernie, suddenly afraid John would wake and see, extricated herself, conscious of Eddy's dampness on her palm.

'Like a baby,' he whispered.

John was curled up, his mouth open, beads of moisture gleaming along his moustache. The small nasal sounds he made reminded Eddy of the crow when it too was about to sleep. The room was stifling. The sleeper stirred and moaned when Eddy struggled to open the window a little more.

'Noisy baby,' Bernie said.

'He'll sleep, all right. He won't wake up.'

Bernie felt a swift contraction of desire in her womb. She did not want John to wake and hear. She wanted a century of she and Eddy alone, to know this stranger whom she had

168

begun to love, despite herself, and be able to explain to the old Bernie where this terrible tenderness had come from.

Yet she looked on the hunched sleeper with pity, wondering if his dreams launched him high into the ether, away from jeering voices. She imagined him poised, then swooping down like a bird. And as she bent to smooth the sheet over his naked chest, she wished for him that freedom, even if only in sleep.

Eddy and Bernie walked hand in hand through the indigo garden, listening to the chatter of night. It's like being drugged, she thought, this heaviness of limbs and eyes, the feeling the world has stopped spinning. Neither of them spoke. They stood looking at the house for a long time, then made their way back to the verandah, where he dragged the old chairs close together and sat her down in one, touching the top of her head with his lips, before taking the other.

Thunder still rumbled in the distance, filling the stillness between them.

'It won't rain,' he said at last.

'I wish it would.'

'There's so many things . . .'

'Me too.'

Without speaking Bernie went into the house for two beers, and they sat drinking and sharing their consciousness of the distant storm, the night, the faint scratching of the crow, the sleeping man inside, and all memories they would surely share if trust could be found.

Then, in a tiny voice, she asked, 'Will you come to my room?'

'Yes.'

She rose and went in, lighting a candle against the untidiness. A joss stick might mask staleness, she thought. It was too obvious to have another shower . . . and after all, he had seen her naked and grotesque already. That memory inspired more shyness. Bernie trembled like a schoolgirl.

When he came in at last she was lying naked, the sheet pulled up only to her waist. He looked at her in the glimmering light, and felt an awe that matched her own – turning away awkwardly to undress like a schoolboy. But he could not prevent her from seeing the bones through his skin, the husk of a desert creature which could easily break and be scattered on the earth.

When he came into bed, he put out an arm, pulling her into

the crook of his shoulder. She waited for him to turn, to throw himself on her as she expected, as she was used to, and yet her own longing receded when nothing happened. Eddy gathered her to his stillness so that they were made into one, more surely than through penetration of the flesh.

'I've never met . . .' she began at last.

'Shhhhhh.'

At last, after a long time, in which both of them stopped shivering and it seemed as if breath itself was no longer necessary, his hand began to stroke the place of her tattoo, tentatively, and explored down as far as the swelling of her breast, but no further. She felt the scratchinesss of fingers used to manual labour, yet blessed with a gentleness she had never experienced, not even with Zippo, who loved her.

(Was he watching, she wondered, did he want her to be happy at last? Were they all watching? She saw the wardrobe looming like a great sarcophagus, and said a prayer for forgiveness.)

Bernie raised her own hand to finger Eddy's wiry curls, then cup his face, as she had longed to do. His mouth in her palm breathed, 'Ah, Bern–a–dette,' almost in sorrow.

And Bernie knew then that they would not make love, perhaps they would never make love, at least not in the way the world understood. Certainly not in the scrabbling, sordid way of her life until that point. But this was enough. To lie dazed with surprise in her parents' old bed, in a house full of shadows, and stroke, and stroke, until they both fell asleep.

Twenty-One

Somebody was shaking him awake. The sheet wrapped round like a shroud.

'Come on, mate, I brought you tea. It's six. You got to get up.'

'No–oo,' he whined.

'I put three sugars in it.'

170

He toppled down again into the void, moaning.

'Don't go back to sleep on me, mate. You've been out for twelve hours.'

'I told you, Nan, I'm going. Stop interfering. Me dad wants it, he told me . . . I heard him . . .'

A calloused hand flattened his forehead, pushing him to earth.

A different voice whispered, 'The sun's fried his brains, Eddy. I seen it before. He's goin' troppo on us.'

'No, he's just hungover. Get a cold facecloth.'

'Eddy, love – I'm going back to sleep.'

'Sure, don't worry about all this. I'll sort it out.'

'You're good, you know that?'

Spots of light raining all around, wrestling the Cessna through pockets of heat, the roaring in his ears – nevertheless John Roper heard something within that tone which stretched his heart on a wire.

The next thing he felt was a cool flannel wiped firmly around his face and neck, bringing back the intimacies of childhood.

He opened his eyes to meet Eddy's, full of concern. The younger man had the facecloth poised, but put it down now and bent to offer the mug of tea instead.

'Get this down you, John, or you'll be late for work. Come on – it'll get cold.'

John allowed Eddy to help him sit up, then took the tea in two cupped hands and sipped.The sugar hit his system almost immediately, making him shudder.

'I'm not going to work,' he moaned.

'Yes, you are. No choice, is there?'

'I hate it.'

'No, you don't. You don't want t' give up just because some drongo said the wrong thing to you. Tell you what, rather be you flying around up there than me pushing a shovel on the ground!'

'You said you've got some days off.' The voice hardened into accusation.

'Yeah, I don't have to go today but . . .'

'Why did you wake up then?'

'Because I knew you wouldn't, mate – and I don't want you to lose your job – OK?'

John stared, then looked away. The knowledge that some-

171

body was being kind confused him. He had no way of responding to the man who squatted by his bed, hands poised to take the mug.

'Finished?'

He nodded.

'Know something, John? You'd be better off if you forgot.'

'Forgot what?'

'Everything . . . the stuff you talk about. None of us can live in the past. And – trust me – it's no good dreaming about who our parents were or what they did. Waste of time really, and sometimes . . . well – blokes don't want to know. Start a new story, John. Try to fit in. Have a few yarns, about *them*. Be better, mate, honest it would.'

'Thanks for the advice,' John said brusquely, and stumbled out in the direction of the bathroom.

They heard the old Moke clatter down the street. Eddy had shut the bedroom door quietly, knowing John would not come looking for him. But when Bernie went to speak he'd held a finger to her lips.

'Shhh.'

'Why?' she'd mouthed, only to receive a shake of the head in reply, as he lay down on his side, head resting on one elbow, looking at her, until she turned away, afraid he would find her ugly in the morning light. She ran her tongue around her lips, dreading her own smell, the sour taste he'd find repellent. But he was curling behind her so that their bodies fitted, and they drifted into a brief doze in the soft, warm stillness.

But when the sound of the engine died away, she turned and asked why they had to be silent.

'I don't want him to know,' Eddy said. 'I mean, about this.'

'Why not?'

'You know.'

'Eddy, I don't know nothing at all! Here we are, you and me, and if you asked me to explain *that* I couldn't.'

He ran a hand over her shoulders, her arms, her breasts, her stomach, so lightly it was barely there. A hovering rather than a touch. 'You don't have to explain things,' he whispered, 'but when I do this, and this, I know it's you – and it's what I thought . . . you'd be my own dreaming, Berna*dette* Molloy.'

He went on stroking as he told her how all the great creatures moved all over the country creating the waterholes, the moun-

172

tains and the rivers, making the animals too, naming every-thing, until at last when it was all done they became part of the earth themselves, marked forever on the landscape in the sacred sites.

'I remember flying over Jabiru, getting a lift back to Darwin because I'd done the pilot a favour – and you can see the animals down there in the patterns of the rivers and the land. All giant shapes, spread out – the black snake, and the croc-odile, and the kangaroo. All down there forever, only nobody knows except the real people.'

'I never met anybody like you, Eddy.'

'So when I touch you, like I'm doing, I can feel my own story, it's another creation story, Bernie – and I started to make it up when I first saw you. I couldn't help it.'

'What does it say?'

'It says – er – there was a guy who'd lost his ancestors and he was wandering about trying to find them, and he went every-where, and then one day he landed in a special place, and it was where he belonged, but he didn't realize. There was a strange woman there with wild eyes and hair, and she lived in a cage in the garden. And maybe she was his ancestor, he didn't know. But he could see she was dying of thirst because some-body hadn't filled up the water bowl. He had to set her free, so when he couldn't find the key to the cage he burrowed beneath the wood and the wire, and he came up inside.

'But the wild woman clawed at his face and blinded him because she was afraid. Still he managed to get hold of her, and pulled her back through the tunnel and out into the air. And when he'd set her free she stopped struggling and looked at him, and she held out her arms to him. But then her arms turned into wings and she was a brolga and flew high up into the sky – away over to the wetlands, where she'd be free. But the man was blind and so he couldn't follow her and couldn't drift on any more. So he turned into a mole, quite happy digging his way through the soil with his scaly hands. Because he knew that his people were from the earth and that's where he'd stay.'

Bernie laughed, daring to put her hand on top of his where it still lay on her belly, insisting that it resume its gentle movement. 'You're crazy, Eddy. And I'm not sure I like the ending to that yarn. I don't get it.'

'Aha, but you don't know if it is the ending, do you? Maybe

there's another episode . . . But it'll do for now. He came to rescue her, even though it hurt him, and he found the place he belonged – his sacred place – and made himself a home.'

She was silent.

Then – 'You made that up?'

'Mmm . . . maybe, maybe not. Maybe it was made up for me, years ago.'

'You're such a strange guy, you know that? But at least you didn't turn me into a chook.'

'You know what a brolga's like?'

She shook her head.

'Oh, she's beautiful – with great legs and a red head.'

They met each other's eyes and started to giggle. Then the laughter faded, as Eddy leaned over to kiss her face and her neck, and then her breasts, so tentatively Bernie guessed he had not made love with many women. There was an insistent sweetness about his every movement which made her heart falter, as if its noise might make him shy away.

Yet the rightness of his touch was a greening for them both, and she touched him gently in turn, exploring his body as she had longed to do last night, feeling his breath quicken at her touch. There was no hurry – the newness of it all required calm stretches of time and the repetition of their kisses became its measure. But at last, as strangeness edged towards knowledge, they became sure. They moved together, inevitably, and she snaked her body beneath him with all the skill she knew – enfolding him with the wholeness of self and soul, to welcome him home.

Twenty-Two

And not so far away John was steering his clattering old Mini Moke – right up into the morning sky.

The smell of the cockpit – a mixture of varnish, oil and high-octane fuel – clings to his nostrils, comforting and intoxicating.

He tightens his strap, swings the rudder with his feet on the pedals, wiggles the stick and thinks about all the kills he's made.

Chocks waved away. An inch or two of extra throttle, then the brakes wailing thinly, and he jerks and squeals downwind along the perimeter track. The drill's automatic: hydraulics on, trimming controls set to zero, one inch forward, mixture rich, propeller controls fully forward, fuel tanks selected, dive brakes in, flaps up, gills closed, then opened, just a fraction . . . All set.

He's not afraid.

My father was a hero, he told them, flying ace, first class, best of his generation.

It's in the blood.

They all knew that.

'Go and jolly well show Jerry who's the bloody boss, Johnny,' called Jim the rigger and Reg the fitter, as they strapped him in the kite. You had to show you were geared up for the jaunt, every time.

The nose yaws one way then the other as each leg comes up. After all this time, ever since being a rookie, he still relishes that lifting into peace – boost and revolution brought back into climb power as the air-speed indicator needle creeps round the dial.

Sun and shade flicker by until a few short, sharp bumps take him through the first broken cumulus. Vapour swirls and streaks the screen, then light flashes bright enough to blind. He opens his mouth and bellows, '*We'll meet again, don't know where, don't know when, But I know we'll meet again some sunny day . . .*' as the whole vault of heaven comes into view, translucent blue flashed with gold and red, beautiful as opal. A rivulet of oil runs along the port engine and dances in microscopically wrinkled, shiny brown patterns as the invisible slipstream lashes it, and light mottles like beaten metal all around – brightly coloured, twice as real as life.

The others are following tightly. They climb in a long slant, until they cross Beachy Head and steer for the French coast. Then Johnny rocks his wings, and they level for the climb, sliding out of their tight pattern and adopting the wider battle formation at 25,000 feet.

Over the Pas de Calais, Me109s swarm round the wing.

The lads fan out four each side. Then he spots a bandit on its own, and drops down like a bird of prey after the kill, taking aim with his cannon at the unarmoured underside. The aircraft shakes.

Da da da da da da da.

He exults as thick black smoke plumes back, and the 109 falls to earth. *Auf Wiedersehen, Hans!* . . . Then another, and another . . . burnt cordite in his nostrils, wrestling the kite, taking aim, again and again . . .

And a yelling all around, like birds calling, as the wing follows his lead, and the remaining Me109s swarm for another try, only to be beaten into retreat as black smoke stripes the hectic air, and fire flashes from the ground.

Top score, Johnny.

Head for home. Back on terra firma, Jim and Reg rush forward, unfastening his straps, pulling him out, wanting to be the first to clap him on the shoulder and call, 'Well done, Johnny!'

For he's a jolly good fellow . . . rings in his ears.

The Moke landed, rattling over the rough earth of the car park. John switched off the engine, and looked around. His head was still hurting. Even at this hour it was far too hot and for the first time he dreaded the pummelling of the cockpit.

He sat listlessly, gazing up at the sky, not wanting to put his feet on the ground and walk to Greg Abbott's tower, already dazzling in the morning sunlight. He looked at the building and narrowed his eyes against the glare. Flat blades of light sliced into his retina.

A blue car pulled up a short distance away, in an emphatic sprinkling of stones. John recognized the BMW, and suddenly everything frightened him – the terminal squatting like a toad, the snake road slithering towards an emptiness of red dust, the shadow of the tower a black maw opening to swallow him. As he watched, two men got out, and he saw Greg stop for a second and glance across at him curiously. Then he said something to the older man, and they started to walk over.

Greg Abbott was dressed in his usual beige shorts and shirt, white socks pulled up to his knees, ankle boots polished. The golden boy in the matching light of morning, about to enter his fiefdom. Lucky blighter, John thought. He was ashamed of the old yellow car he'd bought for a song. There was nowhere to hide.

Greg's burly companion had grey hair and a florid face, and John recognized him, from the portrait that hung in the terminal. This was the legendary Ace, the famous pilot and outback pioneer, who'd been recovering from a heart attack when John arrived from Wyndham.

'How you doing, John?' called Greg pleasantly. 'I'd like you to meet my old man, Ace Abbott. Dad, this is our Pommy flier, John Roper.'

The old man strode forward, and grabbed John's hand with such power he winced. 'Good to meet you, John. Welcome to the lucky country!'

'I came out five years ago, sir,' John said.

'Ah, we don't call blokes "sir" round here, John,' said Greg with a laugh.

'I think it shows respect,' John said. 'That's what I was taught, anyway.'

Ace Abbott's grin faltered for a second; then he clapped John on the shoulder and started to laugh. 'He's kidding you, Greg! Good on you, John! I love a Pom with a sense of humour!'

'Yeah – me too, Dad,' Greg Abbott said, with no smile.

'Greg and me, we got some business to talk. Not that he needs me breathing down his neck, eh, Greg? He's going to make Abbott-Air the biggest and the best in the whole territory, that's for sure! So – you coming in, mate?'

John nodded. There was no choice. Ace Abbott moved slowly, like a man told to take great care. Grounded unwillingly in age, he placed each foot on the earth with deliberation, as if unsure of its trustworthiness. John felt diminished equally by his size and his reputation. Even taller, Greg Abbott strode half a pace in front, as if, John thought, to emphasize his position. The building ahead, the planes on the airstrip, the very lives of the employees of Abbott-Air, were all as much his own as the elegant BMW parked behind them. John fixed his eyes on the man's muscular body as it moved, at ease with itself, towards the inheritance relinquished by the father, the flying ace.

'So what brought you out, John?' Ace asked.

'Flying, sir. What else? It was hard to get the training at

home. I did the ATC, kept going . . . but they turn you down for the RAF if you don't speak with a posh accent . . .'

Ace grunted. 'Typical Pommy snobs, eh?'

'I had all the exams – just about. Kept trying for my English at night school . . . Anyway, on the assessment, they told me I could join as a ranker and try for a commission after three years. I hadn't heard of that. Didn't want it either. I knew it was all because I hadn't been to the right school . . .'

Ace Abbott made noises of disgust. 'Who needs it? No wonder your bloody country's going down the dunny if they think you need Shakespeare to fly a plane! And you heard we're not like that over here? *We* always give a bloke fair goes.'

'Roper worked the trams in Melbourne to pay for NASA,' said Greg.

Ace Abbott stopped dead and swung a light punch to John's arm. '*Good* on you! I like a bloke with guts – eh, Greg? How long was that?'

'Nearly two years. I saved nearly ten thousand dollars, because I didn't know it was going to cost so much at Cessnock. But I made it in the end – and I got the flying prize in my class too, and . . .'

Ace broke in, 'Just the kind of bloke we need at Abbott-Air! Bet you're a bloody hard worker too, eh?'

John faced the older man with a serious expression. 'In my book, sir, when a chap has to do his duty, he will.'

Ace threw back his head and laughed. 'You got a real comedian here, Greg! Deadpan – you see that?'

'No, I mean it,' John stuttered, puzzled by the misplaced mirth. 'I've been brought up . . . to . . . to . . . My father was a pilot, you know, and he died, and I've always believed I had to . . .'

Ill at ease, Greg started to walk again. The other two followed, Ace's laughter swallowed by discomfort. He scratched his head. 'I'm sorry, mate. How's a bloke to know? Commercial pilot was he?'

'No, an American bomber. B17s. He crashed on a top-secret mission at the end of the war. My mother was never allowed to talk about it. She died too – later. My grandmother said her heart was broken.'

Ace Abbott shook his head and let out a low whistle. 'When I think what we all went through . . . I had so many mates

178

who . . . Just like your old man . . .' He stopped, and stared at the distant range, apricot and mauve in the early light. There was a suspicion of moisture in the old man's eyes when he turned to face John and held out his hand. 'Best of luck to you, John. You're good for a Pom! No offence, mate – eh? And, listen, son – wherever your old man is, I reckon he knows you're a credit to him, eh, Greg?'

There was an uncharacteristic shadow on Greg Abbott's face. He stared at John, then collected himself.

'Yeah, Dad, whatever you say . . . Now, go on up to the office while I have a quick word with John?'

Ace Abbott's heavy footsteps echoed down the stairwell. Greg leaned on the metal bannister and folded his arms.

'That charter I booked you for, John . . . er . . . it's not on now . . .'

'Why? Did they cancel?'

'I can't tell you a lie. Truth is, Denny Wilson's taking it.'

'Why? You said . . . And Wilson doesn't need it. He's a senior pilot.'

Greg Abbott sighed. Abbott-Air's client, Barry Fraser, headed the business consortium building the golf course, and once every two or three weeks he chartered a plane to take him down to the Rock, where the new tourist development was under construction. Fraser was a typical Centralian, hard and determined, with a seemingly easy grin beneath eyes which narrowed at the mention of money or opposition. John had flown him three times.

'I know you need the hours, mate, but . . . Baz Fraser's the boss. He's paying, so he calls the shots. He reckoned he wanted a different pilot this time . . .'

'Why?'

'. . . and next time too . . .'

'Why?'

Those flat interrogatives started to annoy Greg Abbott. 'Look, mate, he complained about you, all right? He said last time a bloke'd have thought you were flying in the Battle of Britain, and he didn't like it. Rough and bouncy when you landed . . . Fact, Baz said you were rocking and rolling like a bloody band! That's all. You're a fair enough pilot but you got a lot to learn – about flying, and about getting on with people too. I think I told you this before?'

John looked at his feet. His head was thumping. Suddenly he felt sick and wiped sweat off his brow with the back of his hand.

'You OK?'

Greg Abbott's irritation subsided as quickly as it had flared. Naturally generous, he felt sorry for the Englishman who stood before him like a half-stuffed toy.

'You can take the day off if you like.'

'I said I'm all right.'

Greg shrugged. 'Suit yourself. There's some paperwork for you to do – as always eh? – but before you start, go and get yourself some tea with the other blokes, OK? Try and do yourself some favours.'

John bent to splash water over his face, holding his breath as if he might drown. He raised his head and gazed fixedly at his own reflection until the image in the glass seemed to waver in a pale mist, becoming another face, the one he did not know, the one in a photograph with a shapeless mass of plane behind.

Then, before he could greet it and ask who it was, that image too receded, and for a second the mirror was black and empty, yawning before him. An aircraft screamed outside. His own face swam back, pasty and drawn beneath the sunburn.

Rat-pain bit his guts. He rushed into one of the cubicles, fumbling with his trousers not a moment too soon. The evacuation was quick and foul. It was as if the whole inside of him had been pulled out, and he must flush it away, leaving only a hollow casing. He leaned forward, elbows on his splayed knees, resting his head in his hands, and inhaled his own stink.

Then the outer door banged open and somebody murmured, 'Phew!' John crouched in shame. He dreaded the bang on the door.

But the men were in a hurry. They raised their voices over the sound of urine – long steady streams which testified to the nature of the night before.

'You heard – Den's taking the Fraser charter?'

'My word! What happened to the Pom?'

'Dead loss. Baz Fraser won't have him. Word is, the loser flies like he's that Baron von Munchie bloke!'

'Got tickets on himself, I reckon.'

'Yeah, always crappin' on about his old man being some fuckin' war hero pilot bastard? Roper-the-*Hoper*!'

'Too right.'

'Whatever he was hopin' for – Greg just gave it to him!'

Raucous laughter ricocheted off tiles, porcelain and shiny cream walls. Water gushed quickly, then the door crashed behind the two mechanics and John was left alone.

The lines on the vinyl floor covering reminded him of shopping with Nan when he was little, trying not to step on the lines on the pavement, no matter how quickly she walked. If you step on the lines a black bear will get you. He had no doubt of that, despite the palpable lack of bears in Wavertree, nor did he fail to skirt ladders or throw salt over his shoulder, because that's what she did. She'd take him to school, then catch the bus to clean one of the big houses overlooking Sefton Park, then go to Aigburth Vale to serve dinners to chattering grammar-school girls, clear up, then ride back home in time to meet him. On the way home they'd buy something for their tea, and always a cake for John but none for her.

She was always trying to save money, he realized later, but then there was always enough for a new airfix kit for him, or the Woolworths drawing books which he'd fill with aircraft, copied from library books in fine detail with a hard pencil lethally sharpened and carved with his name. She'd be ironing in the living room, John at the table drawing, *Journey into Space* on the radio, while the fire glowed and shifted comfortably in the grate. Sometimes he'd glance up at her, as she smoothed and folded with rough, reddened hands. She didn't notice. In any case, she would never have believed in the grace revealed only to the schoolboy who loved her.

Lily Roper's bulk made every movement awkward; the roundness of her cheeks and jowels was echoed in the lumpiness of her fat frame. Her one concession to vanity was to set her naturally straight hair, so that it broke around her pebbly face in tired grey waves, like spume on an industrial shore.

Then the the ironing board would go away, and maybe they would get the snakes and ladders out, or Ludo – and, in John's memory, the years folded into one moment in that small back room, hot from the fire, glinting with brass – when he leaned against her, smelling clean clothes, scrubbed skin and, underneath, the faintest trace of something intimate and fertile. He felt her laughter all through him, as she slithered her red counter down, down, down the longest snake, to begin at the beginning again. His yellow counter was a small sun, bouncing up towards the clear blue heaven of the top squares, knowing all the time that the vast, soft cushion of his nan would always be there if he fell.

She did not ask for much affection, it wasn't their way. But sometimes – not very often – she pulled him to her and pleaded, 'You love your old Nan, don't you, Johnny?' Gradually suffocated, he tugged at the ropes which anchored him to her earth, and dreamed of flight. He grew ashamed of her too, embarrassed by the way she waddled down the street in her shapeless felt hat and old blue coat, bent over the bags of shopping. Later, when he worked in menswear, he tried to hide the fact that he still lived with her, but they found out.

His workmates' teens had been played out to the sound of the Beatles; his to Vera Lynn and Tommy Dorsey. They went to discos and picked up girls, and guessed he must be queer, because he showed no interest. And still living at home . . . well, it was obvious, wasn't it? The girls in the shop twittered, saying it was a shame if he was queer, because he was quite nice-looking if only he'd make himself a bit more . . . modern. Ten years passed, when John served suits and shirts during the day, saving and studying, finding out about the assisted migrant scheme, and dreaming of flight.

Somebody was hammering on the cubicle door.

'All right in there, mate?'

At last the external door crashed. Silence flowed back to fill the antiseptic space. John emerged from the cubicle as a small animal slinks from its hole, glancing fearfully around and smelling its own fear as well as danger on every breeze. He stalked along the corridor, grinding his teeth at the thought of paperwork. No job for a real pilot. Then light footsteps tripped up behind him and a girl's voice called his name.

'I'm going for tea, John, do you want to come with me?'

He looked at Hazel, and took a step back. She was pretty, in a thin blue top and a loose skirt of flowered blue cotton. He wondered if she liked him . . . Why else would she run after him? But no – she was too young. It was Bernie Molloy he wanted; you could rest your head on her breasts if only she'd be kind. Maybe he would try again. He could take her to the steakhouse. Women liked a chap to treat them . . .

Hazel knew about the charter. She'd heard her boss on the telephone to Barry Fraser, and to others too. He'd just asked her to look out Roper's file because something was bothering him. She'd heard him saying something to his father about the bloke's yarns changing every time he opened his mouth, and she felt worried for the Englishman. Nobody liked him, and that made Hazel want to try. Something about him reminded her of a teddy bear from a charity sale whose eyes, ears and nose had been placed wrongly, just by a fraction. And its paws were too big too. No wonder nobody wanted it, her mother said. But Hazel had room in her heart to be kind to all broken or ugly things, knowing that even if you can't actually love them, you can try to make them feel better.

'You look like you need a cold drink,' she said.

'I don't want anything,' he replied.

'I hated that party, didn't you? It wasn't very . . . er . . . friendly, was it?'

'Typical, I'd say.'

'You don't look very well today, John. Why don't I tell Greg you've gone home sick? I know he won't mind – he's good like that . . .'

John saw the pity in her eyes, but heard her praise of their boss. He felt the blood hammering in his head.

'I *told* you – I'm all right.'

She froze, her eyes wide. John Roper's mouth was twisted, his face scarlet, eyes full of angry tears. Nobody had ever looked at her like that and she could not understand. Hazel turned sharply, half walking, half running away, before he could see her cry too.

As he stalked along the corridor, one shoulder hunched, John heard a plane ticking over outside. A Beechcraft. He'd never flown a twin-engine. Some lucky man was taking her upon a joyride into the blue today – ascending to the only place that made any sense.'

John frowned and listened hard. *No, it wasn't possible* . . . not that noise, not that muttering out there – talking to him. He smacked a hand on his forehead as if he had just remembered something.

183

Surely they could all hear it? There was no doubt in his mind. That infernal kite was stuttering *Pommiepommiepommiepommie Pommiepommie Pommiepommie* – and no mistake.

Twenty-Three

He carried cinnamon toast and tea to where she sat on the verandah. Bernie's cotton kimono fell back from her arm as she reached up to touch his shoulder. Her skin, still damp from the shower, was miraculous to him now. Eddy stood, mug in one hand, plate in the other, gazing at her as she moved her hand gently down his arm, letting it rest at last on his wrist. For a few seconds, neither of them moved.

When finally she permitted her hand to take the plate, and the other one to accept the mug, the small movements danced. He sat down, his smile reflecting the sun. She returned a nod of thanks.

Eddy thought, we're like people from the same tribe, meeting as strangers, but recognizing each other at last.

There'd been rides in road trains and off-roaders. Jobs digging holes, putting up shelves, cleaning. Yarning in pubs at night with people he'd never meet again. Nights when the implacable sky made him tremble, and mornings when the pale blue air wrapped his solitude like a veil. The time with Tommo was his university, but he took what he needed from all of it, all of them – all the Jims, Daves, Sues, Kerrys, Cols and Brians he'd smoked joints, downed beers and hung out with, before moving on to a new place.

The restless searching seemed so pathetic as to be almost inadmissible. At the mission he saw helplessness on the man's face. So he presented himself to the world as just another teenage dropout, running from repressive parents, and everybody understood that because there were so many of them on the road.

Seven years, and a postcard 'home' once in a while, so they would know he was alive. He imagined the cards stacked in a drawer in his father's desk – a collection delineating the green edges: Geelong, Cape Howe, Sydney, Port Macquarie, Brisbane, Noosa, Rockhampton, Mackay, Cairns, Cape York, Normanton, Gove, Katherine, Darwin, and then turning inland, to the red heart. Those cards must have punished Vernon each time they arrived, and made the woman he'd known as Mum cry for the lost child who was never hers.

Increasingly Eddy found himself remembering the kindness – no, the love – Pam had given.With so much time between them now he knew the punishment should end, yet he had no idea how to go back. On the road you met dozens who had made mistakes, others with no knowledge of who they were, let alone *why* . So many rootless wanderers, he had come to see error and confusion as the order of the universe . . .

Such a long journey, passing people, passing places, until he fetched up here and saw the advertisement for general labourers on the golf-course site. He had grown to like being dirty, the feel of dust on his skin. All he'd wanted was to earn enough to be able to stay for a while, pay for a room, and then move on in the knowledge that he belonged only within the landscape itself. And so then, he thought, I came to stay with Bernie Molloy.

He instructed her to eat the toast, shaking his head at her protest that she never ate breakfast. 'You will now – it's good for you. But don't think you'll always be waited on.'

Bernie chewed, glad of the diversion, because she was not sure she'd be able to control her expression. '*Always* . . .' he'd said. When Zippo died, she'd banished hope from her lexicon. Her life was reduced to a cold beer in her hand, her back against the bar, some guy pressing up to her, the oblivion of music, booze, drugs and sex. She was on the run from the Virgin Mary, she told them, and they laughed.

Later, during the very worst of times, when guilt and grief alike drove her demented, and she lurched zombie-like from pill to pill, anything to blot out the memory . . . she finally understood there was no hope at all, because the last chance of sweetness had been taken from her. In that time of perpetual haunting, her parents' death in their car, head-on with an off-roader driven by teenage drunks, was mere confirmation of what she had told her darkest self: 'It's all shit, Bernie, and you'd better get used to it.'

But now this stranger, the boy who'd arrived on her doorstep three centuries ago (no – eight weeks, was it? – she couldn't remember), had just said 'always', compressing time into two syllables of possibility. She wanted to gasp out her gratitude, but instead she made a play of eating and drinking tea, while he watched. When she'd finished she dared to glance across at him again.

'Thanks, Eddy.'

'See? Good for you.'

'You're good for me . . . Hey, won't it be strange?'

'What?'

'Going back to work. Starting that life again, talking to all those people out there' – she waved a hand to encompass the world – 'when you've changed overnight. And they don't know it . . .'

'*Have* you changed?'

His eyes were grave. She met them without dropping her gaze – afraid the light enveloping them both might snap off, leaving her in the darkness once more.

'Oh yeah,' she replied, nodding slowly. 'No matter what happens – I mean, I don't expect anything to happen, you know? Gave up expecting stuff years ago – Anyway, I'm saying no matter what happens, it's right you and me got together, and yeah – I do feel changed. Does that make any sense?'

He laughed.

'I expect the crow understood.'

'You understand – I know you do, Eddy.'

'Yes, I do. Except – it's still all a mystery to me . . .'

'Why is it?' she asked.

'Because I don't understand how two people can just see each other and *know*. And that's what happened, didn't it? At least, I knew – even that night when you were so disgustingly rat-arsed . . .'

'Oh no . . .' she protested, laughing.

'I used to watch you and imagine what it would be like – er – just to lie down with you, and be peaceful. I used to hear you walking about and I'd feel this little flame – warm, just here.' He pressed on his breastbone.

'Me too! That's just what it was like!'

'Then when I told you about my mother, I knew it had to

happen. Because otherwise I wouldn't have told you my secret. I've always kept silent, wherever I've been. Except, I told Tommo . . .'

''Course you did.'

'. . . and he said that all the spirits who watch over me will always include my mother, so that even if I don't know her, she'll be with me, guiding my footsteps. And her own aboriginal blood is in me, no matter how small a part, and that's why I understand what the land is saying. She'd be singing to me in the wind and winking at me in the surface of the water . . . and I had to learn to listen. That's what he said.'

'That's so beautiful.'

'Yeah.' He sighed. 'But sometimes you can listen too much.' He paused. 'You know something? When I came here, there was something in the house that I could sort of hear. It bothered me . . .'

She tensed. 'What was it?'

'How can I explain? A . . . a . . . crying sound. I thought maybe it was *her*, protesting that I shouldn't have stopped, because everywhere I moved I learned new things. The more I was on the road, the better it felt, making me . . . *like* her. So maybe she was telling me not to stop here. That's what I wondered, those first days. But I couldn't do anything about the fact it felt *right* to be here. Apart from that crying at the back of my mind.'

Eyes fixed dreamily on the crow's cage, he did not see her face, nor the sudden involuntary movement of her hand to her stomach. She let out her breath in a sudden gust.

He turned at that to see her expression contorted. There were tears in her eyes. She shook her head furiously.

'Not now,' she gasped.

At a loss, Eddy reached out and took her hand, and she rose abruptly, pulling him with her. She clung to him, pressing her face to his collarbone, as if afraid she might be dragged away. They stood there for a long time, listening to the *kuk–kuk–kuk–kaark* from the cage, until Eddy kissed the top of her head and held her away from him, looking earnestly into her eyes.

'What is it? You have to tell me,' he said, 'whatever . . .'

'I know.'

'You have to trust me. Or there's no point.'

187

'There's the whole day. I have to go to work at five.'

He tutted. 'I want to *know* you, Bernadette.'

She nodded, then put her finger across his lips. She drew away, tucked her arm in his, and led him down into the garden. They walked very slowly, as if Bernie was an old woman, leaning on him. Maybe that's how it'll be, he thought, and the notion was not strange.

'There's so much to do here,' she said at last. 'I always meant to, but never got round to it. My life was . . . a bit crook. Always.'

'Made some improvements already,' he said.

'My word, yes. And there's more to come, Eddy. There's the very, very important and exciting . . .'

He joined in and chorused, '. . . *Tap*!'

They shook with laughter, and couldn't stop.

This is so easy, Bernie thought. This feels like other people's lives, with silly jokes and time to fill. It's like it was those four years with Zippo, only I was so young then, and we were wild. You never think, then, that anything can go wrong. You wake with a hangover and crawl through the dead-end job, waiting for the night and the parties and the ride-outs up the coast and the camping, blasting to a soundtrack of hard rock. That's how it was. This is different. And happening here, in my parents' house, which I hated so. Eddy's hand already hammered nails and painted where Da once did the same, Ma watching and giving advice.

She could hear them now. How they would approve of a conversation about a necessary kitchen tap, and the fresh yellow he'd chosen to brighten the kitchen. She could imagine her father sitting down to discuss the building trade with Eddy, and the thought made her smile. With a lightening of her soul, she wondered if perhaps she could be normal, like her mother wanted. Not the wild one, after all. But ordinary – with this extraordinary boy beside her.

As if he read her mind, Eddy said, 'I thought you'd think I was too young . . .'

'God, Eddy – it's me who's too old!' she cried, looking away.

'None of that matters,' he said quietly.

'No?'

'No.'

They sat on the edge of the verandah, in the shade of the overhanging roof. He told her he sent the postcards back so Vern and Pam would know where he'd been.

'You should phone them – maybe,' she said.

'Oh I do, the odd Christmas. Keep it very short. What's there to say?'

She nodded. 'It was like that, when I left. Eighteen, and I knew I had to get the hell out of here. I couldn't breathe in this place, with her on at me – do this, do that, clean up, too much make-up, look at your clothes . . . I used to dream of Sydney, but they'd never let me go. So it was the old story. I left a note and took a ride with a guy I'd met in a bar two nights earlier. 'Course, I wrote a couple of weeks after I'd got there, and told them not to worry. But when I called, about a month later, I could hear her crying in the background, and he was . . .'

She stopped and shook her head.

'What?'

'Like he hated me. Patrick was hitchhiking in Europe, and Siobhan and Lou were pulling at the chains already, and so it was all ending. I reckon they wondered if they'd stayed *home* it would've been different.'

'What d'you remember about Ireland?'

'Everything! I was twelve when we came, sick all the time on the boat, and so bored! Never stopped resenting the whole thing. You don't, when you're a kid. You blame your parents for moving you.'

She told him about the O'Donnells and how the other children teased the poor Irish with the bad clothes – and the way her father used to moan and her mother invoke the Holy Virgin, because the streets weren't paved with gold, or whatever it was they'd thought to find.

Eddy laughed. 'Paved with red sand, more like!'

'But it got better for them.'

'Things do.'

'You reckon?'

'Oh yeah . . . Hey, you ever seen what happens after a bush fire?'

She shook her head.

'You see a row of trees, and their burnt trunks like sticks of charcoal at the top, then halfway down there's the new green growth, like a dancer's dress, sprouting out, you know?

189

It makes you believe that everything comes back. It's all going to grow again. Be re-made . . . what happens.'

'Not everything, Eddy,' she said sadly. 'Not everything gets to be green again.'

'But it does,' he said, stoutly. 'It's the way of things – of the land, I mean. It always comes back. You've seen the desert grow overnight, when there's rain?'

She nodded.

'Well, that's you, Bernie. Think of yourself like that.'

She pulled away. 'Oh Christ, Eddy – that sounds like some crap off a birthday card! As if it was so easy! What's bloody easy is to think of *myself* as a fucking desert.'

Bernie rose and stormed through the back door. Eddy waited. But there was silence in the house: no slam of the fridge door, no clatter, no pad of footsteps. After a while, confused, he knew he must follow her.

At the bedroom door he watched her stepping into yellow shorts. She'd already made the bed, but that did little to remedy this room. His eyes roamed over the denim jacket, battered biker's leather, red, blue and black dresses, striped cotton blazer, assortment of shirts – all drooping on wire hangers from the picture rail Sean Molloy had put in all the rooms, as a finishing touch.

The bedroom furniture was fifties' veneer masquerading as mahogany: a chest, a kneehole dressing table with two smaller drawers each side and four tiny ones in a row beneath the mirror, and a wardrobe with a looking-glass panel in the door. Colleen Molloy's furniture, like the sideboard in the living room. Nothing changed. Yet why hadn't Bernie thrown it out?

She was making a show of trying to tidy the dressing table, picking up balls of tissue, and pushing the sun oil, face cream, and body lotion into a row, and banging drawers shut.

'Bernie – I want to know something,' he said. 'This is all so weird . . . why don't you hang your clothes in there?' He pointed at the wardrobe. 'Why have them all round the room?'

'New sort of interior design! Didn't you know?' She chewed her nail and flopped down on the edge of the bed.

'Come on, Bernie! I thought it when I first came, and poked my head in . . . I thought, why's she got a wardrobe in a room if she don't use it?'

Hair obscured her face. She attacked the nail as if to bite

190

it from her hand. Shoulders hunched like a little girl who'd done wrong and was sitting, half sulky, half afraid.

'Bernie?'

She jumped up, muttering that she needed a smoke, and ricocheted round the room looking for her bag. When she found it, the hands that pulled a cigarette from the pack were shaking. The lighter flared and she drew in smoke as if this was her last breath.

'Bernadette?' he insisted.

She whirled round, fists balled at her sides, and her words rose to a scream.

'Stop tormenting me, OK? Stop crapping on about things getting better! You hear me, Eddy – get out of my life right now if you're going to tell me all that garbage about trees getting green! And asking me stupid bloody questions!'

Eddy was still. They stood facing each other, then he turned his head to look at the wardrobe once more – only to catch her reflection, ragged and demented. For a second it seemed to him safer to look at the image than at the real thing, as if he might be turned to stone along with all the tenderness they'd shared. Medusa met his eyes in the glass, and shook her wild head. He saw the snake tendrils whip about, the colour of red earth. Then, as he watched, the face beneath them dissolved, liquefied, melted into a shapeless mass.

He stepped towards her and she put out both her hands, half to ward him off, half begging for help. Eddy plucked the cigarette from her fingers and ground it out on the ashtray by the bed. Then he took her arms and placed them around his waist, gathering her in and soothing as if she were a baby.

The storm broke against him, rocking him with her sobs, making him brace his legs for balance, holding her up.

After a while he realized that there were words within the sounds that came from the creature he held – syllables struggling to be heard.

'You . . . don't . . . I . . . can't . . .'

Eddy knelt before her. She shook her head from side to side, but he caught it between his hands.

'What *is* it, Bernadette? *Please* tell me what's wrong, because if you can't, there's no point.'

The words took a long time to come. 'I want . . . to tell you . . . I want you to know what happened . . .' Her voice started to break again. 'You see, you don't understand. Some things can't ever be put right. So you mustn't try . . . it's no good. It doesn't help to say everything's going to be all right.'

She heaved in a breath, took his hands from her face and held them before her, tightening her grip before going on. 'Because . . . I killed something, Eddy. Somebody, I mean. He'd have made things all right for me – he would. But I murdered him, and . . . He's over *there*, Eddy. I put him there – in the wardrobe. Who you heard crying at night.'

Twenty-Four

John typed with two fingers. She'd be pleased to see the Abbott-Air letterheading. She'd probably show it to her friend. He liked to think of that.

December 27th
Dear Nan,

I'm writing this from the office. I've got my own one now, with light-green walls and a metal desk. The window is big and looks over the runway. There's a Beechcraft Baron out there – it's a twin-engined plane that seats five people. Tomorrow I'm taking some local businessmen on a charter in that.

Today I met the man who owns the company. He's a famous pilot in this area. He was in the war, he told me, and was very nice when I told him about my dad, he said he must have been very brave. I had to "spill the beans" to him because he was so interested. Mr Abbott (they all call him Ace because he's an "ace" flier!!) was very impressed by me and he told me I've got a great future with Abbott-Air. His son is Greg, who's got a bit of a "big head", if you ask me.

Anyway, they've given me my own office as a senior pilot here, and a pretty secretary called Hazel.

The weather is very good, but too hot, and I expect it's very cold at home. Sometimes I miss the snow, and I hope you're keeping my room the way it was because I like to think of it. I hope you're looking after yourself and keeping well and not eating too many cakes!! Don't worry about me. Just "keep your pecker up" and I will write again soon.

From your loving grandson
John

He stuffed it into an envelope with the propeller logo in the corner and glanced around. There was nobody else in the pilots' room, but he knew he shouldn't be caught using the firm's time and stationery. Greg Abbott wouldn't like that.

Upstairs, Ace Abbott's son was sitting at his desk, a piece of paper in his hand. It was the letter Hazel had retrieved from the file, John Roper's job application dated three months earlier. He read it again, frowning   as if some clue to the Englishman's erratic behaviour lay within the stilted phrases of the form letter.

Dear Sir,

I am a Commercial Pilot with limited flying experience and I am interested in the possibilities of working for your organization.

I was trained at NASA in Cessnock, NSW, graduating in November 1981 (?) with a Commercial License, Class 4 Instrument Rating and all Senior Commercial subjects. In addition I won the flying award for my course.

I have recently finished my Instructor Rating with Southern Air Services at Moorabbin, Vic, and I now hold a grade "C" Instructor Rating. My License is endorsed for the AA5, AA1B, PA28, Cessna and PA24-260 type aeroplanes and I have also had experience as Supernumary Pilot on the DH114 at Wyndham.

I have flown extensively in remote areas of Australia and am equally at home in these areas as in the busy terminal areas in which I have conducted the majority of my training.

I am thirty-two years old and single with no ties, and I would accept any offer of flying work whether in

Charter, Instructional or other fields. I am a Freeman of the Guild of Air Pilots and Air Navigators.

My Aeronautical Experience amounts to about 250 hours, including 125 in command, plus about 100 hours supernumary on the DH Heron. I am generally considered to be hardworking and honest, and to have achieved my ambitions since migrating here from the United Kingdom three years ago.

Would you please let me know whether there is any possibility of work with your organization either now or in the future, or if you would like to see me or my references. I would be pleased to comply.

I look forward to hearing from you soon.

Yours sincerely,
John Roper

There was nothing wrong with it. He could see why anybody would give the Pom a job. But to Greg Abbott something didn't add up. And little Hazel had been crying, he could see that. She came back and dug out the letter, as he'd asked, but he could see that her eyes were red. When he asked why, she shook her head. All she would say was she didn't think John Roper was very well. Which in Greg's book meant the Pom must have something to do with it. Or else – why would she mention him, looking so worried? None of it added up.

Twenty-Five

Shocked, Eddy stared at her. The silence yawned, until she spoke again.

'It was all my fault.'

'Don't start at the end.'

'It's all the same. The end started when I was living here . . . Anyway, I left as soon as I could, after all the rows. Yeah, I was bad, Eddy. That's until I met Zippo . . .'

194

'The boyfriend.'

'The big one. We were together for five years, till I was twenty-four. Met him in a bar . . . where else? You should've seen Zippo! He'd have struck the fear of God into Ma and Pa! Y'know – the tough bikie? But beautiful, bit like Frank Zappa, bit like Dennis Hopper. Rode a Triumph – a Bonneville, y'know? Thing is, he looked that way, but underneath he was the gentlest, sweetest guy. Me and Zippo were just like one person. I was his old lady . . . We made all these plans. We'd get hitched and have three kids . . . Baby, this is forever, he'd say. *Jesus.*'

She stopped. Eddy said nothing, just shifted from the floor to the bed beside her, holding her hand.

'No point spinning it out, Eddy,' she sighed. 'You probably guessed. He wiped out one night, something did for him, they never found out what, maybe a piece of wood in the road or something, making him swerve. The Bonnie hit a tree. And that was it. I was in our flat, waiting for him. My Zippo, he took a couple of days to die – really hanging in there, wouldn't give up without a real fight. One helluva strong guy. But they told me if he'd lived he'd never have walked again, let alone ridden. He'd have hated that so much, so maybe it was best he let go . . . But *I'd* have looked after him, Eddy, if I'd been allowed to . . .'

''Course you would.'

'His real name was Kevin, but nobody ever called him that. Zippo was a good name for him. He always carried one, y'know, the lighter? I told him, "Sure babe, you always light me up!"'

Bernie turned with swimming eyes and smiled at Eddy. Who nodded, saying nothing.

'I don't know how to tell it all because I'm nowhere near. Anyway, I came back home just once in that time, not because I didn't want to but because of the money situation. When I showed them a picture of me and Zippo together, her mouth turned right down, and he wanted to know when we were going to do the *daysunt thing!*'

'It's how they were brought up,' Eddy murmured.

'You don't have to tell me that, Eddy! D'you think I haven't thought about it all, so many times, here in this house? But at the time, it just made me mad. I wrote and told them when he died and said I was sorry Zippo didn't ever have the time to make an honest woman of their daughter. She wrote back and said she was sorry for my trouble, and wouldn't I come home now? Ha!'

'What?'

'If she'd known the kind of life I was about to start living she wouldn't have wanted me within a million miles of her. Thing is, there's living wild and there's living *wild*. The first is just having a good time – parties and booze and getting the sack because you've pulled one sickie too many, and moving on to another shop or waitressing or bar job because none of it matters, all that counts is the night time, and you never want that to end. But then there's another sort of wild – which is wanting to destroy yourself, Eddy! That's as crazy as walking through a jungle on your own with no protection at all against whatever's in there waiting in the dark.'

She stopped and ground her fists into her eyes.

'Go on,' Eddy said.

'Something happens to you – well, me at least – when you're really low. It's like you want to kill yourself but haven't got the guts to string up the noose or pop the handfuls – so you do it slowly. You're lying face down in the gutter, and all you want is the rain to come and it to flood through so's you're just breathing all that filthy water, man, and feel it filling your lungs. Like *that*.'

She snapped her fingers.

'So I dropped acid and speed, snorted – you name it. Uppers, downers, everything. All the time. Waking up and lighting a joint and cracking a beer for breakfast, then bingeing all day, so there wasn't no difference between the day and the night because it was all one endless stream of *shite*. You know? Even when I was broke I'd score some whiskey if I had to sleep with the barman to get it. Suze nearly gave up on me. I lost all the old crowd, and lived in some godforsaken room at King's Cross, not caring who I was with. I missed him, see? I was trying to crowd him out my brain. I felt so bad I needed a whole stack of medicine to make me pretend it hadn't happened, and I was somebody else. You know?'

Eddy nodded and pulled her to him. 'It's good you told me, Bernie. But you don't have to remember it now. You go through bad times, but you can still move on . . .'

She pulled away, shaking her head, her eyes wide. 'But

that's not it, Eddy! Not the whole of it. There's more than poor Zippo, God rest his soul! Sometimes I'd think he was watching me, and it just made me worse. When I was out of my skull I'd be hearing all that stuff the priest told us, about sin, sin, *sin*. And I'd think, nobody invented sin till I came along. The more I hated myself, the more I'd . . . Well, you'll be put off me, Eddy, but I can't help that. Not now I've started.

'I'd end up in the cot with some guy I'd been talking to for two hours. Bloke'd give me a couple pills and I'd pay him with a comatose screw. I didn't care. Why should I care? You don't value yourself one cent, so why say no? You're even grateful. All that crap from Father Mullen about stench and filth and what would he know? Ha ha – he should of seen my place on an average night!'

Eddy looked down at his hands.

'OK, so it's not funny. Listen, I had five long bloody years living like that, all a blur, so horrible I blotted it out, until now. Then something happened, and I felt . . . like that stuff about the trees growing green. An old mate of Zippo's came to town, just shooting through, he said. Rode a big Harley, he did . . . an he stayed for about a month and we slept together, of course. I didn't feel guilty. It was a bit like getting back to Zippo, compared to the dross I'd been with. I mean, I *liked* this guy – Steve. We both knew he wouldn't stay. And when he moved on he didn't leave me no address, or nothing, that wasn't part of the deal. Not the way we were. He was headed for Broome, but he wasn't sure . . . Anyway, he's gone six weeks, when I realize something. I'd been on the pill, but with the way I was, well, I'd forget. So when I realize I'm pregnant it's a real shock. Because I think it's Steve's, but well . . . I can't be sure . . .

'At first I reckon to have an abortion. Only thing to do. But I don't get it together, and anyway, I'm scared. One day I'm thinking I want it gone, and the next day I'm dreaming of having a baby, a real baby, a little thing to hold – and make me OK again. Something to love . . . But, Eddy, I don't get my head together to go to those classes they run, and I don't look after myself. I'm a real wreck.

'So . . . the months pass. I'm working in a club at the Cross, getting really tired. I don't put weight on, so when I get myself to a doctor at last, he's quite worried, especially because I'm so mixed up about dates he can't tell how long I've got? He says I got to stop work and rest and eat some decent food for a change, and stop the bloody smoking and boozing. 'Course he's right, but I'm too far gone. He tells me I'm being totally irresponsible – I'll never forget him saying that. Because I know, but I'm so strung out I won't listen to anybody. Even Suze lost her rag with me . . .

'The thing is, Eddy – underneath it all I start to *love* this baby. You wouldn't think it, would you? You can love somebody you've never met. They send me for a scan because of the mix-up over dates and that's how I actually see him on the screen. Just a tiny white splodge on black, that's all. The woman points and says, "Look, that's your baby's head!" And it looks like a planet in the middle of a pile of stars, or something. But I'm staring and thinking – he's real, and he's mine, that little one! I know he's a boy, see. Don't ask me how, I just know.

'So now it's getting near the time, and I'm lying with my hand over my gut, feeling him kick. And I'm so excited I'm going to these baby shops buying stuff for him. A carrycot. Some nappies and those all-in-one suits, y' know? They're in the corner of my place, waiting – and I'm fantasizing I'm turning into a different kind of woman – one who pushes a pram with a baby in it, all wrapped in white. Someone's going to call me *Mum*! It feels like it's a second chance.'

She stopped and threw her head back, staring at the ceiling. Eddy hardly dared breathe. He wanted to hold her but she was too far away from him now. When she continued, her voice had a hard, falsetto edge.

''Course, I went on working. Then one night – I flood – the waters – on the floor, and they call an ambulance and next thing I'm in hospital crying and groaning. But that's just the beginning, Eddy. It goes on for sixteen, seventeen hours, suffering, everything going wrong. I didn't dilate – something like that. Nobody can know what that's like. You think your spine'll snap – like the only way you can jackknife is backwards, cos the baby's in the way.

'I can remember calling for Zippo – and calling for Ma too. But there was nobody there, except the midwife, and a lot of the time she wasn't either. The baby was small, too small. They knew that. So they put a little cot, a special one, in the corner of the room, ready for him – the midwife showed me, she said it was warmed, ready – waiting for him.'

Bernie's voice cracked, but she went on.

'I can see myself there, you know? It's like looking down the wrong end of a telescope and there's this creature on a bed, writhing and screaming and calling for mercy. But there never is none, is there, Eddy? Not for the likes of me. So I see myself surrounded by this dark cloud. That was waiting too – for *him*. For that poor little thing. To take him, Eddy! And I feel so alone. I want my Zippo so bad. I want it to be Zippo's baby and we're married and Ma's smiling at me, and it's all going to be OK.

'So then I'm screaming and they're telling me to push, but there's a funny look on the midwife's face, I can see it now, like she knows something I don't know. And I'm pushing and pushing because even in all that pain I just know this person is the most important thing in the world – this little one who's trying so *hard*. The weirdest thing is, even though I'm yelling fit to bust, I'm happy. Cos this is *doing* something with my life . . . that's how it seems.

'The next bit's a muddle, Eddy. I remember the big push and a kind of slithering feeling and then the world stops – in my memory – because there was a silence. You know, when I talk about it now I can *see* that silence, like a great big ball of fluffy white cotton wool. And I'm just guessing something's bad, something's wrong, when they slug me full of some drug to knock me out – and it's all black.

'Next thing I know is, I wake up in the dark, but there's a dim light in the room. Red. At first I'm dazed. I run my hands down to the bump but it's all different – smaller – and I don't understand. So I press the buzzer on the pillow and a nurse comes in. She's younger than me – I can see that because my eyes are getting used to the gloom. And I say to her, "What happened? Where's my baby?" She says, "Oh, don't you know?" I shake my head. She goes on, "You had your baby and it was a little boy and he isn't alive."

'And she sounds so *sad*. And I say, "I knew that would happen." "Did you?" she says. Then she asks if there's somebody I want her to ring, and I tell her there isn't anybody.

'Looking back, I don't know why I said I knew it would happen. Must of been a voice from deep inside of me, which knew I'd no business to expect anything good. And I lived in the black hole after that. People talk about depression, but the whole point is – nothing happens. It's like the universe has stopped, and you're just crawling through these long minutes, never washing your hair or cleaning your teeth, hardly able to put one foot in front of the other. Like a zombie. Antidepressants make you like that. What makes it worse is – I keep on reliving his birth. I try so hard to remember everything – cos it's all I got – and this picture comes to me, that in the seconds before I go under, when I'm still waiting to hear a cry, they're scooping something up in a green cloth and taking it out the door. So I cling to that little scrap of memory, because that and the scan is the only time I caught a glimpse of him . . . Oh . . . oh . . . Eddy . . . I wish I'd seen him! I wish I'd held him, given him a little cuddle, even though he was dead! Then I'd have that to remember!'

She choked. Eddy wanted to put his arms around her and weep too – but knew he had not earned the right.

'You know something, Eddy – for years after – I wondered what they did with him. But I never asked, because all the time I knew really – they just burnt him up with the rubbish. What else would you do with a dead baby? So *small* . . .'

'Did you . . . did you choose a name?' Eddy asked.

'Yes.'

There was a silence, then she said, 'I never told anybody that. But . . . he was going to be called Tom. That was his name. There – I've said it. I never said it before.'

She turned, her ravaged face alight with a mixture of relief and defiance, the grey eyes like pebbles in a stream. Eddy wanted to reach out but did not dare.

Instead he groaned, 'Oh – Bernie, didn't you tell your mother any of this? Didn't they know?'

She shook her head vigorously. 'Don't be stupid! How could I tell them?'

'It might have been better – for you.'

'I'll get to the end – not that it stops. I often think about my baby, when it'd have been his birthday. October it was, and getting hot in the city. He'd have been twelve last year, can you imagine that? I always get fed-up around then, so I light a candle for him and just sit and think.'

'What?'

'I'll tell you what – I think I gave birth to death. You know? That freaks me out. When your baby's stillborn that's what's going on. You actually give birth to death and it's a contradiction in terms, yeah? And I think how it was all my fault. So I deserved all the punishment I got. Still do.'

'No, Bernie, come on, how was it your fault?'

'Oh, I *know* it was,' she said emphatically. 'If I'd been living a *daysunt* life – just the word Ma and Pa would of used – he'd probably have lived. No argument. There's a trust there and I betrayed it. Simple as that. I was messed up inside they said.

'Anyway – I'll try to cut it short. Suze came back from Brisbane and was really good to me, and after a year the depression began to lift a bit. Maybe it was two years, I can't remember. So I was working in an art gallery then, in the shop part, and that was the best job I'd had. I was trying to clean up my act a bit. So some years go by, and then the next thing is Patrick's ringing me because Ma and Pa have been in a car accident, and they're both dead. Just like that. Clever – wasn't I – to get rid of my folks in one go, like that?'

'Anybody'd think everything was your fault,' he protested.

Her laugh was mirthless. 'Sure! It's all about punishment, Eddy! That's what Father Mullen rammed down our throats back home, so no wonder I'm such an expert! So anyway, I came back, and it was the funeral, and then Patrick, Siobhan and Lou went away again – we didn't have much to say to each other anyway – and I stayed here . . .'

She stared at the wardrobe and started to tremble. Eddy put his arm around her and she hung her head.

'When my brother and sisters had gone, that was when I moved into this room. Me and Lou cleared out all their clothes and Siobhan took them to the St Vincent de Paul. None of us wanted to sleep in here before. But when it was all over, I decided not to be afraid of their ghosts any more. I made myself sleep in their bed. And . . . that night was the worst. You ever had a dream so real it's more real than the daytime? A dream you know isn't a dream, but a kind of message? Have you?'

He shook his head. She raised hers and gazed at the dressing table, speaking rapidly in a low voice.

'I was asleep – yet I wasn't. I thought I could hear them – Ma and Pa – moving around in the kitchen. Filling the kettle like they always did. And I was scared because I was in their room and I shouldn't be. Then – my God – there was this baby crying. Cried and cried like a little animal in pain. Like a knife in my skull. I didn't know where it was coming from, but didn't want them to hear. So I got up. I was all confused.

'And then I saw it, on the bed – a bundle. I opened the bundle and there he was. All red-faced. Mouth open. Crying fit to bust. I didn't know what to do. I wanted him to stop, or else they'd come in. Because I knew he was *my* baby, and they'd go on and on about the sin of it. So I picked him up, all clumsy, and tried to cuddle him to make him stop, but he just cried all the more. The whole room was rocking to the crying – great big waves of sound, shaking the house. And I thought I was going mad. Then I . . . I . . . put him down on the bed, and I got the pillow – and I held it over him, pressing down and down, strong, till he was quiet. No more crying. His little fingers stopped twitching. He was just a doll then, with a sweet face.

'I gathered him up, covering his face with the white blanket, making him a bundle again. Swaddling bands, like in the Bible. I didn't know what to do with him. Then I saw the wardrobe and it looked like a great big coffin to me. So I took the bundle and opened the wardrobe, and laid him in the corner at the back, and closed the door and locked it. It was the only way I could bury him, see? And then I heard *their* footsteps coming along the corridor – and I don't know what happened then.'

She looked round wildly. 'And when I woke up next morning, Eddy, it was like it hadn't been a dream at all. It was real. I can't explain to you the horror of it – I haven't got the words. I was covered in sweat and lay here, sick, staring at *that*. All I could do – in the end – was tiptoe over, turn the key on him, take it out and hide it. And I knew – if the door stayed locked – he couldn't come out and nobody would guess – how guilty I was.'

Bernie's teeth started to chatter, and she clung to him, shaking. Eddy made crooning noises, as if she were a child. They sat for a long while before he said firmly, 'Listen to me, Bernadette – it was a *dream*, a nasty dream, but not *real*.'

'No,' she moaned.

'Are you listening? Are you?'

She sobbed.

'That wardrobe's as empty as when you cleared your parents' clothes.'

Hysterical now, she shook her head from side to side. 'It's not, it's not! You heard it! Him crying in the night! He's in there, and though he's all wrapped up, he's rotted in there, where I put him! It's his spirit crying, making sure I never forget! They told us the souls of the unbaptized go to limbo. What sort of bloody God dishes *that* out to a little thing never did no harm? No wonder he kept on crying!'

'Bernadette, your baby's *not* there!'

'You don't know that.'

'But I do.'

'You're wrong. I can hear him cryin' at night, and he's saying, "*Ma, Ma, why didn't you take better care of me? Why didn't you?*" Then it's like his crying fills my skull and he's rattlin' the door tryin' to get out. Cos the godforsaken person who I was *made* those old rags he's wrapped up in – rotten, you see?'

'No, Bernie. None of this is true.'

'Yes, stupid! We couldn't be separated. He was the same as me, cos he was mine. And because I was rotten but alive, so was he. He was always going to tell me it was my fault. I had a choice. But when I was living on booze and chips and fuck knows what, I was beating the both of us up good, I screwed his little system rotten. And it took him sixteen hours to fight his way out of the cesspit that was my bloody body – where so many losers had been before him – but he gave up the fight just before. You can't blame him, can you? Tell me, Eddy, why would he fight to keep breathing to be with a mother like me? Jesus, what am I sayin'? I'm *not* a bloody mother . . .'

'Yes, you are,' he said quietly. 'That's the whole point.'

'You're a bloody fool, Eddy. I never was. I wasn't made like that. Any stupid hope like that is there, right there, in its coffin. But the walkin' dead – zombies – they cry in the night, and haunt you.'

'You can escape, Bernie.'

'Bullshit! What do you know?'

He was silent.

'There you go!' she crowed, in bitter triumph.

'I was just thinking, some of the tribes, they think a baby who's born dead just goes back somehow . . .'

'Where?'

'Where it came from. To the earth, the water, the air – the whole universe. Even in every fire that's lit, since you say they cremated him. The point is – it's at peace. And in some places in Africa, they believe in a spirit child who wasn't ready to be born. So it waits for the right time, that's all. And it feels just fine about that.'

'It's waiting?'

'That's right.'

'For a different mother to go into?'

'Maybe.'

'But I don't like that.'

'Perhaps it's not for you to like or not to like,' he said gently, laying a hand on her arm, 'because it's only the little spirit that matters, Bernie. Whether it's going to be happy.'

'But *where* is it?' she wailed.

'I don't know. So let's say – everywhere.'

'Not there?' she asked in a small voice, pointing across the room.

Eddy stared at the wardrobe through narrowed eyes, and it was as if it began to tremble, splinter, shatter into its component parts – wood and steel, sand and silica, all falling into the red earth mouth opening in the foundations of the house to receive them. Wood and steel, sand and silica, and the small white bundle of air – all laid to rest.

'Where's the key?' he asked.

She shook her head.

'Please, Bernie. We have to get through this. I'm here. Where did you put that key?'

At last, she pointed to the dressing table, whispering that it was in one of the tiny drawers along the top. Eddy disentangled himself and rose. It took no time to find the small gilt key to Colleen Molloy's wardrobe door and hold it up to Bernie, who covered her face in her hands. Then he walked across the room, and whispered, 'Watch me.'

She closed her eyes.

'All right, Bernadette, you don't have to watch. Just listen to me. I'm putting the key in the lock now. I'm turning it. I'm pulling the door open, Bernie – OK? This is where all your clothes should be – and you know why? Because there's nothing in this wardrobe, Bernadette, nothing except your little ghost . . . and I'm letting him out. Now. *Whoosh.* I can see he's glad to be out of there, Bernie. Always wanted to be free – flying out the door – *Goodbye* . . .'

Slowly she raised her head, to see him standing by the wardrobe, smiling at her. The mirror threw a sheet of light on the wall. 'Come on! – for my sake!' he pleaded. There was something so new and tender in the wideness of his smile, she could not refuse.

Moving stiffly like an invalid, Bernie shuffled towards him. She could hardly bring herself to look into the old piece of furniture. So Eddy swept his free hand out in a theatrical gesture, embracing the orange-brown interior. In the faint breeze of his movement, the metal hangers rattled like bones. Bernie inhaled the dust of her past.

'See – it's empty. Just the old papers on the bottom. Look at them – what's the date on this? – 1963! My God – there's real history in this wardrobe, not nightmares, Bernie. So listen – do you know what we're going to do now?'

She shook her head.

'We're going to clear out the old papers, and wipe it all down, and then we're going to hang all your stuff in there and put your shoes in the bottom. It's going to be given back its purpose, Bernie.'

White-faced, she shook her head again.

'Listen – you've got a choice. You can go back to the garden and sit while I do it all. Or you can help me sort out this room for you. Maybe then – you can move on.'

She pulled a strand of hair across her face and chewed it. Her eyes flickered from the wardrobe to his face and back again. At last she said wearily, 'I'll help you, Eddy, if you can stand having me around. But I . . . I'm sorry I'm such a bloody mess.'

He held her face in both hands, then smoothed her hair.

'You know something, Bernadette Molloy?' he said. 'Some people only become truly lovable when they're fucked up.'

'So . . . does that mean you think . . . *I'm* . . .?' She shook her head in disbelief.

'For definite,' he said.

Twenty-Six

Dick Springville bared his teeth. 'What's with it, Bern? You look like you lost ten dollars and found a cent. That why you so late?'

She wondered why he couldn't see the nimbus. How could people be so stupid? Yet they deserved her understanding – the boss, the bouncer, the early-evening drinkers. Because they might never experience the grace that had been given her. Each day they'd wrinkle up their eyes to face the punishment of the sun, yet never be able to recognize the gift of light.

'Sorry, Dick. Fact is – I found a thousand dollars and had to count it.'

'Turned a couple of tricks, did you? Heh, heh . . .'

Bernie kept silent. Springing Dick squared up for the sassy retort he expected, but looked discomforted when it didn't come.

'How's the boyfriend?' he asked, watching her wipe down the bar.

'Which one?' she smiled.

'That fucking Pom – two-pot screamer can't hold his beer.'

'You gave him whisky as well, Dick. Always been such a kind bloke.'

'Yeah, yeah. Fucking pain in the arse, he was. What'd you see in him, anyway? Must be a good fuck, but I never heard the Poms were any good in that department . . .' He bared his teeth again.

'Listen, Dick, take it easy – we're not an item, OK? I already told you.' She paused, then blurted, 'Matter of fact . . .'

'What?'

She thought better of it and hugged her revelation tight. 'Nothing, Dick.'

He stared at her for a second, but kept silent. Soon the crash of heavy metal filled the room, and the voices rose to match it, as the door banged open and more people crowded in, yelling their orders. Bernie served, threw the money in the till and banged the cans on the bar. It was business as usual in the Zoo.

Yet she kept seeing Eddy's bare back, the vertebrae like pebbles in a stream, as he knelt on her bedroom floor. The soles of his feet grey with dust. Yellowing newspapers folded and shoved in the rubbish bag. A smell of pine disinfectant, and his sinews stretched to scrub.

At last he points silently and she obeys, handing him her garments one by one, to take their place in the wardrobe. Reeboks, sandals, a pair of scuffed leather boots, one pair of improbable red high heels, all lined up in the bottom. He closes the door and smiles. No need for speech. Dust shimmies in a shaft of light. His eyes are golden now, not grey. She leans against the river of his body, feeling his chin on her head. Then, very gently, he puts her away from him and continues methodically, even cleaning where her clothes had hung. Spray polish on the outside of the wardrobe – flower smell, reminding her of her mother. The room is clean at last. Eddy Carpenter has achieved the miracle.

His sweat envelops her again. She leads him to the shower, and gets in too, the deluge cascading over them both as she throws back her head, eyes closed, and feels him wash her. Blindly she reaches out and spreads the foam over him too, hearing him laugh in the rush of water, and she joins in. Then he turns off the spray and wraps her in a towel, sitting on the closed lavatory and pulling her to sit on his knee. His arms tight. A memory then, from so many years ago, when her mother would do that to each of them in turn, sitting them on her damp knee in the close steamy warmth of bath night, holding them close to the buttery smell of her, as the rain drummed down outside.

Bernie can almost taste the comfort of her own thumb in her mouth, from that time. She thinks – what if it were possible to run back shouting for forgiveness, your voice echoing down the corridors which lead back to childhood? Until at last you could enter the crimson darkness, swimming in the waters of all creation, and wait . . . wait . . . for the vast pull of the universe, drawing you out, forcing you to slither across the causeway until, at last, you heard your own vowels hang on the air. What if it were possible to be newborn once more, born into your life?

Then Eddy is taking her back to the bedroom, and laying her down on the bed. He takes the towel from her and drapes it with his on the back of the chair. Even then she thinks, everything this man does has meaning beyond its surface neatness; so may he go on giving order to my life . . . And that prayer slips into the room as they roll together, inevitably, to make love again in the sight of an old wardrobe which throws back their bodies into the fragrant air.

A middle-aged couple began to dance in the middle of the floor, their limbs moving into the memories of their youth with the synchronicity of long familiarity. Bernie watched them with affection, although she had never seen them before and wondered how they had strayed into this pub. She blessed their revolving certainties, the matching gyrations which clicked out a Morse message – that you might try to stay together, if only to dance.

A man leaned on the bar and she realized he had been talking to her. 'So that's why I'm a firm believer in a four-letter word that begins with F,' he said, waiting for just the right amount of time, before he added, 'Fate!'

'That's good,' she nodded.

'It's a Smithy original,' he said proudly, holding out a hand to her. 'Bill Smith.'

She touched his fingers briefly.

'You didn't hear a word I said, did you?' he asked, not seeming to mind.

'Sorry, mate, it's the noise in here . . .'

'I was telling you me business went bust.'

'Aw, sorry to hear that, mate.'

He looked at her sorrowfully. 'You can't sell them shade! Wouldn't you think in a town like this you could sell them shade? But – see – they just want to *hire* shade. Wouldn't you think awnings'd go well in a town like this? Beats me.'

Bernie focussed on the man. He was in his mid-forties, with stringy blonde hair worn too long out of habit, and a beige safari shirt stained with sweat. His pale eyes bulged. 'It's all been a downer,' he sighed, hunching over his whisky. 'See, I came out here nearly twenty years ago. Came from Birmingham. Needed a new start. Everything went wrong, marriage broke up, you name it. I been all over, but always had this dream that one day I'd have my own business. So I thought of . . . shade.'

He emptied his glass and held it out to her.

'Great town for dreaming, this,' she said, handing him the fresh measure.

'Too right, love,' he said sadly.

'So what's your dream now, mate?'

'To go home.'

'Why don't you, then?'

He shook his head. 'Can't afford it. Funny how you get stuck in places, isn't it?'

'Too right.'

But Eddy didn't ever get stuck, she thought. He moved on. How could you cure somebody like that of the habit of leaving? Her longing to wake up with him made her shiver. She told herself not to be a fool, because nothing in her life had ever lasted, except guilt.

'Are you doing anything after?'

'After what?'

His eyes reminded her of frogspawn they prodded as a child – the glopping mass that never, somehow, produced frogs in the numbers it had promised.

'After you've finished here. We could get together . . .?'

'In another century, mate. I'm going home to my boyfriend,' Bernie said, smiling at him with the sheer delight of using the phrase. A *friend*. A *boy*. There was no denying either of the words which sparkled in her mind.

The pale eyes slid away. 'Oh – sorry, always live in hope,' he said, apologetically, then added, 'Hope he realizes he's a lucky bloke?'

'I reckon,' she grinned.

Eddy heard John Roper's key in the lock and called from the kitchen. There was no reply. A door closed.

He went on slicing tomatoes, taking pleasure in his own speed with the knife. Jello taught him that. He smiled to remember the enormous chef at the hotel in Darwin, where he'd taken a job washing up. Jello, christened James, was a man in love with food, as his girth testified. He cursed and yelled at all the staff yet took the odd chance to teach anybody who wanted to learn his craft. In a place where the demand was for steaks and roast lamb, he experimented with the delicate flavours of lemongrass and coriander and told Eddy that one day people would wake up to the possibilities of food from Asia and the Pacific. He said that if he had his way Aussie cooking would be famous the world over.

What happened to Jello? Eddy wondered.

His thoughts turned to Bernie and all the people she must have met, whose names she would not remember. All the men . . .

Sudden jealousy made him slice carelessly. He sucked his finger, put down the knife and walked out into the hall, stopping outside John's door. It was locked. He called, then waited. At last footsteps crossed the room, and the door slowly opened. Still in his polyester work 'uniform' Roper looked hot and uncomfortable – and something else too, Eddy thought. It made him uneasy.

'Come and have a beer,' he said, 'and I'm making a salad. Got ham and cheese – OK for you?'

John Roper shook his head, then shrugged and turned back into the room. He flopped down on to the bed and lay with his hands behind his head, staring up at the ceiling. Nonplussed, Eddy didn't move for a while, then wandered into the room, which smelt of stale sweat. He stood by the bed, looking down. Then he pulled over the wooden chair and straddled it in reverse, leaning on the back.

'What's up, mate?'

'Today – that's all.'

'What happened?'

'I . . . I lost the charter job. They bloody well did me out of it. That Greg Abbott's got a down on me.'

'Why would that be?' Eddy asked.

'They're jealous! They've got an inferiority complex – that's what's wrong with them. That's why they have to sneer and call us all Poms.'

It tumbled out in a sullen rush. Eddy was torn between exasperation and the need to understand.

'Hang on a bit, mate, you're talking to one of *them* right now,' he said.

'Oh, I don't mean *you*,' John muttered.

Eddy leaned his chin on his hands, folded on the back of

210

the chair. 'No worries. Me – I'm not part of any group, so you can insult everybody, far as I'm concerned. But hey – why don't you forget about today, grab a shower and come and have a beer and some tucker? No matter what happened, you'll feel better.'

'Don't tell *her*, will you?'

'Tell her what?'

'About the charter. I don't want her to know.'

'Why?'

'I want her to like me.'

'She does like you, mate.'

'No – I mean *like* me.'

Eddy straightened. He'd had a vague suspicion that John Roper might have cherished fantasies about Bernie, yet pushed it away.

'If she *liked* you, as you put it, she wouldn't give a toss about any job, would she?'

John rolled over on his side and rested on his elbow. 'I know I could get her to like me if she'd only take the time. I always thought girls went for pilots. You know, in the war . . .'

'This isn't the war, mate. And if I were you I'd forget about trying to *make* our landlady do anything. Doomed to failure, that'd be.'

Eddy stared at the other man, knowing he should tell him the truth. Yet he held back. Boiling eyes met his. John's mouth twisted down.

'Don't call me a failure!'

'I didn't . . . I said . . . Hey, come on, you know what I said!'

'You're as bad as the rest.'

'No I'm not.'

'It wasn't my fault.'

'What?'

'Losing the charter . . . and . . . and everything.'

His face began to work, as if two great opposing forces were doing battle on his features. Eddy looked away. He saw the row of books, and the three framed photographs, and the gilt flying trophy, then said, 'Listen, mate, don't get yourself so *upset*.'

'I'm not upset, I'm angry.'

211

'Yeah, but who with?'

'Abbott – and all of them. They don't give a bloke a chance.'

'You got to make your own chances, John.'

'I did! I got myself out here and I worked and I took the course, and all that! I got the trophy in my year! How much do you have to do?'

'People aren't going to like you if they know you don't like them,' said Eddy gently.

'As far as I'm concerned there's no reason to like them – not any of them!'

'There you go again, mate.'

Eddy got up, shaking his head. The greatest test, he thought, is whether you can go on trying to like those who give you so little reason.

'Take a shower, mate. Cool down,' he said.

'Easy to say.'

Eddy shrugged, and jerked a thumb in the direction of the kitchen. 'Like I said, I'm mixing up a great salad. See you later.'

As Eddy reached the door, John called out, 'Anyway – Bernie does like me, oh yes, and I can prove it!'

Taken aback by his tone, Eddy asked how.

'She asked me to spend the night with her – that's how.'

'When?'

'Christmas night. You'd gone to bed. She came in here and asked me if she could sleep with me.'

'No kidding?'

'Abso–bloody–lutely affirmative, old man. So that's how I know.'

'Turn her down, did you, John?'

'I said it was too soon, you know?'

Eddy stood still, allowing the silence to lengthen. His eyes locked on John's, unwavering, until at last the Englishman dropped his gaze. Eddy could not understand why he could still look on this man with pity for his posturing. An image flashed into his mind of his father standing just so in the study, panting with the effort of trying to justify himself yet knowing it was impossible. So often on the road he had remembered Vern-the-bastard with rage and contempt. Now he saw him as weak, just like John Roper.

'She didn't ask you to sleep with her, John,' he said quietly. 'I know it and you know it. The best thing would be if you never mention that idea again, OK? There's things I'd explain to you . . . but not now.'

'What things?'

Eddy hesitated. But he could not bring himself to tell the truth. There was such a gulf between what he and Bernie had exchanged and this man's fervid fantasies that he could not bear to sully it with words doomed to be misconstrued.

'Nothing,' he said.

When Bernie came home from work, her two lodgers were watching a television debate on the dingo baby case. The audience grew heated. A vet was explaining about the animal's jawbone and its relative strength. She stood in silence by the door, meeting Eddy's eyes and trying to fathom the message she read there.

'If you want to go on watching this, I'm away to bed,' she announced. 'I can't stand thinking about it.'

Eaten by a wild creature . . . bury it, oh bury it.

Eddy understood. He crossed the room in two strides and snapped the set off. Then he stood looking at her, registering her anxiety.

John was gaping at her. She looked beautiful to them both, in jeans and a white T-shirt, hair damp on her forehead and shadows under her eyes.

'Thanks,' she said to Eddy, and smiled.

'Had a good night?' John asked.

'Best night, best day – ever.'

'It's all right for some,' said John.

'All right for the whole world, from where I'm standing,' said Bernie. Her smile washed over Eddy, so it took all his will power to stop himself embracing her. There was a short silence.

'Did you tell him our news?' she challenged Eddy.

He shook his head, and rolled his eyes in warning.

'What news?' John asked, suspicion flushing his cheeks.

Bernie said, 'Come here,' holding out a hand, and Eddy knew there was no alternative but to stand beside her. She took his hand.

'Look, John, I don't want you to feel bad, but I can't creep around my own house like some kid. Me and Eddy – well, we've kind of . . . got together, haven't we?' She turned to

213

him, seeking reassurance. He nodded, eyes fixed on her because he was unable to meet the other man's. Bernie shrugged. 'These things happen, you know? You . . . er . . . can't control it.'

Much later, when it had all ended, she would think back to that moment and close her eyes in the effort of remembering. She would try to conjure up John Roper's face, but could only imagine a pink balloon bobbing in the debris after a party.

Twenty-Seven

Over the next two weeks Eddy helped to sow the seed which would form greens where iron would click against ball. One day he witnessed another protest against the flattening of a sacred site, and heard the mockery and abuse from his fellow workers, without saying anything. Realizing that the shift of one letter turns 'sacred' into 'scared', he wondered what it would be like to bury cowardice and shout, 'No, they're not blacks, they're not coons, they're not boongs, they're not wogs – you bastards – they're people, and a small part of *me* is part of *them*!'

Instead he watched in silence as the four ragged men plodded away, heads bent, unable to prevent the digger resuming its work. When a wooden hut, used to store tools, was mysteriously damaged in the night and the contents stolen, he knew who would be blamed. Perhaps they were guilty, perhaps not. He volunteered to mend the hut and wondered whom he was betraying.

Bernie served drinks in a dream, watching benignly as the fights threatened, so that sometimes the toughs paused, troubled by the peace in her eyes, and drifted off in separate directions, the cause of conflict forgotten. Oblivious to innuendo and conjecture, she went through the motions of her job, sustained by the time when she would join Eddy in the little bungalow in Dean Street, and he would help her wash away the beer and sweat, and lie down with her in the room that smelt of flowers. In the morning, amazed by the sweetness of his face, she would cling to him to prevent him from rising for work, then fall back into a sleep undisturbed by dreams of loss. Waking at last in the empty house, she would rise to stand in front of her mother's wardrobe, opening the door of it with awe to see her clothes hanging there like fragments of her soul, brightly coloured and in order.

Sometimes at night one of them would wake and listen to the other's breathing, reaching out a hand to touch. Inevitably they would think of the third person under that roof, and usually wish him gone. Yet Eddy stopped Bernie from giving John Roper notice. He heard her grumble that they'd be able to walk around naked without him, they'd have a chance to have fun, that to see his glowering face depressed her. But she agreed that she too felt sorry for the Pom – and where else would he go?

When she was working, Eddy tried hard to make amends. He knocked at the locked door, offering food and company, knowing he would be rebuffed. But one night, when he knocked and invited John to help him feed the crow, he was surprised when the door opened.

They stood in front of the cage as the tangerine sun hung low, and John held out flesh for the creature to snatch. It was dustier than ever; its eyes suspiciously filmed, no trace of blue in its feathers. When it scrabbled from side to side it looked, for a second, as if it might lose its balance.

'Maybe a bit crook,' Eddy said.

'No wonder.' John's voice was bleak.

'Yeah.'

'You'd be doing it a favour to put it out of its misery.'

'Not yet, mate.'

'*Krrrrrrark, krrrrrrawk.*'

'*She* wouldn't care.'

Eddy suppressed irritation. 'You don't know that, John. Look – we might as well have this out . . .'

'Don't bother.'

'. . . because I know I should have told you, that night, but because it was all so new I didn't like to.'

'I'd rather not talk about it.'

'OK, but I want you to know that me and Bernie . . .'

215

'I can just hear you both – laughing at me!'

John shoved a piece of meat through the bars, and as if to answer his mood the crow snatched at it, pecking his finger. He left it there, inviting a further attack. Gently, Eddy took his arm and pulled the hand back from the cage.

'Shhh,' he crooned, as if to a child. 'Nobody here laughs at you, mate. You got that wrong. Don't put yourself down.'

'Only place to go,' John muttered, his eyes fixed on the bird.

'Come on, John – have a beer with me.'

'You're all the same. You think a bally beer's a miracle cure. Like saying "no worries". It's all a lot of drivel, as far as I'm concerned.'

'Sure it is – whatever you say.'

'Someone will get it in the neck,' said John, in a curious, flat voice.

'Come again?'

The other man laughed suddenly. 'Get my jolly old kite out, Flight Sergeant – it's time for a joyride!'

Eddy pursed his lips. He half expected to see Roper stick his arms out rigidly each side, and run down the garden path, a little boy pretending to be a plane. His instinct was to hold his hands, to catch him before he tripped.

Instead, he clapped him on the shoulder, and returned the laugh. 'OK, old chap – wilco. Now, you come along to the mess, and we'll get ourselves a bite to eat.'

He was rewarded by a twisted smile, which worried him most of all.

Each day John Roper also went through the motions at work. You couldn't reach the clouds, he thought. They were massing above, just hanging there, threatening. He fancied that to ascend to them might bring relief: swirling mist, moisture trickling over the wings and making a delta of the screen. But no, this cloud was like the grey blankets he remembered from childhood, cream stitching around the edges, heavy on the bed, when Nan tucked him in so tightly to stop the bad dreams finding a chink to enter. Comfort in that weight, but none here. No chink above for dreams to punch through. Hot weight on his head, so he could hardly breathe. Almost impossible for the Cessna to rise, with all that above, pressing it to earth. And the currents bouncing up, tossing him sideways.

John glanced down at the map on his knee then out at the land beneath. It was all the same. The orange ugliness stretched to infinity, shrivelling the soul of anyone who dared gaze at it. But there was no choice. He was forced to find the way. The patterns of the map merged with the patterns of the land, and sweat trickled into his eyes. Hot metal corroded his nostrils. The noise crashed about him, reverberating through his spine.

It seemed hours before he dropped to Brookfield Station. As he neared the ground, John was aware of the massive figure of Dave Brookfield standing at a distance near the stockmen's compound, talking to one of the workers. In sudden panic he miscalculated, overshot – and the Cessna just clipped the oil-drum steer with the target eyes, sending it crashing. He heard a cry of rage, and saw Brookfield striding over.

'What the fuck you think you're doing – playing dodgem cars?' he yelled.

John clambered down. Immediately there was a buzzing all around his head.

The usual ragged crowd of women and children material-ized from nowhere and surrounded the boss, some grinning, but most staring at him blankly, faces crawling with flies. Yet he'd done nothing to them, he thought. So why did they look at him like that?

They whispered in their own language. Somebody laughed.

'Listen, mate, the thing's been there since Dad made it, and no bugger's touched it till now. Book in for some flying lessons, why don't you?'

'I said sorry.'

'You sure as hell don't sound it!'

John ran his tongue around his lips. No moisture came from inside him, but when he reached up to smooth his moustache it was sodden with sweat. He touched a fly too, and his stomach lurched. He thought the watching faces dissolved for a second, melting into the air, before rematerializing in a different forma-tion to confuse him. The pewter sky glimmered dully. Dave Brookfield's eyes were diamond chips.

'There's a parcel,' John mumbled, flapping the flies away.

He leaned against the Cessna for a second. The metal was intolerably hot.

He could smell plastic and paper, cooking gently inside – so many letters, so many words bringing news and love to the people on the far-flung farms. Lots of late Christmas cards and parcels still, many from the UK. Brown paper bills that made them groan. Silly postcards. He'd seen them all, delivered them all to the people who watched for the little Cessna but didn't care who piloted it. Except – he remembered how at first they all talked of Al, the one who'd shot through with somebody else's woman, the one they liked because he was big, handsome, easygoing. One of *them*. In John's mind his predecessor merged with Greg Abbott and Dave Brookfield as the type of bluff, rangy Australian manhood he hated most.

Days later Brookfield would tell people the man looked as if he'd faint. 'A bloke didn't know what to do.' Then the Pom straightened up, stroked his moustache and announced, 'The daylight raids on Bremen – sheer suicide missions – but what the deuce could they do?' in a clipped voice.

Dave Brookfield stared, and at that moment Evie arrived at his elbow, looking puzzled. She turned her head from one to the other, and frowned.

'You OK, John?' she asked. 'You look a bit . . . You want a cup of tea?'

'No, I'd like some water – please,' he croaked.

Brookfield snorted with disgust and turned his massive sweat-stained back, stomping off, followed by his men.

John retrieved the Brookfield package and mail from behind his seat, and held it all out to her. He noticed how the faded chambray of her shorts and sleeveless blouse matched her eyes, and how her ponytail swung from side to side with the rhythm of her bottom, legs, shoulders, as she walked with long strides, just ahead of him, towards the house. When they reached the verandah she stopped, and gestured towards one of the rattan chairs. 'Why don't you sit down there, and I'll bring you the water?'

John realized she didn't want him to come inside. He could hear the radio playing a song he'd heard at Bernie's, 'Stay Young' by INXS.

'I bet *you'll* stay young forever,' he said.

'I 'preciate your flattery, mate, but we're all bound for the boneyard sooner or later,' she replied, coolly.

Left alone, John slumped into a chair. He could hear the high-pitched laughter of aboriginal children, punctuated by yapping dogs. Above and beyond that noise the air hummed

– not the testy small irritant of flies around his ears and eyes, not the distant rumble of the Brookfields' generator, but a deeper, more resonant sound from up in the clouds.

'Squadron's on its way back,' he announced.

Looking up, staring fixedly at the sky, he was convinced he saw the black dots appear in formation before his eyes, and tried to count, to make sure they were all there.

Then long brown legs were standing next to him, and a hand thrust a tall glass of iced water before his face, flapping the distant planes away with the other.

'Bloody flies,' she said.

She did not sit down, but lounged in silence against one of the wooden posts, waiting for him to drink his water. Behind her the outback smouldered. She glanced over in the direction of the children's noise, and smiled. That smile excluded him, he knew that. She glanced at her watch. Wanted him gone. The humming began again in John's head, and he wanted to cry out to her to speak to him, to say anything, to drive it away. He gulped so hard the cold hurt his throat.

'Better?' she asked with apparent kindness, so that suddenly he wanted to weep thanks for that small mercy.

'Thank you.'

'No worries.'

He sat still. At last Evie moved towards the steps that led down into the red dirt. 'Well, I got to go and check the kids in the schoolroom. They probably bust the transmitter by now. Any case, you'll be wanting to crack on . . .?'

He stood.

'Might I . . . do you think . . .?'

She sighed.

John headed down the corridor to the toilet and studied the photographs on the pinboard again. Slowly he touched each of the snaps of Evie, letting his finger rest tenderly on the paper.

There was no liquid in him; the sun had evaporated it, as it shrivelled your flesh, sucked the air from your lungs and tightened a burning band around your temples. He turned on a tap, then jerked the handle, so water cascaded into the bowl. The sound was sweet, making him close his eyes for a second. Then he patted cold water all over his face, and turned back to the pinboard.

Her bikini was patterned with blue flowers. He noticed again the way the naked infant's legs wrapped around her waist, so that you could almost feel the warm, soft stickiness of flesh meeting flesh. John stroked the photograph, then carefully hooked his fingernails around the drawing pins that held it, prising them out. He held it in his hand for a second, as he contemplated a picture of Evie Brookfield's husband on his own, tough and debonair, the Akubra pushed back on his head.

Twenty-Eight

At the same time, John Roper's grandmother is wishing there was a downstairs toilet. She stands on the top step. Weight hangs about her. The banister creaks.

Carefully moving her left foot to catch up with the right, both feet placed on each step, before attempting the next one. Halfway down. The wind rattles the letter box. Rain lashing the windows, and making the old roof creak.

The house needs work done on it, but they don't bother, the corporation, they don't care. Poor old Hilda complains of the damp and this place isn't much better.

She told the doctor it was a waste of time to write a letter, because it probably went straight in the bin. Dr Attra didn't agree, of course, but then, she's foreign so she wouldn't know how we do things over here. Or don't do them. If John was here he'd sort them out.

Lily stops, and breathes shallowly. Maybe she should have a commode downstairs, but then there'd be the bother of carrying it up to flush. Hold on to the rail with both hands. Draw strength from the old wood.

One foot, then the other, pause; one foot then the other, pause . . .

Tiny bits of plaster fall in flakes.

About five steps from the bottom, moving more quickly now, left foot too eager, Lily sways for a second, then loses her balance and pitches forward, to land with a crash at the foot of the staircase. Rain is already seeping under the door and turning the coconut mat darker brown. The instant before she lands she puts out both hands in an instinctive bid to break her fall, and believes the crack she hears must be the banister pulling itself out of the wall at last.

Shock and pain plunge her into darkness, but the wind knifing under the front door and through the rattling letter box summons her back. She's lying on her side, with her back wedged against the door. Cold. Her teeth are chattering, hands and feet numb. She can't move yet knows she must. There's a nice fire in the living room. A nice fire always makes you feel better.

Trying to heave herself into a sitting position, Lily discovers her right hand will not work. Flames bracelet her wrist. She stares down, and the universe speeds up, because as she watches she can see her wrist and hand growing, as if inflated by some invisible pump. Maybe I'll float away, Lily thinks, puff up and up, fatter and fatter, lighter and lighter, and float up to the sky in the end. Blow away. Over the rooftops . . .

Look at me, John! I'm flying!

But how would you get out through the roof? That's the trouble. There's no escaping, no matter how you dream. And anyway, the sky's grey and rainy, the wind so cold. It's different out there where he is, where the sky's always blue and the earth so red, and they eat lamb chops for breakfast. You'd *want* to fly up into that blue.

Lily rolls and pulls herself so her weight is on her left elbow. Then she moves it forward a few inches, dragging her bulk behind. She pushes with her feet to give her momentum.

Oh dear God, oh John, please help me.

An hour later, inch by inch along the hall floor, she reaches the living-room door. Sometimes she stops to lay her head down, panting, heart banging to demand release from its cage. At last she can see the fire. Good job she'd built it up, because it's flickering merrily there in her eye-line, between the settee and the armchair. The brasses are bright. She still cleans them once a week, as she always did. You have to keep up standards.

Even now, brain folding up within her skull, Lily Roper can take pleasure in seeing the gleaming companion set, and the square scuttle embossed with a lady in a crinoline to match the ones on top of the poker, shovel and brush, and the three horse brasses hung each side of the mantelpiece. She can see the clock in the middle, showing half past ten. She fixes her eyes on the model planes each side of the clock, each facing into the middle on its perspex stand. John always laughed at her for never remembering their names.

That was like Jimmy the foreman. A laugh a minute, all the other girls said, but you wouldn't trust him as far as you could throw him – you know what these Glaswegians are like.

Jimmy told jokes all right, and made her blush.

'Come here now – what's a wee mouse and a big Scotsman got in common? You dinna know? They both like their wee hole.'

From here Lily can watch the flames. She lies on the threshold, unable to find the strength to move further into the room, one foot left behind in the draughty hall.

Times passes. Lily's eyes are closed, lulled by the gentle tick of her clock, but as it strikes the hour – and again, and again – she opens them to blink at her room. The coals glow and shift in the grate. She's suddenly ashamed of the dust under the settee, and not just there, either. Who'd have thought there'd be so much dust? She only vacuumed yesterday, so where has it come from? It films the whole room, like ash falling. The wind must be carrying it from the whitening fire. And the brasses need a good clean – she thought they were bright but they're not any more.

Oh John, look at the state of the place.

Lily Roper's room slowly darkens. The eye of the last coal goes out.

John Roper outraced the clouds, flying through fire, to land at last by the molten tower of Abbott-Air. As he swung to the ground, he could feel them looking. There were eyes at every window, glittering in the afternoon sun. They wouldn't offer to help, would they? Watching him reach into the back, take out the bags, fold them, and all the time the sweat boiling on him. They should have known he couldn't bear it. But nobody came out to help. His eyes hurt.

When he shouldered the door open, his arms full, he was aware of feet pattering above him, echoing in the stairwell.

'John!' Hazel called. 'You have to come upstairs. He . . . I mean Greg . . . he wants to see you right away.'

'Let me do something with all this stuff first.'

222

'He said right away, John.'

Hazel Cartwright had heard Greg on the telephone, angrier than she had ever known. Her boss never lost his temper, he was too laid back, too ready to give the world fair goes. That's what Hazel told her friends, but today was different and she felt afraid.

John Roper followed her up the three flights. Office doors were open. He could hear low laughter murmuring from those bright spaces, though no heads popped out to grimace in his direction. But he knew they were there, behind the doors. They were always there.

Hazel slipped into her chair, and rested her hands on the keyboard for reassurance. Her spiral notebook was on the left, the growing pile of Greg's letters on the right. The single frangipani stem in a tumbler matched the colours of her cotton dress. She looked down as John passed, whispering that he should go straight through. Then, ashamed of her own cowardice, she looked up again and watched his back as he moved stiffly towards Greg's half-closed door. His shirt was completely sodden; pink skin showed through in patches where it stuck, like scales.

John didn't close the door behind him, nor did Greg Abbott ask him to. And so, like it or not, Hazel Cartwright was a witness to what happened.

'Sit down, Roper,' said Greg Abbott, curtly.

'I'd rather stand if you don't mind. I've been flying . . .'

'Suit yourself. I'd just rather a bloke had a seat when he's about to hear something he's not going to like.'

John Roper stood in silence, his eyes glassy. Greg turned a biro over and over in his fingers, like a propeller.

'Today's just the icing on the cake,' he said, leaning back in his chair.

'I'm sorry?'

'I've had Dave Brookfield on the phone, and I tell you, I've known the bloke for years and I've never heard him go through the roof like that.'

John said nothing.

'Why'd you do it?'

'If you're talking about clipping that oil-can sign they've got there, I told him, anybody can make an error. A small misjudgment, that's all.'

'Small misjudgment?'

'Affirmative.'

Greg Abbott threw the biro across his desk.

'Listen, Roper, you made a big misjudgment – *very* big – when you started messing about with the Brookfields' pictures.'

'I don't know what you mean.'

John glared. It was typical, he thought, that somebody was trying to get him into trouble, and Abbott was more than ready to hear it. They were all the same. They always got in a gang, like the boys at home.

'You know bloody well what I mean! I'm sitting here trying to run this company, and I get Dave on the phone – tells me Evie's upset because she goes to the toilet and sees there's a picture of her gone missing from the notice board they've got in there. You seen that notice board?'

'Can't say I remember.'

'Bloody hell, mate, every time you go there you ask if you can have a comfort stop, so either you're blind or else you've seen the inside of their downstairs toilet! So don't give me that. Anyway, today you were the last in there and Evie finds there's this snap of her with little Tony been taken off the board – it's a personal shot of her in a bikini too, Dave says, and I tell you, to hear him you wouldn't want to go anywhere near that station if you were the bloke stole his wife's picture in a bikini! My God! To make matters worse, there's been a drawing pin stuck into *his* picture that was next to it, stabbing holes in the eyes! Now, who could have done that?'

'I don't know what you're talking about,' John said.

'You've no idea?'

'Affirmative.'

Greg Abbott whirled his chair round in frustration and stared down at the runway, where the Cessna was turning apricot as the sun dropped.

Hazel heard the silence. Not daring to type, she stared down at the hieroglyphics on her pad, knowing there was worse to come.

'Sit down, for God's sake,' Greg said, swinging round. John obeyed, and for a few seconds Greg stared at his employee, wondering what weird brain processes had frozen that sunburnt face into such a mask. 'Anyway,' he continued, 'there's the other matter, the one you didn't tell us about when you came here. I've been doing some checking up.'

John hunched in the chair.

'You didn't think it important to mention you'd had a conviction?'

'What conviction?' John's face was blank.

Greg looked down at the notes on his pad, and sighed. 'You aren't making this very easy for either of us, Roper. You'd been about two months in this country and you must have been desperate to get home, and so you tried to alter an airline ticket, from Sydney to London. You remember that?'

He saw John's face flush an even darker red.

'They spotted the alteration and the police were called. You were ten days in custody and then they convicted you of false pretences and fined you a hundred dollars. After that you moved to Melbourne and drove the trams. You had a couple of crashes, I'm told, and people complained you drove like a kamikaze. You saved up and went to Cessnock – at least that part's true. When you came here you should have been security checked right away, but because of Ace's heart attack and the management changes, things weren't up to scratch.'

'But now they are, I assume,' Roper said, his mouth twisting. 'Too right!'

Greg Abbott had learned to control his temper on the rugby field. Now too, his studies in psychology and management came to his aid. He reached for the biro and turned it into a propeller again, staring down thoughtfully. At last he said, 'What beats me, Roper, is how you thought you'd get away with stealing that photo, like a perv or something.'

'Ah – it's back to that, is it?' said John harshly.

'Yes, it is. You did take it, didn't you?'

'No.'

Greg sighed. 'OK, so you didn't knock the Brookfields' sign over and you didn't mess about with their pictures, and nobody's ever complained about your flying or your attitude, and you didn't have any accidents on the trams, and you didn't have that conviction I found out about two hours ago. So all this is somebody else's fault – but it won't work, Roper! And I don't get it. I'm wondering why you let it all go so wrong – when you did well at Cessnock. I checked. You did get the trophy. There's no taking that away from you, is there?'

Greg Abbott turned away from the struggle within Roper's features, because, despite himself, he felt pity for the man. Gazing over the runway he murmured, 'I suppose the damage was done right at the beginning with that ticket. I don't suppose you thought too much about it, and – mind you – it wouldn't stop you flying in some places. But here we have to get clearance because of the RAF at Darwin, you see? That's why.' He knew he was almost apologizing, anything to make it slightly better. 'So – the ticket business. You wanted to go home, yeah? You must have been homesick, yeah?'

'What would *you* know?'

Greg heard the resentment and tensed. He laid the biro down carefully, parallel with his father's old leather blotter. There was no point in prolonging this, he thought.

'All I do know is – you can't go on working for Abbott-Air,' he said flatly. 'As from today, that's it. You're fired. That clear enough for you?'

Then the man was looming at him over the desk, as he leaned both hands on the edge, and opened his mouth as if to speak. Greg did not flinch but waited, noticing how the veins stood out in the shining, scarlet forehead.

'Hazel will give you all the paperwork,' he said coldly.

John Roper knocked over the chair. At the door he turned and glared at Greg.

'Over and out,' he said.

Twenty-Nine

Eddy instructed her to take the whole weekend off, no matter what Dick Springville said. When she asked why, he laid a finger across his lips and smiled.

'It's a surprise,' he said.

Springing Dick growled that there were plenty of good-looking women in the town looking for bar work, including Joan's daughter Leanne, who was tired of Abbott-Air. Bernie agreed that somebody as young and sexy as Leanne would bring in more punters on a Saturday night. He looked puzzled.

'You tryin' to make out you might jack the job in?' he asked. Bernie shrugged.

'All I'm saying is, I want the weekend off because my boyfriend's planned something.'

'You in *love*, Bern?' he asked, mocking, yet suddenly interested too.

'I reckon!' she replied, enjoying the astonishment on his grizzled face.

Eddy borrowed her car on Friday morning, because he had to collect things, he said. All day she wandered from house to garden, unable to settle. It was like being a child, she thought, back home, when we went on a school trip to Cork, to visit the cathedral.

Bernie fed the crow, watched it for a while, then went back into the house. She opened the door of the room Eddy never slept in now, and saw he'd packed a small roll bag and left it by the door, next to his swag, and the yidaki in its woven cover. He never played, despite her pleadings for a burst of 'didge'. He said it reminded him of his time in Arnhemland, and somehow the sound of it always made him want to move on. It pulled him, he told her, like an echo inside his skull.

'Don't play it then!' she thought.

She experienced a shock of fear at seeing the bag and the the instrument seemingly laid ready for departure, but it was dispelled when she noticed the rest of his stuff – a small amount admittedly – was still all over the room, and the rucksack empty behind the door.

Restless, she moved to John Roper's room and tried the door. Each morning they heard him turn the key when he left.

'What's he got to hide, for Christ's sake?' Bernie asked, more than once.

'Nothing – he's just a funny, private bloke, that's all,' Eddy shrugged.

He was far more concerned by the Englishman's state of mind than she was. 'I think he's getting sick,' he said one night.

'We're not his keepers,' she replied.

Eddy arrived home earlier than usual, and came to find her in the garden. He asked what she was reading, and she turned over the battered volume so he could see the title.

227

'*Irish Fairy Tales*?'

'Ma kept all our old books,' she said.

'But you said you didn't read!'

'I used to. When I was a kid. Maybe I'll take it up again.'

'Everybody needs fairy tales,' he nodded.

'So, you reckon it's true – that they lived happily ever after?'

'In real life? Never. Not in a million years. But that's why people need fairy stories – yarns that tell them about over the rainbow where the bluebirds fly!'

'Or your dreamtime stuff – what's the difference?' she asked, disappointed.

'Not much, I reckon. People need explanations.'

'It's all up for grabs,' she said, waving her book at him. 'I think we should all take over each other's stories as much as we like. People might understand each other a lot more – you know? You could try these. I reckon you're like one of the little people yourself!'

She jumped up and threw her arms around him. They laughed, and then he held her at a distance and asked if she was ready.

'I'm taking you camping, Bernie.'

'*Camping!*' she cried. 'Oh my God!'

'It's about time you did something different,' he smiled.

'Am I going to like this?' she asked, and he nodded.

Eddy was anxious that John hadn't returned at his usual time. He said he felt guilty at leaving him alone for the weekend, but when she tutted in disbelief he looked up with complete seriousness.

'Look, I know you say he's not your problem, but he lives here – and we're the only people he's got. I was going to tell him we'll be back on Sunday and suggest we all go to the Steakhouse that night. Give him something to look forward to.'

'You're a good guy, Eddy.'

'I'll leave him a note, so he knows. He's got to feed the crow anyway. I wish he'd got back so I could say it all to his face . . .'

'Then you'd probably feel even worse about going, y'old softie!' she said.

* * *

They headed west, the Holden rattling and bouncing when they left the bitumen at last. Orange light bounced around them; the sky was turquoise, purple and gold. When she asked where they were heading, Eddy shook his head.

'You're right,' she breathed. 'I don't care. We could just drive now until we drop off the edge of the world.'

It was almost two hours later when he slowed, studied the landscape, trundled on for a while, then turned the wheel, rattling the car over sand, stone and scrub. He braked by a clump of river red gums.

'This'll do,' he said.

'Where are we?'

'Doesn't matter, does it? We'll spend the night here. Collect wood for a fire . . . go on, that's your job while I unload stuff.'

She stared at him.

'Me – collect wood?'

'Yeah, lots of small twigs is good to start. Then some bigger stuff for when it's got going.'

Bernie looked around. Sand and scrub stretched for miles, broken by mulga and eucalpyts in clumps of two and three, trunks mottled and blotched in tones of brown, grey, cream and apricot. She slipped out of her thongs and scrunched sand between her toes.

'This is a dried creek,' Eddy explained, going to the back of the Holden. 'That's why the sand's different here to the earth just over there.'

A short walk away, two low peaks broke the monotony of the landscape. One was little more than a hillock, the other higher and sharper, the two joined by an arabesque sweep of rock, making them one. The rocks were the colour of ripening peaches. The sky behind them glowed purple and red. Bernie heard the eerie buzz of nightfall, a low collective scuttling and shifting all around them. Dreamily she wandered off, bending now and then to pick up a twig, forced at last to pull out her baggy T-shirt to make a cradle for her growing collection.

She turned back to discover that Eddy had already created a small oasis of domesticity in the sand. Her eyes travelled over the two huge eskies, the cardboard box containing a jumble of pans and plates, the blue plastic water carrier, the billycan that reflected the low light, the big rubber torch.

'Where's the tent?' she asked.

His laughter bounced back off the hills. 'Tent? You don't need a tent out here!'

'So where do we sleep?'

Eddy shook his head, and took her arm in mock-solicitude. 'How many years you lived in this country? You never heard of people sleeping in the bush in swags?'

Bernie looked unconvinced. ''Course I heard of it, I just never done it! Never fancied the creepie-crawlies running everywhere.'

'Well, if I introduce you to some, maybe you'll get to know them.'

He fetched his tarpaulin bedroll and set it out, returning to the car to pull out an improvised version, made from a section of tarp enclosing a foam-rubber strip, with a sleeping-bag liner and an old cotton blanket. She watched as he laid this out next to his swag, with pillows from her bed at home. He began to arrange the twigs in a pyramid, and set a match to them at last, crouching to blow the flame into life.

She sat down on her 'bed', and cackled with pleasure. He checked the lengthening flames, then looked over his shoulder with a grin.

'What's so funny?'

'Your bum in the air! Pointy as a pixie's hat!'

'How would you know?'

'Because I'm Oirish, darlin', and we got a direct line to the little people – I told you!'

He sat down and put his arm around her. 'OK, magic Molloy, see if you can read my mind and guess what we got to eat tonight.'

'Er . . . let's think . . . chicken legs and spuds!'

'My God, the woman really does have supernatural powers!'

She swiped at him, but he caught her arm and held it in the air, tickling her with his free hand. She shrieked and begged for mercy, promising him anything if he'd only stop.

The fire crackled. With a loud pop, Eddy opened a bottle of blush, which they drank from plastic wine glasses. He wrapped small potatoes and chicken joints in tin foil and laid the parcels on the fire, then lit a couple of candles which he stuck in the sand each side of the teacloth he'd unfolded with a flourish. Two plastic plates, knives and forks, a box of salad, a bag of tomatoes, bread rolls, a bottle of French dressing – and all the while Bernie watching in silence, and disbelief.

Glasses refilled, they talked of their childhoods. She told him of playing games in the rain, the water streaming, earth-brown, along the side of the lane. He told her about lightning which split the sky, when he would sit by the sliding doors on to the patio, and try to estimate the distance of the storm.

She remembered Da and Ma taking them for a picnic to the stone circle, on a summer day when gulls wheeled and you could hardly tell the difference between sky and sea, the coastline jewelled with islands. She'd lain down on the recumbent stone at Drombeg and imagined the sun striking her, warming her forever – but Patrick jeered she'd be made a sacrifice, they'd carve her up very slowly and lift out her heart and her guts to make the gods happy. She'd cried then, and gone to find Ma. But the turf was bouncy under their feet when they walked back to the van, and there was nothing like an ice cream to solve problems.

'Dad used to say that, when I was little,' Eddy said.

They ate for a while in silence. Then Eddy put the billy to boil and she asked, 'Do you think you'll ever see him again?'

'One day. But I'm not in a hurry. Funnily enough, it's Pam I think about more. She was always a good mother, even though she wasn't really my mum. You can't blame her for not wanting me to know the truth. People never want to rock the boat, do they?' Bernie shook her head. 'Anyway, I bet half the blokes I was at school with are travelling round the world or settled overseas by now. So what's the difference?'

'Unfinished business, Eddy.'

'Yeah, but that's the story of my life. Never *finishing* anything.'

Eddy rose and disappeared into the darkness, returning almost immediately with a short log. A shower of sparks rose into the air. His face flared, set into an expression she could not read.

'Come back,' she pleaded, patting the space beside her.

'I reckon it's time for bed.'

'I need to pee.'

He bent and picked up the flashlight, holding it out with a smile. 'There you are. You won't be seen.'

'Come with me.'

'Why? You scared of the dark?' She nodded. 'What? I don't believe it. You're not scared of those animals in the Zoo, yet you're scared of the dark out here. What is it – scorpions?'

'No – just ghosts. All those spirits. They're everywhere, aren't they?'

'Oh yeah, but *they* don't do any damage.'

She held out a hand and he moved to take it, looking into her eyes for a long time, before he said, 'Let's take our clothes off.'

'All of them?'

'Nobody here to see.'

Bernie felt embarrassed, but did as she was told. This is beyond sex, she thought, surveying his slender limbs, the ochre glimmer of his skin in the firelight.

'You're beautiful,' he said.

'Oh – but you are too,' she whispered.

When they moved, hand in hand, away from the firelight, Bernie looked up for the first time and noticed the stars, so many, as if somebody had poured Christmas sparkle down the length of the sky. She sighed, pointing straight up.

'The Southern Cross,' he explained.

'Can't believe it's so beautiful.'

'That's why you have to believe it,' he said. 'You might not know about God, but there's no arguing with the stars.'

Suddenly she giggled. 'What do you think God thinks of us wandering about here, butt naked?'

'He recognizes the Garden of Eden all over again, of course!'

'Yes, Ed – and by the way, I can see the serpent all right!' She chuckled and pointed at his nakedness. 'But he don't look very threatening to me!'

'No sin in this garden,' Eddy smiled, and when he took her in his arms she felt his innocence loose against her. Resting her head on his chest, she wondered if she dared tell him what she felt.

They lay side by side, locked hands resting on the sand between their beds. Bernie was tense, convinced that nameless, repulsive creatures would drop down from the trees on her face, or that a snake would slither over her in the night. But she did not say so. She knew that she had been permitted to enter Eddy's world. He was at ease here, and she must try to be the same.

Long after she heard Eddy's breathing deepen, and felt his

hand loosen in hers, Bernie remained awake. She let the coarse grains trickle between her fingers, and remembered how, as a child, she would barely dare to breathe in the thick darkness of her room, where the curtains rustled and the old wood creaked – in case the nightmares would discover she was actually there, and punish her. But here? The stars jostled for position in the inky sky.

Thirty

'*Can you hear me, Lilian?*'
It isn't Lilian, it's just Lily. People call me Lily. Lily flower, somebody said once, you want to be my wee lily flower? That's because he wanted . . . But I was never like a flower.

'*Lilian? If you can hear me, just move your hand, love – all right? That's a good girl.*'
Girl?

When I was a girl they all said . . . they all said I was pugugly. Fat face like the back of a bus, that boy said in the Odeon when we were watching *Now Voyager*. Norma and Doris said they were awful, but they still had a laugh. And the boys laughed back, and I know they met them after, when they'd got rid of me. I used to rub Nivea into my face hoping for a miracle, but it never happened.

'*Lilian, now i know you're listening i can tell you what's happening – all right? Your friend found you and called the ambulance, but you'd got very cold, love . . .*'
The fire went out. The room was so dusty, and the fire went out. Then it was all dark, for a long time.

'*You broke your wrist when you had the fall and the doctor's a bit worried about your poor old heart as well, so we'll be keeping an eye on all that too. We've got you on a drip so we can give you your medicine nice and easy.*'
If the door's left open the stair carpet'll get all wet. We've been in that house twenty years, handy for the shops I always

233

said, though John didn't like the area, he said it was a bit common. But I always say, if you keep yourself to yourself and look after your own home as best you can, then that's all that matters. I kept it nice for us, didn't I, John? Nothing wrong with being houseproud, is there, dear?

'Lilian? We're going to put a catheter in now, for your waterworks, all right? We've got the curtains pulled, don't you worry about anything. Jane, give me a hand here – that's right. No, she's too heavy for the two of us, you go and get Pete . . .'

That man made me feel so embarrassed, looking at me. All the girls on the bottling line warned me. But it was all right for them, some of them even looked nice in their turbans and overalls. And all their laughing – taking everything the wrong way. Chat about the night before. They could have their pick, and they knew it. They could send the likes of *him* packing. Not like me . . .

Oh, it hurt, it hurt, it hurt.

'Sorry, Lilian, it's not very nice for you. Come on, love, let's just shift your bottom a bit, there, all done! Now we'll just have to change this drip because it's not going in fast enough . . .'

What was it like for Jesus to have the nails stuck right through his hands? Like that, and that, and that. Prodding away. Jabbing at me. It hurt.

'Look, she's opened her eyes! All right, Lilian? All right, love? You're in hospital, Lilian, all right?'

'Lily.'

'You want us to call you Lily?'

'Mrs Roper. Mrs.'

'All right, Lil! There's a good girl!'

On Saturday morning John Roper found two envelopes on the mat, a brown electricity statement and the familiar small blue oblong, bearing his grandmother's handwriting. He stood turning it over and over. It was much heavier than usual.

He carried it into the kitchen and put it on the side. He pondered the kettle for a long time before filling it, then wondered whether to switch it on. His own face dwindled in its shining surface, curved like the funny mirrors in New Brighton.

'Look at us, Nan, we look like frogs!'
'Speak for yourself, son!'
'Look at me now, Nanny – I'm a plane!'
He thought of his bedroom. Was the Spitfire still there? She wouldn't have changed anything. She never asked if he'd go back home one day, but he knew she was waiting.
How would you go back though?
He let the teabag soak then sloshed in milk and sugar. Then he leaned over and stared into the swirling surface of the liquid, orange-brown, like the colour of the earth he saw far below the plane.

Eddy's note still lay on the draining board:

Dear John,
    I hoped we'd see you before we set off, but you were later than usual. Bernie and I have gone camping for the weekend, just for a change. Sorry to leave you on your own, but I thought we'd all go out to the steakhouse on Sunday night, if you'd fancy that. Don't forget to feed the crow. Plenty of food in the fridge for both of you!
                                                    Cheers,
                                                    Eddy

John stared down at it. Then, very slowly, he tipped his mug so that tea spilled on to the note in a thin stream, and he did not stop until the mug was empty. Tea dripped on the floor, but he ignored it. Then he put the kettle on again. The electricity pulsed like music. He threw his head back, and hummed along, 'In the Mood', hearing the sound in his own head, louder and louder until it was like a plane landing in the garden.

He wished they would kill that engine. It was too close, too close. So he snapped on Bernie's radio to drown it out.

'. . . and on our Saturday chart countdown we're at fifteen now, and it's the old number, made famous by Frankie Vaughan, some of you gonna remember, but now brought to us care of Mr Movement himself, Shakin' Stevens! It is, of course, "Green Door", so take it away, Shakie . . .!'

John listened carefully, then frowned. He felt sorry for the singer, to be left out so. It wasn't fair. He wondered who those people were, 'the happy crowd' who inhabited the world behind that door, where they laughed a lot and played music. Why, he could almost hear the piano – 'hot', the man said. I bet they're having fun in there, John thought. He imagined knocking for entry, waiting for an eye to appear at the peep-hole. You knock once, the door slams, someone laughs out loud behind . . . They wouldn't let him in because he wasn't a member of the club, and it wasn't bloody fair. Who did they think they were? I'll watch until the morning comes creeping . . . Bally sure I will.

The feeling of the envelope calmed him. Smooth Basildon Bond – she always used that. It was easy to know what to give her when he went away. She loved the nice boxed set he chose, paper tied with a navy ribbon, and two piles of envelopes. Later when he wrote to say air letters were better for speed, she still stuck to her Basildon Bond. Lots of sheets in this one, by the feel of it.

John strolled along the corridor, and unbolted the back door. The air punched breath out of him. He stood for a while as the crow hopped in increasing desperation when no food came its way. 'You can wait,' he told it, taking pleasure in the side-ways scrabbling and the raucous *Kraak . . . kraaak . . . kraaak*, which increased in volume as the beady black eye peered at him. And found him lacking.

'Everybody's got to wait their turn,' he snapped, turning away.

Somebody started up a lawnmower. He sat on the edge of the verandah, and watched a beetle picking a laborious passage across the stony path. When it was within reach, he held his foot above its back for a long time, making a shadow the crea-ture could not escape. It did not know how close to death it was; a mere hair's breadth of chance, whilst he was all-powerful. It would be so easy. The carapace would crack, a minute sound in the universe, but satisfying for all that. He used his heel as a pivot and lowered his sole until it was just centimetres from the creature. So easy. Nan used to tell him stories, that somewhere the fly or the wasp or the ladybird had a mummy and a daddy who'd be out looking if it didn't return home.

He decided to show mercy.

An hour passed, and the sun burned his legs, before he stuck his finger into the flap and roughly tore the envelope. She hadn't dated it, and her handwriting looked more wobbly than ever. He looked down at the sheaf of pages.

Dearest John,

It's very cold here, raining buckets as I write this. You'd wonder where it all comes from! Sometimes its hard not to let it get you down but you've got to solder on, I say.

I hope this finds you well, and that everythings going nice as it was in your last letter, thank you for writing. Congratulations on getting that permotion. I know you deserve it. Sounds as if everythings coming together nicely and I was specially interested to hear about your new freind. She sounds really nice. Is she older than you, John? If she has her own house she might be a mature lady, not that I think that matter's. Its whats inside you that matter's not how old you are. I hope shes a kind person looking after you well. Thats' the main thing.

Hilda wants me to join the pensioners club with her, but I don't know about it. But I don't know if I wanted to sit around gossipping with a lot of old women, because I always say I keep myself to myself – as you know, John. But I might go along for Hilda, she get's a bit lonley since Will died.

I'm all right on my own, so dont you ever worry about me. Sometimes I think of all the happy times we had when we went on the ferry or I took you to Speke to watch the plane's. You looked so smart in your ATC uniform too, I was that proud of you. Sometimes when I can't sleep I wonder if we'd do things the same if we all had another go at it. Whats' past, I mean.

Well, here I am rattling on when theres a fire to be laid and some potatoes peeled. It's *The Archers* in a minute, I always like my serial. I'll get the house cosy in a minute and settle down, and every time I look at the planes on the mantelpiece I think of you John. Your room is just like you left it, and I dust it once a fortnight to keep it nice.

Give my best regards to Bernadette, will you send me a photo of the two of you? I'd like to see what she looks like. I could show Hilda and put it on the mantelpiece. Have you told your freind all about me?

I send all my love to you, John, you take good care of yourself and eat well. I must close now, or you'll be bored! Anway, it's time to turn the radio on. We'd always listen together when you were at home. Happy days. Oh well, bye-bye for now, love – at this rate I'll need to buy some new writing paper!!

Love as ever from,
Nan xxxx

The house next to Bernie's had been bought just six months before by a couple called Robert and Nadine Sinclair. They owned a souvenir shop in town, and had plans for expansion, since there was already such a boom in boxes made from Jarrah, coolamons marked in pokerwork, and small digeri-doos virtually impossible to play, but which made striking ornaments with their black and white cross-hatching and swirling patterns of red and yellow ochre dots. The smallest ones could just fit into a large backpack.

Now Robert Sinclair stopped the lawnmower and stood still, pleased at the sight of his freshly painted home, and his pretty wife on the lounger in her swimsuit, whilst Stephen and Myra chased each other through the sprinkler behind the double car port. Contented, he opened his mouth to tell his wife, when she sat up sharply and held up a hand, saying, 'Shhhh!'

A cry came from next door.

'Did you hear that?' she whispered.

The Sinclairs had met their neighbour, asking her over for a beer when they moved in. She had returned their gesture, but Nadine said afterwards the place was such a tip you wouldn't want to spend much time there, and wasn't Bernie Molloy . . . well . . . a bit rough? Other neighbours said they were lucky to have missed the old days, when the place was full of hippies or drunks and the parties never stopped.

The crying was unmistakable. A low, desperate sound that stopped and started like Morse code, short sobs followed by long low groans of anguish, continuing in that pattern as they listened, as if the person was still fighting for control.

Nadine squinted through a hole in the fence.

'A bloke?' Robert mouthed.

Nadine nodded, and beckoned him to move a short way along, where there was a long split in the old wood and they could see through into Bernie's wild garden. At that moment the crying redoubled in intensity, the fight for control aban-doned. Racking sobs shook the still air.

They saw the man sitting on the edge of the verandah, weeping uncontrollably, leaning forward as if he would topple to the ground. As they watched, his fingers let paper flutter to the ground like a flock of small bluebirds.

'One of her lodgers,' Nadine whispered.

'Poor bloke must've had bad news.'

They looked at each other, and screwed their faces up in pity, because they were not indifferent people and the sound reached right into their souls, carrying with it all the unhappiness each of them had ever imagined.

'Maybe we should . . .' she began again.

But Robert Sinclair took his wife's hand and led her into the house to fix some iced tea and drown out that noise with the comforting hum of the air-conditioning. You couldn't just go barging in, he told her, because for all they knew Bernie Molloy had the matter under control. And in any case, it really wasn't their business.

Thirty-One

The kookaburra's demoniacal shrieks woke her. Galahs whirred from the gums, bruising the sky. Just before six, and the sun poured honey and vanilla on the two peaks. Eddy was already hunkered down, brewing tea. Wearing only briefs, his sandy skin gilded by the light, he reminded Bernie of an origami bird.

Bernie raised herself on one elbow and shook her head. He asked if she'd slept well and she nodded. With a small smile he said he knew she'd love camping, and wasn't he right? Again she moved her head, feeling no need to talk. It was enough to observe him, just as she had weeks ago when he was sawing wood. But the woman who'd watched then was that sad stranger she recalled – the one who worked in a bar called the Zoo, lived in a house collapsing around her, and hung her clothes from a picture rail.

239

'I don't want to go on working for Dick,' she said suddenly, receiving the mug.

'Good.'

'I thought you'd ask me why.'

'It's obvious why.'

'But I don't know what to do. That bloke Sinclair next door might let me work in his shop. Be nice to have evenings, Eddy. You and me – we could do so many things. Finish the house. Build a pool in the garden! Wouldn't that be so cool?'

He turned away and began rolling up his swag. Bernie felt her eager face freeze. She could have pulped her own tongue, but it was too late. With this boy, she'd whispered to herself many times, you have to leave the door open. Don't make plans, or he'll plan to take off. But now she'd forgotten. The gold of the morning was tarnished. She was the butt of the birds' mocking cries.

Two hours passed on the road, before he appeared to relax. 'You haven't asked me the next stop on the magical mystery tour,' he said.

Relieved, she smiled. 'That's cos I know you won't tell me.'

'Today you're getting an education,' he said, 'and tomorrow . . .'

'Oh man, there was me thinking I was in for a romantic escape.'

He pulled over suddenly, and pointed to where the stillness of the red and green landscape was disturbed by a turmoil of wings. Bernie could just make out something on the ground, barely distinguishable from its colour, a shape made jagged by the continuous motion in the air. Eddy slammed the door behind him and gestured to her to follow.

The red kangaroo lay on its side, tail stretched out like the stick of an Indonesian shadow puppet. Beneath the pale ribs, the creature's black chest cavity, fringed with flesh, heaved with unspeakable movement, where the two enormous wedge-tailed eagles and flock of crows were feeding on the rotting guts. Appalled, Bernie stared at the gaping red hole which had once held an eye, before her gaze fled across to the delicate paws, resting on each other as if in prayer. The sky flapped savagely about their heads; black shadows cruised on the orange sand like planes across a livid sunset.

Bernie turned away from the scene and retched briefly, bringing nothing up.

'It's horrible,' she gasped.

'No it's not, it's a part of what happens,' he said. 'Look at those eagles – their wingspan's long as my arms can reach and then some. They can pick up a joey, take it off its mother. Nothing she can do. That's how it goes. In the end, that old girl there, she'll be white bones and nothing else. She'll feed crows, eagles, dingos, flies, ants – you name it. And then she'll be her own monument, out here. She's gone back where she came from. Come on.'

They'd walked about fourteen metres back towards the car when Bernie felt compelled to turn again. The birds had descended. They were pecking and pulling in a frenzy, trailing long strings of flesh and sinew from their beaks. She stared in fascinated horror, unaware of Eddy wandering about near her, bending to pick things up from the ground. When at last she turned back, he was walking ahead, his eyes continuously searching the ground.

She caught up with him and he held out a small bunch of feathers. 'Look, these are for you. Those two there, they're from the wedge-tail.'

'I'm not sure I want them, Eddy.'

'It's not a question of wanting or not wanting. You're gonna need them tomorrow.'

'Why?'

He shook his head. 'Just keep your eyes skinned as we walk back. Find us some more feathers. Some small ones too, breast feathers – if you can.'

She obeyed, oddly pleased when he identified the first one she found as from a black kite's tail. Scanning the earth beneath her feet she noticed its variety. What seemed like an unbroken monotony of sand was, in fact, composed of a myriad colours and textures which glittered all around. She bent to pick up a handful, and examined small chunks of rock the size of Smarties: pearly white, beige, vanilla, burnt sienna, peach, orange, purple-grey, chocolate brown, and a black which shone like coal. The little rock fragments were held within countless millions of grains in the same colours, themselves in earlier times ground down by the slow passage of time to create the desert. Eddy looked over her shoulder, and pushed the handful of earth in her palm around with a bony finger, pointing out the tiny fragments of iron mica, dried leaf, grass, insect shell and bone that were there too, making up the whole. She looked down with a mixture of awe and excitement.

241

'And I'm holding it all in the palm of my hand,' she said.

Eddy was transfixed by her expression. It was like opening a book of fairy tales, he thought, and seeing a picture you've always loved come to life, drawing you into the enchantment. He said, 'You know last night we looked at the stars? Sometimes I see just as much in what you've got in your hand. Eons of it. Every little particle with its own story. All going back to the dreamtime.'

'Out here that stuff makes sense,' she nodded, scattering her handful in a wide arc.

'Perfect sense,' he replied.

They stopped frequently as Eddy pointed out things she would never have noticed. He showed her the red nests of the mulga ant, scattered on the ground like bowls beneath the shrubs, and explained that there was a network of tunnels under the ground beneath their feet. He revealed the feathery tracks of the perentie lizard, carefully distinguishing them from those of the goanna nearby, even though Bernie could barely tell the difference.

'But how do you *know*?' she asked.

'Because I was taught,' he replied. 'You know, that time with Tommo was like my uni. It was all I wanted. See that?'

She followed his finger and saw what looked like a misshapen fruit hanging from a branch.

'That's the home of an itchy grub. Moth caterpillar. They hide in there all day and come out at night to feed on the leaves.'

'I used to be afraid of caterpillars,' she said. 'Patrick put one down my neck when we were still at home and I screamed the place down.'

'How can you be scared of something that doesn't want to harm you?'

'Creepy crawlies – you know,' she replied. 'All kids are scared of them. Grown women too.'

'But they're not called creepy crawlies,' he said. 'That's the point. When you give something a name you can't be scared of it.'

'Unless it's the brown snake?'

'I always think it's called that because it was so dangerous nobody *dared* give it a decent name.'

She was taking a turn driving when he tapped her arm and told her to stop. Leaping from the car he beckoned her to follow, and squatted at the edge of the road a few yards away. The bizarre yellow and beige creature froze at their arrival.

'What the hell's *that*?'

'Thorny devil. Fierce, isn't he?'

'You wouldn't pick it up,' she murmured, squatting beside Eddy to look at the small reptile. Its back was covered with spikes; its colouring perfect to render it almost invisible in the landscape.

Bernie knelt and gingerly put her face quite close to the lizard's black, hostile stare. The feet, like little hands, were splayed as if poised for combat. The spines all along the head, back and tail gave it the look of a dragon a child might draw.

'Now I can say I've looked the devil in the eye,' she said.

'Because of the spines it's safe – nothing's going to touch it,' Eddy said. 'Reminds me of you, Bernie – when I first knew you.'

'Too right,' she murmured, and looked up to return his smile.

Then, pulled by the same invisible strings, they stood up to cling to each other, as the thorny creature scuttled away into tussocks of spinifex.

Gradually the landscape changed, the dirt road heading for a long sandstone escarpment that ranged across the horizon like the knubbled back of some vast animal, pressed into submission by the weight of the indigo sky. They hadn't seen another vehicle for over an hour. Woodland thickened each side of the road. Every so often a jewelled lorikeet would flutter across the front of the car, or a flock of finches rise twittering from a stand of gums. Drunk with foolishness, Bernie slid back in her seat, fantasizing that there was nobody else alive. She felt transported to another planet, watching from afar while that shell of a creature which bore her face went about its daily business in the town. Whilst here, her true self could frolic, safe in the knowledge that it was unrecognizable.

'There's a waterhole coming up. We'll swim,' he said.

They picked their way in silence between walls of burnished copper, into a chasm that grew deeper as they walked. At last the track widened and Bernie clapped her hands at the sight of the water. It sheeted beneath the rock face, orange, blue and green. On the far side a skull lay on the sand. Bernie stared across at the wide curving horns, the deep black sockets, and the jawbone's dislocated, ironic grin. She pointed at it.

'Do we want to be watched?'

'Yeah, he's saying, "I was alive once too – so have a good time for me!"'

'Imagine . . .'

'What?'

'I don't know . . . I just had this mad thought . . . you know you get dried food you reconstitute by soaking it in water? Well, imagine if you could do that with everything, so you'd have some dried-up old carcass, some skeleton, and you'd put it in the water, and then later it'd walk out, all whole again. Wouldn't that be something?'

'Him over there – he'd need the rest of him. Couldn't walk about much otherwise. He'd just lie lowing on the edge and be a bit sad.'

'But you know what I mean? That way, everything gets a second chance. Hey, so I'd better move *this* dried-up old carcass in there right away!'

Naked, she ran into the water and struck out, shattering the mirror into a million droplets of colour that shivered around him as he joined her, the sudden cold driving the breath from his lungs. Their voices ricocheted like parrot cries as they dived and raced and splashed each other.

Later, they stood together breathless near the far edge, and kissed for a long time. Then Bernie climbed him like a monkey in a tree, and wrapped her legs around his waist, allowing him to slip into her beneath the ripples. They barely moved, their slow love-making a part of the soft rise and fall of water, the torpor of all living creatures in afternoon heat.

She clung to his thin shoulders, and focussed hard on their twinned still centre, drawing him up, relaxing and contracting her muscles again and again, squeezing him until she thought she'd faint with the mixture of effort and ecstasy. At last she felt him shudder and groan into her neck, and she unfolded herself gently, leaning her head against his chest as the water lapped around them and the wet sand drifted between her toes. From the corner of her eye she could see the steer's skull watching them, and in her happiness she dispatched a thought to it and to all the dead – that she would go on living for them as long as her skin could touch this other skin and be renewed.

Under a sky even richer in stars than the one before, the flat rock felt hot against their backs. They'd made camp near a

244

small creek, built a fire, and eaten boiled rice and tins of mince, washed down with beer that was still cool, but only just. Eddy had learned the art of packing eskies, he said, but not of working miracles.

Now they sprawled hand in hand beneath the illuminated vault. Quietly, as if to raise your voice on a night like this was to shout in church, Eddy pointed out the bright spot of Sirius overhead, Procyon above, and the Milky Way running down between the two. He directed her to Orion a little further to the north, and showed her the Southern Cross and the Pointers rising.

'Can you see which is which?'

'I'm trying . . . But I kind of don't need to know. It's all just . . . there.'

'Once upon a time people used to think the stars were just holes in the sky, and the light of heaven was shining through them.'

'That's nice – if you believe in heaven.'

'That means you don't?'

'I used to think – who'd want to go to heaven if it was full of people like Father Mullen? Rather burn than have to hang out with those creeps prancing about in their nighties!'

He chuckled. 'OK, OK . . . but just look up there. Stare at it, Bernie. Look through the sky to the other side. Just light. That's fine, isn't it?'

'That's fine. Just don't tell me God created it all. That makes it . . . smaller, somehow.'

'Only because those people turned the God they taught you into something small?'

'Good point. But I don't want it to be *made* by anybody.'

'Everything's made.'

'OK then, if I've got to believe stories about it, I'd rather believe the ones that come from here, the rainbow snake and all that, and leave that miserable old bugger of a God back in Skibbereen.'

Abruptly he sat up. 'Tell you what – shall I show you the eyes of God? Right now?'

She sat up too, and put an arm around him. 'I thought we were looking at them up there. Millions and zillions of them – twinkling.'

He loped back towards their camp, returning after a few

minutes with the torch. Then he instructed her to stare hard into the darkness at the opposite bank of the creek in front of them.

The narrow beam moved in a wide slow sweep along the opposite bank. Bernie held her breath as it caught the eyes, green and luminous, bulging silvery like marbles, pair after pair staring unblinking back at them from the black shadows.

'What are they?' she whispered.

'All kinds of things . . . there'll be rocket frogs and burrowing frogs and the odd rat or two, but no . . . never mind . . . *that's* what I call God. Lots of shapes of him. He's been there all along, listening to us. He doesn't miss a thing, Bernie.'

'So – you don't mind if he's a bit slimy down there in the mud, or lives off things you wouldn't want to think too hard about?'

'Fact is – that's exactly what I like.'

He switched off the torch.

That means he could even love me, Bernie thought. Elated, she punched him lightly on the arm and said, 'Anybody told you you're a bit crazy, Eddy?'

'Must be in the genes – no, I'm serious! I talked myself into thinking that's the only good to come out of that stuff I found out – see? I'll never know who half of me is. I know my blood's only an eighth, but that female line going back's pretty powerful stuff. So, if you don't know who you are or where you come from – not *really* – then you have to create the story of your own life.'

'Is that . . . why you move on all the time?' she interrupted.

'What?'

'I mean, like, you *do* one particular place and take what you need from the people you meet – like your mate Tommo, say – then when that's a part of you, you leave to start over again?'

His face was unsmiling. 'Yeah, that's about right. But the way you put it, it's like you think I'm bleeding people dry like a vampire or something.'

'I didn't mean it that way, Eddy.'

'You can get to love people, but still move on. Doesn't mean . . . you're exploiting them, or anything.'

Miserable now, she made her voice as light as possible. 'Oh sure, I know that. A good thing too. It's the way I used to be, and maybe I should go back to it. Means you're always growing, eh, Eddy?' She forced a little laugh.

'Right.'

Uneasy, they stopped talking. Bernie shuddered as a bat whisked by her head. She imagined it tangled in her hair, sharp claws scrabbling at her scalp, leathery wings wrapped in her long curls until, in desperation, the creature was eating its way through into her brain. It would enter through her eyes – just as the whole night was doing now, as she stared into the oily, plop-ping darkness where Eddy had revealed to her the many eyes of his god. Only he wasn't there any more, she knew that. It was all a fantasy. Or Eddy mocking her. Nothing down there but slithering creatures, insects and the dirt, and nothing upwards but those brittle stars – holes in the sky indeed, with the blinding light of nothingness shining through. She shuddered.

'Let's go back to the fire, Eddy,' she said.

He put his arm around her and held her close as they walked back to the orange glow. Bernie's knees were weak; she murmured it was because she'd lain too long on the hard rock, and he supported her tenderly.

Yet with each slow step, as she curved into his body, her arms clasped tight around his waist, Bernie was consumed by the dread of all men and women as they approach their end. Knowing how much she loved this boy (and how she hated the fact that her mind would always express him thus, reminding her of the age difference between them), and that she was doomed to be left alone in the end, sooner rather than later in all probability . . . Knowing that she wanted to lie down on the red ground even then, and disintegrate. End it now.

She steadied her voice. 'Will you do something for me, Eddy? Will you play your didge? You brought it along, I saw you put it in the car, so . . .'

'*Yidaki* – same thing really but – that's its name to me.'

'It'll sound beaut whatever you call it,' she wheedled.

He grinned. 'What makes you so sure?'

'Sure, because everything you do's got a bit of beauty in it, Eddy Carpenter.'

Without another word he went to the back of the car and took out the long woven red bag with its braided handle.

'I haven't played in ages.'

'Why?'

He shrugged. 'I get moods . . . well, I have to be with the right people.'

'What sort of people?'

247

'People with soul, of course.'

He sat upright on his swag, and stretched out his foot to support the plain wooden tube, decorated with four simple bands of red and yellow ochre at the top, beneath a fat beeswax rim, and a wavy line of dots in the same colour at the bottom.

'It's stringybark,' he said, running his tongue around his lips. 'Tommo's son made it for me. Got a good sound.'

The low drone was familiar to her, of course, but she had never liked it much: the threatening sound of an alien culture. But gradually Eddy built up his breathing rhythm, pushing out his cheeks, moving his head then his whole body to the haunting *do–oo–o–rp dooo–oooooo–rrp*, punctuated by occasional yelps, and Bernie was caught up in his music in a way she'd never have thought possible. It became all sounds to her: the guitar, the drum, the piano, the double bass, all the music she'd ever heard, danced to, wept at during long drunken nights. The oscillations relaxed her into a sense that this would go on forever, the rhythm of the moon pulling tides, the dark frequencies of the womb.

He sang her the ugly, guttural noise of their caged crow, the harsh laughter of the kookaburra, the leap of the kangaroo, its death, and the savage whirr of wings as the predators came to feed. He sang her the rapid bark of the dingo in desert wastes, the croak of the bullfrog and the rising screech of parrots at the approach of a storm. His breathing mimicked the rumble of thunder, lightning flashing overhead, and then the hypnotic hum of insects as the sand dried back to its proper form and the pitiless sun rose in the sky once more. The bush fire caught, the trees exploded into flames, the animals raced for their lives . . . Ah, she could hardly breathe for the smoke in that sound.

Then he sang her the night and all the stars, taking her on a journey to where the white gum faded into darkness but the eyes of death blazed forever. But no matter, the universe would go on singing, just like this, beyond our hearing, and the cockatoos would always seek higher and higher, transforming themselves into stars in the trying.

Because – Eddy's music roared – there was nothing else to do.

Thirty-Two

Unexpectedly, it speaks. He hears words amongst the hoarse, ugly cries.

Ah, it is happening . . .

John stumbles over, grasps the bars, and leans his forehead against the metal, kneeling down to meet the angry stare. The heavy, rounded bill jabs forward.

You haven't fed me, you bastard.

'Feed yourself! Nobody's feeding me. Nobody's looking after me. Why should I care about you?'

Because I'm in charge.

'In charge of what?'

Of you. Of all of you. I know what you've been, what you've done and what's going to happen. I know what you're thinking when you don't yourself. I can smell your shit as it forms and you drive it out thinking that'll make you clean. Ha – nothing makes you clean, John. You're made of dirt and that's where you belong.

'No, I don't! Don't talk to me like that, you hear me? I'm growing feathers, just like you. Look!'

That's not a wing! That's a stubby white hand, five worms for me to eat.

'I can still fly better than you!'

It laughs, jumping up and down on the perch with malicious glee.

That's good, you Pommy bastard, because I can't fly at all! Karkk-karkkk-karkkk.

'Don't call me that. It drives me mad. Nan says sticks and stones may break your bones but names will never hurt you. But she's wrong, Crow. I could make fun of you for being stuck in there, I could call you a cripple . . .'

Cripple yourself . . .

'You and me should be friends. Please.'

249

A quick flurry of black and the bird turns its back on him, shuffling from side to side to let a large oily green dropping fall to the floor of the cage. It splatters into a star. John fixes his eyes on its congealing swirls and lumps.

'Talk to me . . . please.'

We haven't been properly introduced.

'I'm John Roper. The English pilot.'

I'm the caged bird . . . krrk-krrrk-krrrk.

John hears its laughter. It reverberates along the metal bars to bounce off his mind's splintering surface. He bangs his forehead rhythmically against the bars, again, again, again.

'Turn round – please. What do I have to do? Feed you?'

No point really, cos I'm heading out anyway. Look at the state of these feathers! She's lost interest in me, and now he's taken up with her . . . well, that means no room for the likes of me or you, is there? I'll be maggot food any minute, so might as well speed it up, eh?

'What are you saying?'

Death.

'What?'

Nothing else for it.

'You want to die?'

What else is there?

'What about flying. Didn't you like flying?'

The bird is silent. It doesn't like the question, and John feels afraid of its rage. The sudden futile flurry of feathers makes him jump. Then the creature settles back on the perch, facing him again, head stabbing left to right, left to right.

Used to fly. Up in the air, you look down, you're in charge.

'I know! I know!'

Grounded.

'I know.'

Don't know anything, Pommy Biggles. Kaaark-karkkkk – ha! Biggles! Got as much in common with him as I got with a sea eagle!

'Biggles is my *friend*!'

No, he's not, mate. You don't have friends.

John bangs his head against the bars again, harder this time. The brief black storm pleases him. A couple of breast feathers drift to the dirty floor of the cage.

'Don't . . . don't . . . don't.'

250

*OK, OK, I'm sorry. Don't get all worked up. That's better
. . . Now – shall I tell you who I really am? Are you ready?*

Ready, she feels, at last. Lily is staring up at the ceiling.
Polystyrene tiles. If you concentrate really hard you can force
your eyes to travel along every line up there, but if you blink
once you lose your place. They told her she was in a 'nice
side ward' so they could look after her better, but they never
seem to come.

It's so cold. The bed is jingling, the noise would keep
anybody awake. Why don't they bring more blankets? Where's
the little button thing? How're you supposed to move with
these tubes tying you up? Why don't they come?

Cold.

Count the squares, count the squares.

Mrs Owen had a pointer for the blackboard, and she'd hit
you with it too, right across the back of the legs, or quickly
on your palm. It hurt. She called me thick, she called me slow,
said I was dim, called me heavy in more ways than one. Oh,
she laughed! They didn't care in those days, did they? They
could do anything they liked. When I told Mam and Dad she
bullied me, they said you have to put up with things. They
didn't expect much, and anyway they were old.

Why don't they come when you ring?

'Nurse, nurse, I'm cold, get me another blanket please,
nurse, I don't want to be a trouble. But please. What's that
jingling noise?'

'Oh God, the bed's shaking, get the thermometer.'

'Nurse, please get me some more blankets, I'm that cold.'

'She's gone and pulled her drip out too.'

'Shushhh. I've got a headache, John, turn that music down
a bit, love. It was always Glen Miller and all the old songs.
"We'll meet again, don't know where don't know when . . ."'

*'Ssh, Lilian, ssh – all right, love? The doctor's coming,
he'll give you an injection.'*

'More blankets! I was counting the squares on the ceiling,
love, I think there's forty.'

*'You don't need more blankets, Lil – you're too hot, lovie,
that's what's the matter, you've got a temperature. But we'll
sort you out soon. Why doesn't that bloody man come?'*

'Nearly forty. And my first time. You wouldn't think that,

251

would you? Not today. But it was different in them days and anyway, nobody wanted me. What're you doing?'

'*All right – er – Lilian, I'm the duty doctor, and listen to me – the nurses are going to roll you over so I can give you your injection. It'll bring your temperature down . . . sorry, old girl . . . we have to do this.*'

'Hurting, hurting. It hurt me. He hurt me so much.'

'*All done, Lil! There's a brave girl! Don't cry, love.*'

'I don't . . . I don't want . . .'

'*Shhh, I'm the staff nurse, Lil. Can you hear me? You're quite poorly so I'll send little Tracy in to sit with you. It's quiet on the ward, Tracy's only a student but she's nice.*'

'I wanted to tell our John about everything I done. It's not his fault – none of it is . . .'

'*She looks bad, Jo . . .*'

'*Keep your voice down!*'

'But I never could. You can't, can you? Then it's all too late. Nurse!'

John sticks out a finger, poking it between the bars.

'*Kerak-kerak-kerak.*'

Blood beads the end. He fixes his gaze on the crimson globule, wondering how many seconds will pass before it drops. There it goes. The crow rises with a clamour of wings to the perch. Blood on the stubby beak. Blood rimming its eye. The dying sun bloodies its ragged feathers. The scaly legs are scarlet now.

'You said you'd tell me who you are, Crow.'

Harak-harak, kraraak, karaak, somebody you always wanted to meet. Haven't you guessed?

'You sound different! Tell me!'

I'm your pop, Johnny-boy.

'You can't be!'

Sure I am, boy! I came back as a bird, and all along I knew it was you. I'da told you sooner but not with those other guys around . . .

'You sound . . . you sound like I imagined.'

Sure I do!

'I'm always thinking about you, Dad. We'd have gone flying together, wouldn't we? You'd have told me all you knew – and that's saying something!'

For sure, boy.

'I've got your picture in my room. And me mam's. She was pretty, wasn't she, like a film star? I don't go anywhere without my pictures. Sometimes I used to sleep with yours under me pillow, and think that if I did that you'd bring me luck. I wouldn't have told Nan that, mind. She says some things are better forgotten.'

Never forget, John.

'Once I thought I could save up and go and find your grave but she said, no, better off spending my money coming out here and learning to fly.'

You're a great pilot, John. You'd have been a hero . . .

'But they don't think so, they fired me, Dad! That Greg Abbott had it in for me. He's jealous, Dad. They've got it in for the British out here, you know that? Pommy this and Pommy that, laughing at you behind your back.'

You see the fires below, bright orange, and all the time you're smelling that gunpowder, oh boy!

'I hate them. All of them.'

Attaboy. Crossed bombs and a death's head on the fuselage.

'Crossed bombs and a death's head.'

You got it!

'I'll give it to them all right, hey, Pop?'

Chip off the old block, Johnny!

'Crossed bombs and a death's head.'

Death's what you deal in, boy. No choice, is there? Up there in the old Fort there's no way down till you've dealt, you know what I'm saying?

'I know, Dad. I always knew you'd come back and tell me what to do.'

Every day we'd lose some of the guys, and every night I'd go to sleep geeing myself up for revenge. Nothin' else for it. We'd be ready for take-off in the Suzy-Mae, *and we'd be shouting at each other over the intercom, 'Kill, kill, kill.'*

'Kill!'

Haraaaaa, kraar-kaar.

'No! I don't want you to go! Come back, Dad – I don't want this old crow – I want *you*. Where've you gone . . .? Dad?'

Biggles, my arse!

'Go away! Crossed bombs and a death's head, I'm warning you! That's what he told me. You must have heard him, because he's *in* you!'

253

He wasn't ever here, you drongo!

'He was, he was. He told me. *He told me!*'

John stands, sweat pouring down his face and stinging his eyes. Numbed, his legs give way beneath him, and he sprawls in the bloody dust of Bernie's garden, where all the trees and the shrubs are dark red now, burning, blackening at the edges of his vision.

Thirty-Three

At first light on Sunday morning Eddy handed her tea and a slice of honeyed damper. Fuddled, Bernie thought she could still hear the reverberations of his playing in the cries of birds. She had no recollection of getting into her swag, of anything beyond his music.

'Last night was brilliant, Ed.'

'Long day today.'

'What's going to happen?' When he shook his head she cried, 'God, you're a mysterious bloke! Every day . . .'

'What?'

'. . . I see more of what you're like.'

'And is that good?'

'It's bloody scary.'

Squatting, he reached out to smooth her ragged hair. 'I thought you were a hard nut, Bernie Molloy.'

'Tough, not hard. Call me tough and I'd say that's what you got to be. Call me hard and I'd say that's an insult.'

'OK, so tough people can still be scared?'

'Scared by you, Eddy. Or rather . . . hell, why shouldn't I say it? Scared by how I'm feeling about you.'

He laid his index finger across her lips and smiled, close to her face. 'Shhhhh, don't say anything, think about all the eyes on us – right now. Better keep some stuff back, hey?'

Bernie lifted her hand, took the finger that silenced her, put it into her mouth and sucked it gently, never dropping her eyes. She tasted salt and sand on him, and ran her tongue around the whorls of his fingerprint, moving the finger slowly back and forward in the tube of her mouth until he closed his eyes and groaned – and she felt in control once more.

'What was it you wanted me to keep back, Eddy?' she whispered, drawing his wet finger down her cheek and neck in a long, slow wipe.

'Nothing at all.'

He leaned forward, tracing the snail trail of saliva on her skin with his tongue, ending at her mouth. They made love quickly, with little need of preliminaries, and when Eddy collapsed on top of her she whispered, 'Well, what d'you think all those nosy little eyes made of that, then?'

'They all wish they were me,' he mumbled into her neck.

'Maybe they all *are* you,' she said.

He rolled off her swag and lay beside it, propping himself up on one elbow, contemplating her face – pink, russet and gold, like the dawn which increased its power now, like the invisible cord of light between them. His pale eyes roved over her features with the minute attention she'd seen him give to leaf and insect, until she dropped her head and begged him to stop. She flipped over on to her stomach, turning her face away.

'I hate you looking at my bloody wrinkles! I don't want you to *see* me! Getting old and ugly, Eddy . . .'

'Hey . . .' He reached out and pulled her round to face him again, and saw the moisture at the corners of her eyes. 'Listen, woman, I *like* your wrinkles!'

She tried to smile.

'You don't know the script, boy! What you're supposed to say is, you haven't got no wrinkles, Bern! I don't see any!'

He shook his head reprovingly, his face serious.

'But that wouldn't be true! One thing I promise you – I'll always tell you the truth. You'll know it when you hear it – OK?'

Twenty minutes later they parked in the open space for visitors to the canyon. Red sandstone cliffs rose sheer from the cleft in the earth, where white cypress pines gleamed in the rifted rock, and vast chunks of fallen stone littered the creek bed amongst gums and thickets of mulga. When he pointed, Bernie grimaced.

'All the way up there?'

'Yeah – it won't take long. It's fine this time of the morning.'

'My God, Eddy, reckon I'm a bloody mountaineer or something?'

He laughed. 'You ever stop grumbling? There's a trail . . . Come on, this'll do you good.'

He busied himself in the back of the car and hefted a small rucksack and the yidaki case. Handing her a water bottle, he marched ahead, forcing her to follow. Flies clamoured in her ears. Bernie hit at them, suddenly wanting to be somewhere else.

What did she know about this man, who marched ahead without looking back? Back then, with Zippo, it was different. They'd been equals. But this one was not her equal: he paid her rent, he was a young traveller, yet he was her superior. This one had the power to make her unhappier than she had ever been, since the baby died. He came from nowhere to transform her house, making miracles out of the mundane, and it amazed her that still she could picture him sawing wood and feel awe.

The ascent was not as bad as it had looked from a distance. Huge sandstone steps made the going relatively easy, and with each step the views became more dramatic. After twenty minutes they reached the top, and paused to gaze across the desert oak and spinifex-dotted sand plains, to a distant mountain range that glimmered lilac in the fresh light. Once she'd have thought it all flat, dry and inhospitable, which indeed it was. Yet with a sudden burst of exhilaration she understood that it is the accommodation of truth which makes the difference. She could embrace the wilderness and accept its counterpart inside her.

Eddy held out a hand, and they followed the trail side by side, past rocks scattered like the toys of a giant child. Queasy at the thought of the five hundred metre drop just a few steps away, Bernie gripped him tightly, until their hands were slippery.

'I hate heights.'

'You never told me that.'

'Lots you don't know about me, Eddy Carpenter.'

'Ditto.'

Suddenly they were walking through a maze of orange sandstone domes, a landscape of science fiction, weathered horizontally into gaping strata where small plants clung for sustenance.

In the distance they heard a small group of tourists with a guide. Eddy frowned. Moving ahead, he turned off the track, walking in the opposite direction from the obvious route around the canyon. At last he stopped at the centre of a rough circle of small red rocks and low mulgas, a few gums on one side, white as bones. 'This'll do,' he said, and dumped his burden on the ground, 'Nobody'll come this way. They tell you to stick to the track . . .'

He sat down, crossed-legged, leaning an elbow on his backpack, the yidaki case thrown down in front of him. Bernie moved to sit next to him, only to have him gesture to the space in front of him. 'Sit there,' he commanded, 'because I have to talk to you. And I need to be able to see you, Bernie.'

Banter rose in her mouth, only to be swallowed and flutter in her stomach. She saw his solemn expression and felt afraid. This is it, she thought, he's leaving soon and he's chosen this place to tell me. Dread pushed her down into the red sand.

Eddy said, 'Once Tommo told me any place would do for a ceremony, if you *thought* it sacred enough. So that's what I'm doing now, Bernie.' He closed his eyes, shoulders back, hands on his knees, palms open to the sky. After a few seconds he looked at her and smiled. 'You should see your face! Don't worry, nothing bad's going to happen.'

He unzipped the yidaki case, but the thing he pulled out was not the instrument itself, but what looked at first like a smaller version, which he passed over to her.

'Here, Bernie, take it. I made it for you.'

She balanced the wooden object across both hands – not a didgeridoo but a hollow branch about the length of her arm, painted with a schematic design in black, white and red. Realizing the painted design needed to be read vertically, she planted the post in front of her, steadying it with both hands.

Both ends were bordered with strong bands in the three colours and in the centre a stick-like woman was painted in a pattern of white dots, heavy oval breasts lolling to each side, arms in the air in a gesture of triumph or despair, head surrounded by hair in waving lines as a child will indicate the sea. The female figure sat with its legs spread crudely, straight out, and between the legs was another stick creature, this one tiny and painted in black.

Bernie glanced up at him sharply, but he said nothing, and her eyes were drawn back to the design. Above the figure's head was a black bird outlined sharply in white and flying upwards towards a large, white five-pointed star. On each side of the star he'd drilled two holes, outlined in black.

'What's it mean, Eddy?' she asked.

'It's a *badurru*.'

'What's that?'

'A hollow log coffin.'

He held out his hand for the painted post, and she handed it over, eyes begging him to explain. 'It's a cross between one of the grave posts the Tiwi people use, and a hollow log coffin. Tommo asked me one day – "What happened to your mother? Where did she go?" Then he told me she sleeps here in the sand. She sleeps everywhere. There's no grave to look for, nothing but sand all over.'

His eyes were far away and sad. 'Tommo helped me, Bernie. And that's what I want to do for you. This woman I've painted here, that's you. And on the ground in front of you, that's your little baby. This bird up here is the baby's spirit. And this is the morning star, which guides the soul to the land of the dead, so it can rest in peace. These holes are traditional – to let the spirit escape. He needs to escape, Bernie, doesn't he?'

A great hurt balled inside her like a boulder at the top of a cliff.

Eddy laid the *badurru* on the sand, then unfastened the ruck-sack and drew out a handful of feathers, which he put on one side. Next came a long piece of thick twine, decorated here and there down its length with clumps of feathers tied together with black cord. Last, he eased out what looked at first like an old-fashioned shopping bag. When he laid it on the ground in front of him – carefully, as if it contained something fragile – Bernie saw that the bag was knitted in three colours of string: red, ochre and black, with long feathers hanging from each end of the handle. It was stuffed with a white cloth bundle.

Puzzled, she watched as he tied one end of the feathered string to the centre of the bag's handles. Every movement was slow and deliberate, his expression grave. He looked up to meet her troubled stare.

'Don't worry, I'll explain. This is a *mindirr* – a ceremonial dilly bag. I've had it since I was in the north, tucked at the bottom of my stuff, waiting for a purpose. Now it's come. What we're going to have here, Bernie, is a funeral – no, don't look like that! It's all *right*. You have to trust me – OK?'

She nodded, her face pale.

'Listen to me – aboriginal people think dying's a part of

life, the great changes that happen . . . But once somebody's dead they have to be let go. There's all sorts of different rituals, and ways of dealing with the dead person's body . . . yeah, but that's *their* business. And this is ours.

'Listen – the main thing worries the people is how to keep the *living* safe. They got to make sure the dead one separates from this world, so it can go on to the next. When the body's buried – or exposed or whatever – one of the elders speaks to the dead spirit, tells it to keep away. "Don't follow us," he tells it. "You have to go the other way now, have to go to your own place, have to leave us alone."

'Because if that doesn't happen, see, they know it'll hang around and spoil things. Not knowing where to go or what to do or where to belong. Tommo thinks the atmosphere's thick with dead spirits, because white people don't know how to let them go. Like a kind of pollution, he says . . . Anyway, the point is, the rituals set the dead spirit free, like it needs to be, and make sure the living can get on with doing just that – living. Like you need to, Bernadette.'

'I know I do,' she croaked.

'Good. So what you got to do now is do what I say. Promise?'

She nodded. He rose, took the hollow coffin post and walked six paces away from where she sat, stopping to push it down into the red earth, so it stood upright. Then, kneeling in front of her, he created a small depression in the sand, and laid the dilly bag there, its feathered handle lying in the direction of the coffin post.

Then he laid both hands on the ceremonial bag. 'Inside here, Bernie, inside my special *mindirr* – is the baby from out of your mind.'

She flinched as if he'd hit her, closed her eyes, and gave a tiny moan.

'Look – he's wrapped in white cloth. Say his name out loud for me.'

Through cracked, dry lips she whispered, 'Tom . . . Tom Molloy.'

'Now say – I'm going to set you free, Tom Molloy. Go on.'

'I'm going . . . to set you free . . . Tom . . . Oh I can't, I can't, Eddy, don't make me!'

'Say it, Bernie.'

'I'm going to set you free, Tom Molloy.'

'Good girl. That's *good*! Now watch.'

Holding the feathered string between the finger and thumb of his right hand, he walked back to the coffin post, uncoiling its length on the ground. He'd paced correctly. The distance was exact. The twine was pale against the red ground, the little bundles of feathers brown and white, stretching away from her, straight towards the painted woman with hair like the ripples of the sea, whose stick arms railed against the sky. Eddy knelt down, facing her, and made another shallow bowl in the sand in front of the post. Then he took up the feathered cord again, holding the end with both hands now, as though it were a steel hawser hard to lift.

'I'm going to pull him away from you now, Bernie.'

He began to pull. The *mindirr* began to move, easing out of the scooped depression, slowly, slowly, making a trail – until Bernie lunged forward, crushing it down, holding it still with both her hands, tears streaming down her cheeks.

'No! I don't want you to do this – I don't want you to take it away, Eddy. Leave him here, please, leave him!'

'Let go, Bernie. You've got to let the spirit child go back where it came from.'

In anguish she lifted her hands from the bundle in the bag and it continued its slow journey from her, leaving a trail in the sand.

'Such a pain – here!' she cried, hitting her chest.

The bag in front of Eddy now, he laid it in the hollow, and coiled the feathered twine on top, placing the end carefully in the centre, as if the smallest movement had significance.

'Now come over here – bring your water bottle – and kneel down in front of us.'

She heard that 'us' with wonder, because now it was true, she realized – there was indeed an 'us' present in that place, more than Eddy and her. She felt the presence of her child in the still clearing, in the glimmering bones of the gums and the drooping grey-green of the mulga pods. It no longer seemed strange when Eddy ordered her to speak again.

'You have to tell him – Now it's time for you to go, and set me free as well. Maybe you'll be reborn, but you have to leave me now and go on your way.'

She hesitated, then repeated what he had said, closing her eyes with the effort. When she opened them she was shocked to see Eddy fishing for a box of matches in his back pocket.

He cut off her protest with a raised hand, and struck the match, holding it to the string until it burned down and hurt his fingers. He lit another match, then another, holding them to different parts of the *mindirr*, while Bernie steadied herself by fixing her gaze on the black stick-baby, the painted one whose soul was a bird.

But soon a small plume of smoke twisted up in front of her, all but obscuring the design on the coffin post. She watched the bag catch, smelt singed feathers, and saw the flame running around the coiled string, crackling yellow into orange into red, as he bent and blew. The flames flickered higher and the dry straw stuffing the cloth bundle caught with a whoosh.

It was nothing, not even a doll, nothing but string, rags and straw, yet as the small fire blazed before her she stared fixedly into the heat and recognized a tiny limpet face, the whorl of an ear, tiny hands starfishing in the air, nails like freshwater pearls, toes curled like shells, the small ribcage cracking open like a crab's claws – the whole thing shifting, settling, collapsing, white and grey, into the red sand.

As she watched she heard Eddy's voice whisper, 'Now – you got to let Bernie go. Let your mother go. You hear me?'

She listened, longing for any reply to Eddy's question, but heard only the high peeling cry of a bird in the distance. There was nothing to do but concentrate on the dying breath of flames. After a while Eddy reached across for the water bottle, unscrewed the lid, and handed it to her. 'Put out the fire, Bernie.'

She obeyed. There was a brief hiss as the hot matter resigned itself to ash, the ash to mud, and the smoke stung her eyes. They sat in silence, looking at the mess where the pyre had been, remnants of string and cloth caked in black and grey. Eddy leaned forward and dipped a finger in the ash paste, making sure it was well coated, then reached across and daubed a line on each of her cheeks, and a dot in the middle of her forehead.

'There – you're marked now. It's almost done. Stand up.'

She obeyed with difficulty because her knees threatened to give way. He told her to bend down and pick up a handful of the remains of the funeral pyre. She obeyed, then stood waiting, hands clasped around the precious mess.

'Put that inside the *badurru* – go on, drop it in there.'

The opening was narrow, but she made a funnel of her palms and let as much as possible slither down into the hole.

He told her to fetch more, and again she obeyed, filling the hollow branch, conscious only of the need to do it right, to pick up the smallest particle of feather and twine and bury it in wood and air. Tears and snot dripped from her nose.

'Now, just sit down back where you were in the first place.'

Bernie turned in silence. From the short distance, she watched as Eddy covered up what remained of the small fire with earth, so that the painted post stood with a small mound in front of it. Then he crossed to her, and bent to take the yidaki from its bag.

'It's funny, I only brought this along so I could hide the post – otherwise you'd have noticed it yesterday. I didn't think I'd play the thing, but you asked me to and I'm glad. So here's a special tune. I'm going to play you the baby's spirit dancing around us, then floating into the trees, then flying further away to the ridge to jump with the rock wallabies, and then he'll drift further away so you'll hardly hear, and then . . . he'll be gone, Bernie, having fun with all the other spirit children, everywhere.'

He set the beeswax mouthpiece to his lips, puffed out his cheeks and drew such miraculously light sounds from the instrument that Bernie heard in them all that he promised. After less than five minutes he let the last, oddly flat and dissonant note drift into nothingness, then laid the yidaki down.

'Eddy?'

'Yeah?'

'Nobody . . . nobody *ever* . . .'

'Sure.'

'I mean it. Nobody. Ever.'

'I know.'

'How?'

'It's obvious.'

'Tell me why.'

'Because of what you're like,' he replied, with the merest suggestion of a smile.

'Is that why I was like that?'

'I reckon.'

'But even before that – I was always angry. Maybe it was in me from birth. You know, they told us about the fires of hell, but nothing they predicted was as horrible as the real thing – so bad, nothing in the world could put it out. Nobody ever had the water. No sky. No person. Till now.'

'I know,' he repeated.

'Sometimes I look at you and I wonder where the hell you came from, Eddy.'

'Too much talking about hell round here!' he laughed.

'No, seriously.'

'I'm being serious. I hate all that Catholic guilt stuff. OK . . . let's go. One more thing to do.' Pulling her to her feet to hold her briefly, he turned to zip the yidaki back into its case, and shoulder it with the rucksack. Bernie stood still in front of the painted coffin post, her hands clasped in front of her breast.

'We don't just *leave* it?'

''Course we do. It belongs out here.'

'Someone might come and find it. Take it.'

He shrugged. 'You'll never know, so it doesn't matter. If anybody wanders over here, like one of the guides, I reckon they'll assume it's proper business been going on here – sacred stuff – so they'll leave it. Any case, they won't be wrong there, will they?'

She shook her head.

'A dingo or something will brush by and knock it over, sooner or later, and it'll just stay here, or get buried if there's a wind, or whatever.' He spread his hands wide. 'It's served its purpose, Bernie.'

Thirty-Four

L ily knew the figure who sat by her side was kind.

'Sometimes I'd daydream about what it'd be like to look like Veronica Lake, and then all the soldiers'd come courting, wouldn't they? If you went to a dance at one of the bases, all the Yanks'd come running – if you looked like that. You're a pretty girl yourself, love, I can just about see you. What did you say your name was?'

'*Tracy.*'

'Ah . . . I'll tell you something, Tracy, I don't think I'm going to get better.'

'Shhh, *of course you will.*'

'Me Ma didn't. It's a hard thing, when you lose them both. Mind you, they had me old. Dad, he was on the dustcarts, fair loved them horses, Suffolk Punches they were called, right big. Ma sewed for Mrs Taylor, the corset maker in Abbeygate Street. Sometimes we'd stand outside the Athenaeum and watch the rich folk going to balls, and once I was in work I'd point out the colonel and his lady and their two girls, and sometimes I'd be able to say I'd actually touched one of the dresses! Madam liked black with a lace trim. People knew how to dress in them days, love. A nice costume of a Sunday, and always a hat and gloves. Slippers on at the door too. We'd go to Ridleys for sugar wrapped in blue paper, and currants and raisins wrapped in the yellow. Hearthstone, bath brick and Sunlight Soap. Funny how you remember the names . . .

''Course, by the time war broke out I was fending for myself. Dad's cart turned over on a corner, and he got kicked. Think of that, he got killed by the thing he loved more than me. Oh aye, he'd have liked a lad, not a girl with less looks on her than one of his Suffolks. So anyway, that was a bad business and Ma was never the same. She didn't want to do much of anything but still went on with the whalebone – until she got the pains. I'd been at the colonel's about fifteen years by that time, and it were all I knew. You didn't want much. As long as you could pay the rent and put bread and cheese on the table, you were all right.'

'*Where did you live, Mrs Roper?*'

'Oh, I'm Suffolk born and bred. A long way from here, love! Best for barley, best for beer – that was Bury St Edmunds. But I couldn't stay. I tried to think of somewhere far away from there . . . couldn't stay there, not with the beer on the air . . . I couldn't have . . . No . . .'

'Shhh, *calm down, now, shhhh.*'

'I looked after Ma as best I could, but it was bad at the end. She blew up like a balloon, love, and her nerves . . .! Get herself in a right state at the sound of Mr Chamberlain's name! She'd shout at the wireless – she didn't trust any of them, because they'd take us into a war sure as eggs is eggs. I'm glad she never saw it.

'Are you still there? I nearly dropped off then. Shall I tell you something? I never had a boyfriend, young Tracy. No lad would of looked at the likes of me. Any road, you didn't meet lads in them days. Not at the colonel's. When the war came I were thirty-three and never been kissed! That's when I went to work at the brewery, and what a change that was! Major Lake, he used to get the lads for the bottling line from the Boys' Brigade, and then they all had to have been in the first eleven at school! He was a fair un, but a stickler.

'Anyway, it all changed because the lads joined up, so they had to bring in the women and girls, even in the brewhouse in the end, and that was the holy of holies. Mind you, there were still the men there – the older ones who couldn't serve. Like Jimmy. Ah . . . Just wait . . . Yes, I'm all right.

'What a time that was, love! Never known nothing like it, in my whole life. We was invaded all right – by soldiers and airmen, never mind the Germans! I'd stand over the road from the Milk Bar on Angel Hill and watch the RAF boys, smashing they looked in their blue uniforms. Oh, the sky was full of planes! Once the Yanks came you'd look up and see these great big ones stacked in the sky, rumbling over your head, to the bases all round. What a sight that was! And then you'd see them coming out of the American Red Cross Club in Westgate Street in their lovely uniforms, not coarse like our boys' ones, but tailored – they were that smart! All the girls liked watching them, not that I was a girl, mind.

'We had all girls on the bottling line. They were all younger than me; it was the best time I'd had. When you started they gave you a chitty and you had to go and get your boiler suit from the store. I had to have a man's one and the legs was that long for the width, I had to roll them, but the girls didn't laugh. We'd wear turbans, of course, and boots, and your hands'd get red from the caustic. Some of them, the young ones, they'd bring lipstick to put on in work because their mothers wouldn't let them cross the doorstep with it on . . .

'They were all so young, and most of them nice-looking with it, and sometimes it fair broke my heart to listen to them. Not that I was jealous, mind, Tracy. They were a lovely bunch of girls and kind to me. But they'd go to dances – the Yanks'd send trucks into town to pick up local girls, and the things they told me about the food on the bases! Once the girls talked me into going with them – anybody could go, you see – and I didn't want to but they said, Lily, this is a chance not to

265

miss, just to see what it's like and hear the band. They said, you can forget ration books for one night, Lil, so I went.

'I'll never forget it as long as I live – seeing those planes there with the paintings on the fronts – the noses – all of women with hardly any clothes on! You won't believe this, love, but there was one there called Luscious Lil. There was! The girls laughed and digged me in the ribs, so I said to them, I said, if I'm luscious then so is any sow in the farmyard!

'Anyway, that night I watched as if I could eat it all up with my eyes and not get any fatter. The band played "Chattenooga Choo Choo", and some of them even did the jitterbug. Nobody asked me to dance, but I didn't mind, not really, because I didn't expect it, I only wanted to watch. You could've loved any one of those Americans, Tracy, especially knowing what they had to do. Some days, on the bottling line, a girl would be crying her heart out, because her special one hadn't come back. So many of them didn't! And at a time like that, girls take risks, they do, I knew all about it, even though I never. But I'd listen to them talk, above the noise of the bottles rattling all day, and then I'd slip away and I'd be hearing "Chattenooga Choo Choo", and making up stories in my head – be dancing with a handsome pilot!

'Every night at seven the town filled up, the Yanks pouring in, some in jeeps and trucks and some on pushbikes. They'd be queuing up Bridewell Street with their bottles, and the pubs were full, and the brewery couldn't keep up with the demand. We ended up making ale from potatoes and all sorts! And the military police would be driving up and down, and little lads shouting at them, "Got any gum, chum?" and every day the girls in work had new stories to tell, some of them not for my ears, they said! Little America we was – oh yes. It fair broke my heart, sometimes . . . Ah.'

'*Are you all right, Mrs Roper?*'

'There's always those as will point the finger. Anyway, I'm getting ahead of myself . . . Hurts.'

'*Shall I find Staff?*'

'No, you stay put, love. It's all right. I like talking to you. And I was coming to when . . . I was . . . I didn't tell you about the man – Jim. He worked in the brewhouse. He was from Glasgow, in his forties, and married with children, they said, but nobody knew that for sure. Some reason he wasn't in the services, but I can't remember why now. He had a look about him, and he said such things! Fair made me blush. The girls used to give him a swipe on the arm and tell him to give over, but me – he saw me go red and it made him worse. And the smell of the grain on him, on all the men! Enough to take your breath away, even if you liked a drop of beer, like I did then . . .

'People started getting the bunting out even before they heard Mr Churchill speak! That was May 1945, you must of read about it, VE Day – seen it on telly. Anyway, it were like a great big holiday – the Tuesday and the Wednesday. Flags and streamers everywhere and people in their Sunday best. I put my blue costume on with the velvet collar, even though it were a bit hot. People made red, white and blue headdresses. And when it got dark they lit up the old Abbey gate and you could see all the stars and twirly bits on it, and you got a lump in your throat, it were that nice. They'd put fairy lights all through the Abbey Gardens, and cherry blossom fell on your head – like . . . confetti. It were thick that year.

'Thousands of people everywhere, arm in arm, dancing the conga all along the Angel Hill and through the gardens. The noise! Course, the pubs had to be restocked, and there was plenty of drinking. I went with some women from work, and they was all – you know – going off with men they knew. They didn't care! It's not every day you see a war end, is it? But it was getting on in the evening, and dancing everywhere, jitterbugging, quickstepping . . .

'I were on my own then. They'd all gone somewhere or other, but I didn't mind much. There was so much to watch and I'd had a couple of glasses of shandy, I don't mind admitting it, I felt that happy. But suddenly that man, Jimmy, was there at my elbow. There'd been a whole pile of 'em outside the Angel Inn when I went past and I thought I heard them laugh, not the laughs that everybody were laughing, but something different. He came along with me. He got hold of my arm and called me his Lilyflower and said I was a fine woman to be on my own. Oh, I knew he didn't mean it! But . . . I wanted him to mean it.

'He gave me a sup from the bottle he was holding like it was precious, and I remember the warmth of it going down. And all the lights all around us, like Christmas, and men and women kissing in the street. Jim saying things to me, nice things. And other types of things too. He asked me to dance – *me* – and I didn't know what to do, but all the people were bouncing around us, so it didn't matter. And he held the bottle up to me mouth while we went round in a circle, and some of the stuff spilt down my chin, and then he . . . he . . . licked it off.'

'*I can't hear you, Mrs Roper.*'

'It doesn't matter . . . My head was in a whirl. Dizzy. And soon he was leading me away, the music was in the distance, and all I remember is walking along Angel Lane, but he was half pulling me, half holding me up, Jimmy, and all the time he was saying those things . . .

'But you can guess the rest, can't you, love? You girls now, nothing shocks you, but it was different then, for me. I wasn't a child, but I didn't know . . . I hadn't . . . And that Jimmy wasn't a bit kind. He put me in a doorway, and then he was pulling at me and I remember thinking about my best costume and I was right frightened then, because he'd stopped saying anything . . . Then he . . . he . . . *hurt* me. My head banged on a piece of flint sticking out in the wall, and I cried out, but he just went on . . . hurting me. It was – it was – it was . . .'

'*Shhhh, shhhhh, don't.*'

'Ohhhh, oh.'

'*There, there.*'

'There's a pain just *here* . . . ahh . . . After, when he'd finished, he took me back to the Angel Hill – I'll say that for him, he did that much – and then he said he had to find his friends, and I stood there with the dancing all round me, then I heard this great roar of laughter, like when Liverpool's scored. I knew what it meant and I wanted to be sick. So I ran all the way home to the house Ma and Pa rented when I was born, and I stripped all my clothes off and do you know what I did? I burnt them all – everything – in the back garden where I'd been digging for victory like they told us. After that I washed myself from top to toe in cold water.'

'*What happened then? Were you all right?*'

'No, love, I weren't. We had the next day as a holiday too and it rained for three hours before the dancing started again, but I stayed home. I sat in Dad's old chair and thought about what I'd done. And I prayed it'd be all right. The day after that, it were back on the bottling line, and at dinner time I walked past the brewhouse with one of the girls, Doris, and

268

he were outside with the men. I went red. I didn't know where to look.

'And he says, he says, cool as cucumber, "How are *you* feelin', Lily?" and the men all laugh their heads off, and one of them, he says, "You should know, Jimmy!" and he grins. Well, Doris stops, and she looks at him, then she looks at me, and sees me fill up, and she gets everything, right away. So Doris goes straight over to him and slaps his face, just like that! She shouts at him to keep his dirty tongue to himself, or sommat like that, and takes me arm and leads me away. And that were that.'

'That's typical of blokes, that is. That's what happened to my friend, just like that!'

'Oh aye, love, but it were worse. Nobody knew for a long time, I was that fat already. I used to go and sit in St Mary's and look up at the big carved angels all along the ceiling, and some of them had right kind faces. I'd look at them so much I got to know them. I used to say, in me head like, that it were all right for them up there, with their wings all spread out like that, looking down on the likes of us who couldn't fly away. But I suppose they couldn't either, could they? Because they was wood. The more I looked at them, though, the more they looked like planes, those big ones, the Fortresses.

'Anyway, I used to sit there and say a prayer for it to be taken away, but after time I stopped doing that and I'd just look up and wonder what to do. There was a big flag hanging near the front, the Stars and Stripes . . . The girls at work knew in the end, and they were good to me, except one or two. When I was showing, I didn't want to go out, I wanted to hide. I was lucky, because I had savings.

'In those days – even after the war, when there was a lot of women in that condition as shouldn't have been – it was still shameful. One day I saw the colonel's lady in Abbeygate Street and she made out she hadn't seen me, crossed the road – and me her maid from when I was fourteen. It was like that. They tried to hide you away, they took you to a special hospital and then you had to work in the laundry so you knew you were a sinner. The babies was all in rows in metal cots and the nurses gave them the bottle, they wouldn't let us. Sometimes I'd be down there with me arms in suds and I'd think I heard him crying, but the supervisor said how could

I know, there was so many of the little buggers. That's what she said. It's a wonder she didn't say little bastards.

'This woman came round, she talked educated, and she had a right hard face, and she'd talk to each one of us and tell us it'd be better to put the baby up to be adopted. She looked at you as if you was dirty – specially me, because I was that much older. I was thirty-nine, mind, and I could see her thinking I should have known better. Ah, it were a terrible place . . . I'd fair break my heart thinking about him being taken away from me. Because I knew that was it. He was all I was going to have for the rest of me life. You can't blame me for wanting to keep him, can you? Nobody could *blame* me!'

'*There – don't get yourself all worked up again.*'

'I walked out of that place one night with him tucked in my coat. Been planning it for days! I went back home, the rent was all paid up, I've never owed anybody a penny – and I put a few things in Dad's old suitcase, and first thing in the morning I was at the bus stop and got the bus to Norwich. Oh, I didn't look back. But I could smell the malt. I could always smell it on me, for the rest of me life. Since then I've never been able to pass an alehouse without feeling sick.

'I didn't know where to go. There I was with John bundled up in a shawl and Dad's case, and all my savings in a bag hanging inside my clothes, except what I needed for the journey. It was funny, I couldn't remember the names of any places except London – and Liverpool. Dad had a friend once, came from here, made us all laugh – so maybe that was in my mind. All I wanted was to get as far away as possible. So that's what I did, I got more buses than I could count and slept in bus stops sometimes because I was that careful, but he was a good boy, our John, he didn't cry. Lucky I'd still got plenty of milk for him . . .

'All the way there I'd sit and think about those angels and the big satin flag, and that's when I decided to make it all up.'

'*Make what up?*'

'I shouldn't say.'

'*But if it makes you feel better, Mrs Roper . . .?*'

'Yes . . . and it don't matter now. Not any more. John won't know. You wouldn't tell, and anyway, he's doing so well for himself out there, he won't come home . . .'

'*Where's that, Mrs Roper?*'

'Australia! He's a pilot now, and I think he'll be engaged before VE Day!'

'Oh, but . . .? That's nice.'

'I didn't want him to know he was illegitimate! So I worked it all out before he was old enough to speak. I told the first place where I got a room I was his nan, and I looked it, especially after what I'd been through. When people asked me more I just shook my head, and there were so many sad stories after the war . . . Nobody would check on you. Where it said "Mother's name" they'd put "Lily Roper", of course, so I worked it all out – I'd had a daughter, Lily, who was born in 1924 when I was only eighteen. I said my husband worked in the brewhouse but he'd died young in an accident so that left just the two of us. My daughter Lil – funny, I sort of came to think she was real – went to work at one of the bases and fell in love with this American pilot, Johnny. He was only twenty-one and she was eighteen. They were going to get married over there, but she'd already fallen pregnant. Then Johnny got killed in a flying accident in Minnesota – I picked that name from a map in the library. Lil had the baby but her nerves got bad, so she went right off her head and jumped on the railway because she said she couldn't live without her Johnny.'

'Oh, that's so sad.'

'I used to make myself cry telling it – how I'd left Bury because of the tragic memories and was bringing me little grandson up alone. I always stopped the conversation right there, and they understood. Even poor John, when he was old enough. I found these two snaps in a junkshop – there was so much stuff after the war, people getting rid of things, things from homes where somebody had died, lots of broken things off bomb sites, rubbish from people's lives. So I found a snap of a pilot by a plane – a stroke of luck, that was, but he was probably thrown over by some girl, or the other way around – and I told John that was his dad. Maybe that lad were killed, but you'd think somebody would have treasured it, wouldn't you . . .?

'Anyway, then I found one of a nice-looking girl who looked like Veronica Lake and said that was his mum, my Lil. He loved those snaps! Had them both in his room, and took them with him when he decided to try his luck out there. Anyway, there it was. Just our John and his nan. I cleaned, I worked in the biscuits, I didn't expect much. Sometimes I'd think I should tell him the truth, but it got harder and harder as time went on, and then you can't, can you? He'd go to the ATC and when you think about it, you'd rather believe *that* about your father than . . . than . . . ohhhh, I'm sor–ry, love.'

'*Shhh, it's all right. Let me get a tissue . . . there, that's better. I'll have to go in a minute – see if Staff wants me.*'

'That's all right. Nothing else to tell . . . Promise me you won't say nothing! I don't want you to say nothing! I don't want people to know. They talk, there's always somebody who'll point the finger . . . Oh, them people aren't kind! *He* wasn't kind! He hurt me . . . Oh, John, John . . . It *hurts* . . .'

'*I'll go and get the staff nurse, Mrs Roper, can you hear me? I'll see if she can get the doctor to come and give you a tablet. Make you sleep . . . Can you hear me, love? I'm just popping out but we'll be back in two shakes of a lamb's tail. All right?*'

'The lad was all I was going to have for the rest of me life. You can't blame me for wanting the best for him, and he always loved his old nan.'

Thirty-Five

B ernie kicked the tyre, hurt her toe and cursed.

A cotton-wisp of moon was rising. Eddy stared at it, then glanced at his watch for the fifth time in an hour, driving her mad.

'Christ, Bernadette, why can't you look after this old thing? When did you last get it serviced?'

'Can't remember,' she snapped.

Bernie turned away, took a couple of paces, then threw herself to the ground, leaning on one elbow and gloomily contemplating the wreck of their weekend.

Eddy smacked the car roof hard. 'What's really bothering me is John.'

'What about him?'

'Bernie, I left him a note saying we'd be back. You know that.'

She shrugged. 'That's the least of me worries.'

He looked at her coldly and she held his gaze until she felt uncomfortable.

'Not so good – letting somebody down. The bloke's uptight enough as it is.'

'Good reason not to bloody want to go out with him then,' she said harshly.

'Christ, Bernie. Sometimes it's like I see you disappearing back to when I first knew you, and I wonder why I bothered.'

Stricken, she stared at him opened-mouthed for a fraction of a second, then turned her back. They'd eaten lunch at the Warra Lodge then fallen asleep in each other's arms under a tree, dazed by perfection. Now the old Holden had died and Eddy was irritated as she had never seen him.

After a short time, she felt him sit, legs outstretched each side, pulling her to lean back against him. Thus cocooned – and forgiven – she found it impossible not to cry.

'Shhhh – don't.'

'It's all . . . spoilt.'

'Of course it's not.'

'Truth?'

'Didn't I promise I'd always tell you the truth?'

Half an hour later a cloud of dust heralded the approach of one of the safari mini-coaches they'd seen at the motel. It stopped, the exhausted French, German and English tourists peering sleepily through the windows, as their khaki-clad guide jumped down and introduced himself as Andy.

After a few seconds of explanation he jumped into the Holden and tried the engine. He nodded, chirped, 'She'll be right!' and went to unstrap his tool kit.

'Bit of a comfort stop, folks!' he yelled at his passengers, who climbed down and stretched, their eyes glazed, as though they had overdosed on scenery and could barely tolerate the lowering red and purple sky.

'Carb, mate – full of dirt? Won't take me long to strip her out . . .?' the guide said, and Bernie blessed the country that could produce such cheerful competence. When he'd finished, and the engine turned over, Andy brushed off their thanks with, 'No worries,' and gave Eddy a clap on the back that almost knocked him over.

* * *

273

It was after ten when they pulled up in front of Bernie's home, behind John Roper's rusty Moke. The bungalow was in darkness. They opened the front door and stood in the hall, listening. The door of John's room was closed. Eddy moved across and knocked softly.

'John?' he called.

There was no reply.

'Listen, mate – it's a real drag, but we had a breakdown. We couldn't get back, OK?'

But the door did not open, and without trying the handle they knew it was locked. The silence rebuked them, and that annoyed Bernie. She turned to Eddy and shrugged. Telling him there was nothing to be done, she led him to the bathroom to share her shower. Red sand was grainy beneath their feet in the shower tray.

It must have been before dawn, but he was unsure whether he'd slept, whether this was a dream, even where he was. Eddy thought he heard a door open and close, but wasn't sure. He listened in the grey-flannel light, but not for long – falling back into a deeper sleep, where he dreamed that he and Bernie were running, hand in hand, from a bush fire that crackled behind them and singed them with its hot breath. He knew he ought to save himself, let her go, run on fast, leave her behind with the animals. But their hands were glued by sweat and he couldn't do it.

He did not catch the quick sound of a car starting up in the street, or the tinny whine of its departure.

'Bernie!' he cried and sat up, sweat running down his chest.

'Shhhhhh, Ed,' she mumbled, turning to snake her arms around his waist, and pull him back down into the tangle of the damp, single sheet.

The light made her blink. 'You would pull the bloody curtains back, wouldn't you?' she mumbled to the empty space in her bed, rolling to press her face into Eddy's pillow. It was his habit to get up early for work but bring her a cup of sweet tea to help her wake, after which she'd usually fall asleep again. Bernie stretched, smiled and waited. She heard the gush of a tap, the slap of his bare feet on the hall lino, the click of the back door opening.

The hectic birdsong from the garden seemed so domestic now, after what she'd experienced. She listened for a while,

274

wondering what Eddy was doing out there, why he didn't come.

'Eddy?' she called.

He moved slowly into the doorway, shoulders sagging, and stood for a moment, staring at her. Then he shook his head, as a dog rids itself of a persistent insect, and glanced back in the direction of the garden, raising one hand to cup his temple.

'What's *wrong*, Eddy?' she called.

He moved towards her, like a zombie. 'I don't believe it,' he said.

'What are you talking about?'

He hunched on the edge of the bed and looked over one shoulder, his mouth twisted.

'The crow's dead,' he said.

'What? How come?'

He shook his head again.

Bernie took his hand and whispered, 'Ahh, but he was a sad old bird, Eddy, with his broken wing. He was bound to turn up his claws sooner or later. I know you liked him, love, and you fed him, but . . .'

'You don't get it!'

'What?'

'He's lying there on the bottom of the cage – feathers all over the place. Somebody's done it to him, Bernie. It's not natural causes. Somebody – somebody wrung his neck.'

Thirty-Six

At the entrance to the car park, Greg Abbott slowed behind a battered Ute stacked with building materials. He watched Hazel's father drop her off then give a thumbs up as he pulled away. Joe Cartwright was a builder who'd worked on the new Abbott tower, one of those whose trade was booming on the back of development in the town. Greg knew he'd already bought Hazel a second-hand Toyota for her nineteenth birthday, coming up in a week, and stashed it in the shed at his yard.

'You won't be needing lifts much longer, chick,' Greg said aloud with a smile, as he watched his secretary click-clack ahead of his BMW in her white-heeled sandals, her pink dress billowing around her calves in the slight breeze.

She stopped and waited while he parked. They exchanged the usual questions about the weekend, then Greg asked after her mother.

'Oh, she's got to have more tests, Greg. Dad's really worried. We all are.'

The freckled face she turned to him was crumpled with concern. A strand of brown hair blew across her mouth, which she seized between a pink-tipped thumb and forefinger, to chew it anxiously.

'Ah, she'll be right, Hazel – you see, Annie's a battler,' Greg said, throwing an arm around her shoulder.

'Hope so, Greg,' she replied, in a small voice. He thought of a little girl who's praying hard for something wonderful to happen, but secretly suspects she's not important enough to be heard.

'Anyway, you got your birthday coming up. That'll cheer Annie up.'

'Oh yes, we're having some people over for a barbie . . . an' you could come if you're not busy, Greg! Next Saturday – I mean, it won't be much, but . . .'

'Will I ever! Would I miss getting your dad to shout me?' Greg grinned, opening the door to let her into the building.

A bottle of some cologne or other, something good for the sweet kid – that's what she'd like, he decided, as he took the stairs two at a time, full of the energy of a new week. On Saturday night he'd had his first proper date with Rosanna, who'd come from Darwin to teach, and charmed him by talking about her class of eight-year-olds as if they were the cleverest children in the universe. Greg found himself watching her over their steaks and imagining what a good mother she'd make, and such a looker too! She was keen on him, she made that clear afterwards – but not too much, which he liked. Greg dropped her off at her lodgings feeling he was definitely in with a chance, and that this time it was what he wanted.

This morning he felt satisfied and excited at once, surprised to find himself daydreaming about her low voice and wishing he didn't have to wait until the evening to give her a call. He twirled his chair to look out at the runway he loved.

John Roper averted his eyes from the patterns on the back of his hands, as he pulled on the control column, feeling the surge with glee. Real power now. This was new, better than anything else. Twin engines! The Beechcraft was a thing of beauty, all right, and he yelled over his shoulder at the four empty seats that they had to realize he'd picked it out specially for them, because he was so pleased to get their charter. He shouted that it wouldn't be long, he'd soon have them all at their destination – 'No problem, old chaps, trust Biggles! Over and out!' He laughed, then pretended the plane was a bucking bronco, just to shake them up a little.

'Roper-the-Hoper says damn you all! Did you hear?' he screamed.

Then he caught sight of his hands again and frowned. Their sun-blotched backs were further disfigured by what looked like spatters of red paint. He'd had to use plasters on the thumb and forefinger of his right hand, which made them clumsier on the controls.

Peck, jab, peck, jab, peck-peck-peck – with the hard stubby beak.

No, you *don't*. Something's got to give, got to *give*, Crow, he thought, as he felt the tiny snap behind that evil little head which had looked on him with such contempt. He saw the ice slide across its eye at last, and let it fall in its straggle of feathers.

'I told you something was due to get it in the neck,' he said aloud, then laughed for a long time.

'What the deuce, old chap?' came the airman's voice from behind him, sounding as if he'd lost ten bob and found a farthing. 'That wasn't a very good show.'

'Don't talk drivel. I gave the chap a sporting chance, Biggles – just look at my hands to prove it!'

'It deserved to die?'

'Affirmative.'

'The crow went west! The crow bought it!' Algy whooped. He must have been sitting next to Biggles, though John hadn't heard him climb in, 'So when do we start the real jaunt, Johnny? Aren't you going to show us some action?'

'Affirmative – and wilco!' smiled John, smoothing his moustache.

He pulled the Beechcraft into a steep climb, then – within moments – they were screaming down towards the burnt-up surface of the earth. Leave it until the last minute, leave it, leave it . . . Orange, red, brown rising, hurtling up at such a speed you wouldn't think, you couldn't possibly do it, unless – that is – you were a genius and born to it, born to fly . . . So – pull out of it again, and yelp with delight to hear Biggles – *Squadron Leader Bigglesworth* – suck his breath in through his teeth, as if he was scared, oh yes!

That'll teach him for not inviting me into the mess!

John glanced at the fuel gauges, sighed and circled slowly, round and round like a crow looking for a carcass far below. He cleared his throat and began to sing, his light tenor pleasing to himself.

'Don't go to work, Ed – pull a sickie, go on!' Bernie pleaded.

'What for? I've finished this now.'

He stood up, and leaned on the shovel, glancing down at the small patch of turned earth where he'd buried the bird. Then he looked up again and met Bernie's troubled eyes.

'He *couldn't* have done it,' she said. ''Cos he felt sorry for it, I know he did.'

'Maybe that's why. He wanted to put it out of its misery?'

'Jesus – maybe. Yeah, that makes it sort of better.'

'We'll ask him tonight. But Bernie, try and watch your temper.'

'He hadn't the *right*! Got a good mind to ring him up at work . . .'

'Wait until tonight.'

'Oh God, I'll have to go to the bloody pub,' she moaned. 'So I won't see him. What an end to our weekend, eh? Bloody ruined.'

Eddy stepped close and held her with his left arm, banging the shovel on the ground to emphasize each slow word he uttered.

'Listen to me, nothing can change what's happened to us!'

She pulled back and stared at him with enormous eyes. 'Truth?'

'What did I tell you?'

Bernie nodded solemnly. They turned towards the house,

278

and Eddy leaned the shovel against its wall. 'Oh please pull a sickie, Ed,' she repeated.

He shook his head.

'I've got things to think about. On the site, doing whatever it is, I can do that. Work things out.'

'Don't think too much, Eddy,' she said, afraid.

At ten, Hazel decided to ask Greg if he wanted coffee or iced tea. Most days she'd play a game with herself to try to guess his choice, which usually bore no relation to the temperature. When it was in the forties he might well choose a cup of scalding black. Sometimes he'd surprise her and ask for a soda.

But now she was afraid to ask. Something was wrong. There was a plane missing. She heard him tell his father on the telephone that he'd something on his mind, that's why he was so annoyed with himself for not noticing it wasn't in the usual place, this side of the runway. Through the open door of her small office she heard agitated footsteps echoing back up the stairwell, after one of the other pilots had been in with Greg, assuring him that nobody put the Beechcraft away in the hangar.

Hazel rose and stood in the doorway, anxiously fingering pink cotton with one hand, and pushing her hair back with the other.

'Greg?'

'Yeah?' He didn't usually sound so brisk.

'Shall I go to the canteen and fetch you a chocolate bar and something to drink?'

He glanced at his watch and shook his head. 'Too early for smoko, Hazel. Why don't you finish those letters I gave you yesterday, they need to get off pronto.'

The testiness in his voice was so unfamiliar Hazel folded her arms in a gesture of defence. 'I wasn't trying to shirk, Greg . . .'

She looked so worried he wanted to get up, lead her back to her desk, and soothe her as you might a small cat. 'I know. I'm not being funny, chick. There's a slight problem on, that's all . . .' He twisted to gaze outside and she heard him mumble, 'What the hell's going on?' before turning back to force a smile in her direction. 'We'll get some iced tea in about forty minutes, OK?'

At ten fifteen exactly Greg was on the telephone to the police, when he thought he heard the sound of an aircraft far off, but it was hardly unusual. Hazel's typewriter was clattering

279

away next door, and he was irritated by the slight obtuseness of the man on the other end of the line.

'I told you, the keys are all in one place . . . Yes, the staff do know that . . .' he explained.

The two air-traffic controllers, Barry Andrews and Steve Smith, were relaxed, chatting about their respective weekends. The mystery of the Beechcraft hadn't reached their eyrie yet, but aircraft engineer Bill Simmonds was at the point of getting up from his seat in a room below Greg Abbott's office, where he sat with his colleagues Mike Chin and Danny Butler, to wander over to the control tower and spread the news. Mike Chin was full of excitement at the birth of his first baby, a boy born in the small hours of Saturday morning, and Danny and Bill, fathers already, were wanting to know when they'd all be going out to wet the baby's head.

Still, the talk about the missing plane took the edge off their camaraderie. Something strange had happened and all the employees of Abbott-Air closed ranks in their disquiet as soon as they heard. After all, Bill Simmonds told Mike Chin, no bloke could walk in off the street and steal a bloody plane, just like that – not like a car or a motorcycle. It had to be an inside job. He shook his head and decided to sit down and have another cigarette, squinting out over the runway, where heat already shimmered in a dream of water. Someone was bound to have picked up the phone to the controllers, he reckoned. They'd know about the Beechcraft by now. He inhaled, and swapped thoughts with Mike and Danny about the likelihood of a tourist joyrider.

'Listen!' said Mike, holding up his hand.

Bill's cigarette was halfway to his mouth, and Danny was just tapping his from the pack. They listened hard. Experts who could identify the noise of any engine.

At first all the controllers heard was the crackle, then laughter, then some words Barry Andrews couldn't make out. He frowned and indicated that Steve Smith should listen.

'He's singing!' he whispered. 'Least – I think that's what I heard.'

They both listened. Clearer now, the voice came in: '*Echo November Alpha to control tower, are you receiving me?*' They waited for the 'over' signal, but it did not come. Instead the song began again, as the two controllers stared at each other in disbelief.

'We'll meet again, don't know where, don't know when, But I know we'll met again some sunny day. Keep smiling through, just like you always do, Till the blue skies take those dark clouds right away . . .'

They'd recognized the call sign and heard the noise of the aircraft, coming in at a low altitude, nearer and nearer. Barry hunched and shouted, 'Come in, Echo November Alpha – come in, Echo November Alpha – can you hear me?'

The voice spoke now, crackling savagely at them and making them shiver – as they would tell their friends for years.

'It's better to die with honour than live with dishonour, old chaps, that's what it told me! My father said it too, and he should know . . . Ha ha! Crossed bombs and a death's head . . . Over and out.'

But it wasn't over and out. He sang again, *'Now will you just say hello to the folks that I know, Tell them I won't be long. They'll be happy to know that as I flew away I was singing this song . . .'*

He yelled the words, and heard the engines match his scream. He saw the sheets of blue and gold ahead – the low-rise tower becoming sun and sky. The runway turned to liquid silver, a river flowing beneath him. The fuselage shuddered. His pecked hands held steady, aiming carefully, making sure he would get this right.

Greg heard the screech as the Beechcraft came in low and straight. He had no time to whirl round in his chair to see what was happening. In the room below him, Mike Chin, Danny Butler and Bill Simmonds jumped up, their chairs crashing backwards, as the banshee din blew away any words, any chance of drawing breath to cry out in horror at the end of things.

Nobody who heard would ever forget the hideous bang and the crash of twisted metal as John Roper flew the Beechcraft straight at the room where he knew Ace Abbott's son sat, carrying on the family tradition. Metal slicing razor-edged, glass exploding, fuel from the wing tank gushing and spraying over the body of Greg Abbot, hurled high into the air . . .

Hazel Cartwright's hands hovered above her typewriter. And the last thing she saw was the head of the English pilot rolling like a watermelon across the floor of her office, before the fireball reached her.

Thirty-Seven

One policeman set the chisel against the doorframe and broke into John Roper's room. His partner stood next to Bernie, waiting. There were reporters in the street, and a small crowd of people come to stare at the house where the kamikaze murderer stayed. Bernie looked out of her window at the set, hostile faces, and felt the taint by association that afflicts the families of the wicked.

'I want to go out there and tell them he's got nothing to do with us,' she whispered to Eddy, who took her arm to lead her away.

'But that wouldn't be true,' he protested. 'He lived here and we knew him . . .'

'No, we didn't!' she cried. 'We didn't know him at all!'

Eddy had been moving soil when he heard the distant crash. He stopped. The other men raised their heads. There was a hush, as if the leaves held their breath, waiting for the black smoke to funnel over the airport. Then, as the hours passed, the news seemed to filter through the streets and homes of the town, nobody quite knowing how, a whisper carried by wind and bird – that there'd been a crash, someone had played kamikaze, nobody knew who, Ace Abbott's son was dead, ten people were burnt, two people had died, two planes destroyed, fifteen people dead, it took them four hours to put out the blaze, they managed to identify the pilot . . . And so on.

After arguing with the foreman, and finally clinching it with the mysterious assertion that he might well be a witness, Eddy biked home to find the police car outside. Bernie ran to him and clung on, her teeth chattering, her eyes red.

The policeman reappeared in the doorway of John's room and called to her. 'You want to come and check out your boyfriend's stuff, Miss?'

'He's not – I mean, he wasn't – my boyfriend!' she protested.

The policeman shrugged.

Eddy followed her across the threshold. The man raised his eyebrows and held out a small sheaf of blue writing paper, covered in round, unformed handwriting. 'Well, the bloke seemed to think different. Check this. He'd chucked it in the waste-paper basket.'

Slowly Bernie held out her hand for the notepaper and read the last letter from Lily Roper. 'This is from his gran, back home,' she whispered, her eyes following the lines, conscious of Eddy reading too, over her shoulder.

Bernie covered her eyes, and thrust the paper back. 'It's not true,' she protested, shaking her head vigorously. 'None of that's true. None of it. It's all his bloody fantasy. Oh, Jesus Christ . . .'

The policeman raised an eyebrow, but his voice was expressionless. 'So – this lady writing the letter's the official next of kin – right, mate?'

Eddy nodded. The policeman shrugged, as if it didn't matter to him whether or not Bernie was the lover of the Kamikaze Pom – as John Roper would come to be known in the days following. The only important thing, the only matter of any significance, for him and the rest of the town – and the whole country as the story hit airwaves and newstands – was that the crazy English pilot had killed innocent people just because he'd been sacked. His was a name, they agreed at the station, only fit to be uttered with a gob of spit.

'You can take a look,' the policeman said, jerking a thumb at the room. 'But don't touch anything. The photographer gets here any minute'.

Eddy took Bernie's hand, and led her a couple of paces forward into the chaos of John's room. The wooden chair was firewood in the centre of the floor, and he'd pulled the sheets and pillows off the bed, and piled them there too, with his clothes and what she guessed were letters from his grandmother. Long rents split the mattress; the Swiss Army knife lay with the largest blade still open. There was a stink of rotting peel and rancid butter from the contents of the kitchen waste bin, upended on the bed, over Bernie's Christmas hat.

'He must've *hated* us,' she whispered.

On top of the pile of wood and bedding on the floor, she was shocked to see John's precious books. Some of them were torn; pages like wings around the pyre. She glimpsed an image of a pilot in a sheepskin flying jacket and leather helmet, goggles pushed on top of his head. 'He started to burn it all – look,' she whispered, pointing to the blackened edges in places, and the singed bedding. But the whole pile was soaked in water, as if he had lost his nerve.

When Bernie dragged her eyes from the mess on the floor to the table beyond it, she could not prevent herself from crying out. On the veneer surface where once Patrick Molloy struggled with his homework, hiding the girlie magazines under his books, John Roper had created a shrine.

In the centre was his trophy from the flying school, set on an upturned mug, itself raised on the walnut box which still contained Mrs Molloy's button collection. Flanking it were the framed photographs John had shown them that first evening – the airman and the pretty young girl, both squinting against the light. Balanced to stand open in front of the raised trophy was a log book.

On the Friday he had written, 'SENTENCED TO DEATH THIS DAY.' On Saturday the entry said, 'BIGGLES WILL FLY AGAIN.' The entry for Sunday read, 'MY FATHER SAYS THE CROW MUST DIE. CROSSED BOMBS AND A DEATH'S HEAD.' The last entry gave an identification number, and the words, 'SUICIDE MISSION . . . THE END.'

Placed precisely in front of the log book was a sheet of cartridge paper Eddy recognized as torn from the drawing book Bernie gave him for Christmas. At the top of the page was a skull, with two crossed bombs beneath it. A speech bubble came from the skull's mouth: 'Time to die!' Below the device was a crude drawing of a plane, viewed from above. Along the wings in thick black lettering was, 'VH – DEATH', and in smaller letters the words 'HELL'S AIRLINES' along the fuselage. Running across the page at the bottom was a message in neat lower-case print:

To Whom It May Concern:
By now you will know that in the early morning of Monday January 10th an aircraft was stolen from Abbott-Air and crashed into the company's office building at high speed. I am the pilot of that aeroplane, and wish to explain why I have been forced to take my own life. I consider that my life has been ruined by Greg Abbott of that

company, who, with no reason AT ALL, gave me the sack last Friday and so ended the happiest period of my life and the career I always wanted. MY FAMILY HONOUR REQUIRES ME TO TAKE REVENGE. My first plan was to use a Cessna 210 for my mission but I decided to switch to the Beechcraft Baron because it would have over three times the energy of the Cessna and do that much more damage. This is the only way I can draw attention to the way I have been treated by Greg Abbott and I hope that others may benefit in some way from this final, ultimate sacrifice of mine. I ask that my grandmother, Mrs Lily Roper of 9 Syton Street, Liverpool 13, is told of my death, and that she knows I died honourably in the name of my father whose flight path I followed.

That is all now. My life is ended.

John Roper

'Jesus,' Bernie whispered, noticing at the same time that the only thing in the room that was still in its original place was the photograph of John's grandmother, still on the shelf.

Eddy looked stricken. 'If we'd known he'd been sacked I'd never've left him alone the whole weekend. He couldn't take it, He *needed* somebody . . .'

'It's not our fault, Eddy. You *can't* turn it into our fault. I won't let you. You sound like you're sorry for him, but all I'm thinking about is those people he took with him. Why'd he have to do that? I mean – top yourself, mate, be my guest! But why the fuck take people with you?'

White-faced, Eddy shook his head.

'Queer the bastard doesn't mention *you*?' said the policeman, turning to Bernie with an odd, unpleasant little grimace.

'No it's not!' she cried, too loudly. 'I told you, the bloke's got nothing to do with me. Nothing at bloody *all*. Do I have to put an announcement in the f— the paper?'

'What you'll have to do is give us a statement,' he said, with dislike.

Suddenly the room was even more hot and crowded. There was a noise from the street. The police photographer's flash crackled in her skull. 'Oh Jesus, I can't stand this,' she groaned, passing a hand across her face. 'Eddy . . .?'

But he had gone.

She found him outside, looking down at the spot where he'd buried the crow, early that morning. A beetle meandered across the soil, its back iridescent blue-green against the dark red. Silently they watched it change direction, and head back past Eddy's boot. Suddenly he raised his foot and slowly lowered it on the insect, crushing it, grinding the ball of his foot into the soil until there were no fragments left. Bernie began to cry.

'Why'd you do *that*? You don't do things like that, Eddy!'

He shrugged. 'It's so easy. Makes me feel like God. And anyway, the poor little bastard's got nothing to do with me.'

'Don't . . .'

'You're crying for a beetle, Bernadette! What I really love to see is compassion in a woman – it gets me right *here*!' He banged his own chest with a fist.

'*Please* don't . . .'

'*You* don't! Don't let me hear you say again John's got nothing to do with us, OK? I don't know how you can look at those pathetic pics in there of his mum and dad, and read all that stuff he wrote, and not feel sorry for him. The bloke was *sick*, Bernie. And I mean, he gave us Christmas presents, for God's sake!'

She was sobbing properly now, babbling that she knew, that he was right, that she was sorry, that it was the shock and so he mustn't be angry with her . . .

Face shuttered against her, he shook his head. 'I just hate it when that hard look's on you. It's like I don't know who you are.'

'Yes, you do, Eddy!' she protested. 'You do know me. You've done so much for me, and it's like – I only know myself because of you. I . . . Oh Jesus, why shouldn't I say it? I'm in love with you, Eddy! I'm sorry – I shouldn't of . . .'

She heard the pleading in her own voice. But his was matter-of-fact. 'All I want to know is – will you write to John's grandmother? The police'll get in touch with her and there'll be what to do with the body . . .' His voice thickened, and he swallowed. 'But somebody proper's got to write to the old lady. Somebody who'll be . . . *kind*. And I think it should be you.'

She nodded.

'I'll do it, Eddy. And I'll tell her – no, I won't tell her he was shooting a line, with all that stuff about me. I'll let her believe what she wants. I'll give her that. Yeah, I'll write a good letter. I'll do it for you, Eddy!'

He stared at her in silence, his ravaged face the mirror of her own. Then he sighed and shook his head. 'You still don't get it, do you? You shouldn't be saying you'll do it for me. You need to do it for John.'

The silence strung out between them. She looked at his earnest, reproachful face and hated him. It had gone. They'd destroyed it all – the two of them, him and John together. Yesterday – a hundred years ago – he had given her something sacred. She'd doused that small pyre with holy water, saving her soul at last. She could close her eyes for a fraction of a second and see a painted woman, a baby and a bird. But now it had gone. The only memory was of predators tearing at rotting meat in the back of beyond, where everything eats everything else because there's no choice, and nothing can be saved.

Her voice clanged, harsh as a vulture's. 'Well, looks like I can't do a single bloody thing right, can I? What's wrong with you, Eddy? We should be . . . we should be . . . *together*, helping each other – and all you can do is knock me. That the *best* you can do? You want me to say I knew him? Well, listen mate, I'm *ashamed* I knew him! You should be protecting me! You should be telling people I'm *your* woman, not his! I don't get you, Eddy! This rat-shit thing's happened to us, and all you can do is make out it's all my fault.'

'It happened to *him*,' he said stubbornly.

In exasperation she slapped her own head. 'You're a fool, Eddy! It's happened to the whole bloody town – and nobody gives a fuck about the Pom, except to hate his miserable, cowardly guts!'

Shocked, he took a step towards her, but she had already swung round to the back door. She turned to shout, 'I'm going to give me bloody statement about how the bloke was nuts – and go to work. Do something useful, will you? Get rid of that bloody crow's cage before I come home! Burn it up. Give it one of your nice Abo ceremonies!'

'Bernie!' he called. 'Don't go to to the pub!'

'Why not? Fuck off, Eddy! I hate the way you make me feel! You went to work this morning, when I asked you not to, so why shouldn't I? At least I'll be talking to my own kind, not a freak like you.'

*   *   *

287

The town hunkered down to lick its wounds. The eyes of the shops were closed, waiting. The fire that had taken four hours to control left fine ash on the air, and a smell of corrosion. People stood on corners, speaking in lowered voices, shaking their heads. Everybody knew somebody who knew somebody who lived next door to one of the dead or injured. Everybody knew of old Ace Abbott, and trembled to think of his anguish. Pity and terror wandered from house to house with the news, closely followed by hatred for the outsider who had done the deed.

Bernie drove to work very slowly. She did not trust herself to go her usual speed, fearing it could be catching – that urge to self-destruct. That the sight of a long, blank wall would exert such a pressure to put her foot down it would prove impossible to resist. She could barely be bothered to change gear, and the Holden protested. The engine's whine juddered across the surface of her brain. Driving like a robot, she glanced down at the wizened, animal claws that clutched the wheel and wondered who they belonged to.

The Zoo was already filling up. When she walked through the door, weary with the effort of putting one foot in front of the other, Dick Springville loomed beside her, shaking his head. 'Jeez, Bernie, what d'you think?'

''Bout what?'

'What your fucking Pommy boyfriend's done, that's what!'

Bernie banged the can she was holding on the surface of the bar, then set up a rapid percussion to punctuate every word she shouted.

'For the last time, he wasn't my boyfriend. He lived in my house, OK? He paid me rent! Anybody says he was anything else'll get this can rammed down his throat so far it'll come out in his pants – you understand, Dick?'

For a second Dick Springville looked as if he might strike her, then he backed off, literally stepping back, one hand raised.

'All right, all right, Bern, only kidding.'

Gradually the noise surfaced again, everybody was talking about the Kamikaze Pom, with none of the wrangling that had marked the endless discussions about the dingo baby case last year. The blunt certainty of this case united everybody in the knowledge that the English pilot was a wicked, murdering bastard.

'Must of gone troppo.'

'Yeah, but Christ – to do it like that!'

'Greg Abbott was a decent bloke. Gave everybody a fair crack of the whip.'

'They was planning her nineteenth. Her mum's sedated.'

'Joe Cartwright's mate told my dad Joe'll never be the same again.'

'What about old Ace? Fucking huns couldn't kill 'im but the bastard Pom might just do it.'

'Why would you do it? Like that? I mean, if he wanted to murder Greg cos he had a beef about getting the sack, he could of knifed him or something. That way, it's bloke to bloke, yeah?'

'A teenage girl never did harm to nobody.'

'Tell you what – good job the Pom made a good job of killing his fucking self.'

'Plenty of people'd like to kill him – real slowly.'

'Takin' Aussies with him – bastard!'

'Chop him into a million bits an' it wouldn't be bad enough for the murdering psycho.'

Bernie served, and listened. Lighting cigarette after cigarette, she took every chance to nod agreement with what was being said. From time to time somebody would throw a nervous question at her, asking what Roper was really like. She stonewalled. All she was interested in was getting her rent, she said. She didn't know anything about the bloke, and didn't want to.

'He used to talk in this Pommy air-force slang, didn't he?'

'Yeah, he was weird,' she shrugged.

'They say he told Ace Abbott that his old man was some American air-force bigwig.'

'Nah, that's not right. He was just a pilot,' she said.

'Dead?'

'Yeah, he never knew him. Died before he was born.'

'Hey, is it true the Pom left a kind of screwy *altar* in his room? And tried to wreck the joint – I mean, your place?' somebody asked excitedly.

The hubbub quietened again. They looked at her. 'Where'd you get that from?' she asked.

'Everybody knows – it's all over town. Must of come from the coppers.'

The noise rose again. Was there a suicide note? Is it true he wasn't qualified anyway – that's why Greg fired him? No, heard he'd been caught thieving. They say he fancied Hazel Cartwright and thought Greg was having a thing with her . . . No, the

Pommy bastard told his folks he was gunna marry B— Shhhhhh, she'll hear you . . .

With no choice but to listen, Bernie did her best to close off. Efficient appendages to her shoulders filled schooners and handed over cans and took money and counted out change and washed glasses. The voices receded, repeating themselves in an endless spiral of anecdote and speculation, yet never running out of curses on the dismembered body of John Roper.

Who had nothing to do with her.

She found herself looking at the two entrances to the bar again and again, as the night dragged on, convinced she'd look up and Eddy would be standing there, as he had been three months ago – just as if he had wandered accidentally from another world. Surely he must come now?

'Need a lock-in tonight, Bern – and you got to stay,' Dick barked.

'Nuthing to do on a night like this, mate, 'cept get rat-arsed,' she said loudly, to be rewarded by a rabbit punch of approval and, 'Goodonya – now you sound like the old Bern.'

How could you avoid it, she thought, if Eddy didn't come?

At two a.m. he let her go, and Bernie drove herself home, surprisingly sober although her chest felt as if she had swallowed a truckload of burning sand. She pulled up, and sat in the Holden for a few minutes, resting her head on the wheel. The thought of turning her key in the lock and walking past John Roper's room oppressed her. Anything might be bearable if she knew Eddy had forgiven her. But supposing her harsh words still filled his head and he despised her?

Ah, but Bernie, she told herself, he's always forgiven you before. He *understands* you.

The bungalow was silent, which didn't surprise her. The doors along the central corridor turned blank faces as she instinctively raised herself on tiptoe. She didn't want to wake him just yet. Yet she had imagined him running to enfold her.

To her surprise the back door was locked. They didn't usually bother when there was somebody in the house, because the fences out the back were so high. But maybe he felt nervous tonight, she thought. Maybe Eddy feared the ghost of John Roper might try to return to the place he had lived, and from which finally he had flown off into the desert, leaving the images of his parents behind. An unquiet spirit, she thought. Maybe that's why Eddy locked the door . . .

The garden smelled of burning. In the moonlight she could see no trace of the crow's cage, but the darker patch where it had been. Bernie thought of her last harsh instruction to him and quailed. He had done as she asked. Always he tried to do what he could to please her. Suddenly incapable of bearing the pain in her chest, she turned and ran into the house, bursting into her bedroom, calling, 'Eddy, I'm sorry!'

But the bed was smooth. The only thing in the room was the faint light from outside, catching the glass of the old wardrobe. In a panic she turned and threw open the door of Eddy's own room, whispering, 'Eddy?'

The rucksack he'd left in the corner was gone, and there was no sign of the drawing book and pencils which usually lay on the table. There was a cleansed, calm air in the room she could not help contrasting – even now in her fear – with the mess John Roper had left next door. Blindly, Bernie turned to the bathroom, but Eddy's brush and razor had gone from their usual place on the shelf, although John Roper's things were still there.

'Eddy!' she called, pulling the shower curtain aside in case he should be hiding there as a joke, to jump out and hug her and tell her it would all be fine. Her voice echoed back off the tiles, the same, but weaker.

'*Eddy!*' she screamed.

Stumbling like an old woman, Bernie walked back to his room, and noticed for the first time that he had left one thing behind. The yidaki in its woven case leaned against the wall behind the door. With a small cry she seized it, and clutched it to her chest, cuddling it between her breasts as she threw back her head to suck in air. Her own last curse echoed in her head – '*Fuck off, Eddy!*' – and she groaned.

Yet he had left the yidaki. Panicking, she ran through the possibilities. He had left it deliberately, as a message that he'd return. But no, she would not allow herself that succour. She saw his boot grind the insect into atoms. Again she heard her ugly voice screaming, '*Fuck off, Eddy!*' and began to cry in the knowledge that Eddy had left the instrument simply because he no longer wanted to play it. She had made him play it for her and that was the last time. Now he'd moved on, as she always knew he would.

Eddy had gone forever.

'Damn you, Roper!' she sobbed. 'It's all your fault! It's all your fault!'

Bleakly she closed the door on his room, still clutching the yidaki to her as if it might transform itself into his sinewy shape, and lie down with her once more.

'I didn't mean it, Eddy – oh I'm sorry, I'm sorry,' she choked, and stumbled towards John Roper's door in the darkness.

The police had told her not to enter the room again until the proper investigators had come from the city and taken everything away. She stood in the doorway, staring at the remains of the English pilot's existence, harshly illuminated in the single bulb. Her eyes travelled over the trophy, the framed photographs each side, the log book, the drawing, then stared at the vandalized bed and the mess on the floor. That must have been for me, she thought. A present for my land-lady – who rejected me, like everybody else.

She stared at the Swiss Army knife, still lying on the bed, and remembered John's puzzled pleasure. She fingered the necklace she never took off, and screwed her eyes tight, conjuring up that day when the wrapping paper had drifted to the floor and they had tried to make each other happy. All three of them.

She opened her eyes again, and the room was so ugly, but so pitiful, her legs could not bear the weight of what she saw. Slowly she slid down the doorframe so she was sitting on the threshold, Eddy's yidaki resting across her knees. She stroked it, then leaned her head back against the wood, looking side-ways at the shrine John Roper had left. For them? For his grand-mother? No, she thought, it was just a statement to himself.

She had no idea how long she sat there, exhausted yet with no need to sleep, before a thought made her scramble stiffly to her feet. Leaning the instrument against the wall, she walked with a sleepwalker's shuffle to the lounge room. There was something that had to be done.

She carried back the twisted brass candlesticks Colleen Molloy had brought from Cork and polished vigorously every week until she died. The cleaning liquid was black on the inside of the twists. The sight of them invoked an image of those broad red arms and hands, polishing and scrubbing and chopping and scouring for ever and ever, Amen.

Bernie set the candles on the floor about three feet apart, just inside the door of John Roper's room, between where she was sitting and the pile of his belongings. Then she took the matches from her shirt pocket and lit them, kneeling for a second before rising to switch off the light. Cradling the yidaki across her lap, she took up her former position across the doorway, like a guard.

The candle flames burned high, throwing a dancing shadow of John Roper's flying trophy on the wall behind and softening the confusion of the room. Bernie's eyes grew used to the darkness and she stared at the shadowy photographs on the table, imagining she could make out the blurred faces which might come alive for one second and tell her . . .

But what?

Awed by the silence, she spoke aloud to the hazy American pilot and the girl with her hair in a roll who looked like somebody called Veronica Lake. 'You have to forgive him. Nobody else will – so you have to. Let's hope everything the priest said was right – and he'll be with you. Oh – Holy Mother of God – I hope so.'

Ah, but wait – she thought. That won't work. The souls of those who have not received holy unction will go to purgatory, Father Mullen had said firmly, frowning at them for daring even to think there might be some mercy.

And my poor little baby in limbo.

'No – it can't be like that, can it, Eddy?' she asked, and stroked the yidaki, bending every so often to rub her face on the coarse cloth of its case. 'I can't believe it's like that. I'd rather have *your* stories, Eddy. Good stories.'

She held the cube he'd carved with her initial, turning it over and over in her fingers, desolately rehearsing in her mind every small thing Eddy Carpenter had said and done since first he entered her house. At last, exhaustion made her head drop. The long candles had burnt down to about two inches when she raised her head from her knees, blinked and looked across at the shrine on the table once more.

Her voice rang back from the crudely drawn skull and crossed bombs. 'Can you hear me – John, Eddy – wherever you are? Are you listening? It's still the three of us, here.'

Thirty-Eight

She bought an aerogramme and wrote the letter with a biro in which Ayers Rock floated. At last, after over an hour of chewing her nails, smoking and biting her lips, she licked the adhesive edges and sealed her words inside their flimsy blue sleeve.

Dear Mrs Roper,

I know you know of me as the person your grandson John has been lodging with, since the end of October. Sadly I think you must probably know by now as well that John met with a flying accident the day before yesterday. ~~He went~~ I won't go into the details of that crash because that is for others to do as they see fit. It was a really terrible thing and I am so sorry to think of you getting such ~~bad~~ tragic news. We were shocked as well.

All I want to do is tell you how sorry I am for your trouble, and that John was a ~~nice~~ good person to have in the house. My other lodger, Eddy Carpenter, was his friend and asks me to say how much he liked your grandson and how sorry he is too. Eddy and I were very fond of John, and I think he was happy living here with ~~me~~ both of us. We had some happy times, specially at Christmas, when we had a good dinner and some fun.

Please believe me when I write that I hope it doesn't make you more upset to read this. It's always hard to know what to say at a time of loss – but I thought you would like to hear that John had been ~~quite~~ happy here and made some good friends. Eddy says that ~~in a way~~ it's important to tell you that.

John told us that you were always a support in his plan to come out here and learn to fly, as he was not able to do at home. So maybe you would like to know that he ~~seemed OK~~ was very good at his job and seemed OK. I know he wrote to you and told you what he was doing, so you know that he had ~~some news he~~ great plans.

The police and special investigators have taken away his personal things, but I reckon they will send them to you in time. I expect John's body will be flying home to you for a proper service and so I wish you would put one flower on – from Eddy Carpenter and myself – and accept our sincere condolences for your terrible loss. It is hard to know what else to say, except repeat how sorry we are, and that we are pleased to have known your grandson.

Yours with sympathy,
Bernadette Molloy

For days after the disaster the national newspapers returned to the story again and again. The headlines called John Roper's life 'A ONE-WAY TICKET TO A NASTY MELODRAMATIC DEATH' and gave full details of how 'FAILURE SET COURSE TO KAMIKAZE DEATH'. The air-traffic controllers told reporters how the English pilot was singing the famous Vera Lynn wartime anthem as he approached the airport, and there were even pictures of the bizarre shrine in his room and a transcript of his suicide note.

There were plenty of photographs of the dead, and colleagues described the virtues of the three hardworking men who left a total of five fatherless children behind. John Roper's picture (dredged from the immigration file, Bernie supposed) looked shifty, which matched the impressions of people he had encountered since his arrival. Their interviews said he was strange and obsessive, and commented on his habitual use of World War II slang. His nickname 'Roper-the-Hoper' was repeated again and again. The nation was united in just outrage at the murdering Kamikaze Pom.

Bernie called in sick, and slammed the phone down on Dick's protests. Then she turned her lie into truth by blotting out most of a week with vodka and white wine, hardly eating, making herself ill. Crawling about, deep within a familiar pit, she read the local paper's accounts of the various funerals of Greg Abbott, Hazel Cartwright, Mike Chin, Danny Butler and Bill Simmonds, and followed the progress of the six others who'd been injured. She heard requiem masses in her head, and waited for word from Eddy.

None came. When disbelief turned to certainty, she could do nothing but sit on the verandah looking out over her garden, turning her eyes again and again to where he had buried the damaged crow, wondering what to do. Only the need for wine and cigarettes pushed her out to the shops – when she picked up snacks as an afterthought. The kitchen sink filled up with used crockery, until she ran out. The house grew dirty. She forgot to wash her clothes and left towels in musty bundles. As she sat smoking, staring into space, listening to sounds once more anonymous, without Eddy, she wondered how it could have happened that she was set back on this course, doomed to career round the circuit, passing the same points again and again, waiting for the flag that signalled the end.

At least John got out, she reflected. At least he did that for himself. She knew he was lying in the morgue while his next of kin's instructions were being sought, and realized she had never felt closer to him than now. She thought of Nembutal, and envied him.

One morning Bernie woke in the squalor of her room to hear somebody rapping on her door.

'Eddy!' she thought, and scrambled from bed, to be halted by her hideous reflection in the wardrobe door. She saw a wrecked creature he might not recognize, had he not seen it like that already. That was before he had held her face and told her – yes, he had, she remembered, and would cling on to that echo forever – that she was lovable.

The letter box rattled again.

Bernie clutched her kimono about her and peered blearily at the policeman on the step. She recognized him as the one who had chiselled his way into John Roper's room.

'G'day,' he nodded.

'Yeah?'

'Should of rung maybe, but I was passing and thought you'd like to be filled in with the latest on your lodger. That right?'

Bernie nodded.

'Seems our bloke's been in touch with the Pommy Foreign Office, trying to get in touch with Roper's next of kin . . .?' She nodded again. The policeman spread his hands in a gesture of indifference. 'Taken a while, but they say there ain't one. No rellies.'

Bernie straightened her back. 'I don't get it – what about

his grandmother? You saw the letter from her, and he put her address in that last message . . .?'

He shook his head. 'Looks like she passed away already. Story is – she was in hospital and didn't make it. Just as well really, eh? Poor old girl got away without knowing what happened.'

Bernie nodded slowly.

'Yeah,' she whispered.

'Reckon if you ring the morgue in a day they'll be able to tell you when the Pom's going to be buried. That's if you want to know . . .?'

Dazed, she nodded. The policeman squared his shoulders and spat lightly on the ground at the right of her short path, making the dust scatter and roll. 'Reckon there won't be many people mobbing his grave with bunches of flowers, eh?'

'That's for sure,' said Bernie slowly, shaking her head.

'Nobody to cry for the bastard, eh?'

'That's right,' she replied. 'Nobody.'

He was turning away when Bernie exclaimed, 'I just thought of something!' The policeman waited, faintly repelled by the hand that suddenly clutched his arm. 'His stuff, the things they took away . . . There were two pictures, photographs of his folks. And his flying trophy as well. I reckon . . .'

She stopped.

'Yeah?'

'Well, strikes me they should go with him, you know – be buried with him? Since nobody wants them. So – can I make that . . . like a formal request?'

He shrugged. 'If you reckon it matters?'

When she nodded he said, 'OK, no worries, I'll tell the boss. You can put a call in too.'

'I'll do just that, mate,' Bernie said. 'Tell them what I think.'

Bernie looked around the yellow kitchen with distaste, reached for the pack of cigarettes on the window sill, paused with her hand hovering, then scooped them into the waste bin in one fluid motion. Leaning back against the sink unit, cradling her mug with both hands, she was unable to avoid a memory of the night she had reached for Eddy and he had rested his chin on her head. As so often in the days since John Roper's suicide, she continued with the one-sided conversation she suspected might never end.

'I did what you told me,' she said. 'You know that? I wrote to Lily Roper, Eddy, but it was too late. Maybe she was dead before he killed himself, maybe it was just after . . . Poor old thing . . . Least she never knew, like the bloke said.'

She waited.

'I was too late, anyway. But I just want you to know I did it, Eddy. And now – you know what else I'm gonna to do? See to this dump like Ma would be proud of me. No – like you would, Eddy. I'm not goin' on living like I've been, OK?'

An answer of sorts came back in birdsong from outside, joining the faint echo of her own voice within the sunny walls, as she reached out and stroked the tap Eddy had mended. Without thinking, she took a tea towel and rubbed it over the surface, then noticed her own face framed in the polished swan neck, elongated as in a distorting mirror. The long pale oval marked with sinuous S-curves of eyebrow and nose, small mouth turned down, recalled images she remembered from the book of Bible stories they read in school, illustrated with details from medieval art – the gravity of the angels and the passive sweetness of the Virgin, who could not turn aside from news she did not want to hear. Then Bernie was overcome by the transformation of the ordinary, the mystery of how such an object could be so beautiful in her eyes it might even redeem the time she had wasted . . .

'The granny had no choice,' she said to the tap, seeing her reflected mouth open into a small O, as if in song. 'But I reckon I do, Eddy. I mean, *you* chose to leave, and John chose to . . . to do *that*, but that poor old soul in Liverpool hadn't any option, had she? So maybe I'll dedicate the rest of today to *her*, Eddy. You'd think that was good, wouldn't you?'

It took eight trips to the garden to clear the mess from John Roper's floor. She dragged the mattress out as well, and heaped the lot into a pile ready for burning. That would have to wait until night, she realized, and she must warn the neighbours. Briefly frustrated by that thought, which obstructed her desire for immediate transformation, she turned back to the house, took Colleen's old bucket of cleaning things, and did not stop until the room smelt only of bleach. She closed the door on it, murmuring, 'There you are, John's granny – old Lily – all cleaned up.'

Methodically she cleaned Eddy's bedroom too, muttering

angrily as she did so, telling him this proved she was quite capable of doing things alone in just the way he'd have done them, and so he could stay on the road and good riddance.

When she closed the door on that room, she pushed her misery aside and crossed into the sunny space she had started to think of as 'theirs', where the double bed reminded her for a second of her parents' red faces side by side, mouths open in sleep. She smoothed the pillows, shuddering at the thought of human excrement lying there – then driving that memory away with a vision of a sock lying on her pillow, stuffed with small packages wrapped in yellow and green tissue. Then the vision of Eddy stroking her asleep.

Working methodically and with such dogged energy there was none left for emotion, she moved through the whole bungalow, even putting polish on Colleen Molloy's sideboard. Sweat soaked her T-shirt and shorts, and she smiled wryly at her own reluctance to sully the shower after she'd cleaned it so well.

By three she was tired, but remembered to call the police station, adopting her most respectable voice, and said that, as John Roper's landlady, and since there was no next of kin, she thought it right that his personal effects should be buried with him. The mantra, 'No worries', convinced Bernie that it would be done as she asked.

She climbed stiffly into the Holden to drive for food. Something else was bothering her too, and she could no longer push it away. It couldn't happen – not to her. After Tom they'd shaken their heads and warned her. In all those years of careless sinning she had watched the flow of her blood, marvelling that it was the only thing regular in her life, ebbing and flowing, obeying the moon.

In the chemist's she hesitated. She walked around, picking things up and putting them down, selecting a lavender bath set like the one that still lay unused in her drawer and raising it to her face to inhale the smell that seemed old-fashioned and healing.

Poor John, she thought, surprising herself.

Miserable, she hesitated over an apricot lip gloss before picking it up and moving over to the counter with her request.

At that moment, far away, Eddy Carpenter felt happy. He stood at the side of the road, and lowered his rucksack with a thump, tipping long draughts of water down his throat. You could never know, he thought, if you'd done the right thing, sometimes until such a long time afterwards. But now, seven years on, he had made his peace. Now it was time to move on again.

Squinting back down the road, he saw dust rise in the distance and heard the rumble through his feet before it reached his ears. The old excitement flared. It meant moving on, shooting through. Heading on and up. He would never lose that, he knew it. Yet this time it meant something else too, and that knowledge reverberated up through his backbone as the cloud of dust thundered nearer.

He stuck out his thumb, stretching his arm wide as he had learnt, with all his muscles flexed to jump back if the driver was feeling mean or if another traveller already hogged the cab.

But this one was going to stop, he could tell. With a sonorous rumble and a series of hisses, the road train came to a halt a way up the road. Eddy gave a small yelp of pleasure, and shouldered the rucksack to sprint towards the front. He gave a thumbs-up signal, and the driver grinned back at him, glad of the company.

Thirty-Nine

She watched the unmistakable ring of colour as if it might change, returning to the bathroom again and again to gaze on the small outline of a new planet until it danced before her eyes wherever she went. There was no mistaking. Panic battled with exhilaration as she slumped on the verandah and wondered what to do.

Yet all the time Bernie knew there was no alternative but to accept. Her anguish at Eddy's absence was countered by a new determination to cope alone, to prove to them all that she could.

With that defiant *them all*, her imagination supplied a series of images – her parents, Father Mullen, the sisters and brother who were as good as strangers now, wild Zippo with his long hair whipping her face as they leaned into the corner, John Roper, and an old woman she had never met who died believing that her grandson had a future here with her, this stranger, Bernadette Molloy.

Eddy materialized as well, his mouth curving, pulling at his curly hair in thought . . . and then his features merged with another imagined face, tiny and pink, like a shell half-buried in the pale, wet strand of County Cork.

She closed her eyes and contemplated the ring of the new planet which would not go away but hung, a glowing purple-red, in the blackness behind her eyes.

'But if it all goes wrong again, Eddy, I won't be able to bear it,' she said aloud. 'You can see that, can't you? I'll bloody well do it better this time, but I'll be forty when . . . Oh Jesus, help me!'

You have to find a way through, she thought, and not like you did last time. You can't destroy *this* one. This one is Eddy's, and will remain as proof.

Half an hour later, calm again, she pressed her neighbours' doorbell, smiling at herself at the two-tone chime. No, she told Robert Sinclair, she wouldn't come in for a beer, but needed to warn him she'd be making a bonfire when it was dark, and the smoke . . .

'I'll come round and give you a hand,' he said. 'See it doesn't get out of control? Now you're on your own?' The last words were said hesitantly, as he was afraid of giving offence. Bernie created a smile.

'Be good to have some help,' she admitted.

Nadine appeared at her husband's elbow, and squealed that of course Bernie must come in and what was Rob doing keeping her on the doorstep? Suddenly Bernie felt weakened by what she heard as the characteristic tone of this country they had transported her to twenty-eight years ago – confident, cheerful and as reassuring as the two-tone bell that opened doors and insisted on hospitality.

'I wanted to come round,' said Mrs Sinclair quietly, fixing her blue-shaded eyes on Bernie's face and reaching out with perfect pink talons to touch her arm in sympathy. 'To say . . . Oh, you know. I felt we should of done something to help, but you don't know what, do you? Don't know what to say, even. Such a terrible thing! I know the bloke was only your lodger, but still – not *nice*.'

Bernie nodded. 'No – not nice,' she said, flatly.

She suffered herself to be led past the TV-watching children, through to the Sinclairs' garden, and be given a tall glass of iced cola which quickly numbed her hand. How extraordinary, she thought, suddenly to be with normal people who cut the grass and tended their borders. She glanced at the fence that divided the two properties, enjoying the sensation of being cut off from her own life. She murmured agreement with everything they said – that the town would never forget the disaster; that they'd heard Ace Abbot was sick again and that was too tragic for words, a hero like that; how scary it is that you can never know when some bloke's a few sandwiches short of a picnic; that on a beautiful afternoon like this one you didn't want to think of it, did you?

'No.'

'So what happened to the other one – the young bloke we saw heading off on the pushbike every day?'

Bernie gave a careful shrug and replied, 'Oh him – he just left.'

Nadine Sinclair glanced at her obliquely. Bernie suspected she must have seen and heard herself and Eddy in the garden, so guessed there was more to the story. But her husband was speaking, so the woman settled back in her chair.

'Bet the kamikaze business got to him – it would, wouldn't it? We used to hear them talking in your garden, him and the English bloke – not that we were listening, mind – and they seemed to be mates.'

'Yes . . . I mean, you're probably right. Eddy couldn't stand it here any more.'

There was a silence.

'So, will you get more – I mean different – lodgers?'

She shook her head. 'Not unless I don't find a job.'

Robert raised his eyebrows. 'I thought you worked at that pub?'

'I did – matter of fact, I still do, in theory. I took sick leave, and now I reckon the boss knows I'm not going back. Want a change.'

Don't look too hopeful, she said to herself, stay cool and play it right. Then added, 'So . . . if you hear of anything!

All suggestions welcome!' Her smile was as dazzling as she could fabricate, willing the reply that came as if she had written the script.

'We–ell, strangely enough – you know we've got the shop?' Bernie nodded, with an air of surprise. Robert leaned forward eagerly, resting his hands on tanned knees. 'Funny you should mention it, but, matter of fact, Caddie, one of the two women in there, she's leaving, and since we're expanding . . . Tourist trade's on the up and up, you know. Nadie was going to help out but . . .'

His wife yawned prettily. 'Got so much to do round here, what with the kids – ferrying them about, getting all their stuff, all that . . .'

'You ever done shop work?' Robert asked.

Bernie's laugh was genuine. 'Oh, I done everything! Waitress, barmaid, chambermaid, supermarket checkout, and I worked in a store, first on the stationery then in accessories. That was years ago – but I reckon I can do anything!'

Her neighbour leaned back as if something had been decided. 'There you go! No worries! As from this minute, you're fixed up!'

When it was nearly dark, Robert Sinclair came round to help her burn the residue of John Roper's life. She stood back and let him take charge, knowing he was the kind of man who liked to do that, kicking the scattered papers and fragments into a more compact pile before taking out his matches. It didn't take long. They watched the flames gain control and stepped back.

'We saw him, y'know,' Robert said, rubbing his chin. 'Through the fence. Not that we make a habit of looking through the fence, but . . .'

'It's OK.'

'He'd got a letter, I think, and . . . he was crying. Sitting there, and just crying. I told the police about it. I guess it just added up to the fact that he'd gone . . . er . . . you know.'

'Crying?' she asked.

'Yeah . . . I mean, I'd say "poor bloke", if it wasn't for what he'd done, you know?'

Bernie stared at him, imagining the sound of John Roper's misery. What had she and Eddy been doing at that moment?

303

They'd been happy, nobody could deny it, and yet the counterpoint to their brief interlude of joy was the sound her neighbours heard, and it was that which remained. She knew she would hear it always, in the cries of birds skeining across the sky.

She fixed her eyes back on the flames, concentrating so hard they began to dry and hurt. A polyester pilot's shirt shrivelled and crisped amid the crackling wood, and the orange wings of a Biggles book flapped up into the air. The bonfire folded in a shower of sparks. She heard her neighbour murmur something, then reach for the bucket to scatter handfuls of water. Smoke blew into her face, making her blink furiously. She wrapped her arms around her stomach and groaned.

'You all right?' he said.

Bernie couldn't speak.

'Tough for you, going through all this,' he said, matter-of-factly.

'Oh, I've been through worse,' she said, attempting a smile.

They watched the fire in silence for a while, then he said, 'Come round? Anytime you want. Whenever?'

'Yeah. Thanks.'

She wanted him to return to his wife and children and leave her alone to watch until the embers darkened. Too soon for her to tolerate a superfluity of kindness. 'Thanks for helping. And for the job,' she said.

'No worries. You OK now?'

'I reckon. I'll stay out here till it's out. Reminds me of being a kid, back home in Ireland. Guy Fawkes' night, you know? We'd wave sparklers around making patterns in the air. Trying to write our names on the night. I loved that.'

'Kids like bonfires.'

'Most years it rained, though, and the fire wouldn't take . . .'

'Rain? What's that?' he grinned, tapping her lightly on the arm.

'Rain made me what I am,' she said.

Bernie was dreaming. She was on a motorcycle alone, riding as she had never learnt to do, her hair streaming in the wind. Heading down the highway she saw smoke in the distance, and suddenly the bush fire was all around, flames leaping across the road. 'No place to run, Zippo!' she screamed, forgetting he was not there, nobody was there, only the flames closing in on all sides and the terrified shrieks of wild things who sensed they could never outrun the blaze. She would melt, bones liquefy – to disappear into steam on the road, and become one with her spirit child in the ether.

Writhing, she cried out in her sleep, and did not hear the key turn in the front door.

Bernie woke in terror, sensing somebody in the room. He was sitting on the bed, making crooning noises as if she were a child. Her scream died. 'It's only me,' said Eddy, laying a hand on her shoulder.

She looked uncomprehendingly at his familiar outline in the gloom, and shook her head. All the days she had longed for his return were reduced to the silence stretched between them.

'I . . . don't know . . .' he began. 'I want to tell you . . .'

He faltered, and reached to lay a hand on her cheek.

She hit it aside. Rage propelled her upwards until she was kneeling to pummel him with her fists, screaming that he had no right to come back like this, without a phone call, he had no business with her any more, not after what he'd done. He accepted her blows until they were too much, and he grabbed her wrists to hold her away from him, crying and cursing as she struggled fruitlessly to pull herself free.

'Stop it!' he pleaded.

She started to cry, racked by sobs, as she accused him again and again in broken phrases he could barely hear. But knew he deserved.

'You . . . just . . . *deserted* . . . me,' she groaned.

There was no strength in her then, so he took her in his arms to rock her into quietness. They sat like that for a long time until Eddy began to laugh. The joyful sound enraged her. She felt him shaking and pulled herself away.

'I'm glad you find something funny, Eddy,' she said. 'You walk out on me . . . *on that day*. You leave me in the shit without a single phone call. You got any idea how I felt? Now you let yourself in here and sit there laughing as if somebody made a joke. Well they did, mate! You're the joker and I'm the bloody victim. I don't know how you've got the nerve to come back and face me, after what you put me through.'

He nodded, and turned his head away. Without looking at her he murmured, 'You've got to let me explain, Bernie. I

305

could sit here all night saying I'm sorry, and I am – I really am. But you've got to let me tell you why.'

'You can start by telling me what's so funny,' she said harshly.

'I was laughing because – this feels so right. I'm happy.'

'Goodonya!' she jeered, in Springing Dick's voice.

'I came all this way but I was still a bit afraid of how I'd feel. Then I had hold of you, and I had my nose in your hair, and – do you have any idea how wonderful you smell? I started to laugh because I'd been crazy, and now I know it's going to be all right.'

'What is?'

'Us – of course.'

'Don't do this to me, Eddy.'

He took her hand, and leaned across her to switch on the bedside light. She cringed back from the glare, covering her face.

'I'm a *wreck*.'

'I was always fascinated by wrecks. Submerged treasure and all that stuff?'

'Very funny,' she said bleakly.

'Not funny. True.'

'Go on then – I'm waiting. Explain, Eddy – for Christ's sake!'

It didn't take long. Shocked by what John Roper had done, and with Bernie's fury loud in his ears, Eddy had decided to run. 'It's what I've always done, and I did it again. I hardly thought, Bernie – just stuffed my things into my backpack and went. Didn't know where I was going either. Then when I got to the end of the road I knew there was only one place for me to go.'

'Where?'

'Home. I knew I had to go back and see them. Something made me.'

'Oh Eddy – after so long?'

He nodded. 'All the way there – one ride from the edge of town, then a couple of cars – I was thinking about John, and you, but I was numb. I blamed myself for everything – for what John had done and for what I'd done to you.'

'And what was that?' She couldn't keep the mocking inflection from her voice.

'Made you love me,' he said simply.

'Oh yeah,' she said bitterly. 'Always knew you had tickets on yourself.'

'Don't, Bernie. Hear me first. I was sitting in that cab, while the driver played music and talked to me, and all the time I was thinking about the *harm* it does – loving people. I thought of my mother and how she must've loved him – my dad. And then her mother, and her mother too – going back, so much pain because they loved men who were only interested in getting what they wanted and dumping them. But then, Pam loved me, like I was really her son, but I was so mad I turned my back on that, and started running. But I never fitted any place. Your word, Bernie – I'm a freak! So I was thinking, maybe if I went . . . home . . . again, I'd be able to sort it out in here.' He tapped his head.

'What happened?'

'They were so shocked! There I was on the doorstep – can you imagine? My dad invites me in like I was one of the staff come round for a yarn. And the first thing I noticed was the paper, on the coffee table, and the headline said, "Kamikaze kills five." Vern was staring at me like I was a ghost, and Pam's mouth was open, but all I could see was that headline. And it was as unreal as me being there with them again. Nothing was real. Not you, even.'

She shook her head. 'Specially not me, I reckon.'

'Bernie – I know I've hurt you. But try to understand – just a bit? I was just a scared kid who couldn't stand feeling so bloody *responsible* for everything. For John and what he did. And for you. I couldn't stand it. But I kind of knew that if I made my peace with my folks, I'd start to sort my head out. It was time.'

'How were they?'

'Oh, where do I start? Grateful for the postcards. Vern was a bit distant at first, but Pam . . .' He paused and smiled. 'She was sweet . . . We talked about the whole thing, over the next few days, and I realized – you can't go on blaming, can you, Bernie?'

She shook her head.

'And the thing was, I knew it was all to do with you. Living here, all I wanted to do was look after you, and that'd turned me into somebody else, not the person I'd been. That other bloke didn't belong anywhere and went on hating his father

307

out of habit. Like shooting through was a habit. Now, back at home, sleeping in my old bed, I stopped that and I started to see that I did belong somewhere.'

Bernie clasped her hands in front of her, as once in church, sending prayers into the incense-laden air.

'You know where I belong, don't you?' he whispered.

Fiercely, she shook her head. 'You could've rung me, Eddy. Not even to let me know you were OK . . . That was terrible.'

'I know. But some things have to be gone through,' he said. 'It's like there had to be a cut-off point, with John's death. Maybe we all had to die that day. And I didn't know if we could – start again. There was only one way to find out. So I thought I'd just show up, and see how you took it.'

'Start again?' she echoed.

'Yes.'

'You never *say* things!'

'Oh, I say things, but not in ways you want to hear.'

'You've never once told me how you feel. You've never said . . . Bloody hell, Eddy, you've never said you love me.'

He shook his head reproachfully. 'Don't try to put words in my mouth, because I haven't got them. I told you what I think about love. It's just a word. It doesn't *mean* anything, not to me, not when I know what it does to people. Anyway, what's more important, what I say or what I do?'

The sweep of his arm embraced the wardrobe, and she felt ashamed.

Bernie pulled on her kimono and walked through to the kitchen. With no choice but to follow, he hesitated then filled the kettle. She dropped teabags into two mugs, added a spoonful of sugar to each and leaned back against the sink, unable to take her eyes from his face. The walls dazzled her, like the glimmer of his skin.

'You'll stay?' she asked at last, frowning in disbelief.

'If you let me.'

'Ah, but Eddy, what will happen later?'

'What do you mean?'

'I'm older than you. You don't want that! What will it be like when . . .?'

'It'll be like it was when we went camping. It'll be *fine*. We'll live in a . . . a . . . bubble we make for ourselves. I'll build a pool, like you wanted. Bernie, I *need* you.'

Bernie groaned. Without realizing it, she was stroking her stomach, moving the fabric in small, nervous circles. She saw his eyes drop, then fix on her face again, puzzled.

'Are you OK? Have you got a pain?'

She shook her head, staring at him with wide, grave eyes. 'But what about when I'm – old, Eddy? Really old?'

'I reckon I'll be around to look after you.'

His grin was so wide and generous she felt a splintering inside and turned her back on him, to hold on to the sink. She rocked backwards and forwards, seeing her image balloon and recede in the tap.

'I got to tell you . . .' she began. 'Something's happened . . .'

He put his arms around her from behind, holding her still. For a long time she couldn't speak.

'I'm pregnant, Eddy.'

He said nothing and her terror increased. Finally she swung round to face him, hands on his shoulders to hold him away.

'Does that make you want to run, Eddy? Because if it does, you got to go *now*. This minute! You hear me? I got on all right without you, Eddy! I even cleaned the place up . . . And I decided I'd have this baby, even if I never saw you again and you never knew about it. I decided I could make myself into somebody else too. I was already different forever, because of my time with you. So I reckoned I could be a good mother, if . . . if . . .'

He watched her face collapse and heard her voice rise to a cry of panic. 'Oh Eddy, I'm so scared it won't be all right. After last time . . . Ah Jesus, Eddy – say something! What do you think?'

Eddy plucked her hands from his shoulders, holding them tight and low between his own, their bodies forming a perfect M. His eyes were wet, and when he spoke at last he enunciated every word as though she were a foreigner who'd asked the way.

'It *will* be all right, Bernie! I know that, just like I know you're the most beautiful woman I ever saw, and that I want to take care of you. Both.'

'But – are you . . . pleased?'

He thought. 'I'm scared, but yes – I'm pleased. The spirit child's chosen us, Bernie! We'll be good at it – being a real family.'

309

'But – you might not be around.'

'Listen, Bernadette – I'm not going anywhere. Not unless you come with me. Both of you.'

There was a long pause, then, in a tiny voice, she asked, 'Truth?'

He shook his head in mock exasperation. 'Oh – *what* did I tell you, Bernie? Don't you ever listen?'

Letting go of her hands, he enveloped her. They stood holding each other tightly, the child between them, as the kitchen filled with steam. Bernie rested her head on his chest and he rubbed his cheek in her hair as he murmured things she only half heard and understood less. At one point she thought she caught the word she wanted to hear, but she couldn't be sure, and anyway it didn't seem so important now. Not when so much else could be put right.

Epilogue

Four days later the local paper led with allegations made by a leading member of the Central Australian Aboriginal Congress, accusing the police of race discrimination. The deaths of aboriginal men in custody were cited, and the police countered that the racism derived from the land rights lobby.

But the newspaper also carried this story, in a column on the far right of the front page.

FUNERAL FOR PILOT

An unannounced funeral in the town cemetery yesterday was the last chapter in the story of Englishman John Roper's kamikaze plane crash.

He was laid to rest only a few metres away from the graves of Gregory Abbott and Hazel Cartwright, two of the five people who died after Roper deliberately crashed a light aircraft into the offices of Abbott-Air three weeks ago. His other victims, aircraft engineers Michael Chin, Daniel Butler and William Simmonds, are all buried on the other side of the graveyard. Six employees of Abbott-Air are still undergoing treatment for burns.

After extensive dealings with the British Foreign Office, it was discovered that Roper had no relatives living in England, but since his stated religion on the immigration documents was Anglican, the authorities took the decision to give him an Anglican funeral here.

Local vicar the Rev. James Barclay told our reporter, 'It is my concern to bury John Roper with proper ceremony because, in the end, judgment on his actions will be made by God.'

Contacted for his views, builder Joe Cartwright said that nothing would bring his beloved daughter Hazel back, so he hoped Roper would 'burn in hell'. Founder of

Abbott-Air, flying hero Adrian 'Ace' Abbott, was unavailable for comment, as he is seriously ill and not expected to recover from the shock sustained at the death of his only son.

Apart from the coroner's constable, two people were at the graveside when the Rev. Barclay conducted a brief service. They were the woman in whose house John Roper had lodged, local resident Miss Bernadette Molloy, and her fiancé Edward Carpenter, originally from Adelaide.

Miss Molloy threw a single gladiolus on the coffin, but had no comment to make. Asked his relationship to the deceased, Mr Carpenter described him as 'a friend'.

Author's Note

I finished the first draft of this novel three months before the terrorist atrocities of September 11th 2001, which made the terrible final action of my character John Roper seem all the more unbearable. Yet this story is based on a real event, which happened many years ago.

The official history of Alice Springs, published in 1988, contains the following paragraph: 'On 5th January 1977 . . . all of Alice Springs was stunned by news of the death of Roger Connellan, two engineers and an office girl. All were killed . . . when a former Connair pilot bent on reprisal for his dismissal from the company crashed his stolen plane into the operation manager's office of the Connair complex at Alice Springs airport.'

Oddly enough, the author fails to mention the piquant fact which seemed to fuel national resentment at this act: the pilot was British and had emigrated to the lucky country to fulfil his lifelong ambition to be a pilot. I was visiting Australia at the time and the dramatic tale of the man whom the newspapers called 'the Kamikaze Pom' lodged itself in my imagination, never to go away.

The details of the real-life story are exactly as in this novel, including the pilot's reported personality and the strange 'shrine' he left in his room; on the other hand, it is important to emphasize that the character John Roper is my own creation, and so are all the other characters. Any resemblance to any living people is totally accidental. To underline that fact, I have shifted the action forward about five years, and do not name one of the most famous towns in my favourite country. I felt these events might have happened in any outback town, or (for that matter) in the middle of Arizona.

Many people have helped (wittingly and unwittingly) with the background to this novel. I am indebted to Geoffrey

Robertson for the original suggestion, and for obtaining the newspaper cuttings which I have carried with me for twenty-four years. The unpleasant incident which closes Chapter One was lifted straight from Robyn Davidson's *Tracks* (1980), a book I admired greatly long before I met the author in 1989 and experienced the pleasure of camping under the stars with her, and sharing a minute portion of her knowledge of the outback.

I've enjoyed the company of good Aussie friends over many years, at home and over there. There are too many books of Australiana on my shelves to name, but *My Place* by Sally Morgan influenced this narrative. I learnt much from from the expertise of guides Noel Wright at Nhulunbuy, Greg Wallis at Kakadu, Brendan Bainbridge and Anthony Noonan at Mount Borradaile and Ben Heaslip at Bond Springs.

I admire the work of Jimmy McGovern and 'borrowed' some words of dialogue from his film *Liam* because few writers can do the haunting of a Catholic childhood as he can. William Lindeiner provided invaluable research on John Roper's flying obsession as well as background books. Lastly, this novel could not have been finished without the peaceful house of Stephen and Penny Faux – as well as the encouragement of my agent Jacqueline Korn and of Jonathan Dimbleby.